SPECIAL AGENT'S SURRENDER

BY
CARLA CASSIDY

First published in Great Britain 2012
by Mills & Boon, an imprint of Harlequin (UK) Limited,
Eton House, 18-24 Paradise Road, Richmond, Surrey TW9 1SR

© Carla Bracale 2011

ISBN: 978 0 263 89511 7

46-0312

Harlequin (UK) policy is to use papers that are natural, renewable and recyclable products and made from wood grown in sustainable forests. The logging and manufacturing processes conform to the legal environmental regulations of the country of origin.

Printed and bound in Spain
by Blackprint CPI, Barcelona

Carla Cassidy is an award-winning author who has written over fifty books. Carla believes the only thing better than curling up with a good book to read is sitting down at the computer with a good story to write. She's looking forward to writing many more books and bringing hours of pleasure to readers.

Chapter 1

It had been another long, quiet day at the real estate office. In the current economy nobody was buying or selling property in the small town of Black Rock, Kansas.

Layla West shuffled her feet beneath her desk, seeking her newest pair of navy sling-back heels. If there was one thing in the world that Layla loved it was shoes. There was also the fact that she'd been left with an inheritance that allowed her to remain calm despite the fact she hadn't made a sale in a month.

With high heels in place, she rose from the desk and grabbed her coffee mug. As she carried it into the back room where there was a bathroom, she noted that darkness had fallen outside.

At least it hadn't snowed yet, she thought as she dumped the last of the tepid coffee down the sink. Early-December often brought winter weather to the small prairie town.

Coffee mug rinsed, she returned to the front office and grabbed her coat from the back of her chair. It was time to get home to her cat, Mr. Whiskers, the only male who seemed content to stick around with her for the long run.

With her coat around her shoulders and her purse in her hand, she locked up the office and stepped outside. She looked around to make sure nobody was lurking nearby and then headed down the street where her car was parked against the curb.

She'd stayed late in hopes that somebody might call, and because she'd been reluctant to go home where lately the silence, the loneliness, had begun to press in around her.

The streets were deserted, most of the stores having closed not long before. She picked up her pace, uncomfortable with being out alone after dark.

She noticed that the streetlight above where she'd parked had burned out and made a mental note to mention it to Sheriff Tom Grayson. The candy cane decorations hanging from all the streetlights reminded her that it was time to get her little fake Christmas tree out of its box and go wild with all her other seasonal decorations. She loved Christmas and always went nuts decorating her house.

Eager to get inside and get the heat blowing, she started to open the car door and realized she'd left her cell phone on her desk in the office.

"Nobody is going to call you," she muttered aloud. Besides, she had a landline at home if anyone really wanted to get in touch with her.

Deciding to get the cell phone in the morning when she returned to work, she quickly unlocked the car, slid in and punched her key into the ignition.

Before she could turn the key an arm snaked around the back of the seat and against her neck. A scream tried to escape her as the arm applied pressure to her throat.

For a moment she thought it was some kind of a weird joke, an old boyfriend trying to scare her, a friend playing a prank, but that momentary thought fled as the pressure on her throat increased, cutting off her airflow.

Wildly, she glanced at the rearview mirror, but realized it had been flipped up so she couldn't see who was in her backseat, who was trying to choke her.

Her first instinct was to grab at the arm, to scratch and claw in an effort to get free. A searing fear gutted her as she thrashed against the seat. Her head pressed against the headrest as the arm tightened; her attacker did not make a sound as he squeezed the air from her lungs.

This isn't a joke, her mind screamed as her vision was narrowed by encroaching darkness. The candy cane decoration hanging from the nearest streetlight began to blur and fade as first tears, then stars danced in front of her eyes.

She tried to scream again, but it came out only as a strangled sob. He was going to kill her. He was going to choke the life out of her. Tears once again blurred her vision and she knew if she didn't do something quickly she was going to die.

The arm around her throat was strong and she knew she didn't have the strength to pull it away and would waste precious energy in the effort. As she realized she couldn't break his hold, she did the only other thing she could think of—she pulled her foot up and took off one of her high heels. Using the heel as a weapon she slammed it back over her head.

There was a low grunt and the pressure against her neck momentarily eased. As she drew in a rasping gasp of breath she slammed her hands down on the car horn.

As it blared in the otherwise silent streets, the attacker jumped out of the car and raced off into the darkness of the night.

She hit her automatic door locks and began to cry in deep, gulping sobs. Still she held down the horn, a bleating plea for help as she squeezed her eyes tightly closed.

Dear God, what had just happened? Why had it happened and who had it been? The questions couldn't maintain any weight as terror still fired through her.

She'd almost been killed. She forcefully coughed, as

if the act could banish the feel of pressure, the terror of not being able to draw a deep breath.

A knock on the driver window ripped a new scream from her, but she gasped in relief as she saw Sheriff Tom Grayson standing next to her car. He'd either heard the horn from his office down the street or somebody had called and he'd come to investigate.

A new torrent of tears escaped her as she unlocked the car and opened the door. "He tried to kill me," she finally managed to gasp as she nearly tumbled out of the car. Her throat burned and her words sounded raspy.

"Who?" Tom asked as he grabbed her arm to steady her trembling stance.

"I don't know who. I didn't see his face. He was hiding in the backseat of my car." She raised a hand to her throat. "He…he tried to choke me. I hit him with my high heel and when I leaned on the horn he ran out of the car."

Tom used his cell phone and called for his brother, Caleb. "Which way did he run?" he asked her as he clicked off the phone. In the distance Caleb left the sheriff's station down the street and hurried toward them.

"Back that way," she replied as she pointed down the street. Her heart banged against her ribs and the taste of horror crawled up the back of her aching throat.

Within minutes Caleb was chasing after the attacker and Tom was leading her down the block to the warm interior of the sheriff's office. Once inside he deposited

her into a chair in his office and instructed Deputy Sam
McCain to get her a cup of coffee.

Layla glanced at the clock above Tom's desk and
realized it had only been about fifteen minutes since
she'd left her office to get into her car to go home.

It felt like an eternity. It felt like a nightmare and
no matter how hard she tried she couldn't wake up.
Somebody had tried to kill her. Somebody had tried to
kill her. The words thundered in her head over and over
again.

She took the coffee from Sam not because she wanted
to drink it but rather because she needed the warmth to
banish the chill that gripped her.

"Tell me exactly what happened," Tom said.

"There's not much to tell," she said, surprised when
a laugh escaped her. Hysterical. She was definitely on
the verge of becoming hysterical.

She took a sip of the coffee and leaned back against
the hard surface of the chair back. "I got into the car, he
wrapped his arm around my neck and he squeezed."

"Was your car locked?"

"Yes. At least I think it was but maybe not. I looked
around to make sure nobody dangerous was lurking
when I left the office and I didn't think about anyone
hiding in my backseat."

"Did he say anything?"

She shook her head. "The only sound he made was
a grunt when I hit him with my shoe. I hope I didn't
break the heel when I smashed him. Those shoes were

expensive." Once again a nervous burst of laughter rose to her lips but she quickly swallowed it down.

It was a fault of hers, the inexplicable need to make light when she was scared or upset. "Why would somebody do that to me, Tom? Why would somebody try to hurt me?"

He frowned thoughtfully. "Can you think of anyone in your personal life who might be angry with you?"

"No, nobody," she said firmly. "You know me, Tom. I don't make enemies."

"What about professionally? Any problems at the office?"

"I'm a Realtor, for goodness' sake. I work for myself and I make people happy." She set the cup on the edge of the desk with trembling fingers.

At that moment Caleb returned to the office. "I didn't see any sign of anyone, but I did a cursory check of the car and grabbed your purse," he said to Layla. He handed her the oversize bag and then turned to Tom. "I also found this in the backseat." He held up a plastic bag with a syringe in it.

"Oh, my God, what's that?" Layla asked as a new horror washed over her. "That's not mine," she exclaimed. "I don't do drugs of any kind."

"I don't know what's in it, but it looks fully loaded," Caleb replied.

Tom rose from his chair and motioned Caleb out of the room. "Excuse us for just a minute," he said as he and Caleb walked out into the hallway.

Left alone, Layla's anxiety flew off the charts as she grappled with what had just happened to her. She couldn't imagine anyone hating her enough to try to strangle her. She even got along well with her ex-boyfriends.

Sure, she knew that a lot of people in town thought she was shallow and superficial, brash and a bit of a wise-mouth. She also knew that there were some who probably thought she was a bit loose, but Layla was the first to admit that she made a lot of mistakes when it came to men.

Even as she thought about her personal life she knew the truth, and the truth was far more terrifying than an ex-boyfriend.

She reached for the cup and took another sip of the coffee, but the warmth of the brew didn't begin to touch the chill that had taken up residency in her bones.

What happened now? Did she just get into her car and go home? The idea of being alone in her house terrified her. What if he knew where she lived? What if he came back to finish the job?

Other women had recently disappeared in the town of Black Rock. A new chill took possession of her body at this thought. They'd disappeared and never been seen again.

Tom returned to the room and sat at his desk, a sober expression on his handsome face. "Layla, you know about the missing women we've had in the last couple of months."

"Of course," she replied. "I was just thinking about

that." There had been four women who had disappeared from Black Rock in the last four months or so, including Tom's own sister, Deputy Brittany Grayson. "It was him, wasn't it?" Her heart beat so fast she felt slightly nauseous. This was the truth she hadn't wanted to think about.

Tom nodded. "Caleb and I think maybe it's possible you were intended to be number five."

His words hung in the air between them as she stared at him in horror. Nobody knew what had happened to the women who had disappeared but the general opinion of everyone in town was that they were all dead.

"We think that all the women were taken from their cars. Most people don't look in their backseats when they get behind the wheel. I would guess that the syringe is filled with something that would knock a person unconscious. He was probably going to choke you unconscious and then administer the drug."

"Or it could have killed me instantly," she said. Her throat began to hurt again, as if in response to their conversation.

He hesitated a moment, his eyes flashing darkly. "We'll know more about that after we send it to the lab."

"So, what happens now?" she finally managed to ask.

"As terrible as this experience has been for you, this could be the break we've been waiting for. We're keeping your car and will go through it with a fine-tooth comb to see if the attacker left anything behind besides that syringe. Hopefully we'll get some hair or fiber or fingerprints that will lead us to an arrest."

"And what about me?" she asked.

"I've called Benjamin. He's going to come by and take you by your house to get some things then we're going to stash you in a cabin out at the ranch until we're certain you aren't in any danger."

"A cabin?" She didn't know about any cabin located on the Grayson property.

He nodded. "It's kind of a family secret, an old care-taker's cottage that my parents renovated years ago."

"What about my cat?"

Tom frowned. "You have a neighbor or somebody who can take care of him while you're gone for a couple of days? Either that or we can see if Larry Norwood can board him."

Layla set the coffee cup on the desk and then leaned back once again, finding it difficult to comprehend everything that was happening. "The only person I'd trust to take care of Mr. Whiskers is Portia and she's allergic." Portia Perez was Layla's best friend and Caleb's fiancée. "I guess it would be okay to board him for a couple of days. I'm sure Larry would take good care of him."

Larry Norwood was the town veterinarian and Layla was comforted by the fact that he seemed like a nice guy who loved animals. Mr. Whiskers already knew the vet, for Larry's office was where she took the cat for checkups and shots.

"I'll see that he's taken care of," Tom assured her. "The important thing is to get you someplace safe until we can figure out exactly what's going on." He leaned forward, his dark eyes piercing into her. "Layla, is there anything else you can tell me about the man who attacked you?"

She thought of those terrifying moments in the car when she'd been certain death was a mere heartbeat away. "Nothing," she finally replied. "It all happened so fast. All I can tell you is that he was strong."

"If you think of anything else, if you think of anyone who might have a reason to harm you, let me know. In the meantime all I need from you is that you tell nobody where we're putting you, and I mean nobody, and that you stay put until we know the danger has passed."

The idea of staying in a cabin alone was nerve-racking, but the thought of going back to her house all alone was absolutely terrifying. "If the culprit is who you think it is, then maybe he won't bother me again since I managed to get away."

"Maybe, or it's possible that he'll be more determined than ever to get to you."

A tiny laugh escaped her. "Thanks for the reassurance."

"I'm not going to waste my breath giving you false assurances," he replied. "There's no way to know if this is tied to the other disappearances or not. We don't have

enough information right now to know what's going on.
But, the one thing I don't want to do is minimize the
possible danger." His mouth was set in a grim line. "I
don't want to lose another woman in this town."

"I don't want to be the one you lose," she replied. "I
know it's hard to believe coming from me, but I'll do
whatever you tell me to do, Tom."

At that moment Benjamin appeared in the doorway.
Benjamin was another of Tom's brothers who worked
as a deputy, but rumor had it he intended to quit his
deputy duties in the spring and focus on ranching and
Edie Burnett, the new woman in his life.

"Layla, heard you've had a bit of a rough night," he
said.

She forced a smile. "That would be the understatement
of the year."

"You ready to head out?"

She looked at Tom, who nodded his assent. "I'll be in
touch to let you know what's going on. And don't worry
about your cat. I'll see he gets to Norwood's later tonight
or first thing in the morning."

She stood in an uneven stance minus one shoe. "Can
I get my other high heel from the car?" she asked.

"It's evidence," Tom replied. "I'm hoping that if you
managed to hit him and break some skin then we might
have some DNA on the shoe."

She took off the shoe she still wore and then looked
at Benjamin. "Then I guess I'm ready to go." A new
burst of fear swept through her as she realized she wasn't

going home to Mr. Whiskers and her own bed, but rather was in effect going into protective custody.

It took only ten minutes for Benjamin to get her from the sheriff's office to her small house. She'd always felt safe in the three-bedroom ranch house she'd bought five years before. But she didn't feel safe now. The shadows in the rooms suddenly felt ominous and she jumped at every ordinary noise. She was grateful to have Benjamin with her.

She packed a large suitcase of the things she considered essential, kissed Mr. Whiskers goodbye and then they were back in Benjamin's truck and on their way to his ranch.

The adrenaline that had pumped through her from the moment the arm had wrapped around her neck eased away, leaving a gnawing fear that had her shaky.

"Please tell me this cabin has electricity," she said as she leaned forward to get the benefit of the warmth blowing from the heater vents.

Benjamin smiled. "Electricity, running water and cable television," he replied. The smile faltered somewhat. "There's something else you need to know. Jacob is staying at the cabin."

Shock waves shot through her. "Jacob? But, I thought he was in Kansas City working for the FBI." As far as Layla was concerned Jacob had always been the hottest of the Grayson men. She'd had a major crush on him before he'd left town to become an FBI agent.

"He was, but he's been back for about six months and staying in the cabin."

"Did he get hurt or something?"

"Or something," Benjamin replied. "He hasn't told any of us what brought him back, but he's not the same man he was when he left Black Rock. Anyway, I just thought I should let you know that you'll be sharing the space with him."

Layla leaned back and digested this new information. At least she'd have some company and it didn't hurt that her company was a man who had always intrigued her. "I'm sure we'll get along just fine," she said. It also didn't hurt that her protective custody involved an FBI agent.

"Good luck with that," Benjamin muttered under his breath as he turned into the entrance of his ranch.

They drove past the ranch house and across the pasture. "How's Edie?" she asked.

A smile flashed across Benjamin's face. "Terrific."

Edie Burnett had come to town to check on the well-being of her grandfather, Walt Tolliver. She and Benjamin had fallen hard for each other and Edie had moved in with him.

A fist of loneliness slammed Layla in the stomach. It wasn't an unfamiliar punch. Sometimes she thought that she'd been born lonely and that she'd never find somebody who might help ease that affliction.

It certainly wasn't from lack of trying. She felt as if she'd dated every eligible bachelor in Black Rock between the age of twenty-one and forty.

She shook her head, wondering if she was losing her mind. Somebody had just tried to kidnap or kill her and she was thinking about her love life. Because that's not scary to think about, she told herself, because that didn't fill her soul with terror.

They drove over a rise and in the beams of the headlights in the distance she saw the small cabin nearly hidden by evergreen trees crowding in on every side.

A faint light glowed at the front window, but it didn't add any sense of real welcome to the isolated place. The front porch was bare and the exterior paint was starting to show signs of age.

"You'll be safe here. Few people even know this cabin exists," Benjamin said as he parked the truck in front of the small structure and turned off the engine.

Layla got out of the truck, a bit unsteady on the uneven ground in the red high heels she'd put on at her house. With her tight jeans and in a new red sweater she felt ready to face whatever life threw at her.

Benjamin grabbed her oversize suitcase from the back of his truck and together they walked up the stairs to the small porch and the front door.

Benjamin knocked and a deep voice replied. He opened the door and Layla stepped inside. Her first impression was that the place was downright cozy with a fire crackling merrily in the stone fireplace and a thick throw rug covering an expanse of the gleaming hardwood floor.

"What in the hell is she doing here?" The deep voice

came from a recliner and a stunned surprise fluttered through her as she got her first glimpse of Jacob Grayson.

His dark hair hung almost to his shoulders and his jaw was covered with a thick growth of whiskers. She could tell from the hollows in his cheeks that he'd lost weight, but his shoulders were still broad beneath the navy sweater he wore and his jeans hugged the length of his long legs.

It was his eyes that made her breath catch in her throat. Dark as night and filled with the shadows of hell, they bore into her with intensity. He looked at her, her suitcase and then at Benjamin. "What the hell is going on here?"

A bubble of laughter unintentionally escaped her. "I guess you didn't get the memo," she said. "I'm your new roomie."

Chapter 2

Jacob recognized her immediately even though the last time he'd seen her Layla West had been about nineteen years old. Even back then she'd liked her jeans tight and her heels high and it looked as if nothing had changed. She'd be about twenty-eight now, definitely not a kid anymore.

There was some small part of his brain that processed the scent of her sexy perfume in the air, part of him that was drawn to the shine of her long blond hair, but the bigger part of his brain stared at Benjamin through angry narrowed eyes.

It would be just like his well-meaning brothers to set up something like this in an effort to pull him from his self-imposed isolation. Nothing like a hot, sexy woman to pull a man back into life. *Yeah, right,* he thought bitterly.

"Is this some kind of a joke because if it is I'm not laughing." What he wanted to do was shove both Benjamin and the lovely Layla West right back out the door. Instead he got out of the chair and approached where Benjamin stood.

"Of course you're not laughing," Benjamin replied tightly. "That might make you human." He dropped Layla's suitcase on the floor and looked at her. "Layla, would you excuse us for a minute?"

He grabbed Jacob's arm and pulled him toward the door. The two men stepped out on the porch and into the cold night air. "This is not a joke," Benjamin said, a touch of uncharacteristic anger in his voice. "This isn't about you and any issues you might have, Jacob. We've all pretty much left you alone out here for the last six months. We've asked damn little of you and hoped to hell you'd pull yourself together."

The cold December wind sliced through Jacob's sweater almost as effectively as the disgust in his younger brother's voice. He jammed his hands into his pockets and waited for Benjamin to finish whatever it was he wanted to say.

"Layla was attacked this evening when she got into her car after work. She managed to get away but she didn't see who was responsible. We need to stash her someplace where nobody will know where she is for a day or two while we figure out what's going on."

"Why don't you put her at your place? You could hide her there. Edie doesn't strike me as the loose-lipped kind of woman." Edie and Benjamin lived at the ranch house up the lane.

"Edie isn't, but you know Walt. He means well but he has never met a secret he could keep." Benjamin jammed his hands into his coat pockets.

Jacob sighed, knowing his brother was right. Walt Tolliver was Edie's grandfather, a nice old man who had become something of a local hero after being responsible for bringing to light a scheme involving illegal experiments on the dead of Black Rock. Walt meant well, but Benjamin was right, the old man had never met a secret he could keep.

"A couple of days at the most," Benjamin said. "Surely you can force yourself to be civil for that long."

Maybe he could pretend she wasn't there for that length of time, Jacob thought to himself. "Whatever," he finally said, the cold seeping deep into his bones.

He stepped back in the door where Layla stood poised for flight next to her suitcase.

"Take off your coat. Relax, you're staying," he said grudgingly as he threw himself back into the recliner where he'd been seated before they'd arrived.

"Great, this should be fun," she said with a touch of sarcasm. She took off her coat and draped it over her arm. "Where do you want me to put my things?"

"There's only one bedroom," Benjamin said. "I'm

sure my brother would want you to have it." He pointed to one of the doors off the main room.

Layla looked at Jacob as if to see if that was okay. He nodded. Most nights he slept in the recliner or on the sofa anyway. Besides, if he was lucky she'd stay in the bedroom and out of his hair until Benjamin came back to retrieve her.

"We'll stay in touch," Benjamin said to Layla as he backed toward the front door. "You'll be safe here, Layla. Just give me a call if you need anything."

With that, Benjamin left. Jacob picked up the remote control to the television and turned the volume up enough that conversation would be difficult. He knew it was rude and he didn't care.

He'd stopped caring about anything six months ago when he'd left his job in Kansas City with the FBI and had returned to Black Rock and this cabin. All he wanted was to be left alone with the crushing guilt that never left him and the images of dead women that haunted him.

"I guess I'll just get settled in," she said, raising her voice to be heard above the television.

He watched as she pulled the suitcase toward the bedroom, unable to help but notice how her jeans cupped her curvy behind. As she disappeared into the bedroom he got up and grabbed a beer from the fridge.

In the past six months beer had become his best friend. Although he never got falling-down drunk, he drank just enough to dull his senses and aid in a little selective amnesia.

Hopefully it would take her at least an hour to unpack that suitcase, which had looked big enough to hold a month's worth of clothes, and hopefully she'd only be in his personal space long enough to wear one of the outfits she'd packed.

He took a long pull on the fresh beer and tried to ignore the scent of her that still eddied in the air. He couldn't remember the last time he'd smelled the pleasant scent of a woman or touched warm silky skin in a fevered caress.

The only women in his life in the last year had initially been faces on flyers who had eventually become bodies in crime scene photos. And their deaths had been his fault.

He shook his head and took another deep swallow of his beer to dispel any horrible visions that might drag across his brain. He didn't want to think about those women, knew that dwelling on them would cast him into the darkest of despair.

As if this personal baggage wasn't enough, his sister had disappeared almost four months before. He'd used what resources he could in an attempt to find any trace of her whereabouts, but had come up empty-handed, as was the case in all his brothers' investigations.

He had a feeling his sister was dead, otherwise they would have found something, heard something by now. It was just a new grief he refused to acknowledge.

He frowned as Layla emerged from the bedroom and sat on the sofa. He glanced at her and she gave him an overly bright smile. "So, what are you doing here? Are you in hiding, too?" she asked.

"Something like that," he replied. The red sweater she wore enhanced the pale blond of her hair and the blue of her eyes. Suddenly his thoughts turned to another woman. Sarah. She'd been wearing red the last time he'd seen her. His stomach clenched tight.

"I usually hear all the gossip but I haven't heard anyone mention that you were back in town." Her voice was raised to be heard over the blaring television.

Reluctantly he lowered the volume. "Besides my family I'd prefer nobody know I'm here."

"Why?"

"Because I want it that way," he replied curtly and hoped she'd drop the subject. He didn't intend to tell anyone what had brought him back here, the culpability he'd had in the last case he'd worked.

She crossed one long slender leg over the other and leaned back, looking as comfortable as if she were in her own home. "So, what do you do to pass the time?"

He sighed. She was obviously determined to have some sort of conversation with him. "I drink beer and watch television or I listen to the silence," he replied pointedly.

"I've never been a beer drinker. I like wine, especially a light blush, and sometimes a strawberry daiquiri is good. But if I'm celebrating something special I love a glass or two of champagne."

Shoot me now, Jacob thought as she continued explaining what drinks she liked and didn't like. She certainly didn't act like a woman whose life had just been threatened. It was just his luck to be cooped up with a superficial woman hell-bent on talking him to death.

When she finally wound down her alcoholic drinks speech, she launched into a monologue about how much she liked Christmas. He tuned her out, making her voice white noise in his head.

"Jacob?"

He reluctantly tuned back in as he realized she must have said his name several times. "Is there anything around here to eat?" she asked. "I skipped dinner and now I'm starving."

He pointed toward the kitchen. "Help yourself." He breathed a sigh of relief as she got up and disappeared into the next room.

There had been a time when he liked nothing more than sitting with an attractive woman and indulging in a little flirtatious small talk, and if it led to something more all the better. But, that had been before Sarah, and before the case that had broken him.

And he was broken.

As an FBI agent.

As a man.

He took another long pull of his beer as he listened to the sounds of rattling pots and pans from the kitchen. Benjamin always made sure he had plenty of groceries so she'd have any number of things to choose to eat.

His stomach rumbled as the scent of frying bacon filled the air. He hadn't eaten supper and he'd skipped lunch, as well, opting for a liquid diet of booze.

Most of the time if he was going to eat he either made himself a sandwich or zapped something in the microwave. Food had lost its appeal, as had most things in life.

Layla stepped into the doorway. "I'm making a bacon and cheese omelet. Want half?"

He didn't want anything from her, but his stomach decided otherwise and he nodded affirmatively. "Okay," he agreed. Within minutes she called to him that it was ready.

"I'll just eat in here," he replied.

Once again she appeared in the doorway. "No way," she said with a hint of steel in her voice. "I've got the food on the table and it's only civilized that we eat there."

"What makes you think I'm civilized?" he countered. God help him, not only did he have a chatty woman on his hands but apparently a bossy one, as well.

"If you want to eat, then you'll come into the kitchen." She disappeared from the doorway.

He stared after her. Who did she think she was to come in here and try to tell him what he should and shouldn't do? If she thought she was going to run this place while she was here then she had another thing coming. Reluctantly he got to his feet.

He was starving and at the moment the issue didn't seem important enough to fight about. He carried his beer bottle into the tiny kitchen where she'd set the small dinette table for two. He dumped the rest of his beer down the sink drain, tossed the bottle into the trash and then took the seat at the table across from her.

Above the scent of the bacon he could smell the ridiculously sexy fragrance of her perfume. Sitting this close to her he could see the gold flecks that sparked in her blue eyes as she gazed at him and to his stunned surprise a tiny flame ignited in the pit of his stomach.

"So, what happened to you?"

The question surprised him, along with his unexpected physical reaction to her nearness. "Nothing happened." He picked up his fork and focused on the food in front of him even though he felt her gaze remaining on him.

"You look like hell," she said.

Jacob set down his fork and gazed at her balefully. "We're here together through no choice of mine. I don't want to share personal feelings and experiences with you. I don't want to make pleasant little chitchat. I just want to be left alone." He picked up his fork and began to eat once again.

"Looks to me like you've been left alone too long," she said as if unable to not be the one who had the last word.

He ignored her and ate as quickly as possible, ignoring the fact that she continued to look at him as she ate her dinner. When he was finished he carried his dish to the sink, washed it and set it in the drainer to dry.

He left the kitchen without saying a word and returned

to the recliner that had become his second best friend, after his beer.

Within minutes she'd returned to the room and to his dismay once again positioned herself on the sofa. "So, Layla, what's been going on in your life for the last couple of years?" she said. "Oh, not much. I own the only realty in town but unfortunately business has been pretty slow lately. I like Chinese food, I'm a Libra and I love to dance."

For the first time in months Jacob felt the urge to smile. It stunned him. It felt like an affront to all the blood that stained his hands.

"Are you always so irritating?" he asked.

She frowned as if seriously considering his question. "I suppose it depends on who you talk to. My friends don't find me irritating, but it's possible some of my old boyfriends might. And just for the record you're more than a little bit irritating, too."

He felt her gaze on him as he stared at the television. "You didn't used to be this way," she continued. "In fact you used to be every teenage girl's fantasy."

"Yeah, well things change, and now I'm going to sleep." He clicked off the television, lowered his chair to a sleep position and then closed his eyes.

He was acutely aware of her in the silence of the room—her scent, the bubbling energy she brought and the faint whisper of the sound of her breathing. He felt her gaze on him but refused to open his eyes.

He breathed a sigh of relief as he heard her finally get

up, and a moment later the door to the bedroom closed. He opened his eyes and frowned thoughtfully.

She was going to be a pain in his ass. Beautiful and sexy, she was apparently a woman who was accustomed to getting her own way. Once again he told himself that she certainly didn't seem to be traumatized by the events of the night that had brought her here.

A day or two, that's what Benjamin had said to him. She just needed to be here for a short time. Surely Jacob could handle her presence for forty-eight hours or so.

He turned off the lamp on the end table and closed his eyes but visions of Layla instantly danced in his head. Even when she'd been nineteen and he'd been twenty-four and home for a visit, he'd been aware of her around town, but she'd been too young and he'd had his job in Kansas City and so he hadn't pursued anything with her.

And now she was all grown up and under his roof. Not that he cared, not that he intended to do anything about it. He had enough dead women in his mind. There wasn't room for a breathing one, no matter how sexy he found her. He just wanted her out of his space.

His head once again filled with thoughts of Sarah. He'd met her when he'd been twenty-six years old and she'd been twenty-four, and he'd fallen hard. She'd been beautiful and fun, bubbling with the same kind of energy that Layla possessed. She loved to talk, loved to dance and had stolen his heart almost immediately.

It had taken Jacob months to get up his courage to ask

her to marry him and when he finally had she'd laughed at him. She'd told him that she was far too young to get married, that she was just having fun and now that he'd gotten so serious about her it wasn't going to be fun anymore.

That had been the last time he'd seen Sarah and his last attempt at a relationship with anyone. She'd devastated him and he never wanted to feel that way again about anyone.

He must have fallen asleep for the scream awakened him. He jerked up, disoriented for a moment as he realized the scream hadn't been one of his own that occasionally woke him from a nightmare.

The fire had burned down to hot coals and the room had grown chilly. He reached out and turned on the lamp next to him. The sound came again, a sharp, piercing scream that sliced through him.

Layla! Full consciousness slammed into him as he recognized her scream. Had the person who had tried to harm her earlier in the evening found her again?

He fumbled in the drawer in the end table and pulled out his gun, then jumped out of the chair and raced toward the bedroom door, hoping—praying—that he wouldn't find yet another woman murdered on his watch.

"Layla, come out, come out, wherever you are."
The familiar voice shot terror through Layla, who was crouched beneath the old front porch.

"Come on, little girl. Take your punishment like a trouper."

Layla's breaths came in rapid, shallow gasps. Don't let him find me. Please don't let him find me. Her heart pounded in her chest so loud she was afraid he'd hear it. Maybe if she stayed hidden long enough he'd pass out and forget that he'd decided she needed a beating.

She screamed as a hand reached under the porch and grabbed her by the hair. Tears filled her eyes as her scalp burned and her body was dragged across the rocks and dirt.

She couldn't breathe.

Suddenly she was in her car and hands wrapped around her throat and squeezed unmercifully. He was killing her and Layla didn't want to die. She wanted to live and get married and have babies. She wanted to have lunch with her friends and be happy.

But she was dying, her throat being squeezed so hard no sweet air could reach her lungs. Inside her mind she screamed for help, but no sound escaped her lips. She knew nobody could help her. She was going to die alone—as she had been all her life.

"Layla!"

The deep voice cut through her, familiar and yet somehow frightening. She struck out with her fists, with her legs, desperate to get away from him, fighting for her very life.

"Hey, hey! Stop! Layla, wake up! It's Jacob."

She came awake with a gasp for air as her heart crashed in a frantic beat. She blinked against the brightness of the overhead light and then Jacob came into focus.

It was Jacob, not the man who had tried to kill her. It was Jacob, not her father who had been the source of so many of her nightmares.

Without thought, functioning only with need, she sat up and grabbed him around the neck, pulling him close as the residual fear from her nightmare shuddered through her body.

"You're okay," he said gruffly, not moving away but not engaged in the hug. "It was just a dream. You should be fine now."

She shook her head and burrowed her face into the crook of his neck where warmth and the faint scent of minty soap and a spicy cologne comforted her. The dream had been a horrifying blend of past and present and her heart still rocked in her chest with an unsteady rhythm.

He released a small sigh and finally wrapped his arms around her. She felt the strength of his arms and shoulders, the very warmth of him that radiated through his T-shirt and her silk nightgown. She closed her eyes and reveled in the moment of safety, of complete and total security.

Even as she began to fully relax she felt the tension that filled him. It was finally he who disentangled himself from her and stepped back, his eyes dark and enigmatic. "You'll be okay now," he said and turned and left the room.

Instantly she was chilled to the bone, bereft with the lack of his presence. She wrapped her arms around her own shoulders, seeking comfort as her mind raced with the images not only from her dream, but from her attack earlier in the evening.

Just go back to sleep, she told herself, but the idea of falling back into those same dreams was terrifying. What she needed was to talk about something, about anything that might take her mind off her dreams, off the fact that somebody had tried to kill her that night.

She eyed the doorway longingly, wanting to get out of the bedroom where she was alone with her thoughts. Jacob certainly wasn't the most sociable creature on the face of the earth, but at the moment he was all that she had.

Making a decision, she slid out of bed, pulled on the sleek, short robe that matched her leopard print nightgown and went into the living room.

She turned on the lamp next to Jacob's recliner and offered him a tentative smile. "I feel like talking. Do you mind?"

"Would it make a difference if I said yes?" One of his dark eyebrows rose sardonically.

"Probably not," she replied truthfully and sat on the sofa. "I can't go back to sleep right now. I'm afraid I'll go right back into that horrible nightmare. Can we just sit here and talk for a few minutes?"

She could tell he'd rather eat nails, but he gave her a weary nod and put his chair into the upright position. "You want to talk about your nightmare?"

"Absolutely not. That's the last thing I want to talk about." She fought against the race of a shiver that threatened to walk up her spine. "I just want to talk about pleasant things." He frowned, as if he couldn't imagine anything pleasant to discuss.

"So, what's your favorite food?" she asked, desperate to talk about something—anything—no matter how mundane.

"Pizza, anything Mexican and I like a good steak." He stared at the blank television screen. "What about you?"

"I think it would be easier for me to list the kinds of food I don't like. Brussels sprouts and lima beans. Other than those, I love almost everything."

He focused his gaze on her and she couldn't help but notice the quick slide from her face to the gaping top of her robe. His frown deepened as he once again jerked his attention back to the television screen.

An uncomfortable silence descended as Layla gathered her robe more closely around her. She knew she should go back to bed, but now she was afraid her dreams would be haunted by his dark gaze.

"What kind of television shows do you like to watch?" she asked in an effort to keep the conversation flowing. "Personally I love most of the sitcoms that are on now. There's nothing better than a good laugh after a day of work. I'm also a reality show freak. They're all so silly but they definitely take your mind off your own problems."

Once again he looked at her, a wry lift to his lips. "And what kind of problems do you have? Whether to buy the shoes you want today or wait to see if they go on sale tomorrow?"

There was a derisive edge to his voice that instantly rankled her. "That's right," she replied with a forced airiness. "I'm all about shopping and going out to lunch and good times." Her voice broke as a sudden wash of emotion gripped her. "I'm sure that's why somebody hid in the backseat of my car tonight and tried to choke me to death."

He cursed silently under his breath. "I'm sorry, that was uncalled for. I've obviously lost my social skills while I've been cooped up here."

He offered her a smile and in that gesture she remembered the man she'd once had a major crush on. "I really don't know anything about you except that you said you owned the realty in town," he said.

She nodded. "I opened the business four years ago, just after my father died. I love finding the right home for my clients and business was good for about two years. But it's been lean lately." She began to relax as she thought about her work. "Hopefully the economy is turning around now and business will get better again."

"What about your mother? Where is she?" His gaze remained fixed on her face.

"She died when I was seven." And that was when all the love in Layla's life had also disappeared. A wave of grief tried to pull her into its clutches, but she fought it, refusing to go there.

"And you don't have any brothers or sisters?"

"No, it was just me. You're lucky to have such a big family. It must be nice to have people who care about you," she replied.

"It has its moments, but it can also be a pain."

"Are you still with the FBI?"

The smile instantly disappeared, as if it had only been a figment of her imagination. "I'm retired."

She looked at him in surprise. "You're awfully young to be retired. What are your plans for the future?"

"To get some sleep before morning comes." His voice was clipped, filled with a new irritation as he reclined his chair once again. Layla knew the moment of tenuous peace and conversation between them was over.

"Then I guess I'll just say good night." She got up from the sofa, turned off the lamp next to him and then went back into the bedroom.

The bedroom was small, the double bed covered with what appeared to be a handmade patchwork quilt. A dresser with a mirror stood against one wall and a nightstand was against the bed.

It was a nice room and there was a photo of the entire

Grayson family hanging on the wall next to the dresser. She moved over to it and studied it.

Mr. and Mrs. Grayson stood together, looking happy and in love. They were dead now, killed in an airplane crash that had left their adult children alone.

The Grayson children all shared the trait of rich dark hair. Jacob stood with his arm around his sister, that charming devilish grin lifting his lips. All the Grayson men were drop-dead gorgeous, but they were also known as men who had humor in their eyes and a flirtatious smile on their faces.

Where was Brittany now? And where were the other women who had disappeared? There had been some speculation that one of the women had simply left town, but the others had seemingly vanished into thin air.

She moved away from the picture and turned off the bedroom light. Instead of getting into bed she moved to the window. It was a perfectly clear night, the moon a gigantic silver orb in the sky.

Her thoughts were momentarily consumed by the man in the next room. What had happened to Jacob Grayson? What had brought him to this cabin, living like a hermit with dark shadows bruising his eyes?

Something had happened to Jacob, something terrible, and she couldn't help but be intrigued. She also couldn't help but remember those brief moments when he'd held her in his arms. It had felt so safe and yet had held just a little bit of dangerous attraction.

And somebody out there in the darkness tried to kill

you tonight. Once again the reality of what had happened slammed into her.

As she finally climbed back into bed, she prayed whoever it was wouldn't find her again.

Brittany Grayson awoke suddenly, her heart beating frantically. She remained unmoving on the cot, eyes open to the utter darkness that claimed the shed or whatever structure they were held in.

How many days had it been? How many weeks or months? She'd lost track of the time that she'd been held captive. There were now four of them, four women held in jail-like cells. The last one had been brought in earlier in the week. Casey Teasdale had hung over her captor's shoulder like a sack of potatoes as he'd carried her in and placed her on the cot in the fourth cell.

"Almost time," he said to Brittany as he'd locked the door to assure Casey's imprisonment. The ski mask he wore effectively hid all his features, making it impossible for Brittany to identify him.

He gestured toward the empty cell. "One more and then the real fun begins, and I've got a special woman in mind to fill that one. A pretty blonde who is a bit feisty and managed to escape me once. She won't escape the next time."

He'd whistled as he'd strolled out of the shed, leaving her with a chill that had nothing to do with the temperature of the building. *One more and then the real fun begins.*

One woman taken was a crime. Two had been a pattern and three made him a serial offender, but four was a collection. The monster who held them was collecting them like fancy figurines and she had a feeling once his collection was complete he'd take great pleasure in smashing his figurines.

She sat up, unsurprised to hear Jennifer's sobs. Jennifer Hightower had been crying off and on since the moment she'd arrived.

Say something to comfort her, a small voice whispered inside Brittany's head. But, as she reached inside herself for the right words she realized she had no more comfort to give.

For the first time since she'd been kidnapped she was without hope, her very soul had been depleted.

Initially she'd been so sure that her brothers would find her. She knew they'd move heaven and earth to find out what had happened to her. But with each day that had passed without rescue, her fear had grown stronger and now it was screaming like a banshee in her head.

Enough time had passed since her disappearance that her brothers probably thought she was already dead. Maybe they'd even stopped looking for her. She lay back down on the cot and squeezed her eyes closed. No, they wouldn't stop looking, but she'd lost the hope that they might find her in time.

One more and then the real fun begins.

She knew in her gut that the real fun meant death to all the women that were in the cells.

Chapter 3

Dawn was just beginning to break when Jacob awakened. Instantly his head filled with a vision of Layla. When he'd burst into her room the night before in response to her screaming, he'd been ready to protect her with his life.

As he'd seen her in the bed, the sheet at her waist and the top of the sleek animal print nightgown barely covering her full breasts, a fist of desire had slammed into his gut. When she'd awakened and pulled him into an embrace, that fist had punched him over and over again as he'd held her in his arms.

He now got up from the recliner and threw a log and some kindling on the hot coals from the night before. Once the fire was blazing nicely, he decided a shower and a change in his thoughts were in order. Stepping into the bathroom he caught his reflection in the mirror above the sink.

You look like hell.

Layla was right. He did look like hell. He scraped a hand across his whiskered chin and then turned away from the mirror in disgust.

Half an hour later he left the bathroom clean-shaven and dressed in a freshly laundered navy turtleneck shirt and jeans. He made coffee, then carried a cup to the living room window and stared outside, his thoughts still on the woman who slept in the next room.

She was so full of life and seemed determined to bring him out of his isolation by talking him to death. She probably had dozens of men lined up waiting to spend time with her.

And somebody had tried to kill her.

He turned away from the window and wished he'd been paying more attention to what was going on in town. He knew his sister and somebody else had gone missing, but whenever his brothers had talked about it, he'd tuned it out, preferring his own drama to theirs. Now he wished he'd listened more carefully to them.

He glanced at the closed bedroom door and wondered how late she would sleep. Not that he cared. As long as she was sleeping she wasn't talking.

She reminded him of Sarah and that was a time in his life he didn't want to remember, a time when he'd had hopes and dreams and everything had seemed possible.

When Sarah had walked away from him she'd stolen his dreams. The final case in his career had shattered his hope.

It was just before nine when Layla finally emerged. Clad in her nightgown and a short matching robe and her hair sleep-tousled around her head, she gave him a heavy-lidded glance and a quick smile. "Coffee, then shower," she said as she disappeared into the kitchen.

His stomach muscles knotted with a tension he recognized. It surprised him that the first real emotion he'd felt for so long was lust. Her long slender legs had looked sleek and sexy beneath the short robe and he hadn't forgotten how her full breasts had looked spilling over the top of her nightgown the night before.

He'd assumed she'd grab a cup of coffee and then join him in the living room, but as several minutes went by he realized she wasn't coming out of the kitchen.

Leave her be, he told himself. After all, that's what he wanted from her. He should be enjoying the fact that she was awake and not talking to him.

Before he realized what he was doing he was on his feet and headed into the kitchen. She sat at the table, her dainty fingers wrapped around a stone coffee mug and her eyelids still lazy with sleep.

"You're obviously not a morning person," he observed as he refilled his own coffee cup. He sat across from her at the table, wondering what in the hell he was doing.

Her face wore a slightly pouty expression that he found oddly charming. "Mornings should be banned," she said, then lifted the coffee mug to her lips. She took a sip and eyed him over the rim of the cup. "Nice to see you have a chin beneath all that hair."

He rubbed a hand across his smooth jaw. "It was starting to bug me," he replied. The last thing he wanted her to think was that he'd shaved for her.

"You have a nice chin. You shouldn't hide it under all those whiskers." She took another sip of her coffee and then lowered the mug to the table. "Did you sleep well?"

"As well as I always do." There was no way he'd share with her the kind of nightmare images that haunted his dreams. "What about you? Any more bad dreams?"

"No. Thankfully I slept like a baby once I finally went back to sleep. Is there a phone in the house? I left my cell phone at my office last night and I need to call Tom to see if he took care of the favorite man in my life," she said.

"The man in your life?" He shouldn't be surprised that she had a boyfriend. What did surprise him was the unexpected sharp edge of disappointment that stabbed him. What was that all about? He sure as hell didn't want anything from her.

"Yeah, he's sixteen pounds of calico fur and his name is Mr. Whiskers."

"Any men of the human variety in your life?" he asked.

"Passing ships, not that I care." She lifted her chin slightly as if in defense of whatever he might say. "What about you? Is there some woman pining for you back in Kansas City?"

"Nope, I was too devoted to my work to have any real relationships." It was the easiest way to reply and it was somewhat the truth. After Sarah he hadn't wanted anything that might somehow involve his heart. "I'm not a relationship kind of man."

He could tell Layla wanted to ask him questions about what had happened in his work, about what had brought him back here, questions that he didn't want to answer. He stood and motioned to the old harvest gold phone hanging on the wall. "Feel free to make whatever calls you need. Just remember you aren't supposed to tell anyone you're here."

He got up and left her alone in the kitchen. He told himself it was so she could make her call in private, but the truth was something about Layla West had him off balance.

From the moment she'd breezed into the place the night before she'd brought a spark of life that had been missing. He felt the spark deep in his soul and he wasn't sure whether he liked it or not.

For the last six months he'd been immersed in his self-imposed isolation, bitter with memories and drowning in guilt and remorse. He didn't want to be rescued from himself by anyone.

He'd just gotten settled back into the recliner when she came out of the kitchen. "Mr. Whiskers is now in the care of Larry Norwood, so all is right in my world, and I'm going to take a shower."

The minute she disappeared into the bathroom Jacob was visited by images of her naked body standing beneath a steamy spray of water. He closed his eyes as he imagined the slide of the soap down the hollow of her throat, across her delicate collarbone and then on to her full breasts.

He could easily imagine himself stepping into that spray of water next to her and taking her into his arms. A vision of their hot soapy bodies sliding together tensed all the muscles in his stomach.

He jerked out of the fantasy as his cell phone rang. He pulled it from his pocket and saw from the caller ID that it was his brother, Tom.

"I just talked to Layla and she didn't sound too worse for the wear so I figured I'd better check in with you and see how it's going."

"It's going," Jacob replied, irritated by where he'd allowed his fantasy to take him. "You have any clues as to who attacked her?" Hopefully the crime would be solved and Layla could get out of here.

"Nothing. I was hoping to get some DNA off the shoe she used to whack him with, but we'll have to wait to see what comes back from the lab. Same thing with the hypodermic needle the perp dropped."

Jacob felt as if he'd entered an alternate universe. Layla hadn't mentioned anything to him about hitting her attacker with a shoe or a needle being involved. "Whoa, take it from the top. Layla didn't tell me much about the attack on her."

There was a moment of silence. "Are we talking about the same Layla West? Usually Layla tells anyone who will listen whatever crosses her mind. I imagine you shut her down before she could say much of anything about it to you."

Tom was right. Jacob had made it clear to Layla the night before that he didn't want to talk, that all he wanted was for her to shut up and go to bed. A sliver of shame worked through him.

As he listened to Tom relating the details of the attack, a grudging admiration for his roommate filled him.

She'd fought back. It sounded like she hadn't panicked, but rather had fought back using whatever resources she had at her disposal, in this case her shoe.

Even though she'd acted unconcerned about the attack, it was obvious from her nightmare that she'd been affected more than he'd initially thought.

"When you get a chance, I'd like to sit down with you and hear about these cases you're working on," Jacob said. He could tell he surprised Tom by the moment of stunned silence that followed.

"I'd like that," Tom finally replied. "Maybe a pair of fresh eyes will see something that we've all missed. You want to come here or meet me someplace else?"

Jacob still wasn't ready for his presence in town to be known. "Why don't we meet this evening after dinner at the big house? I'm sure Benjamin and Edie won't mind."

"I'll check with Benjamin and set it up. I'll bring Peyton and Lilly along. The women can chat while we talk."

"Sounds like a plan," Jacob agreed. "Then unless I hear something different from you, I'll see you this evening about seven."

The men hung up and by the time Jacob had poured himself another cup of coffee and settled back in his recliner, Layla was out of the bathroom. She was clad in a pair of jeans and a royal blue sweater that did amazing things to her eyes.

"Now I feel more human," she said as she sat on the sofa.

As he told her about the meeting with Tom that evening her lips curved in a happy smile. "I adore Peyton and little Lilly and I've been looking forward to getting to know Edie better. This will be a perfect opportunity."

Peyton and her daughter had been relative newcomers to Black Rock when Peyton's daughter, Lilly, had been kidnapped. As Sheriff, Tom had been on the case and when Lilly was found alive and well, the two had realized they'd fallen in love.

All of Jacob's brothers had found the loves of their lives, although none of them had married yet. They all were waiting for Brittany to return, a study in futility as far as Jacob was concerned.

"How about some pancakes?" Layla asked as she got up from the sofa.

"I'm really not hungry," he replied.

"Nonsense. Didn't anyone ever tell you breakfast is the most important meal of the day?" She flashed him a bright smile and then disappeared into the kitchen.

Jacob released a small sigh. There was no question that he had a strong physical attraction to Layla, but the last thing he wanted to do was follow up on it.

He didn't want to get involved with any woman; he still remembered too clearly the pain of Sarah's rejection. And if that wasn't enough he had a head full of dead women silently accusing him for botching their case, for being the impetus that had resulted in their murders.

He was a man meant to be alone and that's the way he liked it.

It was what he wanted.

It was what he deserved.

Layla was grateful when it came time for them to leave for Benjamin's place. Jacob had been a bear all day, barely speaking to her and playing his television loud enough that the cows in the distant pasture had probably heard the noise.

There was a tension in the cabin that palpitated with its own energy. She wasn't used to being cooped up and after a single long day she was ready to scream. If Jacob had been living this way for the past six months it was no wonder he was half-mad.

She now gave herself a final check in the bathroom mirror and wondered if Caleb and Portia would also be at Benjamin's house. Portia Perez was dating Caleb Grayson and she was also Layla's best friend. Layla hadn't talked to Portia since she'd been attacked, although she was certain that Caleb had probably told her what had happened.

She and Portia talked to each other almost every day and at the moment Layla would love to see her friend and tell her about the horror of what had happened. She'd also like to whisper to Portia that despite his grumpy attitude, in spite of his brooding and downright rudeness, she was intensely drawn to Jacob Grayson.

"If that's not a heartbreak waiting to happen, then I don't know what is," she muttered to her reflection in the mirror. Not that she was a stranger to heartbreak, most of her relationships ended in that state.

She'd realized long ago that she was a woman who seemed to inspire great lust in men, but nothing deeper, nothing more lasting. She'd given up on finding true, long-lasting love a long time ago.

You aren't good for anything, girl. No man is ever gonna want you. Her father's voice thundered in her ears and she shook her head to cast it out.

From the time her mother had died when she was a child to the time of her father's death four years ago, she'd felt inadequate, lacking in any qualities that would make her worthwhile to anyone.

Her father had been a brutal man, both physically and

mentally abusive. "But you survived," she whispered to the woman in the mirror. "And you thwarted an attack by a madman."

"You going to be in there all night or are you ready to go?" Jacob's voice called from the other side of the bathroom door.

"I'm ready," she replied and left the bathroom. He stood by the front door, car keys in hand and a familiar scowl riding his features. She grabbed her coat and pulled it on, then gave him a bright smile. "What are we waiting for?"

He opened the door and they walked out into the cold night air. "Wait here," he said and then he walked off into the darkness of the night.

She stood on the porch, wondering where he had gone, but moments later a black pickup pulled up in front of the cabin with Jacob at the wheel.

"Where did this come from?" she asked as she slid into the passenger seat.

"There's a shed not far from here. I figured there was no way you could walk the distance to the house in those shoes."

She glanced down at her blue pumps and then looked at him. "You'd be surprised what I can accomplish in a pair of sexy high heels."

He grunted and pulled away from the cabin. It took only minutes to travel the lane that led to the big ranch house that had been the Grayson family home where Benjamin and Edie now lived.

All the lights were on, creating a welcoming glow as Jacob pulled up beside Tom's car. Edie greeted them at the door and ushered them inside as Benjamin's dog, Tiny, danced at their feet.

The house smelled of evergreen and cinnamon, and Christmas decorations adorned every available surface. Layla shoved aside a wistful twinge as she thought of the little tree she'd intended to unpack and put out the night she'd gotten attacked.

"The men are in the study and the ladies are in the kitchen," Edie said as she linked arms with Layla. "Come on, Layla. I've got chocolate cake and coffee and Peyton and I can't wait to chat with you."

As Edie pulled Layla toward the kitchen, she saw Jacob disappear into the next room with Tiny following close behind him.

The minute Layla entered the kitchen and saw Peyton with her daughter, nine-month-old Lilly, on her lap, Layla's heart swelled with a new wistfulness she rarely allowed herself to feel.

"La-La," Lilly said at the sight of Layla. She squealed in delight and held out her chubby little arms for Layla to take her.

"Lilly," Layla exclaimed as she scooped up the little girl and kissed her on her dimpled cheek. Lilly giggled and smacked her lips as if finding everything around her absolutely delicious.

"Here, I'll take her and you take off your coat," Peyton

said as she grabbed her daughter and returned to her chair at the table.

Layla slid out of her coat, which Edie took from her and hung on a hook near the back door. "That cake looks positively sinful," she said as she sat in the chair next to Peyton. "Are Caleb and Portia coming, too?"

"No, although Portia said to send you her love. Caleb is on duty tonight and she had something going at her daycare—a parents' night," Edie explained as she set a cup of coffee in front of Layla.

"Shouldn't you be there?" Layla asked Peyton. "Lilly goes to Portia's daycare."

"Tom and I decided to skip it." Peyton tucked a strand of her long blond hair behind her ear. "It's not every day Jacob emerges from his cave."

"How are things going there? I couldn't believe it when Benjamin told me he was putting you in the cabin with Jacob." Edie sat across from Layla.

"Yes, has he said anything to you about what brought him back here from Kansas City?" Peyton asked. "Tom has been so worried about him."

Layla shook her head. "No, nothing. He isn't the chattiest person in the world. I've only been there one night and a day and I already think there have been times when he'd gladly wring my neck."

She raised a hand to her throat as a flash of memory snapped through her—an arm wrapped around her throat, squeezing, choking her to death.

"Are you all right?" Edie reached across the table

and touched her hand, jerking her from the terror of that remembered moment. "You just went ghost pale."

"I'm fine," she replied with a forced smile of brightness. "I just...this has all been so crazy."

"Crazy scary," Peyton said. "Tom is beside himself trying to find out who is behind all the disappearances. He's not sleeping. He's barely eating and I've been worried sick about him."

"I just wish I would have paid more attention when I was attacked. I wish I would have twisted around enough to see who it was, or scratched his face enough that there would have been DNA under my fingernails," Layla said with frustration.

"You did what you were supposed to do, you survived the attack," Edie replied sympathetically.

"Yeah, but I just wish I could have survived the attack and identified the bad guy," Layla said.

She was grateful when the talk turned to more ordinary things, the forecast for snow in the next couple of days, the argument of which was better comfort food, chocolate cake or cookie dough ice cream.

As they ate cake and drank coffee, the conversation remained light and easy and Layla found it a relief from the tense air that had surrounded her all day in the cabin with Jacob. But it wasn't long before the conversation circled around back to Jacob.

"It has to be a woman," Peyton said as Edie picked up the cake plates from the table. "Somebody broke his heart badly and that's what brought him back here."

"I don't know, he doesn't seem to be the type to have much of a heart to break," Layla replied ruefully.

"Don't let that fool you." Edie returned to the table. "I think we can all agree that the Grayson men come off tough and immune to emotion, but if you dig deep enough you find a wealth of vulnerability."

"The tougher they are, the harder they fall," Peyton said with a nod of agreement.

"All I really know is that something bad happened to him, something that haunts him." Layla had seen the utter darkness in his eyes, but there had been a moment when he'd looked at her that she'd seen something else, something that had made her heart beat a little faster and her palms grow slightly damp. It had been a flash of naked hunger, a spark of want that had immediately been doused.

She had no illusions where Jacob was concerned and the last thing she needed in her life was another meaningless sexual encounter that would only leave her raw and bruised. Besides, he didn't even seem to like her very much.

"Earth to Layla." Edie's voice pulled her out of her inner thoughts and back to the conversation.

"Sorry, I drifted for a minute," Layla replied.

"I was just saying that I think nothing will be right with the Grayson men until they find out what happened to Brittany," Peyton said.

"Benjamin thinks she's dead." Edie whispered the words as if afraid to say them aloud.

"Tom refuses to accept that," Peyton replied. "He thinks as long as there is no body then there's hope. He wants her home for Christmas. That gives him less than three weeks to find her."

"There are a lot of places to hide bodies around Black Rock, places where nobody would find them," Layla said, fighting against a shiver that threatened to sweep over her.

She could have been one of the bodies left in the woods or buried out in some field. If she hadn't managed to hit her attacker with her shoe and scare him away, Peyton and Edie might have been sitting at this table wondering what had happened to her and speculating about where her body might be found.

The conversation was halted by the men coming into the kitchen. "Are you trying to keep that chocolate cake all to yourselves?" Benjamin asked as he placed a kiss on the top of Edie's head.

"You know how we women are about our chocolate," Peyton answered as she handed Lilly to Tom.

Layla watched Jacob, who stood slightly apart from his brothers. Whatever conversation the men had shared hadn't lifted the shadows in his eyes. If anything, they looked darker.

"Jacob, you ready for a piece of cake?" Edie asked as she got up from the table.

"No thanks, none for me," he replied.

"He's probably worried that a little bit of sugar might sweeten up his mood," Benjamin replied drily, then grunted in surprise as Edie elbowed him in the stomach.

At that moment the doorbell rang and Edie left the kitchen to answer it. She returned a moment later with Caleb in tow.

"What's up?" Tom asked, obviously surprised to see his little brother.

"I left the office to get a cup of coffee from the diner and when I came back I found this taped on the door." He held up an envelope with a gloved hand and looked at Jacob. "Somebody knows you're in town because it's addressed to Special Agent Jacob Grayson."

Jacob froze, his features not betraying a single emotion as he stared at the envelope. He made no move to reach for it and for a moment it was as if everyone was freeze-framed in a still photo.

"Open it," Jacob finally said, his voice deeper than usual.

Caleb nodded and opened the envelope and withdrew what appeared to be a plain white note card. "'Hello Agent Grayson,'" Caleb read aloud. "'Hope you've enjoyed your time off. I'm ready to play again. Are you?' It's signed 'The Professional' and there's a P.S. 'Brittany says to tell you hello.'"

Layla gasped aloud and looked at Jacob, who had gone sickly pale. He stumbled back a step, his mouth opening and closing as if he couldn't get enough air.

"No." The single word finally escaped him in a strangled whisper. Before anyone in the room could move or guess his intent he flew out of the kitchen and a moment later the front door slammed shut.

Nobody stirred as the roar of Jacob's truck filled the air. It was only when the sound drifted away that Tom looked at Layla. "Looks like you need a ride back to the cabin."

"What just happened? What does that note mean?" she asked.

Lilly began to cry, as if aware that something bad had just happened. Peyton comforted her while everyone looked at Tom.

Tom frowned. "I don't know what's going on, but Jacob obviously has some answers and I intend to stay in that cabin until he gives them to me. Sooner or later he'll have to show up there."

It was quickly decided that Benjamin would drive Peyton and Lilly home while Tom went to the cabin with Layla. As Layla got into Tom's car it was fear for Jacob that caused her heart to beat frantically.

That note had shaken him badly and she knew with certainty that Jacob wasn't a man who got shaken easily. Something bad was in the town of Black Rock and that bad had just reached out and touched Jacob Grayson.

And she knew with all her instincts, with all her heart and soul, that the bad had only just begun.

Chapter 4

Jacob roared out of the driveway that led onto the Grayson property and out on the highway. He slammed his foot down on the gas pedal as he clenched the steering wheel so tightly his knuckles were white.

Not again. The words screamed inside his head. He couldn't go through it all again. He *wouldn't* go through it all over again.

He reached out and flipped the heater fan on high, but he knew he'd never be warm again. The chill of pure evil had gripped him and would never let him go.

Eventually he eased back on his speed, not so much concerned for his own safety but for that of anyone he might meet on the road.

His thoughts raced. How had the bastard found him?

He'd been so careful to lay low. When he'd left Kansas City he hadn't told anyone where he was going. Only a handful of people knew he was back in Black Rock and he'd trust those people with his very life.

Maybe he didn't know for sure that Jacob was in Black Rock. Maybe it had just been a guess that Jacob had come home to the bosom of his family to lick his wounds.

This thought brought him little comfort. The madman was in Black Rock and, if his note was to be believed, he had Brittany in his grasp.

He wanted to stay in his truck and drive forever. He wanted to continue west until he reached California and drove into the ocean. But, he'd driven for twenty minutes when he finally turned the truck around and headed back toward the cabin.

Although he wished he could drive to the ends of the earth, he knew he had to go back. There was no way to escape, no matter how far he drove.

He had no intention of getting involved in a madman's game again, but Tom needed to know what he was up against. It was time for Jacob to let his brother know what had brought him home.

If Jacob had paid more attention to the crimes happening in Black Rock, to the disappearances of women over the last couple of months, he might have guessed sooner that The Professional was back at work.

Now there was no guessing. The Professional was

back and if they didn't find him then the women he held
would die. His own sister would be killed.

But I can't do it again, he thought as he turned onto
the Grayson property. He refused to be a part of the game
a second time.

When he drove past Benjamin's house he noted that
all the vehicles had disappeared from out front. Caleb
would have probably gone back to the sheriff's office
but he wasn't sure where Tom or Benjamin might have
gone.

Layla. He hadn't even thought about her when he'd
reeled out of the house. Surely somebody had taken her
back to the cabin.

When he reached the cabin he had his answer. Tom's
car was parked out front and he saw the slender silhouette
of Layla watching from the front window.

For some reason, the sight of her standing there, as if
anxiously awaiting his safe return, touched him. But any
positive emotion he might have felt couldn't be sustained
beneath the weight of what had happened, what he now
knew to be true.

The Professional was back.

He turned off the truck engine but remained seated,
dreading the idea of going inside and facing the demons
that had been chasing him for the last six months.

Faces flashed before his eyes, the faces of the women
he'd let down, women who had wound up dead because
of him. Raw emotion churned in his stomach, making
him feel half-nauseous.

When he finally did step into the cabin Tom was seated in his recliner and Layla rushed toward him, her eyes filled with concern. "Are you all right?" she asked anxiously.

He was surprised that it mattered to her, that she cared at all. He hadn't been particularly kind to her in the time they'd spent together. He reached out and touched her cheek, a gentle touch as he shook his head. "No, I'm not all right, but I'm here now."

"And you're going to tell me what's going on," Tom said, the familiar hint of steel in his deep voice.

Jacob nodded wearily and stepped away from Layla. He sank down on one end of the sofa while she sat on the other. He looked at his brother and for a long moment wasn't sure where to begin.

"Who is he?" Tom asked.

"A serial murderer," Jacob replied. His chest tightened painfully. "He contacted the FBI after he'd kidnapped three women in Kansas City. He gave us their names and the locations he'd taken them from. I was put in charge of the case and coordinated with the Kansas City Police Department." The words fell from his lips with the bitter taste of dread, of failure. "Everything he told us checked out so we knew he was the real deal."

He leaned back against the sofa cushion, as if the softness might alleviate the difficulty of talking about the events that had unfolded in that case.

"I don't know why he focused in on me, but he did," he continued. "He started calling me, taunting me with details of the kidnappings and the women he had in captivity. He told me what he was feeding them and how they all begged for their lives. He said he was taking care of their basic needs like the wicked witch who plumped up Hansel and Gretel before trying to cook them in her oven."

Neither Tom nor Layla said a word, but waited for him to continue. His thoughts reeled him back in time and his stomach knotted tight. "He alerted me when he took the fourth woman and said he had room for five. Told me that when he got his fifth victim it would be party time."

"Party time?" Layla finally spoke, her eyes huge and her pretty features unnaturally pale.

Jacob looked at her and frowned. "Maybe you should go into the bedroom while Tom and I talk."

Her chin lifted and her blue eyes narrowed. "Not a chance. If what we believe is true, then I was almost at one of his parties and I want to know everything."

Once again he was struck by the strength that shone from her eyes, a strength that radiated from the square set of her shoulders. Once again he realized there was definitely more to Layla West than her love of high-heeled shoes and her need to fill any silence with the sound of her own voice.

He looked back at Tom. "He called himself The Professional and his plan was that once he had five women he'd torture and kill them one by one. He fed not so much on the actual kills themselves, but rather on the terror of the women as they waited their turn to die."

"Dear God," Layla murmured softly.

"So, what happened?" Tom asked, a muscle knotting in his jaw line.

A blackness reached out to Jacob, the darkness of utter despair, of a pain too deep to acknowledge, too wide to endure. He clenched his hands in his lap and stared down at them as he was cast back to the past.

They'd interviewed hundreds of people, checked and double-checked family members and friends of the victims in an effort to find a connection that might lead them to the guilty party. But it had all been in vain.

"Jacob?" Tom softly prompted.

"We did everything we could to figure out who this man was, what his connection was to the victims, and we eventually came to the conclusion that it was random, there was no connection that we could find."

"And random makes things even more difficult," Tom said.

Jacob nodded. "Anyway, the story was picked up by a reporter and became a big deal," he continued. "These kidnapped victims weren't prostitutes or drug addicts, they were all from good families, young women with jobs and people who loved them. The press ate it up. Somebody leaked that I had personal contact with the perp and the reporters were all over me."

It had been a terrible time. He'd been eating, breathing and living the case. "I was exhausted, sick by the conversations I was having with the creep, suffering nightmares when I did finally manage to close my eyes. A reporter caught me at the wrong time and I snapped. I told him that the perp called himself The Professional but he was nothing special, just another garden-variety creep preying on helpless women."

He raised his head and looked at his brother, his heart beating a thousand miles a minute. "That night after the piece ran on the news The Professional called me. He was crazy with rage. He told me he was smarter than all of us, more cunning than any killer we'd ever chased. He promised to show me just how good he was and when he hung up I knew it was going to be bad."

Once again the darkness threatened to consume him. He got up from the sofa, unable to sit still as he finished the horrible story.

He picked up a log and threw it on the already hot flames in the fireplace, needing more warmth as he continued. "I got a call from him the next morning. He told me I'd pushed him over the edge, that he'd gotten his fifth victim and had his party and now he needed a little party cleanup crew."

Jacob turned and faced the fire and in the dancing flames he saw the faces of the women who had been depending on him to find them, the faces of the women he'd let down. He squeezed his eyes tightly closed, but the accusing faces refused to disappear.

The air in the cabin was suffocating and held an air of dreadful expectancy. Above the crackle of the fire he heard Tom shift positions in the recliner, felt Layla's gaze burning into his back.

"He gave me the address of an old abandoned warehouse in the river district of Kansas City. He said that if we hurried we might find them all still breathing. My team rushed to the location." He paused, the emotion he'd been fighting crawling up the back of his throat, constricting his chest to the point that he wasn't sure he could continue. He turned around and looked at his brother.

"And they were all dead," Tom said flatly.

Jacob nodded and drew in a deep breath. "They'd been tortured and killed sometime during the night. According to the coroner, there was as much as two hours between the first death and the last."

"Jacob, they were dead no matter what you did. You aren't responsible for what happened," Tom said, his gentle voice doing nothing to ease Jacob's torment.

"Don't you get it? If I hadn't shot off my mouth when I did then maybe we would have had more time," he exclaimed. "Maybe we would have been able to find those women before he killed them." A flash of anger swept through Jacob. It was so easy for somebody who had not been involved to attempt to absolve him of any guilt.

He sank down on the sofa once again and buried his face in his hands. For a long moment nobody spoke. Jacob's heartbeat thundered at his temples, making him feel sick to his stomach.

He finally raised his head and looked at Tom. "I'm not going through this again. I can't get involved with this. I came here so that I wouldn't be involved in any more crimes he might commit."

"According to the note you got, you are involved," Tom replied. "He knows you're here, Jacob."

Jacob shook his head. "He might know that I'm somewhere here in town, but he must not know that I'm here at the cabin. Otherwise that note would have been left here on my doorstep, a way to show his power and control." He shook his head more vehemently. "I'm not playing his game. I'll tell you what you need to know, what information we got before, but I'm out of this." Unable to stand himself or the situation another minute, he got up and went into the bathroom.

Once there he sluiced cold water over his face and dried off with a hand towel, refusing to look at his reflection in the mirror.

He threw the towel on the sink and then leaned against the door. He couldn't be responsible for what was going on now with The Professional. He couldn't be a part of it again. If he said something or did anything that resulted in more deaths, he'd never survive.

It was better to do nothing.

If he hadn't shot his mouth off to that damned reporter, if he hadn't belittled the killer, then maybe the murders wouldn't have happened when they did. Maybe he would have been able to glean more information from the phone calls he received from the man. Maybe…

maybe…maybe…all the maybes in the world didn't change what had happened.

He stayed in the bathroom until he could no longer hear any conversation going on in the living room, then he opened the door and walked out.

Layla was alone, seated on the sofa where she'd been when he'd exited the room. He didn't look at her but rather threw himself in the recliner and stared at the blank television screen.

"Tom said to tell you he'll call you first thing in the morning," she said.

He gave her a curt nod and then closed his eyes, as if he could shut out the world with a flip of his eyelids.

"Jacob, talk to me." Her voice was a soft plea. "Don't shut yourself off."

"Do me a favor and just leave me alone," he replied without opening his eyes.

Silence reigned for a moment and he wondered if maybe she'd gotten up and left the room. He cracked open an eyelid and saw her still seated on the sofa, her gaze lingering on him. He quickly snapped his eyelid closed once again.

"You can't keep yourself out of this," she said softly. "You can't hide anymore, Jacob."

He opened his eyes and glared at her. "What do you know about it? What do you know about anything? I can do whatever the hell I want to do. Just leave me the hell alone."

She got up from the sofa and walked to the side of

his chair. The scent of her perfume surrounded him as she leaned down to face him eye-to-eye. "I know that I think it's damned arrogant of you to believe that you and you alone were responsible for those women's deaths."

"I was," he half yelled.

"That's a bunch of nonsense," she retorted. "You didn't hold a gun to this Professional's head and force him to kidnap that last woman. You didn't force him to kill those women. It was his fault and nothing you said to that creep could have made a difference."

He wanted to tell her to shut up, that the last thing he needed or wanted from her was her input into the situation. He got up from the chair, not wanting her hovering over him. He stalked into the kitchen and opened the refrigerator door and grabbed a beer.

He was about to unscrew the top when she came into the kitchen. "Are you going to drink this away?" she asked. "Is that what you've been doing here for the last six months? How's that working for you, Jacob?"

"Don't push me, Layla," he warned. "Just back off and leave me alone."

With a stubborn glint in her eye, rather than doing as he asked she advanced toward him. "You've been left alone to wallow in your self-pity for too long."

She walked closer to him and when she was close enough to touch him she took the beer bottle from his hand and set it on the counter.

"I felt his arm around my neck, Jacob," she continued, her gaze steady and determined as it held his. "I felt his malevolence, the very evil inside him. He likes it. You said it yourself, he gets off on the terror he creates. He was responsible for those deaths, not you. Surely somewhere in that hard head of yours you know I'm right."

Although he'd heard those very words from his supervisors and coworkers before he'd left his job, he hadn't believed them, at least not then when it had all been so fresh, so terrible. But, now the words coming from her found the wound in his soul and somehow eased a bit of the pain.

"They haunt me, you know," he confessed. "The women he killed. I see them in my dreams."

Her eyes were shiny with emotion and he knew it was for him. She placed a hand on his arm, her fingers warm through the thin fabric of his cotton shirt. He welcomed her warmth, wanted to pull her against him and lose himself in her heat.

"Jacob, you have to play his game again. You have to forget about those other women and focus on the ones who are hopefully still alive."

Her touch no longer felt welcome, but rather burned him. He jerked away from her and stepped back, but she came forward as if refusing to acknowledge his retreat.

"Jacob, for God's sake, he has your sister," she exclaimed. "If for no other reason you have to be involved in this for her."

The words pierced through the veil of denial he'd

tried to erect. Brittany. His heart cried her name and for a moment he felt too weak to stand.

Layla stepped forward and wrapped her arms around his shoulders and pulled herself tight against him. He grabbed on to her as if she were an anchor in a storm-tossed sea.

He felt her heartbeat racing as fast as his own and remembered that she was a part of this, that she had nearly been The Professional's victim.

She trembled in his arms and he tightened his grip on her. She raised her head and looked at him and in her eyes he saw his own emotions mirrored there.

"I'm going to play," he said, knowing he really had no other choice. "I'm going to play his game and hope that this time I find them in time."

Somehow in the depths of his soul he'd known from the moment he'd received the note that he would once again be chasing The Professional and hoping that this time had a different ending.

"I'm afraid, Jacob," she whispered softly.

He once again tightened his grip on her. "It's going to be all right," he replied. He didn't have the heart to tell her that he was absolutely, positively terrified of what was to come.

Chapter 5

Layla awoke to the sounds of men's voices coming from the living room. She assumed Tom and Jacob were having a meeting. She rolled over and grabbed her wristwatch from the nightstand and saw that it was just after eight.

Too early to get up and she didn't want to intrude on the crime-fighting talk going on. She definitely didn't want to know any more details about The Professional and his crimes. She knew all she needed to know about the horror of what he had done, promised yet to do.

Her heart ached as she thought about Jacob. Now they all knew the terrible events that had brought him home, the trauma that had left him with haunted eyes and a scarred heart.

After Tom had left the night before and as she and Jacob had embraced, she'd been afraid for herself, but she'd also been afraid for him. She knew if he was forced to play the madman's game again and things went badly and his sister was murdered, he'd probably never recover from the guilt and grief.

And for a moment, as she'd stood in his embrace, she'd felt connected to him in mind and soul like she had never felt connected to another man. Bound by fear and circumstance to each other, not exactly a good basis for a relationship, she reminded herself.

"Not that I'm looking for a relationship," she muttered aloud.

It wasn't long after that embrace that Jacob had insisted she go to bed. She'd done that, but it had been a long time before sleep had finally found her.

She must have fallen back asleep for when she opened her eyes again it was just after nine and the cabin was silent. Outside the wind whistled, promising a frigid, blustery day. The sunlight was muted, as if its shine was bothered by low-hanging clouds. Maybe the winter storm that had been forecasted for next week was coming in faster than expected.

She got out of bed and pulled her robe on, then left the bedroom to find Jacob standing at the front window, a cup of coffee in his hand. Even though she didn't think she'd made a sound he turned to face her as if he'd sensed her presence.

"I'm going into town around eleven to meet with

Tom and go over his case files on the missing women," he said.

"Then I'm coming with you," she replied. "I can make arrangements to meet Portia or one of my other friends for lunch."

"I don't think that's a good idea," he replied. He looked cold, distant, very different from the emotional, vulnerable man of the night before.

"It's a perfectly fine idea," she countered. "I can ride with you to the sheriff's office and then go to the café for lunch. I'll be surrounded by people and I'm sure I'll be perfectly safe." She didn't want to stay here all alone. "Jacob, we can't be sure that he doesn't know you're here at the cabin. I don't want to be left here without you."

A muscle knotted in his jaw. "You could stay with Edie at the big house," he countered.

She shook her head. "I want to eat lunch out and I'll be just fine."

He frowned. "Okay, you're coming with me but if you can't find a lunch date then you'll have to cool your heels in Tom's office. I don't want you wandering the streets all alone."

"Trust me, I'll find somebody to have lunch with me," she replied and headed for the phone in the kitchen. Portia was thrilled to hear from her and immediately agreed to meet her for lunch.

When it was finally time to leave, Layla couldn't wait to get out of the cabin. Jacob had retreated so far into himself she couldn't reach him. He remained at the window...watching...waiting, an air of expectation keeping his shoulders rigid and his back straight.

Whatever tenuous connection they'd made the night before was gone, swallowed by the darkness of his eyes. She had a feeling he didn't like the fact that she'd seen him vulnerable, that she'd momentarily been his comfort.

A man like Jacob wouldn't tolerate pity and would hate to be seen as weak. She hadn't thought him weak, rather she thought his inner torment spoke of a good man's battle against evil.

At a quarter to eleven they were in his truck and headed into town. "I think it's going to snow," she said as she held her hands out to the warmth of the heater.

"Feels like it," he replied.

"I always hated winter. It's so quiet when the snow falls and my dad didn't work much when it snowed." She turned and looked at Jacob. "He was a construction worker so winter meant he was home most of the time."

"And you didn't like having him home?"

"Not much. He wasn't a very nice man, but that's a whole different story. I hate winter but I love Christmas." She frowned. "And I'm missing the fun of putting up my tree and decorating it. At least it will be fun to have some girl time with Portia."

"Just make sure you stay with her and then come straight back to Tom's office. I don't want anything to happen to you."

"Keep talking like that and I might think you care about me," she said teasingly.

"Strictly business," he replied curtly. "Tom is holding a news conference at noon to remind women to check their backseats before they get into their vehicles and to not wander off alone. He's going to announce that the women of the town shouldn't trust anyone."

"That will stir things up," she replied.

"At this point it's necessary for him to repeat the warnings. Now that we know what we're up against it's important that every woman watch their backs."

"Most of us were already doing that with the disappearances," Layla replied.

"And yet he almost got to you in your car," Jacob countered.

"I got careless," she replied. She frowned thoughtfully. "Tom said that he thought all the women had been taken from their cars. I know Suzy and Jennifer's cars were left at their workplaces and Casey's was still parked in her driveway, but Brittany's was hidden in an old barn."

"Tom and I talked about that this morning. We think maybe he hid her car because he wasn't ready for anyone to know what was going on yet."

"He's smart, isn't he?" She watched as Jacob's features tightened.

"Like a fox."

"Did the FBI ever get close to catching him?"

He hesitated a long moment. "No. We never got close. He was like a ghost in the shadows, a phantom that gave us just enough information to whet our appetites, but he didn't make any mistakes."

Chilling. The whole thing was chilling.

The rest of the ride was accomplished in silence. Layla stared out the window and tried not to think about the killer who was working in their town. Instead she thought about how nice it had felt both times that she'd found herself in Jacob's embrace.

After her nightmare his arms around her had made her feel safe, and last night there had been an intimacy between them that had felt right despite the horrible circumstances.

She glanced at him now and was struck again by the fact that he looked so self-contained, like a man comfortable in his utter aloneness.

He'd told her he didn't do relationships and she wondered what had brought him to that decision. Certainly at the moment he appeared to be a man who needed nobody, but had it always been that way?

By the time they reached the sheriff's office Portia was already there waiting for her. After saying hello to Tom and Sam McCain, one of the other deputies, Layla and Portia left to walk the short distance to the café.

"I've been worried sick about you," Portia said as she leaned into the wind and pulled her collar up closer around her face.

"I'm fine," Layla replied, the wind nearly carrying her words away. "We'll talk when we get inside."

There were few people walking the streets and when

they reached the café they found that many of the usual lunch crowd had apparently opted to spend the bitterly cold day in the warmth of their homes.

They sat at a table near the back and shrugged out of their coats. "Now, how are you really?" Portia asked.

"I'm okay." Layla smiled to assure her friend. "Really."

"When Caleb told me about the attack on you my heart nearly stopped. You must have been so terrified."

"I was," Layla admitted. "But, I feel better staying in the cabin with Jacob. Nothing like having a real live FBI agent at your beck and call."

"I doubt that Jacob is at your beck and call," Portia replied drily. "I can't imagine him doing anything for anyone that he doesn't have to do."

"He's not so bad," Layla said, feeling the need to defend him. "He's had a rough time. Didn't Caleb mention to you what we found out last night?"

"I only saw Caleb for a few minutes this morning and we had some other things to talk about. So tell me what you know."

In a lowered voice Layla told her everything that had transpired the night before. Portia listened wide-eyed as Layla told her about the dead women in Kansas City and The Professional who they now suspected had the missing women from Black Rock.

"That's horrifying," she said when Layla was finished. "It's scary to realize how evil people can be. And it's possible it might be somebody who grew up right here, somebody we all know."

Layla nodded and for the first time looked around at the people inside the café. What would a killer look like? Would he look like Buck Harmon? Buck sat at the counter eating a burger, his long dark hair unruly and his shoulders set in defensive arrogance.

Buck frequented The Edge, a bar on the outskirts of town where Layla occasionally went to dance and have fun. He'd asked her out a couple of times but she'd always turned him down. Buck was trouble and she wanted nothing to do with him.

Or was The Professional an older man? Maybe one of the men seated in a group in the corner? John Mathews, a pleasant-looking man who worked in the bank next to Layla's office, caught her eye and raised a hand in greeting.

The Professional could be anywhere. He could be anyone, somebody they all knew and trusted. He was a monster wearing an ordinary face. Or was it possible he was hiding in the shadows in town? Not somebody they all knew, but rather a drifter who had no real ties to the area?

"Afternoon, ladies. What can I get for you?" Katy Matherson, the waitress, interrupted the direction of Layla's thoughts.

Layla ordered a burger and fries and Portia ordered a salad. Once Katy had departed, Portia leaned back against the red vinyl booth and eyed Layla with concern.

"How are you and Jacob getting along?" she asked.

"I think maybe I'm driving him a little bit crazy," she admitted. "You know me, I like to talk and I don't think he likes to listen to me." She frowned and took a sip of her water. "I think he thinks I'm shallow." She thought of that moment when Jacob had asked her what she had to worry about except the next sale on shoes.

"Then he just doesn't know you very well," Portia replied. She reached across the table and grabbed Layla's hand. "The important thing is that you stay there with him until this crazy man is caught. It doesn't matter what he thinks of you, that's the safest place for you to be right now."

"I know." Layla sighed, her thoughts filled with a vision of Jacob. "I'm attracted to him."

Portia looked at her in dismay. "Oh, Layla, why do you always find yourself attracted to men who are emotionally unavailable?"

"That's not true," Layla protested. "Jackson Michaels wasn't emotionally unavailable." Jackson was the last man she'd dated. The relationship had been hot and heavy for two months and then he'd stopped calling her.

"Then why aren't you still with him?"

Layla frowned thoughtfully. "I don't know. He just stopped calling and that was it." To be perfectly honest, she hadn't been heartbroken. Jackson had been a nice guy, but he hadn't taken her breath away, he hadn't made her wild with desire. He'd just been a comfortable date on lonely nights. "I guess you'd have to ask him why he stopped calling," she finally said.

"Didn't you?" Portia asked.

Layla shook her head. "No, I just figured if he didn't want to see me anymore then that was that."

"Sometimes you have to fight for what you want, Layla. You've dated a lot but you've never fought for any of those relationships to last."

"Life is too short to have to fight for a man. Besides, who needs one? All I said is that I was attracted to Jacob."

The last thing Layla wanted to do was any sort of self-analysis on why she was almost thirty years old and still alone. In her heart she thought maybe her father was right. She was a good-time girl, but not worth a lifetime of love. In any case, she was sorry she'd brought the whole thing up.

"Jacob is damaged goods and that's the last man you need to get involved with," Portia exclaimed.

Thankfully the food arrived and the conversation turned more pleasant. Portia entertained her with stories about her children at the daycare and extolled the virtues of the new assistant she'd hired.

As Portia talked about the kids, Layla found her heart filled with the familiar wistfulness that struck her sometimes when she thought about family. She wanted children. She wanted to be the mother she'd never had to a son or a daughter.

She'd already decided that if she wasn't in a committed relationship by the time she was thirty-five she would either be artificially inseminated or adopt. She wasn't going through her life without knowing the joys of motherhood.

"I've got a secret to share with you," Portia said.

"You know I love secrets," Layla replied. "Spill the beans."

Portia leaned forward, her eyes shining brightly. "I'm pregnant."

Layla stared at her in stunned surprise and then exploded with happiness for her friend. "Oh, my God, that's wonderful news. I know how much you've wanted this."

Portia nodded. "I love taking care of other people's children, but I can't wait to take care of my own."

"I'm assuming you've told Caleb?"

"This morning, that was the only serious conversation we had. He was thrilled, but insists that we need to get married as soon as possible."

"So, you're planning your wedding. How exciting!"

"Nothing big," Portia replied. "Both Caleb and I agree that we're just going to have a quiet, intimate ceremony. Anything else would feel wrong with everything that's going on right now."

Layla felt a whisper of cold breath on her neck as the reality of what had happened once again slammed into her. Four missing women, and she had almost been the fifth.

"I have a huge favor to ask you," Portia said, pulling Layla back from her fear.

"You know I'd do anything for you," Layla replied. She and Portia had been best friends since grade school and it had been Portia's friendship that had gotten Layla through her terrible childhood.

"Be my maid of honor at my wedding."

Layla's heart swelled. "You know I'd love to," she replied. "Now, tell me all the details you're planning for the big day."

They talked about the wedding and were in the middle of talking about Christmas plans when Portia gazed at her wristwatch and frowned.

"I've got to get back to the daycare," Portia exclaimed. "I'm already twenty minutes later than I intended to be. The kids will be wondering about me."

The two women got up and headed to the cashier where they paid for their meals and then stepped out into the cold wind. Portia's car was parked in front of the café but she looped an arm with Layla's. "Come on, I'll walk you back to the sheriff's office."

"Nonsense," Layla exclaimed. "Your car is right here. Get in it and go. Besides, I'm going to stop in my office for just a minute. I left my cell phone there the night of my attack and want to grab it." She untangled her arm from Portia's.

Portia hesitated, a frown tugging across her forehead. "Are you sure? I don't mind going with you."

"You already said you're late. Just go. I'll be fine. It's the middle of the day and I'm sure I can walk a short block without any trouble." She gave Portia a quick hug. "Now get in your car before we both freeze to death."

Before Portia could protest further, Layla started down the sidewalk. The wind seemed to have grown even colder while they'd been eating and she pulled her coat collar up around her neck as she headed toward her office. At least with her cell phone she wouldn't feel so cut off from her normal life.

Two minutes, that's all it would take her to run into her office and grab the phone off her desk. She passed a couple headed toward the café and exchanged a quick smile with them.

The candy cane decorations swung back and forth on the streetlights, buffered by the wind that almost screamed in intensity. They'd be lucky if this cold front and the heavy clouds didn't dump a foot of snow by nightfall.

It wasn't until she dug into her purse for her keys to her office door that the first stir of uneasiness whispered through her. The last time she had left here she'd been attacked. She'd tried to downplay the whole thing at the time that it had happened but now that she had more information about The Professional and the game he liked to play, the horror of how close she'd come to being one of his victims rose up inside her.

Her hand trembled slightly as she shoved the key into the lock. *Get a grip,* she told herself. The danger was past and she'd survived, just as she'd survived every bad moment that had ever happened in her childhood.

She opened the door and stepped inside, immediately spying the blinking light on her answering machine and the jeweled cell phone just where she'd left it.

As she dropped the cell phone into her purse she punched the button to play her messages. "Layla, it's Ginny Sinclair. I was just calling to tell you that I've finally decided to put my mother's house on the market and of course I'd like you to handle it. Call me when you get a chance and we'll meet."

"Yes!" Layla said and pumped her fist in the air. She'd been hoping Ginny would contact her when she was ready to sell. And she already had a couple of buyers in mind.

A second message began to play, the voice a deep, unfamiliar male one. "Yes, my name is Michael Fields and I'm thinking about making Black Rock my permanent home. I'd like to set up a time and place where you could show me some available properties. I'm staying at the Black Rock Motel in unit seven."

He ended the message with his cell phone number, but there was no way Layla intended to plan a tour of properties with any male stranger, not until Mr. Professional was behind bars.

Deciding to make a quick pit stop, she left the main reception area and went down the hallway and into the bathroom. She should tell Jacob and Tom about the caller from the motel. They should check him out to make sure he wasn't dangerous.

When she was finished using the restroom and had washed her hands with the orange-scented soap she loved, she stepped out into the hall and he was there.

She barely had time to process the ski mask that covered his features and the hypodermic needle he held in his hand before he lunged forward to attack.

She screamed and threw her purse at him, adrenaline spiking through her as she turned to run. She'd gone only two steps when he crashed into the back of her.

Her knees smashed to the ground as she fell and she cried out in pain at the same time she tried to scrabble forward like a crab, but he managed to grab her ankle and held tight.

She kicked and screamed again as terror crashed her heart against her ribs. *Get away,* that was the only thought that resounded in her head, obliterating any other thought or sound she might hear.

She had to get away! She didn't want to be a missing person. She refused to go to his party.

Twisting onto her back she managed to break his hold on her ankle. She kicked both legs like motor pistons, gasping in relief as she connected with his hand and the needle flew out of it and skittered along the carpeting to the side of the hallway.

He roared with rage and once again managed to grab

her leg. She twisted and turned in an effort to get free, but his hand was like an iron vise.

Slowly, with deadly intent, he began to pull her along the carpeting toward the needle that she knew meant her death. She knew screaming was useless, that the howl of the wind outside would steal away the sound from anyone who might hear and rush to help.

It was at that moment that Layla knew she was going to die. She was going to be the fifth victim. She'd be the guest of honor at his party. She was going to die because she'd come after her stupid cell phone.

Chapter 6

"We can't assume that he followed me here from Kansas City," Jacob said to his brothers seated around the conference table. "Kansas City is only a three-hour drive from here. It's possible he could be a longtime local and came to Kansas City to commit his crimes."

"That's a scary thought," Benjamin said.

"Were you working with any kind of a profile?" Tom asked Jacob.

"We'd profiled his age to be between thirty and fifty. He's organized with above-average intelligence. He's probably single and is either self-employed or works a job that allows him to work alone for long hours at a time." Jacob leaned back in the hardback chair and frowned as he tried to remember everything they had learned about The Professional, which was damned little.

"You know, the usual stuff, maybe a bed wetter and a fire starter and he probably abused animals at some point in time in his youth," Jacob added. "He's probably narcissistic in personality and suffers from delusions of grandeur, that's evident in the fact that he likes attention."

"Just another garden-variety creep," Tom said with a small smile at Jacob. The smile lasted only a second. "I got a report back early this morning that the drug in the needle found in Layla's car contained a combination of Valium and Versed."

"Versed?" Benjamin looked at him curiously.

Tom nodded. "It's a drug most commonly used for minor health procedures. It would render a person unconscious."

"So, we know our perp either has some medical training or has access to drugs," Jacob replied.

"Nothing any of you have said has narrowed our pool of suspects at all." Frustration was evident in Benjamin's voice.

Jacob looked at Tom. "In all these missing women's cases you didn't find any kind of physical evidence at all?"

"A button," Tom replied. "In Casey Teasdale's car we found a button on the floor of the backseat. It's a slightly oversize white button, but unfortunately there's no way of knowing how long it had been there or if it had anything to do with her disappearance. We tested for fingerprints, but couldn't lift any."

"Right now we don't even have a potential suspect. How are we going to find this guy?" Benjamin exclaimed.

Tom looked at Jacob. "I have a feeling he's going to find Jacob. Didn't you say he communicated with you by phone during the last case?"

Jacob nodded and his cell phone in his shirt pocket suddenly felt as if it weighed a thousand pounds. "To be honest, I'm surprised he hasn't already called me. I never changed my number. I knew he was through with me after the Kansas City debacle."

"Maybe the note that he sent you was just the first contact and the calls will soon start coming," Tom said.

Jacob's stomach turned at the very thought of having to endure another round with the killer. "Maybe this time during the calls he'll make a mistake, give us a clue that we can use to find out his identity. One thing is certain, if he has four women and he's working as he did last time, then he's got them alive and stashed someplace nearby. Maybe an old barn or shed or an abandoned warehouse of some sort."

"We're in the middle of ranch and farming country, almost everyone outside of town has a barn or shed on their property. It's going to be like looking for a needle in a haystack," Benjamin said.

"And Brittany is the needle we're hunting for," Tom

replied, a wealth of emotion in his deep voice. It was the first time any of them had mentioned her name, had acknowledged that she was in the hands of The Professional.

Once again Jacob's stomach churned as he thought of his younger sister. Brittany, with her zest for life and easy sense of humor, had been spoiled by all of her brothers.

They were all different men under their skin, but they all shared a tremendous love for their only sister with her bright green eyes and long dark hair. The idea of her being in the grips of this psychopath made Jacob want to throw up.

As his brother began kicking around ideas and rehashing the details of the kidnappings, Jacob suddenly thought of Layla and how cold he'd been to her throughout the day.

He'd found comfort in her arms the night before and it had surprised him. He'd thought there was no place in the world he'd ever find comfort again. But Layla's arms had been warm and welcoming and it had scared him more than a little bit.

He didn't want to like her but he did. He didn't want to respect her and yet he did. He definitely didn't want to desire her but he burned with it. What he wouldn't do was allow himself to care about her in any way that involved his heart.

Caleb's cell phone rang. With a quick apology he answered, his face paling as he listened to the caller. "Be right there," he said. "That was Portia. She's at Layla's office and Layla was attacked."

Jacob was out of his chair before the words had fully left Caleb's mouth. As he tore out of the office and into the winter air, a tumble of thoughts went around in his head.

What were they doing in Layla's office? The deal had been she could have lunch with Portia and then return directly to the sheriff's office. Irritation battled with fear as he raced down the sidewalk toward the real estate office.

He was vaguely aware of his brothers' footsteps pounding the pavement just behind him but all he cared about was getting to Layla and making sure she was okay.

He told himself the frantic beating of his heart had nothing to do with his feelings for her, but rather because he felt responsible for her safety.

When he reached her office he slammed through the front door and found the two women in the hallway. Layla lay on her side, curled into a fetal ball and Portia knelt beside her, her pretty face pale with fear.

"He went out the back door," Portia said as she rose to her feet and stepped back against the wall to get out of the way.

As Jacob knelt next to Layla his brothers ran past them to the back of the building. They could deal with the attacker; Jacob's main concern was the woman who looked like a broken doll against the thick beige carpeting.

"Layla, are you all right?" he asked. She nodded her head. Her eyes were closed but silent tears trekked down her cheeks. "Can you sit up?"

He breathed a sigh of relief as she opened her eyes and pulled herself to an upright position. "What happened?"

"I thought I'd just run in and grab my cell phone. I left it here the night I was attacked. No big deal, right?" The words came haltingly from her. "I came in and got the phone off my desk and then decided to use the bathroom. When I came out he was here in the hallway waiting for me."

"Who was here?" Jacob asked even though he suspected what her answer would be.

She shook her head. "I don't know. He had on a ski mask and he had a needle in his hand. I threw my purse at him and tried to run, but he grabbed me from behind. I kicked him and I thought I was going to die. I thought for sure I was going to be another missing woman, and then Portia came in."

She'd begun to tremble, first her lush lips, then her slender shoulders and finally her entire body. It was the tremor of terror.

"I knew she was coming in to get her cell phone and I got in my car and waited for it to warm up before I left. By the time the engine was warm she still hadn't come out," Portia explained. "I don't know why, but I got worried and decided to come in and check on her."

"Thank God you did," Layla exclaimed. She looked up at Jacob, her eyes the color of midnight and haunted. "He wants me to be his number five. I thought maybe he'd just go after somebody else, but he came after me again. He must have been watching me…stalking me." Her voice rose higher and higher in pitch.

Jacob yanked her up to her feet and wrapped an arm around her shoulders, afraid that she was about to get hysterical or go into some sort of shock.

She leaned against him and buried her face into his chest as the tremors continued to suffuse her body. At that moment Tom came back up the hall from the back door.

"Whoever it was, there's no sign of him now." Tom swiped a hand through his dark hair. "The back door lock is broken. We'll need to get a locksmith over here to fix it."

"I'll take care of it," Benjamin said from behind Tom.

Caleb shoved past the two men to get to Portia. When he reached her he pulled her into an embrace. "You could have been hurt," he exclaimed, emotion husky in his voice.

"I'm okay," Portia assured him. "I was never in any real danger. He was already gone by the time I got back here to Layla."

Layla straightened her back and stepped away from

Jacob. "This was all my fault. I was foolish to come in here alone. I'm sorry," she said to Tom. "I'm so sorry," she said to Portia as tears once again began to course down her face.

"Take her back to the cabin," Tom said to Jacob. "We'll take care of things here and I'll come out later to talk to her."

Jacob nodded and once again placed an arm around her shoulders and led her toward the front door. He didn't know whether to be angry with her or feel sorry for her, but one thing was certain, he was afraid for her.

Everything had conspired to make it easy for The Professional to make a move to take Layla. The inclement weather had people staying off the streets, so there had probably been no witnesses. Even if anyone had seen a man in a ski mask they probably wouldn't pay attention to him with the wind howling so bitterly.

He'd apparently jimmied the door lock in anticipation of her eventual return to the office and Layla had presented to him a perfect opportunity by coming in here all alone.

That meant she was right. He'd been watching her… stalking her. She was also correct in her assessment that he wanted to make her, in particular, his fifth victim.

Jacob's heart felt like stone in his chest as he realized it was up to him to keep that from happening. It was up to him to make sure The Professional was caught before he had his party—with Layla as the guest of honor.

* * *

Jacob was quiet on the drive back to the cabin and Layla was grateful. For the first time in her life she didn't feel like talking.

She found herself in a familiar dark place, like the one she'd often found herself in throughout her childhood. It was a place of danger, of uncertainty, and all she wanted to do was find a safe hiding place where nothing and nobody could hurt her.

She'd managed to process the first attack on her. She'd been at the wrong place at the wrong time, a convenient victim he'd thought would be easy to take. She'd been out after dark alone and had probably left her car door unlocked. She'd made herself an easy victim.

But this second attack spoke of something darker. He had to have been watching her, waiting for her to return to her office. He didn't want another woman. He'd chosen her and he wouldn't be happy until he got to her.

"Are you okay?" Jacob finally asked.

"Not really," she replied truthfully. "I'm trying to go to a good place in my mind, but I'm having trouble finding that place."

He flashed her a glance that let her know he had no idea what she was talking about. "Whenever I'm stressed or scared I make a picture in my mind of doing something I like to do," she said in explanation.

"Like buying new shoes."

She nodded. "Something like that. I might imagine myself in a store, or at Portia's daycare with the kids.

When I was younger my favorite place to go in my mind was to imagine I was with my mother. We'd have lunch together or she'd sing to me, you know, I think about the things that make me feel safe and happy."

She looked out the window in time to see them passing the entrance to the Grayson ranch. "Where are we going?"

"I'm going to go to the cabin by some back roads that lead to the property," he replied with a glance in his rearview mirror. "I want to make sure we aren't being followed."

A new chill filled her at this thought. Would he find them at the cabin? Had their security there been breached? "Who is he? How did he know I'd stop in the office today?"

"My guess is that he saw you leave the café and he followed you. Did you see anyone who seemed to be paying particular attention to you in the café or out on the streets?"

"Not really. John Mathews waved at me when I first arrived in the café and Buck Harmon was sitting at the counter. Buck has asked me out a couple of times but I've never gone out with him. You think this might be personal?"

Once again he glanced in the rearview mirror, but apparently saw nothing that alarmed him. "I think all of the women were random victims, chosen only because he knew their routines and knew he could get into the back of their cars. That's one thing that's going to make it more difficult to find him, the fact that the victims were random, and talking to friends and family isn't going to help further the investigation."

"I had certainly become a creature of habit," she said thoughtfully. "Most nights I stayed late at the office and I wasn't always good about locking my car." An edge of anger swept through her. "I made it so easy for him."

"I don't think it started personal with you, but we both know it has become personal." His dark eyes found her again. "There's already been two attempts on you. We don't want a third. We might not get so lucky next time."

Layla leaned forward to adjust the heater vent as his words caused a new chill to race through her. "Do you have nice places you go in your head when you're stressed or upset?" she asked, wanting something to take her mind off the attack.

"I usually go to wherever the bottom of a bottle of beer will take me, but it's usually not a nice place. It's always filled with darkness." His hands tightened around the steering wheel and she knew he was regretting giving her just that much personal information.

Silence reigned for the rest of the drive and finally after twists and turns down back roads they arrived at the shed where Jacob kept his truck. He parked in the shed and they walked the short distance to the cabin.

Overwhelmed. That's what Layla felt as she shrugged out of her coat, sank down on the sofa and watched as Jacob placed a log on the fire and stirred the embers with a poker. He messed in the fireplace until he had flames dancing then he took off his coat and sat in his recliner.

"You want to talk about it?" he asked.

"There's a first, you're inviting me to talk?" She released a deep sigh. "There isn't much to say. I pretty much already told you what happened."

"Did you get any sense of his height? His weight?"

She frowned thoughtfully, remembering that single moment when she'd left the bathroom and had been confronted by the man. "He wasn't as tall as you. I'd say average height and weight. He had on black pants and a brown coat."

"That's good, that's the kind of things we need," he said with encouragement. "Anything else you can think of? Did he talk to you?"

"No, he never said a word. Maybe he was afraid I'd recognize his voice."

"Maybe. Tom is going to be here in a little while. He's going to bring me copies of the case files of all the missing women and he'll want to question you again. Maybe you should make a list of all the men you noticed in the café."

"I can do that," she agreed. "Although I didn't really pay attention to everyone who was there." She opened her purse and pulled out a pen and a diary-size notebook. "I carry this with me and jot down notes about my days," she explained.

She'd always done a little journaling, had started it

when she'd been in fifth grade. It had been a safe way to vent emotions she couldn't speak of out loud. She stared down at the paper and realized her body was beginning to ache from the attack.

"I think before I do this I want to go take a hot shower," she said. "Now that I've started to calm down I'm feeling some bumps and bruises."

Jacob's eyes darkened. "I'll kill him if I get the chance."

The words spoken so calmly, so filled with certainty, shot a mini-chill through her as she got up from the sofa.

Minutes later as she stood beneath the hot spray of water, she understood the darkness that had become Jacob Grayson. The experiences with The Professional had damaged him and there was no way of knowing if that damage could ever be healed.

And now she was wrestling with her own darkness. What worried her more than anything was that since the attack she hadn't found that safe place in her head. The fear from the attack still had her in its grips and no scenario she came up with in her head could take it away.

As a child the mental form of escape had been what made her strong, what had allowed her to endure. Now without that coping mechanism she felt lost.

When this was all over how damaged would she be? Would she ever feel safe again?

By the time she'd finished her shower Tom had arrived

and another round of questions ensued. She could tell him no more than she'd told Jacob although Tom pressed her hard for any impressions she might have gotten from the man who'd attacked her.

She made the list they wanted of everyone she could think of who had been in the café, but there was little more she could do to help with the investigation.

"It's possible you didn't even see him before the attack," Tom said. "He could have come from any of the buildings near your office and sneaked right into the back alley. I've got a couple of men questioning the business owners in the area to see if they saw anything or if anyone suddenly went missing from their work."

"If he can't get to Layla eventually he'll take somebody else," Jacob said. "Eventually his need will drive him to act again."

"All the women in town are on notice, there isn't much else we can do," Tom replied.

He left as dusk was falling and Layla went into the kitchen to cook something for dinner. As she was putting together a meatloaf, Jacob came into the kitchen and sat in one of the chairs at the table.

"It's not your responsibility to cook for me," he said. "I'm sure you probably don't feel like it, especially after the day you've had."

"I like cooking," she replied. "I learned early in life to be good at it." She finished forming the loaf in the pan and then put it in the awaiting oven. "It will take about an hour for that to cook. You want mashed potatoes? Or

I can do scalloped potatoes. Some people like them cut up in wedges and cooked with the meatloaf, but I'm not a big fan of that. Or I could just scrub a couple and put them in the oven to bake." She paused, aware that she'd been rambling. "You really don't care about potatoes, do you?"

"Not really."

She sat opposite him at the table. "I don't know if you've noticed or not but when I'm stressed or upset I tend to talk too much."

"I've noticed." His lips curled up slightly.

For just a moment she thought she saw a faint twinkle in his eyes, like the ghost of the man he'd once been shining through. Her heart did a crazy flip-flop and she wished she'd spent more time with him before The Professional had stolen his soul, wished she'd met him before so much damage had been done.

The twinkle disappeared and the distance she'd come to expect returned as he got up from the table. "Just let me know when it's time to eat," he replied.

Dinner was a silent affair with Jacob not engaging her in any way. When the meal was over and the kitchen was clean, Layla decided to call it a night. It was still relatively early but she was beyond exhaustion and only hoped that she would sleep without dreams.

"I'm going to bed," she said to Jacob, who was once again in his recliner.

"Good night." He remained distant, not taking his eyes off the television screen that played an old movie.

She'd thought that sleep would come quickly due to her exhaustion; however, once she was alone in the bedroom sleep refused to come at all. She twisted and turned, playing and replaying the attack in her mind.

Who was he? Who was this man who called himself The Professional and what was broken inside him that allowed him to do such heinous things?

He'd been so strong as he'd dragged her across the carpeting. If he'd managed to get to that needle and inject her, she now knew she would have gone unconscious. Then it would have been easy for him to carry her out of the building and take her wherever he was holding the other women.

She pulled the quilt up closer around her neck as a shiver worked through her. Twice she'd nearly been a guest at one of his parties. Jacob was right, she might not be so lucky the next time.

What she wanted was somebody to hold her, somebody to tell her everything was going to be all right, but there was nobody. Jacob certainly wasn't up for the task. She wished she at least had Mr. Whiskers with her. He might just be a cat, but he was warm and furry and liked curling up with her during the night. She made a mental note to call Larry Norwood and check how Mr. Whiskers was doing without her.

Mr. Whiskers had been the only male she'd ever been able to count on to love her unconditionally. In her past she had only a father who had abused and belittled her;

in her future she had the potential of becoming a victim of a serial killer. In her present she was completely and utterly alone.

Chapter 7

Jacob sat at the kitchen table, the case files of the missing women spread out before him. He'd contacted his superior at the Kansas City FBI field office to see if he could get any information they might have found on The Professional's crimes since Jacob had left the department. He'd also wanted to find out if there had been any similar crimes committed anywhere else in the country.

His boss had confessed that there had been no further leads on the case and had told Jacob that if Tom wanted FBI assistance in Black Rock all he had to do was request it.

Jacob knew his brother Tom was a prideful man, but that he wasn't so proud he wouldn't ask for help if he needed it. The truth was if The Professional was one of Black Rock's own as they suspected, then the brothers of the Black Rock law enforcement were the best men to find the criminal.

There were no records of similar crimes that had taken place anywhere in the country. It was as if The Professional had come into the age of his reign of terror in Kansas City and now was continuing in Black Rock. Jacob knew that if he was successful here, then it wouldn't be long before another place would soon suffer the same kind of attack.

Criminals like The Professional didn't suddenly stop unless they were placed behind bars or dead. The dark desires that drove him wouldn't be sated for long after one of his parties. He'd soon need another…and another. He had to be stopped here and now.

Was he from Black Rock or had he followed Jacob here? That was the million-dollar question. If they could just pinpoint where The Professional was from they might have a better chance of figuring out who he was.

Jacob leaned back in the chair and glanced at the clock on the wall. Almost midnight. He'd been poring over these files for hours, ever since Layla had gone to bed.

He was looking for something, anything that his brothers and the other deputies might have missed, but so far he'd been unsuccessful in finding anything that might point a finger to any one person in Black Rock, or anywhere else.

He'd asked Tom to come up with a list of people who had recently moved to the area, on the chance that The Professional had followed him from Kansas City to his hometown. He also wanted background searches done on all the doctors in the area and any other hospital personnel who might have access to drugs. An average Joe wouldn't have access to the kind of drugs that had been in the hypodermic needle they'd found in Layla's car.

His brother was returning the next day and hopefully would have a list of names they could begin investigating. It wasn't much to go on, but they had to start somewhere. To keep Layla safe.

Layla.

He got up out of his chair and poured himself a fresh cup of coffee, then returned to the table. Something about Layla was bringing him back to life and he wasn't sure he liked it.

She was making him feel, and he'd believed himself incapable of ever feeling anything again. When he'd seen her curled up on the floor in her office, his heart had nearly burst out of his chest with fear for her.

He didn't want to care about anyone ever again, but Layla had made a chink in his armor, a chink that made him wary. Hell, he was even beginning to find her incessant chatter oddly endearing.

He looked up and nearly jumped in surprise as he

saw the object of his thoughts standing in the doorway wearing that sexy nightgown and matching robe. Her hair was tousled around her face and only made her look sexier than ever.

"Can't sleep?" he asked as a knot of tension wound tight in his stomach.

"No." She walked barefoot to the coffeemaker and poured herself a cup, then grabbed the chair opposite him at the table. She took a sip of the coffee and then lowered the mug from her lips. "I've been tossing and turning and finally decided to give up the battle." She looked at the paperwork in front of him. "Are those the case files of the missing women?"

"Yeah." He stared down at the file in front of him, finding it less provocative than looking at her. "Unfortunately, I haven't been able to find anything that might move the investigation forward in any way."

"So, really the only thing you all have to go on is the drug angle from the syringe that he left in my car."

"That and a button that might or might not have been left by the perp."

"A button?" she asked curiously.

He finally looked at her once again and tried to keep his gaze on her face, not allowing it to drift south. "A white button to be exact." He opened one of the file folders. "There's a picture of it someplace in here. Ah, here it is."

He slid the picture across the table toward her. She picked it up and studied it. "Too big to be a shirt button," she observed. "Looks more like a coat or some sort of decorative button. Where was it found?"

"In Casey Teasdale's car. Did you know her?"

She nodded and slid the photo back to him. "Casually. She was a trendy dresser. It's possible the button came off a dress or a jacket of hers."

"Did you know my sister?" He wasn't sure why he'd asked or why it was important to him. For the first time since this all had begun he wanted, needed, to talk about his sister.

"I know Brittany," she replied, making him realize he'd spoken of his sister in the past tense. "We're friendly, but don't really hang out together. She's a beautiful woman, Jacob, and I know you and your brothers are going to do everything in your power to bring her home."

Emotion pressed thick and tight in his chest. He'd tried not to think about his sister at the hands of The Professional, but now thoughts of Brittany filled his head, his heart. Would she be home for Christmas? Or would they find her body after The Professional had enjoyed his party?

"She's tough," he finally said.

"Tell me about her," Layla urged him, as if sensing his need to talk about her.

"She's sometimes irresponsible, which is why my brothers didn't realize she was initially missing. It wasn't until she'd missed a couple of days of work that we realized there was a problem. Still, she'd missed work before and Caleb, Benjamin and Tom had always covered for her. We all spoiled her terribly over the years."

"I imagine having four big brothers isn't the easiest thing in the world at times," Layla replied.

An unexpected laugh blurted out of him. "She used to complain that it was like having four overly protective fathers." He leaned back in his chair. "She loves to sing and is completely tone-deaf, but she has a heart of gold and would do anything for anyone." Any laughter he might have felt faded away beneath a crushing weight of anguish. "She's got to be all right."

"She's still alive, Jacob. Hang on to that," Layla said softly. "He hasn't had his final party yet, and as long as he doesn't there's still a chance for Brittany and all the other women."

He nodded. "If anyone can survive this ordeal, she can. We just need to find them before he snaps again."

"Or before he gets me." Layla's voice held a slight tremor that spoke of her own fear. "I don't want to be a guest at his party."

"We're not going to let him get to you," he said, a rough edge to his voice.

"Promise?"

He sighed. "The last time I made a promise I made it to Carrie Walker's mother. I promised her I'd find her daughter before The Professional killed her, but Carrie was one of the women we found in that warehouse. I don't make promises anymore, not about anything."

"Well, I can promise you that I don't intend to go

into my office alone again until this is all over." She wrapped her fingers around her mug and brought it to her lips. He couldn't help but notice that her hands trembled slightly.

"I'm sorry you're frightened," he said.

She lowered her cup and offered him a small smile. "Thanks. I'll be fine. This isn't the first time in my life I've been afraid. True fear is being eight years old and hiding under a porch. Real terror is knowing that if your father finds you it might be the time he finally beats you to death."

Jacob stared at her in stunned surprise. "Your father was abusive?"

She set her cup on the table and her eyes were dark with memories he could only guess were terrible. "My father was a brutal bastard. The only good thing he did for me was die. Surprisingly, he had a very big life insurance policy on himself and left me as beneficiary. And you probably think I'm terrible for saying that."

"I don't think you're terrible at all." He'd sensed that there was more to Layla West than her chattiness and superficial values. He realized now there had been clues about her father, he just hadn't picked up on them. "You never tried to get help from anyone?"

Again she smiled, a small gesture that didn't quite lighten the darkness of her eyes. "For a long time I just assumed everyone's dad was mean. By the time I knew that something was wrong I was too scared of him to tell anyone. The day I turned eighteen I left his house and got myself an apartment. Between then and the time of his death we didn't have a relationship at all."

"It was his loss," Jacob replied.

This time her eyes lit up. "Thanks. Anyway, I figure I survived him. I can survive this." There was a hint of steely strength in her voice. "And that's why I like shoes," she added.

Jacob frowned in confusion. "What do shoes have to do with all this?" Sometimes the way her mind worked fascinated him.

"Shoes are my rebellion against the man who raised me. Every year at Christmas he bought me a pair of shoes, the ugliest sturdy brown shoes you'd ever want to see. I hated those damned shoes. Kid at school made fun of them. I decided when I got old enough to buy my own, I'd make sure they were pretty, sexy high heels and I'd have a different pair for every day of the year."

"You don't owe me any explanation for what you buy," he protested.

"I know, but I suspect you think I'm kind of shallow and I just wanted you to know that there is a method to my madness. I paid my penance for future sins by enduring my father and now I just want to live life to its fullest. By the way, I think you've more than done your penance for a sin you didn't even commit." She leaned forward, her eyes ablaze with emotion. "Just catch this man, Jacob, and in the process give yourself permission to live again."

He wanted her now, with her eyes so bright and the

sweet words of redemption on her lips. He wanted to carry her into the bedroom and take her until they were both left gasping and spent.

But he knew he wasn't going to do that. He had nothing to give her except his momentary passion, his quick-fire desire, and it didn't seem fair to offer her that and nothing else.

"Why aren't you married, Layla?"

She shrugged her shoulders. "I'm just not the marrying kind," she replied.

"So, you have no desire to have a family?"

"On the contrary, I definitely want kids," she replied. "I figure by the time I'm thirty-five if I haven't found a man who'd be a good father, then I'll just get artificially inseminated and have my baby. I don't need a man in my life to be a good mother."

He wondered how deep the scars were from her childhood with her father. Was his brutality why she wasn't the marrying kind, why she didn't think a father was important in the life of a child?

"There are men out there who would make great fathers," he said.

"I suppose. And on that note, I think maybe it's time for me to try to get some sleep." She stood and carried her cup to the sink.

"Yeah, I need to do the same," he agreed. He closed the case files and stacked them, then got up and took his cup to the sink. He turned to tell her good-night and found her standing far too close to him.

The flowery, feminine scent of her filled the air and the desire he'd tamped down only moments before roared to life once again.

"Then I guess I'll just say good night," she said. She licked her lower lip and Jacob knew in that instant that he was going to kiss her.

She must have sensed it as well, for she made no move to back away from him or go to her bedroom. Instead she leaned forward at the same time he took a small step to close the short distance between them.

The instant his mouth touched hers, he knew he was in trouble. Hot and greedy, her lips instantly yielded to his, opening enough to allow him to deepen the kiss.

At the same time her arms went up to his shoulders and he found himself gathering her close, the slick material of the silk robe warming as his hands splayed across her slender back.

The kiss spiraled out of control quickly. He tangled his hands in her soft, scented hair as their tongues swirled in a fevered dance.

Her robe gaped open as she pressed even closer to him, so close he could feel the fullness of her breasts against him, felt the hard pebbles of her erect nipples through the thin material of her nightgown.

She was fire and vibrant energy in his arms and he wanted to take whatever she offered, whatever he needed from her. He wanted to take until she had no more left to give and then he'd take some more.

For the first time in over six months he felt wonderfully

alive, his mind emptied of all thought except his want of the woman he held in his arms.

He moved his mouth from her lips to her jaw, then down the length of her neck, his heart pounding rapidly in his veins. She dropped her head back, allowing him access to the column of her throat, and as she released a small moan, his desire torched hotter, brighter.

There was no thought of what he couldn't give her, no thought of how wrong this moment was for both of them. There was only her heat, her fire that warmed him in places that had been cold for a very long time.

"Jacob," she whispered, his name a fevered plea for more and more.

And he wanted more. God help him but he wanted all of her. He released his hold on her and stepped back, giving them both a moment to draw in deep breaths, to ground them in reality.

She obviously didn't want reality. She held out her hand to him, her eyes speaking of her own desire, and he knew he was going to take her into her bedroom and stay with her until their desire was sated.

The bedroom was dark when they entered and she dropped his hand only long enough to turn on the bedside lamp. It created a soft pool of illumination that loved the hues of her skin.

She shrugged off her robe and his gaze was drawn to the flush of her cheeks, then the fullness of her breasts beneath the animal print gown.

He'd been numbed by his pain, by his very solitude

for some time. But he didn't feel numb at the moment. Rich and raw desire filled him as he advanced toward her.

"No promises," he said, his voice sounding deeper than usual.

"None needed," she replied easily. "Just give me tonight with you, Jacob. I won't ask you for anything more."

That was all he needed to hear, the acknowledgment that she expected nothing from him except this night and his passion. He took her back into his arms.

At that moment his cell phone rang.

The musical ring sliced through the sexual tension as confusion washed over him. Who would be calling him at midnight?

The confusion swiftly gave way to a fear that instantly washed all his desire away. He dropped his arms from around Layla and stared at her as the phone rang again.

"Don't answer," Layla said urgently as he dug his cell phone out of his pocket. "Please, Jacob. Just don't answer it." It was as if she knew who might be on the other end of the line.

He stared down at the number on his caller identification, not recognizing the digits that were displayed. He opened the phone and placed it against his ear, but said nothing.

"Hello Agent Grayson. I've missed you. Are you ready to play?"

The deep, familiar voice cast Jacob back into the darkness and it was only the touch of Layla's hand that kept him from drowning in it.

Chapter 8

"I couldn't hear anything in the background of the call that might point to a location," Jacob said to his brothers, who were all squeezed around the cabin's small kitchen table. Outside the day was as dismal and gray as the mood among the men.

"We've gone over this a dozen times already," he said impatiently. "I didn't recognize his voice, it was distorted as it's always been. All he said was that he's looking forward to playing the game with me, that Jennifer Hightower cries all the time and Suzy Bakersfield appears to be in a mild state of shock. And Brittany said to tell me hello."

As the men continued their discussion Layla silently refilled their coffee cups. She'd gotten up early that morning and fixed Jacob breakfast. He'd said he wasn't hungry, but she'd insisted he eat, knowing that it was going to be a long day.

The night before had seemed endless. After the phone call, Jacob had insisted she go to bed, and sensing he wanted time alone, she'd complied. She'd found sleep impossible and knew he'd suffered the same fate as she'd heard him wandering around the cabin until nearly dawn.

She hadn't been sure if it was the phone call or the fact that they'd almost made love that had kept sleep at bay for her. The contact with the killer had been disturbing, but so had the intimate contact with Jacob.

Jacob moved her as no other man in her life had ever done before.

She would have fallen into bed with him last night if the phone call hadn't interrupted them. And he would have taken her to bed. He'd kissed her with raw desire. There had been no mistaking what he wanted from her.

And she'd wanted him like she'd never wanted before. She would have willingly capitulated to her own wants, her own needs, if that horrifying call hadn't happened.

She tucked a strand of her hair behind her ear and tried not to dwell on the thoughts of what might have been, but they kept intruding into her brain.

She knew better than to chase what she couldn't have, and Jacob was in that category. Oh, she might get his passion, enjoy his lust, but she knew there would never be anything deeper, more lasting.

Sometimes she felt as if her father had cursed her just to be spiteful. He'd made a deal with the devil to keep her from finding real love.

Jacob looked both tired and slightly dangerous in his black turtleneck and jeans and wearing his shoulder holster. He'd had the gun on when she'd gotten up that morning, the result of the contact with the killer and a reminder that danger could come at any time.

She finished pouring their coffee and then resumed her stance in the corner, her gaze lingering on Jacob. The lack of sleep the night before showed in tired lines that bracketed his mouth, in the faint shadows beneath his eyes.

What she'd like to do was pull him into her bed, force him to sleep without dreams and sleep wonderfully well-embraced in his arms. She closed her eyes and for a moment imagined herself there, in the safety and security of his strong arms.

"Okay. So we didn't get anything from the phone call. I've got a couple of the men searching all the abandoned buildings here in town," Tom said as Layla tried to focus less on Jacob and more on the conversation. "And when we're finished in town we'll spread out and begin checking buildings around the area."

"That's going to be a huge job," Benjamin observed.

"I agree," Tom replied. "I've called up all the volunteer deputies to come in and help with the search and the men from the fire department have also offered to step in and do whatever they can to help."

"This is a good town," Benjamin added. "People will step up to stop this lunatic."

"Caleb came up with a list of people who have moved to Black Rock in the last six months or so," Tom continued and looked at his youngest brother.

"There's only been a couple of people," Caleb said as he pulled a piece of paper from his pocket. "Jerry Tipton is thirty-two and moved here four months ago. He's divorced and works as a traveling salesman for some grocery company. Then we have Greg Todd. He's twenty-nine and moved here a couple of months ago and works as a nurse at the hospital. Finally, there's the Norwood family. Larry, his wife and their two daughters moved here about seven months ago."

"I investigated Larry Norwood when Lilly was kidnapped," Tom replied. "He doesn't exactly fit our profile in that he appears happily married and obviously has a love for animals, since he's a veterinarian."

"The profile is sometimes wrong," Jacob replied. "We can't overlook anyone."

There was no way Layla would believe that Larry Norwood could be The Professional. He was caring for her cat, for goodness' sake.

"We'll do full background checks on these people," Tom said. "At least it's a place to start."

"I'd like to talk to all of them," Jacob said. "If one of them is The Professional I might not recognize the voice but I could pick up something in their speech patterns that would identify him."

"I'll arrange interviews with all of them in my office," Tom said.

"As a nurse it's possible that Greg Todd would have access to the kind of drug we found," Benjamin said.

"Anyone can access any drugs on the internet these days," Jacob reminded them.

"A traveling salesman would have opportunity," Caleb added.

"We'll check them out," Tom said. "Once they're cleared with alibis or whatever, we'll move to long time residents of Black Rock that might be responsible."

"Like Buck Harmon?" Layla asked.

Tom leaned back in his chair and smiled at her. "Buck is a pain in my ass, there's no question. He drinks too much and when he drinks he gets stupid, but I'd bet my badge he isn't a killer."

"Buck Harmon isn't organized enough to find his way home on a Saturday night," Benjamin said wryly.

"I just thought of something," Layla said, suddenly remembering the phone message she'd received in her office. "When I was at my office I listened to my messages and there was one from a man. He said his name was Michael Fields and that he was planning on making Black Rock his home. He's staying at the motel and he wanted me to take him out to look at properties."

"Did you contact him while you were there?" Tom asked.

She shook her head. "I wrote down his phone number but I didn't call him back. He's staying in unit seven at the motel. Maybe it's him. Maybe he's The Professional."

She frowned as she thought of what might have happened if she'd taken him out. Would she have shown him an empty house where he could have overwhelmed her and carried her off?

"We'll definitely check it out," Tom replied.

"Maybe it's him, but I'm inclined to think not," Jacob replied. "As far as we could tell in the other cases, he never contacted his victims."

"And there's no evidence that he did so in these current cases," Benjamin added.

"But somebody here in town is a killer," Layla replied. "And he wants me."

"He doesn't like to lose," Jacob said. "And you've thwarted his efforts twice now." His gaze held hers for a long moment and in his eyes she thought she saw a hint of softness. "Is there someplace else you can go?" he asked. "Family or friends or somebody you can stay with until this mess is all over?"

She shook her head. "I don't have any family and all my friends are right here in Black Rock." She raised her chin defensively. "Besides, he's got me staying here in this cabin where no hint of Christmas exists, he's got my cat boarded at the vet's office and me staying away from my office. He's taken enough from me already. I'm not leaving town."

She was suddenly aware of Tom staring at her, his eyes narrowed thoughtfully. "I'm not sure I want you to leave town," he said slowly. "Maybe it's a good idea for you to be seen in town, to let him know that you're still here and aren't afraid. Maybe it will push him to do something stupid."

"Whatever I can do to help, I'll do," Layla replied, ignoring the flutter of fear that winged in her stomach.

"Or it will push him to do something terrible," Jacob said darkly.

Layla wanted to place her hand on his shoulder as she saw the shadows that had crept back into his eyes. She knew he was remembering when he'd thought he'd been the one who had pushed the killer too far and death had resulted.

"He's going to do something terrible whether we push him or not," Tom replied. "And we'll do whatever is necessary to keep Layla protected."

As the men continued to discuss their plans to further the investigation, she remained in her place in the corner, listening to the conversation that eased none of her fears.

It was almost noon when Layla and Jacob were alone again. Jacob was quiet, but it wasn't the morose kind of silence she'd endured the first night and day with him. It felt like a focused silence, as if his head was filled with plans and thoughts that brooked no discussion.

"No more fires," he said when she started to place a log into the fireplace.

She looked at him in surprise. "Why not?"

"We don't want to send up any more smoke signals that will let anybody know that we're here."

His words sent a new sense of disquiet through her as she placed the log back in the wooden box by the fireplace. "Does this mean we'll freeze to death?"

He cast her a tired smile. "No, it just means I need to turn up the thermostat on the furnace." He sank into his recliner with a deep sigh.

"Portia is pregnant," Layla said, suddenly remembering her friend's good news from the day before. She had no idea what made her think of it but suspected it was her mind subconsciously working to stay positive.

Jacob raised an eyebrow. "She is? Caleb hasn't mentioned anything about it, but I guess the circumstances haven't exactly been great for him to make an announcement. He must be thrilled. He always wanted a family."

"Did you ever want children?" she asked.

"I thought about it once, but things didn't work out." He leaned back in the chair and stifled a yawn with the back of his hand. "It was a long time ago and I was a different man then." These words were spoken with an edge of bitterness in his voice that invited no further questions.

"Why don't you take a nap while I make us some lunch," she suggested.

"That sounds like a plan," he agreed. "And for dinner tonight you and I will eat at the café."

"Why do I suddenly feel like a minnow?"

"Layla, you know I won't let anything happen to you, but I think maybe Tom is right. Both of us need to be seen around town. Maybe if we flaunt our presence in his face, he'll get so angry he'll show his hand." His eyes suddenly went black. "Let's just hope we don't push him so hard that those women wind up dead before we catch him."

"That's not going to happen this time, Jacob," she said fervently. She knelt down next to his chair and laid her head on his upper arm. "This is going to have a better ending."

"You promise?" he asked softly, his voice already filled with imminent sleep.

Before she could reply she knew he'd fallen asleep. She rose from his side and watched him for several long moments. His chest rose and fell in a slow, deep rhythm and once again she thought of what it would be like to be held in his arms. She found herself wondering what it would be like to be loved by a man like Jacob.

Irritated with this kind of thought she left him and went into the kitchen to prepare some sort of lunch for them. Within minutes she was engrossed in putting together a quick sauce for spaghetti.

So, there had been a woman, she thought. Things didn't work out, that's what he'd said and that implied there had been a relationship once.

Whoever she was, Layla suspected she had broken his heart. Once again Layla found herself wishing she'd connected with Jacob sooner, before the woman, before The Professional.

She chided herself inwardly. The last thing she wanted to do was develop any real feelings for Jacob. She didn't want to feel that heady rush of emotions, the hope that somehow she'd find her soul mate. She'd been disappointed so many times in the past and didn't want to go through it again.

It was easier to not involve her heart, to go through the motions of a relationship without expecting, without hoping for anything other than a few laughs and a couple of nights. Loving Jacob would be the worst thing she could do.

It took her nearly an hour to get the sauce and spaghetti ready. She made a salad and broiled some bread with a little butter and garlic topping, then set everything on the table.

Satisfied that it was ready to eat, she stepped into the living room and froze. Jacob wasn't in the recliner. Her gaze shot to the bathroom door. It was open and it was easy for her to see that nobody was inside.

Don't panic, she told herself, but when she checked the bedroom and didn't find him there, a sweeping anxiety overtook her. Where had he gone?

On wooden legs she walked to the front door. His coat was no longer hanging on the hook next to hers. She looked outside, but saw no sign of him.

The anxiety blossomed into something stronger. Had he tired of her? Had she pushed him too hard with personal questions, talked too much and driven him crazy?

Or had he somehow gotten a clue who The Professional was and gone after him without the support of his brothers, with only his rage to back him up?

No, she didn't believe he'd done that. She'd sat in on the conversation that had taken place around the kitchen table. There was no way Jacob could have gleaned the identity by that conversation.

It was more likely she'd driven him crazy, with her talk about shoes and children, with her endless nervous chatter about everything under the sun.

She remained at the door, staring outside as a new emotion shoved up in her chest. A weary resignation filled her. She shouldn't be surprised if he'd left for good. Even with the threat of death hanging over her head she couldn't keep a man at her side. It was just like her daddy had always told her.

Jacob made his way through the thick woods near the cabin, wondering what in the hell had possessed him. But he knew. Layla. She had possessed him.

He knew this land as well as he knew the sound of his own breathing. During the last six months of isolation he'd often walked these woods at dusk, thinking about the past and the part he'd played in the deaths of The Professional's first victims.

Somehow over the last couple of days rational thought had sliced through the fog of despair that had settled over him since he'd arrived back in Black Rock.

He no longer carried the weight of those deaths in his heart. Layla had been right when she'd told him that the women were already dead the moment The Professional had taken them. Jacob also suspected The Professional had meant to make Jacob feel responsible when he'd claimed Jacob had pushed him over the edge. The killer was already over the edge and his words to Jacob had just been more of his manipulation and game-playing.

At least there had been no report of any other woman missing. Tom's press conference had put the women of Black Rock on notice. There was a killer among them and care should be taken not to be out alone.

Of course, Jacob still believed that Layla was the chosen fifth victim and The Professional wouldn't be happy with anyone else, but the problem was he wasn't sure. He couldn't anticipate anything when it came to this particular serial killer.

It took him only minutes to find what he was looking for. Using the ax he'd brought with him he cut down the small evergreen tree. He'd also brought with him a bucket perfect to fill with dirt to stand the tree upright.

He had no idea how long he and Layla would be cooped up together in the cabin. It was possible they would be there through the holidays and she was missing the Christmas season, so he'd decided to bring a little of it into the cabin.

With the tree set in the bucket he picked it up and headed back and his heart felt lighter than it had in a very long time. He had no Christmas decorations for the tree, but he had a feeling Layla was creative enough to make a purse out of a sow's ear.

When he reached the porch she flew out of the door, her face pale as she trembled with something that looked very much like anger.

"How could you?" she demanded and slapped her hands against his chest. "How could you just disappear like that and not tell me where you were going?"

"I thought I'd surprise you," he offered, aware that it had been a mistake on his part not to tell her he was going out. He'd been alone too long and it had been thoughtless. "Get inside before you catch cold."

She turned on her high heels and stomped back through the door. Jacob followed her, aware that he owed her an apology. "I'm sorry," he said as he set the tree down next to the fireplace. He shrugged out of his coat and hung it up.

"I just thought you'd left, that maybe I'd driven you away because I talk too much." Her voice trembled slightly.

"I hate to admit this, but I'm getting used to your chatter," he said with a small smile. "You'd mentioned a couple of times that there was no Christmas here, so I thought I'd bring you a little." He sat on the sofa next to her. "Layla, I'm not going to leave you until this is all over, until I know for sure you're in no danger. Again, I apologize for scaring you. And now I smell something delicious so let's eat and then you can figure out how to make this little evergreen tree into a Christmas tree."

She could have held a grudge. God knew Sarah had been able to hold a grudge for hours, even days, over some perceived slight. But, Layla was back to herself as they ate lunch, chattering about the holidays and asking him about favorite Christmas traditions from his youth.

"Aluminum foil stars," she said suddenly. "That's how we can decorate the tree. And popcorn." She jumped out of her chair and went to the pantry. "Got it," she exclaimed triumphantly as she pulled out a box of microwave popcorn. "This will be so much fun," she said as she returned to the table. "We'll spend the afternoon creating a stunning masterpiece."

"Whoa, the tree was a project for you. I've got other things to do this afternoon," he protested.

"Like what?" she demanded. She leaned forward and grabbed his hand across the table. "Let it all go, Jacob. For just a couple of hours let it go and let's have fun."

Fun? He couldn't remember the last time he'd allowed himself that. Staring into her hopeful eyes he realized he wanted a little fun with her. He wanted those couple of hours of not thinking about danger and death, of not allowing The Professional to enter his mind.

"You're going to have to teach me how to make aluminum foil stars," he replied.

She smiled in delight. "I'd be happy to."

Within thirty minutes they had finished the meal, cleaned up the dishes and were seated at the table with a box of aluminum foil while the scent of freshly popped popcorn filled the air.

"Christmas was never any big deal when I was growing up," she said as they worked the foil to create stars. "Once I left my father's house I made it a big deal every year. I usually decorate my house like the North Pole, bows and ribbons and holly everywhere."

"Christmas was a big deal at home when I was a kid," he replied. His head was suddenly filled with the memory of those days when his parents had been alive and all his brothers and his sister were beneath one roof.

He'd loved being part of his family unit and at that time had promised himself that when he got older and married he'd fill his house with children and laughter.

He'd not only done a disservice to himself, but also to the memory of his parents by closing himself off from his family the last six months.

"Mr. Whiskers loves Christmas, too," Layla said, pulling him from his thoughts.

"How long have you had Mr. Whiskers?" he asked.

"Two years. I got him as a kitten because I felt like I needed something living and breathing in my house besides myself. I wanted something to come home to, something to take care of and Mr. Whiskers was my answer."

He nodded, but in her words he sensed a depth of

loneliness that was belied by his perception of Layla West. She was vibrant and beautiful and he couldn't imagine a woman like her ever being lonely.

"Maybe you need a pet," she said and smiled at him. "Have you ever considered getting a dog or a cat, something you could take care of? Something that would love you unconditionally? You know studies say that pets are good for your mood and good for high blood pressure."

He laughed. "What makes you think I might suffer from high blood pressure?"

"I don't see how you wouldn't have high blood pressure considering the job you chose." She set aside the star she'd just finished. "Did you like your work…I mean, before The Professional?"

He stared out the window where a false twilight had fallen despite the fact it was only four o'clock. He felt as if he'd been in the middle of a false twilight for months.

"Yeah, I loved what I did," he finally replied. He got up from the table and walked over to the window where he stared out unseeing. "I felt like I was doing something good, something important. I like law enforcement and I allowed him to take that away from me."

He wasn't aware that she'd left the table until she touched his back. It was a soft touch, meant to comfort. "You could go back, couldn't you?"

He considered her words thoughtfully and then shook

his head. "No, I don't think so. It's been too long and it wouldn't be fair to the other agents who stuck it out."

"Then what are you going to do? You can't stay here, cooped up for the rest of your life."

He turned to face her then. "To be honest I haven't given it much thought. Maybe I'll see if Tom could use another deputy here when this is all over." He smiled then, hoping to take away the concern that darkened her beautiful eyes. "Or maybe I can set up a booth and sell aluminum stars."

She smiled then, just as he suspected she would and the warmth of it sizzled through him, along with the memory of the kiss they'd shared.

He wanted to kiss her again. He knew it would be a mistake, but he didn't care. He had scarcely moved a muscle before she was in his arms, her mouth locked with his in a kiss that took his breath away.

Someplace in the back of his mind he knew this wasn't right, that there was no way he was willing to put his heart on the line again. But another voice reminded him that he'd made that clear to her, that she knew the score and it didn't seem to matter to her.

Take what she gives, the voice said. Don't overthink it, just go with the flow. The flow was in the sweet spill of her hair in his fingers, in the heat of her lips against his.

"Oh, Jacob," she murmured against his mouth. "I want you. Take me into the bedroom and make love to me."

His heart accelerated in rhythm as his body responded

to her nearness, her words. But he had to be certain that she understood. He had to tell her again that she should expect nothing more from him than a physical connection that had no future.

"Layla." He stepped back from her. "If we do this then you have to understand that it's a one-shot deal and there's no future with me."

"I live in the moment, Jacob. Besides, I already told you I'm not the marrying kind." She moved back into his arms, her eyes shining overly bright. "Just give me this moment with you."

How could he deny her what he wanted most? Together they left the kitchen and went into the bedroom. Once there he kissed her again, the kiss quickly growing to a fever pitch.

He knew there were condoms in the bottom drawer of the nightstand. Throughout the last couple of years his brothers had occasionally entertained women in the cabin.

He broke the kiss once again, this time to remove his holster and set it on top of the nightstand. As he did that, Layla pulled her sweater over her head, revealing a black lace bra that nearly had him finished before he'd begun.

Yanking the turtleneck he wore over his head, his heart thundered. It had been so long since he'd enjoyed the pleasures of a woman's body, so long since he'd felt this well of need.

She kicked off her high heels and then peeled off her

jeans, revealing panties that matched the black bra. "You are so beautiful," he said softly.

She smiled and slid beneath the quilt on the bed. "And right now I'm all alone."

He was just about to unfasten his jeans when a bang of metal came from outside. Somebody was out there! Instantly he reached for his gun, all thoughts of lovemaking banished by a different kind of adrenaline.

Layla shot up to a sitting position, her eyes huge with fear. "Jacob?"

"Stay inside. Don't open the door to anyone but me," he said as he ran for the front door. His thoughts zoomed through his head. Who was outside? If it was one of his brothers they would have made themselves known.

Was it possible their hiding place had somehow been found? Was it The Professional outside seeking a way in? Even the reassuring weight of his gun in his hand couldn't take away the chill of imminent danger that worried through him as he opened the door and stepped out into the shadows of pre-dusk.

Chapter 9

The minute Jacob left the bedroom Layla scrambled out of bed and pulled her robe around her. Her heart banged painfully fast against her ribs as she hurried toward the front door and peered outside. There was no sign of Jacob or anyone else.

Had The Professional found them? There was no question in her mind that he would kill Jacob to get to her. Tears blurred her vision as she gripped the door frame on either side.

Jacob! Her heart cried with fear for him. He shouldn't have gone outside. He should have called for backup. He was just starting to live again and it wasn't fair that he might die in his effort to keep her safe.

She should have grabbed her cell phone as she'd run

from the bedroom. She was just about to go retrieve it and call for help when Jacob appeared at the door.

Quickly she unlocked it and threw herself at him. "Oh, thank God," she exclaimed.

"It was a false alarm," he said. "A stray dog was trying to find a meal in my trash can around back." He patted her back. "It's okay, you're safe."

"I wasn't worried about me, I was terrified for you," she confessed as she clung with her arms around his shoulders. She buried her face in his chest, his skin cold from his outing without a shirt. "I was afraid it was him and that he'd kill you."

"Nobody is going to kill me if I can help it," he replied, his voice lower than usual as he tightened his arms around her.

She didn't reply. She wanted to warm him, needed to continue to touch him, to assure herself that he was alive and well.

The moment in the bedroom had been broken by the noise and Jacob's rush outside, but it hadn't taken away her intense desire for him, it hadn't banished her need to belong to him completely, even if there was no happily-ever-after attached.

She finally raised her head and looked at him. "Now, where were we?" She was determined to get what she wanted, and she wanted Jacob.

His eyes flashed with fire that threatened to combust her where she stood. "I remember exactly where we were."

"Then why don't we resume where we left off?" She

stepped out of his arms and turned to go back into the bedroom, confident that he would follow.

Once again he set his gun on the nightstand within easy reach as she shrugged out of her robe and got into the bed. She watched silently as he took off his shoes and socks and then shrugged out of his jeans.

As he stood at the side of the bed clad only in a pair of navy briefs, her breath hitched in her chest. He might think she was beautiful half-clothed, but he was absolutely magnificent.

His torso was long and lean, his shoulders broad and his legs powerful. But it was those eyes of his that captured her, so dark and hungry as they gazed at her.

He slid into the bed next to her and she shivered in sweet anticipation as he drew her into his arms. His body was no longer cold, but rather wonderfully warm.

Their lips met in a kiss that stole her breath and made her utterly boneless in his arms. She suspected she'd wanted him the moment she'd walked into the cabin and saw him, so brooding and broken. But he didn't feel broken now—he was filled with vibrant energy.

He splayed his fingers across the naked skin of her back, his touch hot and welcome. She wanted his hands everywhere, on her back, on her breasts and anywhere else. She felt as if her skin was starved for his very touch.

"I feel like I've wanted you forever," she whispered.

"I feel the same way." His hands found the clasp of her bra and in the blink of her eye she felt it unfasten.

She rolled over and straddled him as she allowed her bra to fall from her shoulders. She closed her eyes as he reached up to caress her bare breasts and then moaned as his thumbs raked across the tips.

She could feel his arousal beneath her and she wanted him on top of her, inside her. She rolled back to the side of him and stripped off her panties, then tugged impatiently at the waistband of his briefs.

"Not so fast," he protested. "Slow, Layla, I want to take it slow."

And he did take it slow. His hands moved with languid but studied intent, as if memorizing the weight of her breasts and the span of her waist. His lips moved slowly, too, drawing in each of her nipples in turn, into his mouth and creating exquisite sensations that shuddered through her.

Magic. He was sheer magic and he made her feel like the most beautiful woman on earth. As he gazed at her with his onyx eyes that sparked with such fevered need, she felt his magic in the very depths of her soul.

When his hand moved down the flat of her belly, a small moan escaped her. And when he touched her as intimately as a man could touch a woman she was instantly at near-orgasm.

As he moved his fingers against her, she cried out his name, stunned by the tidal wave of pleasure that swept over her again and again until she was weak and gasping for breath.

It was then, when she was limp and shuddering in his

arms, that he moved away from her just long enough to take off his briefs.

He fumbled in the nightstand and then she realized he'd grabbed a condom wrapper. "Wait," she said as he tore it open. "I want to touch you before you put it on." She wanted to feel his warm flesh in her hand, feel the pulse of the power inside him.

As she took hold of him he groaned in pleasure and when she stroked her hand up and down the hard length of him he stopped her. "Don't," he said in a voice that sounded half-strangled. "I don't want it to be over this way."

Neither did she so she pulled back her hand as he put on the condom. When it was in place he rolled on top of her and took her lips in a surprisingly gentle kiss.

The kiss spoke not so much of hot, unbridled desire and greedy want, but rather of something deeper, something beautiful and caring that made Layla want him more than ever.

She opened her thighs to welcome him and he slid deep into her with a sigh. For a long moment neither of them moved. She clung to him, her arms wrapped around his back as their heartbeats mirrored each other in a wild rhythm.

He began to move then, slowly and with long deep strokes that began the rise of a new tension inside her. All her nerve endings were enflamed and she arched beneath him seeking another release. When it came she cried out his name and realized he was there, too, crashing back to earth as he whispered her name.

Almost immediately he got up from the bed. "Are you coming back?" she asked. "Please come back," she added.

"All right," he replied simply and then left the bedroom.

She got out of bed and grabbed her nightgown and pulled it on over her head and then got back beneath the warm sheets that smelled of Jacob.

She hoped he'd come back to the bedroom. She wanted him to have the comfort of the bed for the night. She also wanted him to hold her close to him until she drifted off to sleep.

Her heart swelled as he returned and slid back beneath the sheets. She snuggled next to him, pleased as he turned on his side and pulled her against his chest.

"Now I suppose you're going to do a verbal replay of everything just so I can hear the sound of your voice." His voice held a relaxed, teasing tone.

"Hmm, actually, the whole experience has left me rather speechless," she replied.

"I hope that's speechless in a good way."

"Definitely. If I was a cat I'd be purring."

He stroked a hand down her thigh. "And if you were a bunny the possibilities would be endless."

She laughed. "Why, Agent Grayson, nobody mentioned to me that you actually have a sense of humor."

"There was a time some people thought I was quite witty."

Layla inched away from him and propped herself up on her elbow so she could see his face in the fading light that whispered through the window. "Tell me about the women in your past. Were there hundreds?"

He laughed, the sound deep and pleasant. "No, just a few. The last couple of years I'd focused almost exclusively on work."

"Any heartbreak in that few?"

"What, are we playing Twenty Questions?" he protested.

"I will if you want to, but it might just be easier to appease my naturally curious nature." She reached out and shoved a strand of his dark hair from his forehead, unable to fight her need to touch him.

"There was one," he said. "But doesn't everyone have at least one heartbreak in their past?"

She frowned thoughtfully. "I don't. I have a lot of broken relationships, but I'm not sure my heart has really been broken before. I just refuse to allow that to happen."

She was too embarrassed to admit to him that the men in her life didn't stick around long enough for her to become truly emotionally involved with them.

"So, tell me about this woman who broke your heart," she said, wanting to know everything about him.

He pulled her back into his arms and kissed her on the forehead. "We were young, she was pretty and I thought it was love, but she was just having fun. It seemed like a big deal at the time, but not so much now."

"Is she why you decided not to do relationships?"

"Enough, Layla. Enough talk for one night."

"You know there's really only one way to shut me up," she said as she allowed her fingers to smooth down the flat of his abdomen and down to his inner thigh.

He drew in a breath and chuckled. "I had a feeling there might be a little bit of bunny in you," he said softly just before his mouth claimed hers.

It was almost an hour later that Jacob slept with her curled up in his arms. The howl of the wind outside sounded bitterly cold and lonely, but she was warm and sweetly sated next to Jacob.

He just might become her very first real heartbreak, she thought as the wind rattled the glass in the window frame. He'd walk away from her when this was all over just like all the other men she'd slept with or dated. But, this time she had a feeling it was going to hurt more than it ever had before.

She closed her eyes as sleep threatened to overcome her. One thing was certain, in the future whenever she needed to go to a safe and happy place in her mind, she'd come back to this moment in his arms.

He was a patient man. The Professional sat in his favorite chair and listened to the wind screeching outside his windows while he took a sip of hot cocoa.

He knew Jacob Grayson had Layla stashed someplace

here in town and it was just a matter of time before he found them. The others were hidden in a place he was confident they wouldn't be found, and as far as he was concerned he was above suspicion anyway.

Smarter than the FBI, better than the local yokels, he could have made Black Rock his hunting ground forever, but after his party he'd be gone. Like a shadow in the night, like a phantom in a dream, he'd disappear and set up shop in another place.

As the howling wind got more intense, he decided he'd go someplace where it was warm. Maybe Florida or California. He smiled at the thought of all those beach bunnies just waiting to be plucked for a party.

Yes, it was time to head to a warmer climate, but first he had to get to Layla West. Then the real fun would begin.

It was snowing when Jacob got out of bed the next morning. Not a pretty, gentle fall of flakes, but a wheezing, icy blizzard. It must have started several hours before because the ground already sported at least two inches.

"Terrific," he muttered drily. This would only hurt the investigation, making the search more difficult.

He poured himself a cup of coffee and then moved back to the window, grateful that Layla was still asleep. He'd awakened spooned around her warm body. Before he opened his eyes to face the day he'd been happy.

Frowning, he felt a restless adrenaline try to take

hold of him. He wanted to be investigating instead of cooped up here in the cabin. He knew protecting Layla was important, but right now an edge of impatience, of urgency, filled him.

He suspected these new emotions were in response to his growing feelings for the woman in the next room. He didn't want to care about her, but he did and with each minute that passed, each hour that went by, that feeling grew stronger.

She'd made it clear to him that she wasn't the marrying kind, and he knew that his involvement with her could only lead to a new kind of heartbreak, but he didn't know how to protect himself from her.

She was bigger than life with her infectious laughter and depth of compassion. He knew she was loyal to her friends and had a side that was very nurturing. She'd make a good mother.

Again he frowned as he thought of her plan to be a single parent. No man? No problem. That had been her attitude. She didn't need a partner, wasn't in the market for one. In this particular aspect she reminded him of the woman he'd thought he'd once loved.

As he stared out to the drifting, blowing snow he realized his love for Sarah hadn't been as deep as he'd thought. Sure, he'd enjoyed her company and there had definitely been an element of lust involved. A marriage proposal had seemed like the obvious next step in their relationship, but he was grateful now that Sarah had turned him down.

It felt like fate that he was here now with Layla, but he reminded himself not to get used to it, that she was a temporary woman in a temporary situation and he'd do well to remember that.

By the time she got up he'd worked himself into a foul mood. She saw the snow as a wintry delight and he saw it only as an impediment to them getting out of the cabin for good.

His thoughts were echoed by Tom, who called just after nine. "I was hoping to set up a face-to-face meeting with you and the three men we discussed the other day. Unfortunately, this weather has thrown a wrench in the plans."

"Yeah, I figured," Jacob replied, trying to ignore the jiggle of Layla's bottom as she whipped eggs in a bowl. This morning she was dressed in a pair of black jeans and a white-and-black striped sweater that clung to every curve she possessed.

"Michael Fields turned out to be a dead end," Tom continued.

"Michael Fields?" Jacob frowned, for a moment unable to place the name.

"The man in unit seven at the motel who wanted Layla to show him property," Tom reminded him. "Turns out he's from Texas. He's retiring and he and his wife are looking at several small towns to relocate. They'd driven through Black Rock in the fall and were charmed. We checked him out thoroughly and he has solid alibis for all the kidnappings."

"So, that's one name to strike off our very short list of suspects," Jacob said in frustration.

"Jacob, we're doing everything we can."

"I know, I know," Jacob replied hurriedly. "I'm just getting cabin fever." He left the kitchen and walked into the living room. "I feel the need to be more involved. I want to find this creep and I can't do it from here."

He needed some distance from Layla, who was making him breakfast like she had every morning they'd been cooped up here. He needed to escape the domestic life they were building day by day, a life that was far too appealing.

"There's nothing that can be done today," Tom said. "We even had to call off the search because of the weather. It's supposed to clear up by nightfall. Maybe tomorrow I can get you in here for those interviews. You're the only person who has talked to this madman and I'm hoping something will come from that."

"Let's hope," Jacob agreed. By the time the two men had hung up Layla had French toast ready for them.

She was unusually quiet during the meal and he found himself wanting to know her thoughts. "Why so quiet?" he finally asked.

She poured more syrup over her French toast and didn't meet his gaze. "I feel like I'm keeping you from the rest of your life, from doing what you really want to do."

He realized she'd been listening to his conversation

with Tom and she was hurt. His heart softened. "Layla, look at me."

Slowly, as if with great reluctance, she met his gaze and in the depths of her beautiful blue eyes he saw a whisper of pain, an edge of guilt.

"If it wasn't for you I'd still be wallowing in self-pity and drinking myself into an early grave," he said. "You brought me back to life." As he said the words he recognized the truth of them and saw the lightening of her eyes.

"Really?"

"Really," he replied. Once again he felt he was getting too close, feeling too much for her. He cleared his throat and focused back on his breakfast.

He'd made love to her the night before and already he felt the burn of desire for her once again. He needed to get out of here, needed some distance from her. But there was nowhere to go to escape her presence in the small cabin.

She was everywhere, in every corner of every room, her scent in the very air he breathed. He had to focus. He sat down in the recliner and picked up one of the files on the missing women. Suzy Bakersfield had been taken after her shift as a cocktail waitress at The Edge.

Her car had been left out front of the bar and for several days the speculation was that she'd met some man and gone off with him, even though Suzy's current boyfriend had insisted that wasn't true.

Jennifer Hightower, the first missing young woman,

had been taken after she'd finished work at a local convenience store. And speculation was that Casey Teasdale had been taken early in the morning as she'd gotten into her car to go to work. The crime scene in all cases had been the women's cars, but other than the button in Casey's car, nothing else had been found. And there was no way to know for sure if that button was even connected to the crime.

He barely glanced up as Layla came into the room and sank down on the sofa. She pulled out the journal he knew she kept and began to write in it. She wrote for only a brief time and then closed the journal, set it on the coffee table and looked at him.

"Jacob, if you need to do something besides sit around here all day and babysit me, I'm okay with that. I could spend time with Portia or I'd even be all right staying here alone."

He eyed her in disbelief.

"Seriously," she exclaimed. "He doesn't know we're here and there's no reason to believe that he'll find us if we continue to be careful."

There was no question in Jacob's mind that The Professional didn't know their location. If he did know, something would have happened by now, another attempt would have been made on Layla.

"It's a moot point right now," he replied and gestured toward the window. "Nobody is going anywhere today."

"But I want you to know that you're free to do what

you need to do to catch this man. And if that means working the case outside of this cabin, then so be it."

He looked for signs of fear in her eyes, in her features, but saw no indication of that emotion. "Why the change of heart? It was only yesterday you were terrified when I disappeared for a few minutes to get that Christmas tree."

She shifted her gaze away from his and sighed. "I'm tired, Jacob. I'm tired of being here. I want my life back. I want my cat. We can't stay here forever. I mean, what if this killer doesn't do anything for weeks, for months?"

She sat up taller and straightened her shoulders. "As long as he's out there the women in this town are in danger. You know this killer better than anyone else because of your previous contact with him. Therefore, you're the best chance we have of catching him. You need to be actively working this case, not sitting in that chair reading the facts from a file."

She continued to surprise him. "We'll see," he replied. "I'm hoping to meet with the three men who have recently moved to Black Rock at Tom's office to see if something about their speech patterns is familiar to me." He glanced toward the window once again. "Hopefully I can do that in the next day or two."

"And while you do that I'll see if Portia wants to hang out," she replied. "I just want this over," she said firmly.

Jacob stared back down at the folder in his lap. She was ready to move on, he thought. She was probably tired of his company, eager to get back to real life and other men.

He jumped as his cell phone rang. He pulled it from his pocket and checked the caller ID. An unrecognized number. Jacob answered.

"Good morning, Jacob," The Professional's altered voice came across the line. "Are you enjoying this wintry weather?"

"What do you want?" Jacob asked, his stomach tightening with tension.

"Ah, surely you remember that I'm a sociable kind of man."

"Why don't you give me a name?" Jacob asked. "Your first name."

The caller laughed. "And why would I want to do that?"

"Just to be sociable," Jacob replied.

Again he laughed and Jacob tried to memorize the sound. "I just wanted to let you know that I bought party favors the other day. You know, that kind that you blow in and a long tongue of paper comes out."

"Tell me where you have those women," Jacob said, aware of Layla getting off the sofa and moving to crouch by his side.

"No can do," the caller replied.

"Then tell me your first name," Jacob pressed, his voice louder than he'd meant it to be. Layla placed a hand on his thigh, as if to calm him.

"You're as tenacious as a terrier. My name is The Professional and that's all you need to know."

"You say you want to play a game, but a game isn't fair unless there are clues."

"Who said I play fair?" His voice was filled with a smug amusement that ripped at Jacob's insides.

"Invite me to your party, you spineless creep," he exclaimed, unable to control the frustration that roiled inside of him. Layla's fingernails dug into his jeans and he drew a deep steadying breath. "Why don't you meet me someplace and we'll party together, just the two of us."

"Sorry, you're just not my type," The Professional replied and then clicked off the line.

Jacob closed his phone and muttered a curse beneath his breath.

"He just calls to stir you up," Layla said softly. "He calls to get under your skin because he knows he can. He feeds off you. Maybe you shouldn't take his calls anymore." She took his hand in hers, the warmth of the touch soothing his ragged nerves.

"I have to take the calls," he replied. "In one of them he might slip up. He might say something that will be a real clue to his identity."

He was grateful when she dropped his hand and returned to her place on the sofa, grateful because he'd liked the feel of her hand in his and knew that she had been offering him support.

And even though he hadn't believed he'd gotten

involved with her, even though he'd warned himself not to get emotionally attached, he realized that once this was all over, Layla West would leave a new scar on his heart.

Chapter 10

The weather in Kansas was crazy. The snow stopped falling midafternoon and the sun came out in all its glory, quickly melting what had fallen.

By the next morning there were only patches of snow left around tree trunks and in the thickest part of the woods that surrounded the cabin.

Layla stood at the bedroom window and stared outside, her thoughts on the man in the next room. They'd made love again the night before. It had just happened…the spark of passion, the uncontrollable need to be in each other's arms. It had been sheer magic.

It was getting more and more difficult for her to pretend that she didn't care about him, more difficult to maintain the distance that had always served her so well when it came to men.

She didn't want to get involved with him, and more than that she didn't want to feel any hope of a future with him. She knew she'd only be deluding herself and would ultimately be devastated.

Tom had called to let Jacob know he'd set up a two o'clock meeting with Jerry Tipton, the traveling salesman, and a two-thirty with Greg Todd, the nurse. He'd also set up a four o'clock meeting with Larry Norwood at his house because he was not working at his office that day.

Jacob appeared in the bedroom doorway. "Ready?"

She nodded and picked up her purse from the bed. "I'll spend the day with Portia at the daycare and she can bring me back here around five."

He frowned but said nothing as they left the cabin and headed for the shed. She'd insisted that Portia bring her back here rather than have Jacob drive out to the Norwood place and then back into town to get her and then back to the cabin.

"You know I don't mind backtracking to pick you up."

"I know, but this works out better. We'll be careful and make sure we aren't followed and everything will be fine," she assured him. She needed to prove to herself that she could be okay without him for a little while. It wasn't like she was going to spend the night there all alone. It would probably only be a matter of minutes that she would be by herself.

They were silent on the ride into town. Layla suspected Jacob had already gone into investigation mode, that his thoughts were consumed by the need to crack this case, save his sister and the other women and then get on with his own life, wherever it might take him.

"I'll see you back at the cabin," he said as he pulled up in the driveway of Portia's gingerbread-trimmed house.

"I just hope the next time we talk you know who The Professional is and he's behind bars," she said as she opened the truck door.

For a moment the demons were back in his eyes and she wanted to climb back in the truck and wrap her arms around him, she wanted to say something that would put a glint of laughter there. Instead she got out of the truck and closed the door.

He remained parked in the driveway until she reached the door to the detached garage where Portia's daycare business resided.

As she turned to wave to him, she was gripped by a sudden, inexplicable sense of dread. She told herself it was just because this was the first time they'd been separated since the attack on her in her office.

Portia and the kids quickly took away any disquiet she felt. The afternoon sped by with plenty of kisses and hugs and laughter. Layla gave herself completely to the joy of being with the kids, but couldn't help but wonder what life would be like if she was together with Jacob and had his baby. She knew instinctively that he would be a wonderful father.

"I'm in love with him," she confessed to Portia as the two of them went into Portia's private office. Portia's assistant was having reading time with the children, which gave Portia and Layla time for a little girl talk.

"Are you sure you don't feel that way because of the circumstances you find yourself in?" Portia asked. "There's no question that Jacob represents safety for you. Maybe you're just confused about your feelings for him?"

Layla considered her words. "There's no question that he makes me feel safe and secure," she agreed. "But he's also passionate about things and has a wonderful sense of humor, and even if there was no danger at all in my life I'd be in love with him."

"Does he feel the same way about you?"

"I'm sure he doesn't," Layla replied with a wistful pang in her heart. "He's physically attracted to me, but you know that's always the easy part for me. Men want to take me to bed but they never want to marry me." She forced a smile to her lips. "Don't look so concerned. Once this is all over Jacob will just be another passing ship in my life and I'll be fine."

Portia looked at the clock on her wall. "And if you want to stop by the vet's office and visit Mr. Whiskers, we'd better get out of here." She got out of her chair and grabbed her coat and purse while Layla did the same.

She'd asked Portia to run her by to see her kitty on the way home. She desperately missed the cat and hoped he wasn't grieving over the separation from her. She knew seeing that he was being well cared for would ease her heart.

"So, are you going to tell Jacob how you feel about him?" Portia asked when they were in her car and headed to Main Street.

"No. What's the point?" Layla countered. "If he wants something to happen between us then he'll tell me. I definitely don't want to get my hopes up and be disappointed again. It's easier to have no expectations than to have them crushed."

"Sometimes I think that's your problem," Portia replied. "That you have no expectations for yourself or your happiness. You just assume you won't be happy, won't be loved, and so it doesn't happen for you."

"Please, let's not turn this into another counseling session," Layla exclaimed with a small laugh.

"You should have had counseling years ago because of the abuse from your father," Portia retorted.

"I don't need counseling," Layla replied. "I survived and I'm doing just fine." She put a note of finality in her voice, hoping Portia would drop the whole subject.

Thankfully by that time Portia had pulled up and parked in front of Larry Norwood's veterinarian office. "Are you coming in?" Layla asked as she opened the car door.

"Are you going to be long?"

Layla shook her head. "Not at all. Why don't you sit tight and keep the car running and warm? I know Larry isn't here today so it should just take me a couple of minutes to check on my baby."

Portia frowned and Layla knew she was probably remembering the last time she'd let Layla go off alone. "I'll be fine," she exclaimed to her friend as she got out of the car and shut the door.

Once inside the office she was greeted by Margaret Wisong, the receptionist. "Dr. Larry isn't in today," she said after greeting Layla.

"I know, I was just wondering if I could have a quick visit with my cat, Mr. Whiskers," Layla explained.

"Oh, my, that cat is a lover." Margaret smiled and gestured to exam room one. "Why don't you go in there and I'll bring him to you."

The examining room was typical, with a sink and cabinets and a stainless steel table. Margaret came in carrying Mr. Whiskers and as Layla took the cat from her arms, he began to purr loudly.

"I've missed you, too," Layla murmured as she stroked his soft fur and cuddled him like a baby against her chest. "Is he eating okay?" she asked Margaret.

"No problems, and he's sleeping fine, too," Margaret assured her. "And don't worry, he's getting plenty of play with everyone here. He's become one of our favorites."

"Good," Layla replied. "It won't be too much longer and you can come home," she said to the cat. She felt better now, knowing that he was doing fine. "Thanks for taking such good care of him," she said to Margaret.

"No problem." Margaret took the cat from Layla's arms. "We love taking care of doggies and kitties," she said. "Is there anything else I can do for you?"

"No thanks, I was just feeling a little homesick for my cat," Layla replied.

As Margaret left the examining room Layla started to follow behind her. She had no idea what made her glance at the white lab coat hanging from a hook in the corner, but her gaze fell on the sleeve and the row of decorative oversize white buttons on the cuff.

Her heart stuttered to a near stop as she saw that one of those buttons was missing, a button that looked just like the one that had been found in Casey Teasdale's car.

Larry Norwood. Her brain fought to make sense of it. He could have lost that button anywhere, she tried to rationalize. On wooden legs she left the examining room. Or he could have lost it in a struggle with Casey Teasdale.

Was it possible the friendly vet was the monster they sought?

She felt half-dizzy, sick to her stomach. *Don't jump to any conclusions,* she told herself. There might be several people in town who wore those kinds of lab coats. But even as she told herself this her heart thundered with the weight of her discovery.

Once outside she slid into the passenger side of Portia's car. "Everything all right with Mr. Whiskers?" Portia asked.

"Fine. Everything is fine," Layla replied. She was bursting with the need to tell Portia what she'd seen, but she was afraid to involve her friend. She didn't want to malign the vet if he wasn't guilty.

Besides, she didn't want anyone to know until she had a chance to tell Jacob. He'd know what to do. He'd be able to clear the vet or make sure that Norwood was put behind bars if he was guilty.

She glanced at her wristwatch and saw that it was quarter to four. He'd be on his way to the Norwood farm to interrogate the vet. As soon as Portia dropped her at the cabin she'd call him.

Layla pulled her journal and a pen from her purse. Portia glanced her way and grinned. "Are you still journaling all the time?"

"Every day," Layla replied. "Sorry, I just need to make a quick note to myself." She jotted down the words *Larry Norwood, missing button, lab coat* and then closed the small book, some of the pressure of the secret diminished just by writing it down.

The drive seemed to last forever. Portia chatted about her pregnancy, the kids in her daycare and Caleb. Thankfully, she didn't seem to notice that Layla was unusually quiet, her thoughts consumed by the possibility that Larry could be The Professional.

Where had Larry and his family lived before coming to Black Rock? Hadn't he moved here about the same time that the case in Kansas City had wrapped up? She wished she had the answers, and she definitely wished she knew how he'd lost the button on his lab coat.

Maybe she'd just found the clue they needed to crack the case. Surely Tom and Jacob would be able to match the missing button on the lab coat to the one found in the car.

"Are you sure you'll be okay here by yourself until Jacob gets home?" Portia asked as she parked in front of the cabin. "I could hang around until he gets back."

"Absolutely not," Layla replied. "Besides, you mentioned earlier that you have a parent-teacher meeting to get back to."

"I could call the parents and cancel," Portia said. "I just wanted to talk to them about their little boy's penchant for hair-pulling."

"Nonsense, go to your meeting. I'll be fine until Jacob gets home." Besides, if what she suspected was true, then she didn't have to worry about Larry Norwood finding her. He was at this very moment being questioned by Jacob and Tom.

"Thanks for letting me spend the afternoon with you," she said as she got out of the car.

"You know I always love spending time with you. Take care, Layla, and I'll talk to you later."

Layla's heart still thundered as she watched Portia pull away. Larry Norwood! She couldn't believe it, but the evidence didn't lie.

She turned and hurried up the steps to the cabin. Once

inside she pulled her journal from her purse and carried it with her into the kitchen and the phone.

She picked up the receiver and frowned. "Hello?" Her stomach plummeted. There was no dial tone. The phone was dead. It was at that moment she knew she was in deep trouble.

She turned to run into the living room to get her purse and her cell phone when the back door that led into the kitchen exploded open and her nightmare grinned behind his mask. "Hi, honey. I'm home," he said as Layla screamed.

The interview with Jerry Tipton and Greg Todd had been another study in frustration. Jacob and Tom were silent as Jacob drove toward the Norwood farm on the outskirts of town.

"Greg Todd is some piece of work, isn't he?" Tom finally broke the silence.

"Arrogant young kid with an attitude as bad as his complexion," Jacob replied. "But, he's not smart enough to be our man."

"Why would somebody that age decide to move to a little town like Black Rock?" Tom asked.

"My guess would be he was having trouble getting hired in the bigger hospitals."

"What about Tipton?" Tom leaned forward and adjusted the heat vent to blow more directly on his body.

Jacob thought about the traveling salesman who had seemed very eager to cooperate, but had been unable to provide any real alibis for the times of the kidnapping. "I think we need to look closer at him. Check his financials and see if we can pin down where he was and when. He has the perfect job to fit the profile and he seemed bright to me."

"And way too eager to please," Tom added. "Did you notice how he kept wanting to know all the details about the crimes?"

"Could be morbid curiosity or something more malevolent," Jacob replied. "I know it's not unusual for these guys to try to insinuate themselves into the investigation. What frustrates me is that I didn't pick up anything in their voices or speech patterns that made me believe one of them was The Professional." He tightened his hands on the steering wheel.

He just wanted this over. He wanted Brittany and the other women safe and sound, wanted the killer dead or behind bars and needed to get Layla out of the cabin and out of his life.

Because he wanted her in his life.

He shook his head as if to dislodge that particular thought. He couldn't want her because she didn't need a man. She was just another heartache as far as he was concerned and he'd suffered a lifetime of heartbreaks in this life already.

"You know, it's possible these three are just dead ends," Jacob said. "He might not even be on our radar at this point."

"Don't remind me." Tom's voice held the same kind of weariness that Jacob felt.

Jacob felt like he'd spent his entire life chasing this killer and he feared that once again they wouldn't find him in time and there would be another party to clean up after.

His stomach twisted as he thought of the killer's last party and that his sister might be a part of the next one. No, they couldn't let that happen.

"He's just not making mistakes," Jacob finally growled and slammed a hand down on the steering column. "And we need the bastard to make a mistake before we lose Brittany, before we lose them all."

A wealth of despair filled Jacob and pressed so tight against his chest he could scarcely draw a breath. He felt as if they were running out of time. He knew that eventually The Professional would no longer be able to control his compulsion to kill.

As far as Jacob was concerned they were already on borrowed time. He'd tried to act on his compulsion both times he'd attempted to kidnap Layla. He should be ready to explode at any moment, like a bomb that killed everything and everyone in his path.

Not Brittany, he thought. *Please, not Brittany and not Layla.* Somehow they had to stop this man before more women died, before more families were destroyed by grief and despair.

"What are your plans when this is all over?" Tom asked, pulling Jacob from his inner torment.

"I plan on staying here in Black Rock. I'm kind of hoping there will be an opening for a deputy." He slid a glance to his brother.

"With Benjamin quitting in the spring I'm sure we could use you, but are you sure you don't want to go back to the FBI? You could. Your supervisor has kept in touch with me."

Jacob once again looked at Tom, this time in surprise. "He has?"

"He was worried about you and told me that when you were ready to let you know you still have a job there if you want it."

Jacob digested this information and then shook his head. "No, as much as I appreciate knowing that, I won't go back. I'm not cut out for the kind of work I was doing. I allow myself to get too emotionally involved."

"That particular trait is highly desired in one of my deputies," Tom replied. "You know there's nothing we'd all like better than to have you here. But I wanted you to know that you have options."

"Thanks," he replied, but he'd already made up his mind that he wanted to stay in Black Rock. He hadn't realized how homesick he'd been until he'd come back here. He hadn't recognized the depth of his loneliness in Kansas City until he'd returned here to the warmth and caring of his family.

He knew that if he went back to the FBI he'd immerse himself in his work and would probably never build a life that included a real home and family. He was stunned to realize he wanted that.

He wanted a woman to come home to, somebody who would force him to eat breakfast because it was the most important meal of the day, somebody who would warm his nights and brighten his days. He wanted a woman who talked too much and loved high-heeled shoes, a woman exactly like Layla.

As he turned into the long winding driveway of the Norwood place, he shoved everything out of his head except the investigation.

On paper Larry Norwood looked the least likely to be a serial killer. He was a successful businessman with a wife and two children and was well-respected in the community. But Jacob reminded himself that John Wayne Gacy had been a beloved and respected member of his community who dressed up like a clown to entertain his friends and neighbors, and he'd killed thirty-three young men and boys.

The killer's profile was only as good as the paper it was written on and there was always room for error.

The Norwood home was a small, neat ranch. A bright red barn sat near the house, along with a gardening shed. Beyond the house was a rolling rise of pasture.

The barn was too close to the main residence to house the missing women, Jacob thought as he parked the car and turned off the engine.

"This doesn't look promising," he muttered.

"If nothing else, after this interview 'Norwood' is a

name we can cross off our list of potential suspects," Tom reminded him.

The two men got out of the truck and Jacob felt the bite of the cold north wind. The slight respite they'd had of winter weather that had quickly melted the snow was gone, replaced by the promise of another storm soon to arrive.

Tension twisted Jacob's gut as he and Tom approached the house. They needed answers and he felt as if they were spinning their wheels while time ran out for the victims.

Tom knocked on the door and as they waited for a reply Jacob once again scanned the immediate area. The barn door was open, indicating that there were probably no secrets inside. He turned back to face the door as it opened.

An attractive blonde offered them a tentative smile. Two little girls peeked out from behind her. "Sheriff Grayson, didn't Larry call you?"

"Call me about what?" Tom asked.

"He got an emergency call about a sick horse and had to leave. He said he was going to let you know." She looked from Tom to Jacob. "He must have forgotten. I'm sorry about the inconvenience."

"Do you know who called him about the horse?" Jacob asked.

She shook her head. "No, I'm sorry I don't." She hesitated a moment, and then continued. "Would you like to come in and wait for him?" It was obvious she was uncomfortable with the idea of the two men coming inside.

"We'll just hang out in the truck for a little while and see if he shows up," Tom replied. "If he happens to check in with you would you get his location for us?"

"Of course. I'm sure he won't be too long." With another smile she closed the door and Jacob heard the click of a lock being turned.

"You can't blame her for being cautious," Jacob said as they walked back to the truck. "For all she knows we're the men who are responsible for the disappearances of the women. Just because we have a badge doesn't mean we're the good guys."

Once they were in the truck Jacob looked at his watch. "Maybe I should call Layla and let her know I'm going to be later than I thought." He pulled his phone from his pocket and punched in the numbers to her cell phone, then frowned as it went directly to her voice mail.

"No answer?" Tom asked as Jacob hung up.

"It went to her voice mail." An uneasy tension began to build inside him.

"She and Portia are probably in the middle of shopping or talking and Layla didn't hear the phone," Tom said as if to assure Jacob.

"Maybe." Jacob punched in the numbers to the phone inside the cabin, but hung up after it rang four times without an answer. Surely Tom was right. She was with

Portia and hadn't yet made it to the cabin. He hoped that was the case, for any other scenario was absolutely unthinkable.

Chapter 11

Layla screamed as the man advanced on her. She turned and ran from the kitchen, terror shouting in her head as her heart raced frantically.

She knew there was no place to hide in either the living room or the bedroom, so she headed for the bathroom, where she could at least lock the door.

She flew into the small room, twisted the lock and only then released the sob of horror that had welled up inside her. If she could just stay safe until Jacob got home.

Confusion played in her mind. She'd been so certain that Larry Norwood was The Professional, but Jacob and Tom were interviewing Larry, so he couldn't be the man in the house. So who had broken in the back door? Who was behind that mask?

A loud bang resounded on the bathroom door and a scream once again clawed up her throat. She stared at the door, her entire body suffused with a trembling that kept her frozen in place.

"Come out, come out, Layla," a deep voice called from the other side of the door.

Instantly she was cast back in time. She was a little girl hiding under the porch, hoping and praying that she wouldn't be found. The trembling inside her grew more intense and she slid down the wall as tears began to flow down her cheeks.

Don't let him get me, a childish voice whispered urgently in her head. *Please don't let him get me.* Ancient fear mixed with present terror, making it difficult for her to draw a breath, to think clearly.

She tried to think of what she'd done to garner his violence. Had she washed the dishes wrong? Had her bed not been made properly? She'd tried so hard to be good, but it was never good enough.

She shook her head. No, this wasn't about her father. This was about The Professional. There was no sound on the other side of the door. Rather than the silence making her feel better, it horrified her.

What was he doing? Surely he wouldn't just give up so easily and just go away. Her sobs halted as she caught her breath and waited in dreadful anticipation. Every nerve in her body screamed. Every muscle she possessed tensed.

A bang sounded on the door and the wood in the center cracked, exposing an ax blade. Layla jumped to her feet in panicked horror.

She fought through her fear, knowing that if she froze she was dead, that if she stopped thinking she would be his last victim. The window!

With adrenaline-fueled strength she raced to the small window and gasped in relief as it slid open easily. As the ax slammed into the door again and again she punched out the screen and began to climb outside.

She almost made it. Her upper body was outside when he crashed into the bathroom and grabbed one of her legs. She kicked and twisted to get free, unable to summon the strength to scream again as she fought to get free.

She kicked so hard she felt as if she'd thrown her leg out of the socket, but she was rewarded by a gruff grunt and suddenly she was free and falling to the ground.

Run!

She hit the frozen earth hard, her breath whooshing out of her. She got to her feet and took off, praying she could get to Benjamin and Edie's house before the masked man caught her.

She'd gone only a few feet when she realized she'd lied to Jacob. There were some things she couldn't do in high heels, like run fast enough to escape a serial killer.

She kicked off the shoes, not breaking her pace as she ran for her life.

His laughter rang in the air, far too close behind her. Tears blurred her vision as the cold ground froze her bare feet. *Don't look,* her mind screamed. *Don't waste the time to turn and look behind you.*

She didn't look but she felt him, felt the malevolence rolling off him as he closed the gap between them. She wasn't going to make it. Sobs ripped inside her chest. She wasn't going to get to safety.

He grabbed her then, pulled her down by the shoulders. Once again she hit the ground and rolled, still trying to get some distance from him.

He jumped on her, laughing once again as if it were all nothing more than a game to him. "That's it, fight me," he exclaimed as he managed to straddle her chest with her arms trapped beneath his legs. "There's nothing I love better than a good fight."

She would have continued to fight, but at that moment she recognized his voice. She'd been right. "Larry? Larry, what are you doing?"

Without warning he slapped her, the blow ringing bells in her ears and scorching her cheek with stinging heat. "My name is The Professional and don't you forget it."

Layla watched in horror as he pulled a hypodermic needle from his pocket. "Please, no," she begged, even though she knew her pleas would fall on deaf ears.

The sting of the needle in her arm was nothing compared to the ache in her heart as she thought of Jacob. She'd never see him again. She'd never know the glory of being held in his arms, of tasting his lips against hers just one last time.

It was over. This was the end. Her life was over and it was Jacob's beautiful face that filled her mind as darkness overwhelmed her.

Jacob checked his watch for the tenth time in twenty minutes and then sighed in frustration. "I say we go home and arrange to meet Dr. Norwood another time. For all we know it could be hours before he gets back here."

"You're right," Tom said, sounding as defeated as Jacob felt. "I'll call him in the morning and see if we can meet with him then."

Jacob nodded. He was eager to get back to the cabin. He'd tried to call Layla several more times but she hadn't answered.

A thrum of anxiety had begun inside him and with each minute that passed it grew more intense. The only reason he wasn't completely in panic mode was because he'd tried to call Portia and she hadn't answered her phone, either. He could only assume it was possible the two were still together and had their phones buried in their purses or shut off altogether.

"You know the number of Portia's daycare?" he asked Tom. "I'll call there and see if maybe they haven't even left there yet."

Tom rattled off the number and Jacob called. "Portia," he exclaimed with a sense of relief when she answered. "It's Jacob. Can I talk to Layla?"

"She isn't here, Jacob," Portia replied with a touch of unease in her voice. "I dropped her at the cabin about thirty minutes ago."

A new sense of urgency swept through him. "Thanks." He clicked off and shoved the truck into gear. "Something's wrong at the cabin. Portia said she dropped Layla off thirty minutes ago."

He roared down the road that led away from the Norwood farm, his heart stuttering wildly in his chest. Why wasn't she answering her phone? What the hell was going on?

"Don't jump to conclusions," Tom said. "Maybe she's in the shower or taking a nap and hasn't heard the phone."

"Maybe." Jacob tightened his hands on the steering wheel. He didn't believe she was showering or napping. All his instincts were screaming that Layla was in trouble. Jesus, he should have left the Norwood place the first time he'd called and been unable to reach her.

Ignoring the legal limits he stomped on the gas pedal, wishing he had wings to fly at the speed of sound. Tom said nothing and for that Jacob was grateful. He didn't want to listen to all the logical reasons why Layla wasn't answering the phone. He just wanted to get to her as quickly as possible.

"I wonder what kind of a horse emergency kept Norwood from the appointment?" Tom finally said.

Jacob shot him a quick, questioning glance. "You think there wasn't an emergency?"

Tom released a sigh of frustration. "I don't know what in the hell I think anymore."

Jacob's mind raced over everything he knew, everything he thought he knew about the killer. "In one of our phone conversations he told me I was as tenacious as a terrier. Sounds like a comparison a vet would use."

"That's speculation, not evidence," Tom reminded him.

Where was Larry Norwood? Was he really dealing with a sick horse or was he at the cabin now with Layla, planning his final move in the Black Rock area?

"I don't get it. Why would he blow off an interview with us when he knows we're going to check his alibi?" Tom said. "He knows he's on our radar, so why would he take chances like that?"

"I don't know. I can't think about it right now." As Jacob turned onto the Grayson property, the tension in his stomach twisted so tight he felt sick.

They flew past the big house, rocking over bumps in the lane as Jacob scarcely let up on the gas. He braked hard in front of the cabin, his heart pounding in dread as he then flew out of the truck.

Before he reached the porch he saw something bright and colorful lying on the ground on the side of the cabin. On leaden feet, his heart pounding so hard it hurt, he walked over and stared down at the pink-and-yellow-flowered high heel. He spied the second shoe nearby.

The ground spun beneath him and bile rose up in the back of his throat. *No.* The single word repeated itself over and over in his head. Had the shoes fallen off her feet as she'd been carried away by The Professional or had she taken them off to run? There was no way she'd just tossed the shoes outside for no reason.

Too late. The words pealed in his head like a bell gone mad. *Too late.* He was too late to save her, just like he'd been too late to save the others. "She's gone." The words fell like stones from his lips. It was his worst nightmare come true and he didn't know how to awaken from it.

Tom grabbed him by the arm. "Come on, let's check inside."

Both men drew their guns as they approached the cabin, even though in his heart Jacob knew The Professional wouldn't be inside. He was already planning his party, with Layla and Brittany as guests of honor.

When Jacob saw the shattered bathroom door and the ax lying on the floor next to it, he nearly fell to his knees in agony.

He couldn't imagine Layla's terror. A fine mist covered his sight as he thought of the utter fear she must have experienced. And he hadn't been here for her.

Damn him. Damn Larry Norwood and his sick, twisted mind. An edge of anger began to grow inside Jacob. He wouldn't blink if he got the opportunity to kill him.

It was easy to understand the chronology of events by the evidence left behind. He'd come through the back door. Layla must have run to the bathroom. The open window there indicated that she'd managed to crawl out and run, but she hadn't been able to run fast enough to escape her pursuer.

Numb. Jacob was numb as he and his brother stood in the kitchen and Tom called for help. He'd get men there to process the scene and others to search for Layla.

Jacob's gaze fell on the notebook laid open on the table. Layla's journal. He frowned. She never left it laying out where he could thumb through it. It was always in her purse.

He took a step closer and his heart nearly stopped once again as he read the words on the page. *Larry Norwood. Missing button. Lab coat.*

"Get somebody to Larry's office to collect all his lab coats," he told Tom, the numbness gone as he realized Layla had given them the clue they needed. It was all circumstantial, but it was enough for him to know that the friendly town vet was The Professional. "It's Larry."

Tom looked at the journal and a knot pulsed in his jaw. "Now all we have to do is find him before he kills anyone."

Flashbacks shot through Jacob's head, visions of dead women who would haunt him in some measure for the rest of his life. As Layla's face superimposed over the features of one of those women, he felt as if he'd been punched in the gut with a killing blow.

It was at that moment he realized the depth of his love for Layla, and what he feared more than anything was that he'd be too late for her, too. To make matters worse, it had begun to snow again.

Brittany sat up as the masked man carried in Layla West and placed the unconscious woman on the cot in the last cell. Her heart cried in anguish.

The cells were all full now and she knew that meant death wasn't far behind. She got up from her cot and grabbed the bars that held her prisoner as the man locked Layla's enclosure.

"My brothers will kill you for this," she said as he walked back toward the door.

He laughed. "Your brothers couldn't find a hole in the bottom of their socks." He pulled off his ski mask and she gasped in surprise as she realized it was Dr. Norwood.

She'd had little interaction with the vet before being taken by him. She also knew that he'd taken off the mask and allowed her to see who he was because he was certain there was no rescue for her or the others, that none of them would live to identify him to the authorities.

"They'll never stop looking for you," she replied with a lift of her chin. "They'll hunt you to the ends of the earth."

He laughed again. "They don't even know who I am, and by the time they figure it out I'll be long gone from Black Rock with a new identity and new hunting grounds."

"What about your wife and children?"

"What about them?" he replied. "They're nothing but a drain on my finances, a distraction I no longer want."

Cold. He was like a block of ice, a sociopath with no empathy, no feelings for anyone other than himself. She couldn't imagine now how he'd managed to maintain the facade of a caring veterinarian.

He gestured toward Layla. "She should be awake in just a little while and then we're going to have a party. I've got some special party favors out in the shed and I can't wait to share them with you all."

As he left the building Jennifer Hightower began to sob. "We're going to die. We're all going to die."

"No, we aren't," Brittany said vehemently. "You know what I'm going to do when I get out of here?" She didn't wait for a response. "I'm going to hire a carpenter to build a deck on the back of my house and when it's finished I'm going to throw a big barbecue and invite all my friends and family. Casey, what about you? What are you going to do when we get out of here?"

"I'm going to marry my boyfriend," she said. "He's asked me twice and both times I told him I wasn't ready. But when we get out of here I'm going to plan the biggest wedding this town has ever seen."

"I'm going to quit my job and go back to college," Suzy Bakersfield said. "I always wanted to be a lawyer, but I've been afraid to go for it. I'm ready to go for it now."

For a moment hope filled the air, a shining hope that Brittany grabbed on to and embraced in her heart, drew into her very soul. He might take their lives, but he'd never have their spirits or their dreams.

All too quickly that moment of peace was shattered as Layla moaned with the first stirring of consciousness. *She should be awake in just a little while and then we're going to have a party.* Larry's words whirled around in Brittany's brain and brought with them the hopeless despair of the doomed.

Chapter 12

Consciousness came in tiny bits and pieces. First Layla became aware of the aches of her body—her knees, her hips and finally her face. Everything hurt and she was reluctant to leave the sweet oblivion of the darkness behind for the cold harsh reality of the pain.

The second thing she became aware of was the fact that she was lying on a cot of some kind that smelled of mildew. She frowned, surfacing slowly into the here and now.

The last thing that pierced through her brain was voices…women's voices. They were soft whispers edged with fear and it was then total consciousness struck and Layla knew exactly where she was and what was happening to them all.

They were going to die. She didn't move, didn't open her eyes to let the others know she had awakened. She listened to them talking about all the things they were going to do when they escaped here and her heart felt heavier than it had ever felt in her life.

Jacob. He was an unfinished song in her heart, an ache in her very soul. She knew he'd blame himself for this, would probably retreat back into his self-destructive isolation and that broke her heart as much as the knowledge of her imminent death at the hands of Larry Norwood.

She'd never believed that they had a future together, but that didn't stop her heart aching with all the what-ifs.

"Layla?"

The soft voice drifted to her and she immediately recognized it as belonging to Brittany. "I'm here," she whispered.

"Are they looking for us? Do they have any idea who might be responsible?"

"Jacob should know by now," Layla replied. If he'd found her journal. If he'd bothered to read it. Oh, God, so many ifs to depend on for their rescue.

"Jacob? Isn't he in Kansas City?" Brittany asked. "At least he was there when I got abducted."

For the next few minutes Layla caught Brittany up on all the family news she'd missed while she'd been imprisoned.

As she talked, she realized how much she would have

loved being a part of the Grayson family, how much she would have loved to build a family with Jacob.

What she didn't share with the others was that Larry Norwood had committed this crime before and the result had been the deaths of five women. Even though she knew that they were aware of the danger they were in, she couldn't tell them about the real horror that was The Professional.

"Layla, when he comes back, you have to act like you're still unconscious," Brittany exclaimed. "It's the only thing that might buy us all some extra time."

"I can do that," Layla replied with an assurance she didn't feel. If he got too close to her he'd surely hear the pounding of her heart, the rapid breathing that she'd be unable to control. "Where are we?"

"We don't know," Suzy replied. "We've tried to figure it out, but we have no idea."

"For all we know we could be hundreds of miles from Black Rock," Casey added.

Layla looked at her wristwatch. It was just after six. "No, we're close to Black Rock," she said. She hadn't been unconscious very long. He must have used a light dose of the drug. *Couldn't wait to have his party,* she thought fearfully.

How long could she fake being totally drugged out? How much time could she buy them all before Larry lost his patience and started his sick party?

Remaining on the cot where she lay, Layla looked around, trying to figure out where they were being held.

It appeared to be a barn or some sort of shed that had been renovated for torture and imprisonment. Were they on property that belonged to Larry or somebody else?

Tom and Jacob had been to Larry's place that afternoon. Wouldn't they have noticed a big shed and gone to investigate?

As the only Realtor in the area she knew how many empty properties were around the town and knew that many of those places had structures just like this on them.

How were Jacob and the other men ever going to find the right place in time to save them? If it were humanly possible then she knew Jacob would be the man who could find them, but she wasn't sure it was possible.

As if to punctuate her dismal thoughts the door to the shed opened and he walked back in. Layla closed her eyes and focused on slowing the rhythm of her breathing, knowing that not only her life, but also the other women's lives might depend on her acting skills.

"No party is complete without balloons," he said. "And party favors, girls," he said. Layla tensed as she heard the sound of items being dropped on the floor, and Jennifer Hightower began to sob hysterically.

She couldn't even imagine what he'd brought in as "party favors" but she knew she had to keep her breathing slow and steady and not react to anything that might go on around her.

He began to whistle and she could tell from the

sound that he was approaching her cell. A rattle of keys indicated he was unlocking the door.

She considered springing up and attacking him. She'd have the element of surprise on her side, but quickly dismissed the idea as she remembered his strength and the fact that she was weak and banged up.

Instead she focused once again on playing dead, praying that she did nothing to let him know she was no longer unconscious.

The cell door squeaked open and she felt his presence next to her cot. *Stay focused,* she told herself as she drew in deep and even breaths. She kept her body boneless, her mouth slightly agape.

"Hey, Bozo," Brittany called out and Layla knew she was trying to distract him. "Why don't you open up my cage and fight with somebody who isn't drugged to the gills?"

He laughed and Layla nearly jumped out of her skin as she felt his breath on her face. Tears burned beneath her closed eyes, surged up in her chest and she feared if he remained so close to her for another second she'd lose it.

"I'm going to enjoy partying with you, Brittany," he said, his voice moving farther away from Layla. The door to her cell closed again. "But the party can't begin without Layla. She's been a real pain and I have special plans for her, but she has to be awake to really enjoy them."

She heard the scrape of chair legs against the floor.

"I'll just sit here and enjoy the atmosphere while we wait for Layla to join us," he said.

The only sound was the quiet sobbing of Jennifer and Casey and Larry's low melodic whistling as they all waited for the party to begin.

Jacob, where are you? Layla fought the emotion that threatened to erupt from her on a torrent of tears. *Please, find us,* she mentally begged. *Find us before it's too late.*

The snow that had begun as fat fluffy flakes had transformed into smaller, more serious frozen precipitation, only adding to Jacob's sense of urgency.

They were headed back to the Norwood farm, hoping to get answers there. The kid gloves were off as far as Jacob was concerned. If Larry wasn't there, then Jacob had some hard questions for Norwood's wife.

Benjamin was processing the cabin and before Tom and Jacob had left he'd picked up a couple of hairs just inside the back door that he suspected were dog hairs. They wouldn't know for sure until they were sent to the lab, but it was the final clue that Jacob needed to be certain that The Professional was, indeed, Larry Norwood.

They were in Tom's official car, with Tom at the wheel, leaving Jacob to clench his fists at his sides as he thought of Layla, of Brittany and all the other women who were in danger.

"How big is his property?" Jacob asked, knowing Tom

had asked Caleb to find out what property the Norwoods owned in the area.

"Almost two hundred acres."

"A big area," Jacob replied more to himself than to his brother. And the snow was falling and time had possibly already run out.

"I've got some men meeting us there. It's mostly pasture, so it shouldn't take us long to search."

Jacob said nothing. He knew an extra second, an added minute could mean the difference between life and death, and the thought of Layla no longer in this world nearly destroyed him.

He knew she wasn't interested in a long-term relationship. She hadn't even indicated to him that she felt anything about him except a flash of passion and perhaps some natural sympathy for all that he'd been through.

What surprised him was that he'd realized he was capable of loving again. Somehow in the past couple of days with Layla he'd rediscovered the hopes and dreams he'd believed were lost forever.

He might not have Layla in his life forever, but he wanted her in this world, needed to know she was alive and well even if she wasn't with him.

And he couldn't even think of his little sister in the hands of Larry Norwood. The rage of knowing the man had the two women Jacob cared about most in the world threatened to spiral him completely out of control. He knew he wouldn't be any use to anyone if he allowed that to happen. He had to stay in control, stay cool and calm despite his inner turmoil.

By the time they reached the Norwood place the snow had changed back to a hard-driving sleet that bounced off the windows and quickly slickened the roads.

Deputy Sam McCain and several others were already there waiting in their cars for Tom and Jacob's arrival. As Tom parked all of the men got out of their cars.

"Wait here," Tom instructed the others. "I'm hoping we can get Mrs. Norwood's permission to search the premises and just in case she balks Caleb is working at getting us a search warrant."

The last thing any of them wanted to do was gain evidence that a good criminal defense attorney would be able to get thrown out of court on a technicality. Jacob followed behind Tom as they approached the front door for the second time that day.

It was like déjà vu and memories from the last time he'd faced off with The Professional once again filled his head. That time the creep had won. But they couldn't let him win this time. This had to have a different ending, he prayed.

Larry's wife opened the door, her eyes widening as she saw the men standing in the yard. "Sheriff, what's going on?"

"Has Larry gotten home?" Tom asked.

"No, I haven't heard from him. Would somebody please tell me what's going on?" The fear that had widened her eyes now crept into her voice.

Behind her came the sounds of little-girl giggles and Jacob realized she and her daughters were just more victims of Larry's madness.

"Tracy, we need to get your permission to search your property," Tom explained. "We need to search both inside the house and outside."

"I don't understand. What are you looking for?"

"The women who have vanished from town," Jacob said, the urgency he'd been feeling reeling out of control. The sleet bounced on his shoulders, stung his face. "We think your husband has them stashed someplace out here."

"Oh, my God." Her face paled, but she didn't waste time asking more questions. "Of course," she replied, her voice shaky. "Do whatever you need to do."

Tom motioned three of the men toward the barn, two more men into the house and indicated that the others follow him and Jacob into the pasture.

Even though there was no way the missing women were hidden in the house, they were hoping to find something that might be used as evidence or a clue as to the women's whereabouts.

It took the men only minutes to spread out and begin to walk the property. As the sleet continued to fall and Jacob looked ahead to the empty pasture, the sick reality of failure ripped through him.

What if he was wrong? What if it wasn't Larry and while they were here wasting their time The Professional was having his party with the women at another location?

As far as his eyes could see there was no structure that could house the women, nothing at all to break up the empty landscape. Where were they? Where could he have stashed them?

It didn't take long for the ground to become more overgrown with tall dead brush and groves of trees, and with each step he took Jacob's last vestiges of hope began to wane.

It had been at least an hour and a half since Layla had been taken, too long to hope that she might still be alive. The darkness of night wasn't far away, adding to Jacob's sense of urgency and his utter despair.

The sleet once again turned to snow as Tom motioned for the others to join him. The five of them came together and Jacob saw that the hopelessness he felt inside himself was mirrored in his brother's dark eyes.

"I'm calling for more men," he said. "There's no way the five of us can cover all this property efficiently."

It would take more precious time for anyone else to arrive on scene, Jacob thought. Too late. They were going to be too late.

"I'm going to press on," he said and motioned toward a rise in the distance. "Maybe from there I can get an eagle-eye view of the rest of the property."

Tom nodded. "I'll go with you." He instructed the others to fan out once again and then fell into step next to Jacob.

The rise in the land was steeper than it had initially appeared and once they crested the top Jacob's heart nearly stopped. Below them, nestled in another grove of trees were two wooden sheds, one small and one large—large enough to hide kidnapped women.

Both buildings were weathered and looked like a hundred other structures that had been built years ago and then left abandoned by the construction of newer buildings.

Adrenaline spiked through him as Tom grabbed his arm. It was obvious his brother thought the same thing that Jacob did, that they'd found Larry's lair.

"We can't just rush in," Tom said with renewed urgency in his voice. "You go to the left and I'll go to the right. We need to take a look inside and assess things before we just barge in."

Jacob nodded, his gaze narrowed as he surveyed the geography. Although there appeared to be nobody around, the last thing he wanted was to be seen approaching the building. Right now the element of surprise was on their side and he wanted to keep it that way.

His heart thrummed a rapid pace as he drew his gun and split up with Tom. Was this it? Was this the place where Larry had planned his party?

When they got inside would they find the same kind of carnage he'd found in the warehouse in Kansas City? His entire being rebelled at the very thought.

The closer he moved to the building the faster his

heart beat. The snow had picked up in pace, lessening visibility and in this case working to their advantage.

This felt right. The location was isolated and if the women were capable of screaming there was nobody around to hear them. It provided easy access for Larry and probably had a way into this area without going past the main house.

By the time he reached the building itself all he could hear was the pounding of his heart in the unnatural silence that snow always brought.

He was glad to see that this side held a side door and that some of the wood had decayed, leaving cracks that would allow him to peer inside.

Before he could look, a scream ripped through the silence, followed by a deep male laugh that Jacob recognized. His blood ran cold and he knew he couldn't wait to assess the situation. The party was happening now and it had to be stopped.

Using his shoulder, he burst through the door and into the shed, his gun in front of him. Everything happened in a split second.

Amazement filled him as he saw the five jail cells constructed inside. Bright red balloons danced around the ceiling, a macabre touch to a scene of horror.

Relief flooded him that all the women were still alive, and a new horror filled him as he saw Larry in the cell with what appeared to be a doped-up Layla.

Before Jacob could act, Larry yanked Layla up before him and held a knife at her throat. "Drop your gun,

Agent Grayson. Drop it or she dies right before your eyes."

Layla's eyes were closed and she was obviously dead-weight in his arms, but the knife at her throat would kill her whether she was conscious or not.

He was vaguely aware of somebody screaming, of another woman crying, but his sole focus remained on Larry and the woman he held in his arms.

"Let her go. It's over," Jacob said. At that moment Tom entered through the front door of the building. Jacob held up his hand to keep his brother back, not wanting anything that might force Larry's hand. He tightened his grip on his gun.

"I don't think you heard me, Jacob," Larry replied. "I said drop the gun—both of you—or I'll slit her throat."

"It will be the last act you do before you die," Tom exclaimed.

Larry grinned. "But while I'm in hell I'll enjoy the fact that the last thing I saw was the look on Agent Grayson's face when I killed Layla."

Layla's eyes suddenly opened and in that instant Jacob realized she was not only conscious, but alert. Without warning she shot back her elbow, connecting with Larry's side. He grunted and released his hold on her. Layla flew to the ground and Jacob fired.

The bullet caught Larry in the chest and he reeled backward and fell as a sobbing Layla got back to her feet. She flew out of the cage and toward Jacob and he dropped his gun to grab her as she threw herself into his arms. He hugged her tight as she wept.

Tom rushed to Larry's side and checked his pulse, then nodded to Jacob, indicating that the man was dead. He called for more help as Jacob continued to hold Layla. "It's over," he said to her. "It's finally over for good."

Tom grabbed the keys from Larry and hurried toward Brittany's cell. "No," she said. "Get the others out first."

Within minutes the shed was filled with men and weeping women. There would be much evidence to gather, statements to get, cleanup to do. But this time the cleanup was on their terms, not the terms of the man who had called himself The Professional.

"I knew you'd find us," Layla said as she finally moved out of his arms. "I knew if I could just play at being unconscious long enough you'd have the time you needed to get here."

A sweet admiration filled him as he thought of what she'd done when she'd surprised him with the elbow and then had dropped to the ground, giving Jacob a perfect shot at Larry. "You're amazing," he said to her and stroked a finger down the side of her beautiful face.

She gave him a tremulous smile. "I'm a survivor from way back when."

Then Brittany was in front of him and Layla stepped back so he could hug the sister he'd thought was lost forever.

His happiness nearly overwhelmed him, until he realized that now it was safe for Layla to return to her normal life, that now it was time to tell her goodbye.

Chapter 13

It was just after dawn when Jacob and Layla left the sheriff's office and headed back to the cabin. The night had been filled with happy reunions, making statements and gathering facts.

Brittany had gone home with Benjamin and Edie, deciding that she wanted to stay in her childhood home for a while before returning to her house in town. Layla knew it would take a while for Brittany to return to the vivacious, fun-loving woman she'd been before becoming a victim of Larry Norwood.

The other women had been reunited with family and friends and had gone home to heal from the trauma they had endured and the weeks of time that he had stolen from them.

"I feel so bad for Larry's wife and kids," Layla said as she gazed out the passenger window of Jacob's truck. The snow had stopped once again, although it promised to be a cold, blustery day.

"She'll be okay. Apparently she's planning on moving to Chicago where her parents live," Jacob replied. "She had no clue what was going on. She said Larry was always a private man who spent a lot of time out of the house."

"Sounds like their marriage wasn't a good one." She glanced over at him. He'd been unusually quiet on the ride and Layla figured he probably couldn't wait to get rid of her.

"It won't take me long to pack up my things and then if you could just drop me by my house I'd appreciate it."

"No problem."

A wave of depression settled over her. She wasn't sure what she'd wanted him to say, but that wasn't it. There had been a small part of her that had hoped he'd tell her he didn't want to take her home, tell her that he wanted to keep her with him forever.

But, you've never been a forever kind of girl, she reminded herself, and Jacob wasn't a forever kind of man. It was time for her to get back to her sad, lonely life and pretend that it was exactly as she'd planned it, exactly what she wanted.

When they reached the cabin her heart squeezed tight in her chest once again. This was where she'd fallen in love for the very first time. It had only taken days, but she felt as close to Jacob as if they'd been together for months. It felt as if all the other relationships she'd had in the past were just practice for the real thing with him.

Tell him how you feel, a little voice whispered inside her as they entered the living room. But she knew she wasn't going to do that. What was the point? It was better to just walk away than to put her heart on the line and let him reject her. She'd been able to handle other rejections, but his would destroy her.

As she walked into the bedroom to gather her things, he threw himself on the recliner. Whether he knew it or not, he was a much different man than he'd been when she'd first arrived.

She knew he'd always be haunted by the women they hadn't been able to save, but his nemesis was dead, his sister had been found and Jacob had reawakened to life in the days Layla had been with him.

She told herself it was enough for her, that she was content knowing he'd get on with his life and be in a better place than when she'd first arrived here. But as she began to pack her clothes back in the suitcase hot tears burned at her eyes.

Was it so wrong to want to be a forever kind of woman? Was it so wrong to love Jacob enough to want to spend her life with him? They'd been through so much together. They belonged together, but her wishing it didn't make it so.

By the time she had her suitcase packed she had her

emotions back under control. As she reentered the living room Jacob got out of his chair to take the suitcase from her.

"All set?" he asked, his eyes shuttered and showing no emotion.

She nodded. "Back to real life." She forced a cheerfulness into her voice. "At least I'll be home for Christmas." She glanced at the silly little tree they'd decorated with aluminum stars and emotion once again threatened to consume her.

As he carried the suitcase out the front door Layla took one last look around the cabin, remembering laughing with him as they'd talked about Christmases past and decorated their little tree, comforting him as he'd sat in the chair after telling them about The Professional and making love with him beneath the homemade quilt in the bedroom.

There was no question she'd carry a piece of him with her for the rest of her life. He had imprinted into her heart in a way nobody else had ever managed to do.

Leaving the cabin, she hurried to the truck where Jacob was waiting to take her back to her life. "What are your plans now?" she asked when they were headed into town.

"Spend some time with Brittany and the rest of my family, help Tom finish up the last of the details with the case and beyond that I'm not sure. Why?" He didn't look at her but rather kept his gaze focused on the road.

"I was just curious," she replied with forced lightness.

"You know, if you're ever in the market to buy a house I know the best Realtor in town."

He gave her a faint smile. "Yeah, so do I."

The closer they got to her house the tighter emotion pressed thick in her chest. Saying goodbye was never easy, but telling Jacob goodbye seemed like the most difficult thing she'd ever done in her life.

Sure, they would see each other around town, maybe bump into one another on the streets and each time they did she knew she'd feel the ache of his absence deep within her.

"It's going to be a special Christmas for all of you with Brittany finally home," she said. How she wished she were going to be a part of their celebration.

"Yeah, it's definitely going to be a Christmas to remember." His voice wasn't cool, but she felt the distance radiating from him. It was as if he'd already moved on without her and had no desire to look back.

By the time they reached her house she'd fallen silent, had no more words to give him. Her heart weighed a million pounds as they walked up to her front door and he set the suitcase down on the porch.

"Thanks doesn't seem enough for what you did for me," she said.

For a moment she saw something soft in his eyes. "I didn't do for you anymore than you did for me." That softness fled as if it had never really been there. "I'd say we're even."

Even. The word resonated in her soul. She didn't want

to be even. She wanted him to need her, to want her for the rest of their lives. *Even* felt cold and impersonal.

"Be happy, Jacob," she said with her love for him nearly choking her throat.

"You do the same." Before anything else could be said he turned on his heels and walked back to his truck. She watched from the front porch as he drove off without a backward glance.

As she unlocked her door she fought back the tears that threatened to fall. *Silly to be so upset,* she thought as she dragged her suitcase over the threshold and into the entryway.

She was used to men walking away from her, but what made Jacob different was that this time her heart had been completely involved. This time she'd been desperately, hopelessly in love.

Dragging her suitcase into the bedroom, she tried to focus on all the things she needed to do to get back to her normal life. First on her list was to retrieve Mr. Whiskers from the vet's office. Second on her list was to try to figure out a way how to stop loving Jacob Grayson.

At this thought she sat on the edge of her bed and let the tears that she'd desperately been trying to hold back fall.

"So, now that you've rejoined the living when are you going to get out of this place?" Caleb asked Jacob. He and Portia had stopped by the cabin for a visit and Jacob was more than happy for the unexpected company.

It had been a week since Larry Norwood had been killed and all the women had been rescued, seven full days since he'd taken Layla home.

"I don't know, I'm thinking maybe I'll stay here through the winter and then look for something to buy in town in the spring." Jacob frowned thoughtfully. "I'm still not sure I'm ready to rejoin all of humanity."

"What are you brooding about now?" Portia asked.

"I'm not brooding," he protested.

"Yes, you are," she countered. "You've been moody and brooding for the last week. I would think you'd be on top of the world with that creep dead and all the women safe and sound."

"I am on top of the world," Jacob replied, his frown deepening as Portia gave him a disbelieving look. "I'm fine," he assured her, but the truth of the matter was he wasn't fine.

He'd always been a man alone, but he'd never been a lonely man until now, without Layla. She'd breezed into the cabin and had not only brought life back to him, but had also brought love.

He missed the sound of her voice and the clack of her high heels on the floor. He ached for the softness in her eyes and her breathy little sighs as he'd made love to her.

Since she'd been gone he felt as if he'd lost his very best friend, the person who stirred not only his passion but made him laugh and made him want to share all the pieces of himself.

He'd thought she cared about him. There had been moments when she'd gazed at him with such a lightness in her eyes, when she'd touched him with such sweet tenderness that he thought he felt her love for him. And yet she'd walked away without a word, letting him know he was not important in her life.

"You've heard that we're doing a big Christmas gathering at Benjamin and Edie's on Christmas Eve," Caleb said, pulling Jacob from his thoughts of love lost.

"Yeah, Tom mentioned it to me."

"According to Edie, Walt and Margaret are already fighting over who is going to cook what for the meal," Portia said.

Edie's grandfather Walt had briefly moved in with Benjamin and had battled with Margaret, the woman who had been the housekeeper, over the cooking. Somehow in the midst of those initial battles love had blossomed between the two senior citizens and Margaret had moved with Walt to his house in town.

"What do you want Santa to bring you, Jacob?" Portia asked.

"Layla." The name left his lips and he stared at Portia in horror. He'd only meant to think it. He hadn't meant to say it out loud.

"Ah, so that's how it is," Caleb exclaimed with a grin. "I thought I sensed something going on between the two of you."

Jacob stared at his brother and then looked at Portia.

"I'm in love with her," he confessed and he knew his heartache was evident in those five words.

Portia sat back on the sofa and held Jacob's gaze. "That's interesting because she's in love with you."

"Yeah, right," Jacob replied drily. "Trust me, she made it clear to me from the very beginning that she didn't care about relationships."

"But that's not true," Portia replied. She leaned forward. "Jacob, I've known Layla since we were both in grade school. I've never known a woman who needs to be loved more than her, but for years her father told her that she wasn't worthy of love, that she was worthless and no man would ever want her."

Jacob's stomach twisted as he thought of Layla as a vulnerable child dealing with the abuse of her father.

"I've tried to explain to her that love is a verb, that when you're in love you have to do things to show it and you have to talk about it, but she has her defenses so high she doesn't understand." Portia grabbed Caleb's hand. "She's used to men walking away from her, and they walk away because she doesn't give them a reason to stay, she never tells anyone what she wants. But she told me how much she loves you and she's been sick since you two parted ways."

Was it possible what Portia said was true? A tiny ray of hope flared in his heart. Was it possible that both of them had been so afraid of being hurt again they'd let the best thing that could happen walk out of their lives?

"You know, when we Grayson men finally figure out what we want, we usually go after it," Caleb said.

What if Portia was wrong? What if he went to her and spilled his guts and she laughed at him? What if he put his heart on the line with her and she turned him down?

It couldn't hurt any more than it did now. Suddenly what he wanted to do more than anything was let her know that she was worthy, that he loved her with a depth that would last through eternity.

He got out of his chair, driven by the same kind of urgency that had driven him when he'd been hunting for her when she'd been kidnapped. He felt that if he didn't tell her how he felt right now, if he didn't take a chance with her in the next few minutes, he'd explode.

"She's probably at her office," Portia said as he pulled on his coat. She and Caleb got off the sofa and Portia grabbed Jacob by the arms. "If this isn't for forever, if you don't love her with every fiber of your being, then don't bother with her and just leave her alone."

"I can't imagine living without her." His voice was husky with emotion.

Portia nodded and smiled. "Then go get your woman, Jacob."

Minutes later as Jacob drove toward town, doubts began to assail him. What if Portia didn't know what was truly in Layla's heart?

For all he knew in the last week Layla had started dating somebody else in town. He thought of a stop he needed to make before he saw Layla…if he decided to see Layla.

Maybe he was just one of those fools who were forever destined to fall in love with women who didn't have the capacity to love them back.

He eased his foot up on the gas pedal, suddenly unsure what he was going to do.

Layla stared out her office window and tried to fight against the depression that had been a constant companion for the last week.

There was nothing worse than being depressed at Christmastime. The night after she'd gotten home she'd spent the evening decorating her house for the holiday, but all the tinsel and bright lights couldn't pierce through the hollow ache that had invaded her chest. Nothing in her life had prepared her for this kind of heartbreak.

She should just go home. Nobody was going to buy or sell a home so close to the holiday. She was just wasting time sitting here when she could be home with Mr. Whiskers.

Deciding to do just that, she grabbed her purse from the floor and set it on her desk, and it was at that moment she saw him approaching from across the street, a bright red box tucked beneath one arm.

Jacob. Even as she stared at him, she told herself she didn't want to see him, wasn't ready to face him yet. Still, her eyes drank in the sight of him.

At some point since she'd last seen him he'd gotten

a haircut and he walked with a new sense of pride, of confidence that only increased his attractiveness.

As he saw her through the window he smiled and she wanted to weep. She steeled herself as he opened the door and came in, bringing with him the scent of the cold air and a faint whisper of his cologne.

"Well, look what the wind blew in," she said as she stood and forced the lightness into her voice that had always served her well. "If it isn't the town's latest hero and the newest member of law enforcement."

"So you've heard that I'm going to be a deputy," he said, stopping just short of her desk.

"The whole town has heard and has applauded the move by Tom to hire you. You couldn't come with better credentials than being an ex-FBI agent and the man who brought down The Professional."

She wanted to touch him, to run her fingers over the curve of his lips, to press herself against him and feel safe and loved for one last time.

Instead she sat back in her chair to give herself as much distance from him as possible. "So, what are you doing here?"

"I brought you something." He set the red package on the desk in front of her.

She stared at it and then back at him. "Why?"

He jammed his hands into his pockets and shrugged. "Because I felt like it. Go on, open it."

What was he doing? Why was he torturing her? Her

fingers trembled as she unwrapped the paper to reveal a shoe box. She looked up at him again in confusion.

"I couldn't find shoes like the ones you kicked off the day Norwood grabbed you, the ones that were ruined by the snow," he said.

She opened the box and pulled back the inside paper to reveal a pair of bright red sling-back pumps with tiny white bows. They were the most beautiful shoes she'd ever seen.

Tears blurred her vision and suddenly she was mad, mad that he thought she'd want a pair of shoes when all she really wanted was him.

"You crazy fool," she exclaimed. "I don't care about shoes. All I really care about is you." She stared up at him, appalled by her outburst.

His eyes narrowed and he pulled his hands from his pockets. "Do you mean that?"

Tension filled the air, a tension of expectancy that pressed tight against Layla's chest. Did she tell him the truth or did she make a joke out of it? Before she could decide he walked around the desk and pulled her to her feet.

"I just had a talk with Portia," he said. "She reminded me that love is a verb and that it's something you do as well as something you feel. I feel it, Layla, and I decided it was time I act on it."

Her heart began to beat faster but fear kept her frozen in place. "Is this some kind of a joke?" she finally asked.

"Does this feel like a joke?" He pulled her into his arms and took her lips with his in a kiss that sang of hot, sweet desire.

She pulled away from him as tears stung her eyes. "It doesn't feel like a joke. It feels like passion, but I know how that works and eventually that will be gone and there will be nothing left. I don't want you for a little while. I can't stand the thought of you being just another man who leaves me when the passion is gone."

"Oh, Layla." He reached out and embraced her close again. "There's no question that I feel passion for you. But I also want to be the man who holds you when you cry. I want to listen to everything you have to say, even if it sometimes makes my eyes cross. I love you, Layla, but more importantly I need you. I know what your father did to you, how he told you for years that you didn't matter, and I want to spend every day of the rest of my life showing you how important you are to me."

He stroked a hand through her hair and smiled and in that smile she saw his heart, and she knew that it was hers for the taking.

"I do talk too much," she admitted.

"A charming trait."

"And I don't do mornings very well."

"I can give you plenty of space in the mornings," he replied.

"You'd have to like my cat."

He grinned. "I love Mr. Whiskers and I haven't even met him yet."

"I love you, Jacob." Once again tears burned at her eyes, but this time they were happy tears. "And I want you in my life forever. I love everything about you. You're the man I've waited my entire life to find, and contrary to what my father thought, I am worthy of love. I am worthy of your love."

"Layla, you talk too much," he said as he lowered his lips to hers once again.

This time as his mouth plied hers with heat, she tasted not just his passion, but also the kind of love she'd only dreamed about, the kind that would last for the rest of her life.

Epilogue

The noise in the Grayson house was just shy of deafening. Caleb and Benjamin were in a good-natured argument about football. Peyton's daughter, Lilly, was laughing as Tom tickled her tummy and Edie and Benjamin were refereeing Walt and Margaret as they argued about whose dessert was best, Walt's apple pie or Margaret's pumpkin.

Layla sat in a chair next to the grand Christmas tree and breathed in the sense of family that surrounded her. It was magical, as everything had felt since Jacob had come to her office and proclaimed his love for her.

He'd moved from the cabin into her house that day and for the first time in her life Layla felt as if she was where she belonged, that he was where he belonged.

She now smiled as he came into the living room. He'd left a few minutes before to have a chat with Brittany. "How is she?" she asked as she stood.

He wrapped an arm around her shoulders as they stood before the glittery tree. "She's still pretty fragile."

"It hasn't been that long. She just needs time to heal from the ordeal," Layla replied.

"I don't think she's coming back to her job as a deputy."

Layla leaned into him, loving the way she fit so neatly against him. "Did she mention what her plans are?"

"She wants to stay here with Benjamin and Edie for a while longer and she doesn't know for sure what she wants to do after that."

"She'll be okay, Jacob. She's tough and she's a survivor. You all just need to give her some time and space for her to figure it all out."

"I know," he agreed, then laughed as Lilly released a new giggling scream of delight. "Just think, next year there will be another little one with Portia's baby here."

"If we work really hard we could make it two new babies here by next Christmas," she replied.

His eyes burned with a new intensity as he pulled her even closer to him. "I'd like that."

She grinned at him. "You just like the working on it."

"That, too," he agreed with his sexy grin. He sobered and released the sigh of a contented man. "It doesn't get any better than this—family all together, the scent of great food in the air and the woman I love more than life itself standing in my arms."

As he kissed her he warmed her from the very top of her head down to her toes that were encased in the red high heels he'd bought for her.

She returned his kiss and realized all she'd really needed to find happiness was Jacob Grayson and the belief that she was worth every good thing that came her way.

He broke the kiss and held her gaze. "I promise you, Layla, I'm going to love you for the rest of my life."

She gazed up at him with wide eyes. "But you never make promises."

"I only make ones that I intend to keep," he replied. "Now, let's go eat some of that apple and pumpkin pie and then get home so we can work on giving Lilly a new little cousin."

She thrilled not just with the promise his lips had made, but also with the promise that warmed his eyes, the sweet promise of enduring love.

* * * * *

TOOL BELT DEFENDER

BY
CARLA CASSIDY

First published in Great Britain 2012
by Mills & Boon, an imprint of Harlequin (UK) Limited,
Eton House, 18-24 Paradise Road, Richmond, Surrey TW9 1SR

© Carla Bracale 2012

ISBN: 978 0 263 89511 7

46-0312

Harlequin (UK) policy is to use papers that are natural, renewable and recyclable products and made from wood grown in sustainable forests. The logging and manufacturing processes conform to the legal environmental regulations of the country of origin.

Printed and bound in Spain
by Blackprint CPI, Barcelona

This book is dedicated to my very own tool
belt defender, Frank.
After all these years you still know exactly what tool to
use to keep me feeling safe and protected and
loved. Thank you and I love you.

Chapter 1

He was a hot hunk in a tight white T-shirt, a pair of worn jeans and a tool belt riding low on his lean hips. He was nothing like what Brittany Grayson had expected.

When she'd called Chad Warren, one of the local carpenters in the small town of Black Rock, Kansas, to see about him building a deck on the back of her house, he'd told her he was already booked for the spring but would send an old college friend of his who had recently moved to town.

Chad was a good old boy, fifty pounds overweight, who believed beer pong should be a nationally recognized sport. It was silly, but she'd just assumed his college buddy would be like him. But the man standing on her front porch didn't look like a peer of Chad's;

rather he looked as if he'd stepped off the slick pages of some hot-hunk calendar.

"Brittany?" His voice was deep and pleasant and made her realize she'd been staring at him open-mouthed through the screen door.

"Yes, I'm Brittany and you must be…" Her mind suddenly went blank.

"Alex. Alex Crawford, Chad's friend. You called him about a deck?"

"Yes, I did." She hesitated before opening the screen door to allow him inside. There had been no men except for her brothers inside her home since she'd moved back in a little over a month ago.

As she unlocked the screen, she realized she wasn't quite ready yet to allow a stranger inside, especially a male stranger. Instead she stepped outside where the late April sun was warm and the air smelled of newly bloomed flowers.

"It's nice to meet you, Alex. Let's walk around back and I'll show you what I have in mind," she said. She frowned as she realized there was no car in her driveway. "Did you walk here?" she asked.

His eyes were a warm blue that stood out against his tanned face and were complemented by his slightly shaggy dark hair. "I live three doors up." He pointed up the street to the Walker home that had been on the market for a while.

"How long have you lived there?"

"I moved in about six weeks ago," he replied as they walked around the side of the house toward the back.

That explained why she didn't know the Walkers

had moved out and Mr. Hardbody had moved in. Six weeks ago she'd still been living at her brother Benjamin's house trying to heal from the trauma she'd lived through.

As they reached the backyard she motioned toward the small broken brick patio that existed just outside the back door. "What I'd like is a wooden deck big enough to hold a barbecue pit and an umbrella table and maybe some plants and, of course, lots and lots of people."

He nodded and pulled a tape measure from his tool belt. "An outdoor entertainment area," he said.

"Exactly," she replied and watched as he began to walk the site. The last thing Brittany had wanted to think about over the past eight months of her life was men. But looking at Alex Crawford definitely gave her a slight flutter of pure feminine pleasure.

When she'd been held captive by a serial killer for four long months, she'd spent her time thinking about all the things she would do if she escaped, if she managed to live.

She hadn't fantasized about love or having babies. She hadn't thought about men or hot sex. Rather she'd thought about a deck where she could invite all her friends and family to share good times with her. And now she was finally going to see those fantasies come to fruition.

"I'd say what you want is about eighteen by twenty-four," Alex said as the tape measure zipped back into its metal case.

"And I'd like a railing around it with an opening to step down into the yard," she said.

He nodded and smiled. "I can do that."

The man had a smile with the capacity to stop time. A wave of warmth washed over Brittany as she tried to stay focused on the matter at hand. "How long will it take?"

He frowned, the gesture doing nothing to detract from his attractiveness. "It will take maybe a week once we get started. I work weekdays from about eight in the morning until about three-thirty and I have a couple of young men who help out, but I don't work on the weekends."

Probably he took the weekends to spend with his family, she thought. A man who looked like Alex Crawford probably had a wife who looked like a supermodel. "So, you'll call me with a bid?"

"If you give me just a few minutes I'll have a bid for you now." He pulled out a small pad and a pencil.

His dark hair shone richly in the overhead sunlight and Brittany suddenly felt the need to get some distance from him. "Why don't I go get us each a glass of lemonade?" she suggested.

He looked up and smiled again and another rivulet of warmth swept through her. "That sounds great."

She escaped back into the house and went through the living room to the kitchen. For a moment she stood at the window and watched him as he once again walked off the area where the deck would be built.

Surely her response to him was nothing more than a healthy awakening of emotions that had been dormant for far too long. She moved away from the window and poured the lemonade into two tall plastic tumblers.

She would be twenty-six in two months—it was only natural that she might appreciate the sight of a good-looking man. She should be glad that normal feelings were finally beginning to return to her.

For the past several months she'd alternated between numbness and an irrational fear as she'd tried to reintegrate back into the life that had been stolen from her for four agonizing months. Nightmares, panic attacks—she'd had them all and had begun to believe she'd never have a normal moment again. It was nice that this normal moment was a healthy dose of lust.

She walked out the back door and motioned him to one of the four chairs at the old table that was on the broken brick patio. "Thanks," he said as he took the drink from her. "I've got some figures for you." He handed her a piece of paper that had his bid written on it. "If you agree, then I'll write up a contract for you to sign."

The figure was about what she'd expected. "Looks good to me." She leaned back in her chair and offered him a tentative smile. "Chad mentioned that the two of you went to college together."

"We did. I went on to law school and got a job in Chicago and Chad came back here."

"From lawyer to carpenter? Quite a leap," she observed. "What brings you back to Black Rock?"

"My wife's family is from here and after several

years of doing the high-powered, high-stress corporate thing, I decided I was ready for a change of pace."

A small laugh escaped Brittany. "The difference in pace between Chicago and Black Rock, Kansas, is like the difference between a pit bull and a stuffed dog." She wasn't surprised that the man was married.

He laughed. "You've got that right, but Black Rock is just what I needed." He tilted his glass up and drained it and then stood. "If you agree with everything I can start work tomorrow, given I can get a lumber delivery."

She got up from her chair and took his empty glass and together they walked around the side of the house to the front.

"Is it your birthday or something?" he asked.

She looked at him in confusion. "No, why?"

He pointed to her mailbox where a bright red balloon was tied and bobbed and danced in the slight warm breeze. Shock ripped through her and the glasses slid from her hands, crashing to the grass at her feet.

It's party time. The nightmarish voice whispered in her brain as memories attacked her. The cell where she'd been kept, the promise of a party when all the cells were filled with helpless women, the final moment when red balloons had danced up to the ceiling of the old shed. *It's party time.*

"Brittany, are you all right?"

Alex's voice pulled her back from the dark abyss she'd nearly fallen into and she tore her gaze from the balloon and looked into his concerned eyes.

"I'm fine," she replied, aware that her voice was shaky and hoping he didn't notice.

"Are you sure?" He bent down and picked up the glasses.

She nodded, even though she wasn't at all sure that she was fine. Thank God the glasses were plastic and hadn't shattered when she'd dropped them. She took them from him, hoping he didn't notice the trembling of her hands. "Silly me. Just a touch of clumsiness. You'll call me and let me know if you're coming tomorrow?"

"I'll head home now and order the necessary lumber and other supplies. If they can deliver tomorrow then I'll give you a call." He eyed her worriedly, but she forced a cheerful smile to her lips.

"Do you need me to write you a check now for the materials?" she asked.

"That's not necessary." His eyes gleamed with a teasing light. "I know where you live."

"Thanks, Alex. Hopefully I'll see you tomorrow." She turned on wooden legs and headed for the house, an urgent need to get inside and lock the door filling her.

She didn't wait to watch him walk down the sidewalk toward his place; rather she turned on her heels and half ran toward her front door. Once inside she slammed it shut and locked it.

Leaning heavily against the solid wood door she told herself she was overreacting, that maybe there was a child's birthday party someplace on the street or a graduation celebration and somebody had just tied the balloon on her mailbox by accident.

Surely there was a logical reason for the balloon. It had nothing to do with the man who had called himself The Professional. He was dead. She'd seen his body after he'd been killed. He was no longer capable of having a "party" complete with red balloons and death.

Still, the legacy he'd left behind sickened her and even though she knew it was totally irrational, that balloon tied to her mailbox made her fear in her heart that somehow The Professional wasn't done with her yet.

As Alex walked back toward his house his head was filled with thoughts of Brittany Grayson. She was something of a celebrity in the small town. Last fall a serial killer had held the town of Black Rock hostage when he'd begun kidnapping women. It had taken all four of Brittany's brothers, who were the law in Black Rock, to figure out that The Professional was actually the town vet, Larry Norwood. They'd managed to rescue the women and Norwood had been killed.

It was discovered that he'd committed the same crime in Kansas City, but unfortunately authorities hadn't been able to catch him before he'd tortured and killed the women he'd held captive there.

Brittany had been the first woman kidnapped and the one who had been held the longest. Still, it wasn't the crime that was uppermost in his mind—it was the woman herself.

Brittany Grayson was stunning and something about her had instantly struck him right in the solar plexus.

Her long dark hair had shone richly in the sunshine and although initially her chocolate-brown eyes had been wary, they'd warmed as she'd talked about the deck she wanted.

The gold, sleeveless blouse she'd worn had emphasized intriguing golden flecks in the very depths of her dark eyes and her jeans had hugged her slender frame and showcased her long legs.

As he approached the two-story house he now called home, he noticed it was time for the first lawn mowing of the season and reminded himself that he wanted to plant flowers in the bed along the porch and down the walkway.

Coming from a high-rise condo in Chicago where there had been no outside maintenance or yard work for him to be responsible for, moving into this house had been daunting but would definitely be worth it in the long run.

As he opened the door he heard the sound of little feet running and before he could prepare himself completely six-year-old Emily launched herself into his arms.

"Daddy!" She placed her hands on both of his cheeks, making it impossible for him to look at anything but her, which of course he didn't mind. The pint-size blonde with her bright green eyes and long pigtails was the most important thing in Alex's life.

"What?" he asked as he carried her into the living room and then leaned down to place her on the floor.

"Grandma said I've been so good while you've been gone, I should get ice cream after dinner tonight."

"She did, did she?"

"Guilty as charged," Rose Tyler said as she walked into the living room.

Alex smiled warmly at the older woman. She was an attractive woman, her short gray hair perfectly coiffed, clad in a pair of navy slacks and a tailored white-and-navy blouse.

She had certainly been instrumental in Alex's decision to move to Black Rock. When his wife, Linda, had died eighteen months ago, Alex had tried to be a good and present single parent, but with his work schedule as a lawyer in a big firm Emily had spent more time with babysitters than with him.

It had been an unacceptable reality for a little girl reeling from her mother's death. Here in Black Rock not only did Alex have a new occupation that he found far more rewarding than what he'd been doing and allowed him more time with his daughter, but Emily also had a loving grandmother who only lived a block away from their house and was available to babysit day or night.

"Then I guess ice cream it is," he agreed and laughed as Emily clapped her hands together and then did a little dance to show her pleasure. "I have to go tell Lady Bear. She'll be so happy." She dashed from the room and up the stairs toward her bedroom.

"You've done such a good job with her, Alex," Rose

said with a smile. "And I'll never be able to thank you enough for moving here so I can be a part of her life." Her smile wavered slightly and she placed a slender, wrinkled hand over her heart. "When we lost Linda I was afraid that I'd lose you and Emily, too."

"Don't kid yourself, this move was as much for me as it was about you and Emily," he replied. "I was more than ready for a change of lifestyle and I think this is going to be a great place to raise Emily."

"Did you get the job?" Rose asked as she pulled on the white cardigan sweater she'd brought with her when she'd arrived to watch Emily.

"I did. If all goes well, starting tomorrow morning I'll be working on a deck at Brittany Grayson's house."

Rose frowned. "That poor girl. I can't imagine her having the courage to move back to her house all alone after what she's been through. She'd got to be one of the strongest people I know."

"She definitely seems ready to move on with her life," he replied.

"Speaking of moving on, I'd better get out of here," Rose said, as she picked up her purse from the sofa.

Alex walked to the bottom of the staircase. "Emily, Grandma is leaving. Come down and tell her goodbye."

Emily came down the stairs, her favorite pink stuffed bear in her arms. "Lady Bear wanted to say goodbye, too."

"By all means, I wanted to say goodbye to Lady Bear," Rose replied as she shook the bear's pink paw.

Alex watched the goodbyes exchanged between

Rose and Emily and Lady Bear and tried not to worry that Emily's attachment to the stuffed animal bordered on obsessive.

The bear had been a gift from a friend attending Linda's funeral and Alex had a feeling that all of Emily's love for her mother had been transferred to the stuffed animal.

"Are you sure you don't want me to drive you home?" Alex asked Rose when the goodbyes were finished and Emily had gone back upstairs to her room.

"No, thank you. A little exercise is good for me, and besides, it's only a block. You'll call me later and let me know what the schedule is for tomorrow?"

"Yeah, but I should be able to work it so that I'm home when Emily gets off the school bus," he replied. "If something changes I'll let you know."

A few minutes later he stepped out onto the porch and watched as Rose walked up the sidewalk. Rose had lost her husband in a car accident five years ago and then had lost her only child, Linda. There was nobody Alex admired more in the world than his mother-in-law, who, despite the tragedies she'd suffered, continued to not only put one foot in front of the other but seemed to seek out happiness whenever and wherever she could find it.

She'd been by Alex's side when Linda had died, and he knew the anger she'd felt toward her daughter, an anger that still burned inside Alex when the grief wasn't filling him up. But Rose had hidden her anger well as she'd tended to her daughter in Linda's last days.

When Rose disappeared from his sight he turned and went back into the house. As he climbed the stairs to Emily's room, he checked his wristwatch. It was only a little after four.

He found Emily sitting at the child-size table and chairs in her room. Lady Bear sat in the chair opposite her and there was a coloring book open not only in front of Emily, but also in front of the bear.

"Hi, Daddy. We decided to color you a picture," she said as Alex folded his long legs and sat in the little chair next to hers.

"You know how much I love your pictures," he replied. In fact, the front of his refrigerator was laden with Emily's artwork. He watched for a few minutes as she colored a blue sky and a pink house. When she started in on the yellow sun he spoke.

"You know, I was thinking, maybe since you were such a good girl for grandma while I was gone, we might have ice cream before dinner."

Emily's green eyes opened wide and the yellow crayon rolled out of her small hand and across the table. "Before dinner? Like right now?"

"Like right now," he replied. He laughed as Emily was out of her chair with Lady Bear in her arms before he could blink his eyes.

"Now, that's a good plan," she exclaimed.

"But only one scoop. I don't want to completely ruin your appetite for dinner."

"Okay, maybe one scoop before dinner and one scoop after," Emily replied, making Alex laugh.

Ten minutes later they were headed down the sidewalk to Main Street where Izzy's Ice Cream Parlor had quickly become their favorite shop in town. He'd managed to convince her that Lady Bear didn't need to come with them, that she'd much prefer some pretend honey when they got home than an ice cream cone now. As they walked Emily regaled him with stories about her day in school.

Thankfully, Emily had adjusted well to changing schools, loved her teacher and had already made new friends. She also loved having a backyard and had begun making noises about getting a dog. So far she'd adjusted to the move far better than Alex.

Although he'd been ready for the change, looked forward to a new occupation, a new lifestyle, he hadn't expected the loneliness.

In Chicago there had been business dinners, fund-raisers and late nights at the office to keep the loneliness at bay. Here most evenings existed of a bottle of beer and the sound of crickets from outside the window. He definitely hadn't expected this kind of aching loneliness.

But he didn't intend to ever marry again, and was reluctant to even date. The last thing he wanted to do was invite a string of women into Emily's life, women who would never be more than temporary.

As they walked by Brittany Grayson's house his thoughts returned to her. According to the local gossip she'd been strong and courageous during her captivity, and the other women who had been held captive had given her credit for keeping them sane.

If he did ever decide to marry again, which he seriously doubted he would, he would choose a strong woman. He'd loved Linda, but it hadn't taken him long into the marriage to realize she was childlike in her fears of life and that fear was ultimately what had led to her death.

Still, even though he told himself he had no desire to get involved with any woman right now, he couldn't help the anticipation that swept through him as he thought of seeing Brittany again.

He couldn't help but wonder if she was the fearless heroine everyone called her or just a damaged victim of a heinous crime.

Chapter 2

"Maybe you moved back here too soon," Brittany's eldest brother, Tom, said to her the next morning. He'd stopped by on his way into work as sheriff of Black Rock. He was a handsome man in his khaki uniform, but he had that stern big-brother look on his face that drove Brittany crazy.

"I mean, if the sight of a balloon threw you for a loop, then maybe you weren't ready to be out on your own," he added.

"It was time for me to get out of Benjamin and Edie's place. They're newlyweds and need their own space and it was time for me to get on with my life." Brittany got up from the table to refill her coffee mug. "Besides, it didn't throw me for a loop. I just wondered who had tied it to my mailbox and why." She topped off her coffee and then rejoined him at the table. "It was just natural curiosity."

Tom smiled at her knowingly. "Most people's voices don't quiver when expressing their feelings of natural curiosity."

"I'm sorry I even mentioned it," she retorted ruefully.

"You know you could always stay with us if you aren't ready to be out on your own. Peyton wouldn't mind having you with us."

Love for her brother surged up inside Brittany. He and his wife were newlyweds, as well, and had Peyton's little daughter, Lilly, to dote on. Besides, Brittany didn't want to live with any of her brothers anymore. She wanted…needed to be out on her own.

"Thanks, but I'm fine here. In fact I'm having a new deck built."

"Chad doing it?" he asked.

Brittany shook her head. "He was busy so he recommended a friend of his, Alex Crawford."

Tom frowned. "I don't think I've met him."

"He's only been in town about six weeks. He moved into the Walker house."

He nodded. "Have you given any thought to coming back to work?" he asked.

Before her kidnapping Brittany had also been a member of the Black Rock law-enforcement team. She'd worked beneath Tom as a deputy along with her other brothers Benjamin and Caleb. Her brother Jacob had worked for the FBI in Kansas City, but during the time Brittany had been kidnapped he had returned to Black Rock and was now also a deputy for the town.

"I'm not ready yet," she replied. "I hate to leave you shorthanded but to be perfectly honest, I'm not sure I want to return." The words formed a lump in the back of her throat.

Tom lifted an eyebrow in surprise. He leaned back in his chair, his eyes studying her. "You don't have to come back if it doesn't feel right, and don't worry about leaving me shorthanded."

"But isn't Benjamin leaving in a week or so?"

"Two weeks."

Brittany's brother Benjamin had for years divided his energies between the jobs of working as a deputy and ranching on the family homestead. He'd finally decided to ranch full-time and was quitting his duties as deputy.

"Have you given any thought to what you'd rather do if you don't come back?" Tom asked.

"Not really. I thought I'd take some online college classes and keep my options open."

"What about money? Are you okay?"

Brittany smiled. "I'm fine. I had some savings and I'm using some of my inheritance for the deck."

"I figured you'd already spent all that money on shoes and purses," Tom said teasingly and then checked his watch. "I've got to get out of here. If I don't check in soon, Caleb will be sitting in my chair with his feet up on my desk." He downed the last of his coffee and then got up from the table and carried his cup to the sink.

Brittany walked him to her front door where he turned and touched her lightly on the tip of her nose. "You'll be okay. Go shopping, buy yourself something completely frivolous. That's always made you feel better in the past."

She watched him as he walked toward the path to his patrol car parked at the curb. She knew he meant well. All of her brothers did, but they all interacted with her as if she were the same person she'd been before the kidnapping, and she wasn't.

She closed the door and locked it, then returned to the kitchen and grabbed her coffee cup. She walked to the back window and stared out at the patio.

A little over eight months ago, before she'd been taken captive, she'd been a spoiled, indulged princess. She'd loved hanging out with her friends at Harley's Bar, a rough-and-tumble tavern that boasted live music on the weekends. She'd loved shopping and lunch out and dating men that weren't necessarily husband material.

She'd often been late to work, knowing that her brothers would cover for her, and living each moment without thought for the next had been her specialty.

She wasn't that woman anymore, but her brothers had failed to see that although her life had been spared, the immature, irresponsible girl she'd been had been killed, leaving her floundering to discover exactly who she was now.

She rubbed her eyes, feeling the grit of exhaustion. The balloon had been gone when she'd gotten up that morning, but the sight of it had kept her awake far too long the night before. She hadn't been able to shake a sense of foreboding that in the light of day seemed rather silly.

She jumped as her phone rang. She didn't recognize the number, but picked it up and answered.

"Brittany, it's Alex."

His deep voice washed over her with a welcome heat and she reminded herself that he was a married man. "Hi, what's up?"

"I thought I'd let you know that the supplies should be delivered around noon today and if you don't mind I'd like to be there when they drop them off."

"No problem. I just can't wait for the project to be done."

"Then I'll see you just before noon."

She hung up and smiled ruefully. It was just her luck that after everything she'd been through the first man who sparked any kind of interest in her was totally off-limits.

Reminding herself that the last thing she needed at this moment in her life was a man, she set about making herself breakfast.

It was about midday when she looked out her back window and saw Alex seated in one of the chairs on her patio. She opened the back door and stepped outside.

"You should have told me you were here," she said as he smiled at her and stood.

"I didn't want to bother you. They told me the delivery would be around noon, but that usually means anywhere between noon and four."

She waved him back down and sank into the chair opposite his and tried not to notice that he looked just as handsome today as he had the day before. "Would you like something to drink?" she asked.

"No, thanks. I'm good."

He was better than good, she thought. "It's a gorgeous day to start the project," she said.

He smiled. "Nothing better than a perfect spring day for a little work outside."

"Have you had a chance to explore Black Rock?" She just wanted to make conversation, to have a reason to remain sitting across from him and enjoy the view.

"We've definitely discovered Izzy's Ice Cream Parlor. I think it's going to be our favorite hangout until winter comes."

"When winter does arrive then you'll have to go out to Mathew's pond on the north side of town. If the temperature is right he sets up fire barrels around the edge of the pond and half the town shows up there on the weekends to ice-skate."

"Sounds like fun."

"How's your wife coping with small-town life?" she asked, needing to remind herself that that he was a married man and then maybe that thousand-watt smile of his wouldn't have so much power over her.

"Actually, I lost my wife almost two years ago. Being a single parent was part of my reason for changing careers and deciding to move here. My wife's mother lives here and I thought my daughter could use the support of a loving grandmother."

"I'm so sorry," Brittany said, knowing the simple

words weren't adequate for the depth of loss he'd suffered. Her heart went out to him. He had not only
lost the woman he loved, but apparently had made the
choice to leave his career behind and move because
in his mind it was the best thing he could do for his
daughter.

Someplace in the back of her mind she realized this
meant that Alex was a single man. Not that it mattered to her. No matter how hot he was, she just wasn't
ready for a man in her life.

All she wanted from Alex was a deck where she
could have her friends and family over for barbe-
cues and good times. Beyond that she knew what she
needed most was time to heal, and that was something
she had to do all alone.

"It's all right," he replied. "Time passes and life
goes on. My main goal is just to make sure that Emily
is okay. Emily is my six-year-old daughter."

Now she understood why he didn't work weekends
and worked relatively short days. "You mentioned that
your wife's mother lives here. Would I have known
your wife?"

He shook his head. "Linda never lived here in Black
Rock. Her parents, Rose and Harry, moved here after
Linda and I got married."

"Rose Tyler," Brittany said.

"That's right."

Brittany smiled. "She's a nice lady. She does a lot
of charity work here in town."

"She's the greatest," he agreed. "And best of all

she's a babysitter who never complains about long hours."

"What about your parents?" she asked.

"They live a wonderful life in Italy. They weren't exactly what you'd call doting parents and so I knew not to turn to them when Linda died."

At that moment the conversation was cut short as the truck from the lumberyard arrived. Brittany stood to the side and watched as it was unloaded. The truth of the matter was she watched Alex as he helped Ed Burton from the lumberyard unload. She watched in fascination as his T-shirt stretched taut across his back with each load he lifted.

She'd found the tidbit of information about his parents intriguing but told herself she didn't want to know more intimate details of his life.

Even if she were ready for a man in her life and even though she found Alex incredibly sexy, she still wouldn't want to have any relationship with him.

Brittany wasn't sure she wanted children of her own. There was no way she'd want to take on somebody else's. She still needed to work on herself and wouldn't have the time or energy to deal with a grieving child.

No, she would be happy to admire Alex's taut body over the next couple of days but there wouldn't be anything more between them, not that he'd made any sign that he was even remotely interested in her.

Within twenty minutes everything was off the truck and stacked neatly on one side of the yard and Ed Burton drove away. Brittany was surprised when

Buck Harmon and another young man appeared in the backyard.

"There you are," Alex said with a smile to the two young men.

"Sorry we're late. Gary had to stuff his face with a sandwich before we left his house," Buck said. He raised a hand to Brittany in greeting.

"These are my helpers," Alex said. "I'm assuming you know Buck and Gary."

"I know Buck," she replied. And what she knew of him she didn't like. At twenty-four years old Buck had a reputation for trouble. He worked odd jobs, drank more than he should and could be a hothead. More than once as a deputy she'd had to give him a stern warning about some infraction or another. "But I don't believe I've met Gary before," she added.

"Gary Cox." He strode over to her and held out his hand. The freckles on his face danced as he offered her a friendly smile and shook her hand with an adult firmness. His coppery hair gleamed in the sunlight as he stepped back from her. "I'm Buck's friend and I've been helping Alex on some of his jobs."

He looked like an odd companion for Buck. Gary gave the impression of being a puppy dog, eager to please and slightly goofy. "Nice to meet you, Gary," she said.

"Now that the introductions are out of the way, it's time to get to work," Alex said.

"And I'll just get out of your way," Brittany replied. She went back inside the house but stood at the back window and watched as Alex and the younger men got to work.

She wondered if Alex knew that Buck wasn't the most trustworthy person in town. Buck had had more than his share of run-ins with all of the Graysons. If she got a chance she'd mention her concerns about him to Alex, but in the meantime she watched as the work began on the dream that had helped keep her sane through her months of captivity.

Watching Alex work should become a national pastime, she thought as she watched him pick up a hole digger and hand it to Buck.

She turned away, deciding she needed to stop watching Alex and find something more constructive to do. She'd been meaning to clean out her closet since moving back into the house. She'd lost about fifteen pounds while being held by The Professional and intended to donate a lot of the clothes that were now too big for her to charity.

She kept her mind blank as she worked, knowing that if she gave it free rein it always went back to the filthy cell where she'd been held, counting the days, the very minutes to death.

It was just after three when she heard a knock on her back door and hurried to answer. Once again a rivulet of warmth wiggled through her as she saw Alex.

"We're knocking off for the day," he said when she opened the door. "We've got the posts up but they need to set. Since tomorrow is Saturday we'll give them the weekend and we'll be here bright and early on Monday morning."

"Sounds good," she replied. "Then I'll see you on Monday."

"Have a good weekend," he said and then he was gone.

She hadn't realized how much the sound of the male voices coming from the backyard throughout the afternoon had comforted her.

Now she found the silence slightly oppressive. She moved the box of oversize clothing she'd packed next to the front door and then called a local charity for a pickup the next day.

Sitting down on the sofa, she punched the remote control to turn on the television, just wanting the noise to fill the emptiness of the otherwise silent house.

For almost three months she'd been alone in the shed, with only the sound of The Professional's voice to occasionally break the silence with his taunts and threats. She'd discovered that now she didn't do silence well.

Her thoughts instantly drifted back to Alex. There was no question that she felt a visceral physical pull toward him. And why shouldn't she? He was definitely attractive and she was definitely lonely.

She only left the house for grocery shopping and then only when it was absolutely necessary. She told herself it wasn't fear that kept her inside but rather the stares and whispers that followed her anywhere she went.

A couple of the friends she'd had before being kidnapped had contacted her after her rescue, but she'd realized they seemed more interested in finding out the grisly details of the crime than her well-being.

Although she was happy that her brothers had all found love while she'd been gone, the fact that they were now building lives with loved ones and had a place where they belonged only made her loneliness deeper. She didn't know where she belonged anymore.

The late afternoon and evening crept by. She fixed herself a salad for dinner, then watched some more TV. Finally at nine o'clock she went into her bedroom and got ready for bed.

She'd just turned out the light and closed her eyes when her phone rang. Fumbling on the nightstand, she turned on the lamp next to the bed and looked at the caller ID on the phone.

Anonymous caller.

She frowned and sat up. Probably a sales call or some stupid survey, she thought as she grabbed the receiver.

"Hello?"

Nobody replied, although she knew somebody was on the other end. She could hear the soft sound of breathing. "Hello?" she repeated, this time more firmly. "Who is this?"

Still nobody answered, but the breathing grew louder and she was suddenly cast back in time, back to when The Professional would breathe a little harder, a little faster as he talked about the party of death he intended.

Trapped in a moment of sheer terror, her heart beat frantically and she couldn't catch her breath. Frozen with fear she heard nothing but the sound of the caller breathing...and waiting.

She finally managed to crash the receiver back into the cradle.

She drew several deep breaths and then released a shaky laugh. The Professional was dead. She was safe and a prank phone call had nothing to do with the man who had once planned her death.

The phone call, along with the balloon, had been nothing more than coincidences that had triggered bad memories. There was absolutely no reason for her to be afraid, yet she couldn't stop shaking and she couldn't quiet the dreadful sense of foreboding that slithered through her.

It took a very long time for her heart to finally return to a normal rhythm and even longer before she was ready to turn out the light.

Alex spent much of Saturday working in the yard with Emily. He cut the grass while she raked and bagged the clippings and then they went to the local nursery and picked out flowers to plant along the walk leading from the street to the house.

As they worked Emily kept up a string of chatter, asking him if there were flowers in Heaven, what kinds of flowers they were planting and anything else that entered her brilliant little mind.

It was after dinner and cleanup that he announced he thought a trip to Izzy's was in order to reward them for all their hard work during the day.

At just after seven they left the house and headed

down the sidewalk toward Main Street. It was a beautiful spring evening, unusually warm and with the scent of newly bloomed flowers hanging in the air.

Emily alternated between hopping and skipping next to him. She was a child that rarely just walked. She oozed energy and an exuberant happiness that filled Alex's soul. In the weeks immediately following Linda's death he'd feared that his daughter would never know real happiness again, but she was a testimony to the resilience of the human spirit.

"I'm thinking strawberry," she said thoughtfully as she jumped over a crack in the sidewalk.

"Really?" he replied with amusement. They had this conversation each time they walked to Izzy's. She professed to be thinking about eating some flavor of ice cream but always opted for chocolate ice cream with sprinkles when they got there.

"What are you thinking, Daddy?" she asked.

This was also part of the tradition that had been established in their walks to Izzy's. Alex frowned in mock thoughtfulness. "I'm thinking maybe worm-flavored ice cream."

He was rewarded by her infectious giggles. "Daddy, that's so gross," she exclaimed.

As they walked in front of Brittany's house he was surprised to see her sitting on her porch. "Wait up, Emily," he said. He jogged up the walk to her porch. "Good evening, Ms. Grayson."

"Good evening to you, Mr. Crawford."

Her smile warmed him as Emily came running to

join him. "Emily, this is Ms. Grayson," he said. "My daughter, Emily."

"Hi, Emily. You can call me Brittany," she replied.

"We're going to get ice cream at Izzy's. Want to come with us?" Emily asked.

"Oh, I don't think so. I don't go into town much," Brittany replied, but Alex thought he saw a touch of wistfulness momentarily flit across her beautiful dark eyes.

"Emily, why don't you show Brittany how you can do a cartwheel in the grass?" Alex said.

Emily's face lit up. There was nothing she loved more than showing off her gymnastic skills. "Okay." As she raced off the porch Alex turned back to Brittany.

"And why don't you go into town much?" he asked.

"Watch this, Brittany," Emily yelled from the yard.

She focused her attention on Emily. "You've probably heard about what happened to me."

"I've heard a little bit about it," he admitted.

"That's super, Emily," she called out as Emily performed two perfectly executed cartwheels. "People stare and whisper," she said softly. "It makes me uncomfortable so I just don't go out much."

He heard a hint of loneliness in her voice and it called to his own loneliness. "We're not going to traipse down Main Street in a parade. We're just going to Izzy's for some ice cream."

"This time I'm going to do four cartwheels in a row," Emily yelled.

"Tell you what," Alex continued. "If you feel somebody staring at you and you get all uncomfortable, I'll stick an ice cream cone on my nose and cover my head with sprinkles. Trust me, nobody will be staring at you after that."

She looked at him in surprise and then laughed. By that time Emily had rejoined them. "Did you see me do four cartwheels?"

"I did," Brittany replied. "That was so totally awesome."

"So are you joining us?" Alex asked, vaguely surprised at how much he wanted her to come with them.

She hesitated a long moment and then nodded. "Okay, just let me grab my purse."

"She's pretty," Emily said as Brittany disappeared through her front door.

"Yes, she is," Alex agreed.

"Do you like her?" Emily slid him a sly glance.

"I'm building a deck on the back of her house so she's kind of like my boss right now." The last thing he wanted was for Emily to get any ideas about a budding relationship between him and Brittany.

Since they'd moved to Black Rock Emily had learned about stepmoms and had decided it would be nice to have one. Alex had explained to his daughter that finding a perfect stepmother was more difficult than it seemed and that she shouldn't count on it ever happening.

Brittany stepped back out the front door with her purse slung over her shoulder. "All set."

The two of them fell into step on the sidewalk while

Emily danced just ahead of them. "What kind of ice cream do you like, Brittany?" she asked.

"I'm definitely a chocolate lover," Brittany replied.

"Me, too!" Emily exclaimed. "Daddy says he's going to get worm-flavored ice cream today."

"That's gross," Brittany replied.

Once again Emily laughed in delight. "That's what I told him." She fell into step next to Brittany and gazed up at her. "Since you're daddy's boss, maybe you could tell him that he should let me get two scoops of ice cream instead of just one."

Brittany laughed again and Alex thought he could listen to her laugh for a long time. He was also aware of the scent of her, a clean, fresh floral with a touch of jasmine that teased his senses.

"Let's see when we get there how much arm-twisting we need to do to get your daddy to agree to two scoops," she said.

Emily nodded and then once again danced ahead of them along the sidewalk. "She's a doll," Brittany said.

"She's far too smart for her own good, as stubborn as the day is long, but best of all she's my heart," he replied.

"That's nice. Every little girl needs a father in her life."

"Are your parents here in town?" he asked.

She shook her head, her rich dark hair gleaming in the sunshine. "My parents died a long time ago, but I have four brothers who stepped into the role of father figure and sometimes that feels like four too many," she said ruefully.

He grinned. "One of them is the sheriff, right?"

"Yes, that's Tom. Then there's Jacob, Benjamin and Caleb. Right now they all work as deputies, but Benjamin is quitting in a couple of weeks to ranch full-time."

"And from what I've heard you were also a deputy at one time."

"Before the incident." Her voice held a slight edge of stress. *The incident*—such pitiful words to use to describe what she'd gone through.

"It's been a beautiful day, hasn't it?" He quickly changed the subject. The last thing he wanted to do was ruin this time with her by discussing something she didn't want to talk about. "Emily and I spent the afternoon planting flowers along the walkway to our front door."

"We got flowers with a name like what my daddy sometimes calls me," Emily quipped. "Impatients."

Brittany laughed again and Alex could tell she was relaxing with each minute that passed. There was something tragic about a woman who had lived through what she had and wound up being afraid to leave her own house because of the whispers and stares of the other people in town.

"Once you have my deck up I intend to plant flowers everywhere in the backyard," she said. "I want that deck to be the prettiest place on the planet."

"Then I'll have to make sure that I'm on top of my game and give you a deck that will be the envy of everyone in town," he replied.

By that time they'd reached Izzy's. The ice-cream

parlor was a small shop with half a dozen small round peppermint-pink tables inside and a long refrigerated counter displaying almost every flavor of ice cream imaginable. Much to Alex's mock dismay and Emily's giggles, they had no worm-flavored.

They were the only customers inside, and once they'd ordered and been served the three of them sat at a table near the window where the last of the day's sun was visible, slowly sinking lower onto the horizon.

The conversation centered on the merits of ice cream and the variety of flavors available. Brittany was good with Emily, talking to her with an easiness and respect that Emily responded to in the same way.

There was no question that he was drawn to Brittany. Her thick, shiny hair begged him to tangle his hands in it, her plump lips seemed to ask for a kiss and that scent of her half dizzied him with a simmering desire to seek its source.

He didn't know if his reaction to her was just a manifestation of his loneliness. Or maybe he was drawn to her because she seemed so different from his wife. A core of inner strength shone from Brittany's eyes, a strength he found vastly appealing.

"This was nice," Brittany said as they left Izzy's and began the short walk home. Twilight had fallen and night shadows were beginning to creep in.

"I'm glad you came with us," he replied.

"Me, too," Emily added. "I think you should come with us every time we go to get ice cream."

Brittany smiled at her. "That's just because you got two scoops with me along."

Emily giggled and then sobered a bit. "But I also like you because you're really pretty and you make my dad smile really big."

Alex felt his cheeks warm and tried to find something to say, but Emily wasn't finished yet. "Did you know my mommy is in Heaven?" she asked Brittany.

"Yes, your daddy told me that," Brittany replied.

"Do you think there's ice cream in Heaven?"

Alex saw a whisper of compassion in Brittany's eyes at Emily's question. She stopped walking and crouched down to Emily's level.

"I'd like to think there's ice cream in Heaven. You know, my mommy died, too. Maybe your mommy and mine are having ice cream together right now."

"That would be good," Emily replied with a little smile. "Now, watch how I can jump the cracks in the sidewalk really fast." She raced ahead of them, her pigtails dancing.

"That was nice," he said to Brittany.

She nodded. "It must be tough to be a single dad."

"Emily makes it relatively easy. She's a good kid. Would you like to have dinner with me tomorrow night? I cook a mean steak."

He wasn't sure who was more surprised by the invitation, Brittany or himself. The words had just tumbled out of his mouth as if with a life of their own.

"Thank you, but I always have Sunday dinner with my brothers and their families," she replied.

"Then what about Monday evening?" They stopped in front of her house.

Her brown eyes studied him thoughtfully. "Alex, I'm not looking for any kind of romance."

"I'm not, either," he quickly replied. "I have no intentions of ever marrying again. But I'm new in town and to be honest, I've been a bit lonely. I just thought it would be nice to have a friend to share a meal or spend some time with."

"Okay," she agreed. "As long as we both understand where we're coming from, I'd love to have dinner with you on Monday."

"Great! Why don't we say around six-thirty?"

"Sounds good and thanks for the ice cream." She looked down the walk to Emily. "Bye, Emily," she called.

"Bye, Brittany." Emily waved. "See ya later."

Brittany looked back at Alex. "And I'll see you Monday morning, right?"

"Bright and early," he replied. They said their good-byes and he watched as she climbed the stairs to her porch and then disappeared into her house.

Emily fell into step beside him and began chatting about her plans to play with the neighbor girl the next day. Alex listened absently and wondered why he wanted to kiss a woman he'd just told he only wanted to be her friend.

Chapter 3

She shouldn't have agreed to dinner. Brittany walked into her kitchen, dropped her purse on the counter and then sank down into one of the kitchen chairs.

Alex Crawford disturbed her in a distinctly pleasant way. Something about him made her heart flutter in her chest and caused her palms to dampen. She liked the way he looked, the way he smelled. She liked the sound of his laughter, so rich and deep, and she liked the way he interacted with his daughter.

As she'd watched him eat his ice cream she'd found herself wondering what his lips would taste like, how his arms would feel wrapped around her.

Dangerous thoughts.

She knew she wasn't ready for a romantic relationship, and as cute and sweet as Emily had been,

Brittany definitely wasn't ready to be a mom. Her brothers would laugh at the very idea and remind her how flighty and immature she was.

Still, she could use a friend and apparently that was what Alex was looking for, too. He was new to town and obviously hadn't made any real friends, and hers had all pretty much deserted her in the months following her rescue while she'd been living with Benjamin and Edie on the family ranch just outside of town.

"Two less lonely people in the world." The words to an old Air Supply song filled her head. Maybe Alex was supposed to be her transitional man, the one who, through his easy friendship, could bridge her way from recovering crime victim to healthy young woman ready for love.

Dinner at Alex's place was nothing to be concerned about, she told herself. Emily would be there, and besides, Brittany had made it clear to Alex she wasn't ready for romance.

She was about to get out of the chair when a shadow darted across the kitchen window. Every muscle in her body froze—except her heart, which roared to a painful gallop.

Somebody was in her yard...just outside of her window. What was he doing out there? Had the person been watching her? Why? The inertia left her and with her heart still beating far too fast, she got up from the table.

Her feet felt leaden with fear as she tentatively approached the window and cautiously peered outside.

Nothing.

Although the evening shadows had thickened, there was still enough ambient light to let her know that there was nobody lurking in her backyard.

Had the shadow just been a figment of her imagination? Had a cloud danced over the moon to create what she'd thought was somebody just outside the house?

She drew a deep breath and backed away from the window, her heart not yet finding its normal rhythm. She felt foolish and yet couldn't halt the feeling of threat that combined with a deep sense of dread that washed over her.

She wished she had her gun, but she'd turned it in to Tom just after she'd been rescued, knowing it would be some time before she was ready, if ever, to go back to work as his deputy.

The fear kept her awake until near dawn when she fell into a restless sleep. She didn't get out of bed until almost noon the next day and as always the sunshine made her fears of the night before seem silly.

She hated the fear, was ashamed of it. It was part of the reason she knew she wasn't ready to go back to her job. A good deputy didn't feel fear. A good deputy didn't think the way she'd thought when she'd been held by a madman.

It was just before six in the evening when she left her house to drive to the family ranch on the edge of town. Since the crime that had taken her away for four months, it had become a tradition that on Sunday the whole family got together at the old homestead for dinner.

As she parked in front of the large, rambling ranch

house, she tried to slough off the exhaustion that had been with her all day long. Two nights of too little sleep had definitely taken its toll.

She was the last to arrive and when she walked through the front door the chaos of family greeted her. Her brothers were all in the great room, Tom's wife Peyton's little girl, Lilly, tottering back and forth between them with squeals of delight.

"Hey, girl." Caleb got out of his chair and greeted her with a kiss on her temple. He stepped back from her and frowned. "What's up with you? You don't look so hot."

She punched him in the arm. "Thanks, you're terrific for a girl's ego." She worried a hand through her long hair. "I'm just tired, that's all. I didn't sleep very well last night."

"Bad night?" Benjamin asked, his dark eyes filled with compassion.

She shrugged. "I thought I saw somebody outside my window. It freaked me out a little bit and I had trouble getting to sleep." She watched as they all exchanged glances.

"You know, Brittany, maybe you should talk to somebody," Jacob said. "You won't talk to us about what happened for those four months. Maybe you need a little therapy."

"I don't need therapy," she replied with a touch of irritation. "I just need a good night's sleep, that's all." She left the great room and her brothers and went into the kitchen where the wives were all gathered.

Of all the women who had become sisters-in-law,

Brittany felt the closest to Layla, Jacob's wife. Layla had been the last victim kidnapped and placed in a cell to await The Professional's final party of death. Although she'd only been captive for a few hours before they had all been rescued, Brittany knew that Layla understood at least part of the kind of terror that Brittany had tasted, had endured throughout her ordeal.

"Mmm, something smells good," she said as she entered the large, cheerful kitchen.

"Roast and potatoes, green beans and hot rolls," Edie, Benjamin's wife, replied. "And Portia brought pies."

Portia, Caleb's wife, patted her five-months-pregnant belly. "I've been dreaming about peach pies for the past week. I keep telling Caleb it must be some sort of strange pregnancy craving."

"I wish I could blame pregnancy hormones for my dreams of chocolate fountains, doughnuts and candy bars. God, I've become such a sugar addict," Layla exclaimed. Brittany laughed and sat on the stool next to her at the kitchen island. "How are you doing? You look tired," Layla said.

"I am," Brittany admitted. "But on a positive note I've started work on the deck I've been talking about forever."

"That's great. Who's doing the work?" Peyton asked.

"A new guy in town. His name is Alex Crawford." Even saying his name created a pleasant pool of warmth in the pit of her stomach.

Layla released a wolf whistle. "I sold him the house. That man is pure sin walking. What? I'm married, not dead," she exclaimed as the others looked at her. "I'm still allowed to look and admire."

"He is easy on the eyes," Brittany admitted, but she didn't mention that she'd agreed to have dinner with him. There was no point when she had no intention of it being anything but a pleasant dinner between friends. Still, she couldn't stop the small shiver of delight that worked through her as she thought about spending more time with him.

Dinner was a wild, chaotic affair with everyone talking over each other and plenty of laughter served all around. Brittany found herself once again counting her blessings that she had such a strong support system in her family.

Still, there was no question that when she saw the small smiles and secretive looks that flew from husband to wife, the touches that spoke of a deeper, lasting intimacy, a wistful ache filled her up inside.

Eventually she wanted what her brothers had found, a love that made a couple into something more, a commitment that was meant to last a lifetime. Even though she yearned for that, she didn't think she was ready for it at this time in her life.

She still jumped at shadows, trembled when nobody talked on the phone. She didn't particularly like the dark and knew it was going to take time for her to finally be one-hundred-percent healthy.

"Just think, within a couple of weeks I'll be able to have you all over for a barbecue on my new deck," Brittany said as the meal was winding down.

"I like my burger medium well and my beer ice-cold," Jacob said. He shot a glance to Layla. "And my woman silent and naked."

Layla snorted. "I have no problem with the naked part, but you know you aren't ever going to make me into a silent woman."

Once again everyone laughed and within minutes the men had returned to the great room while the women cleared the table. "One of these days we're going to make them stay here and do the dishes while we go into the other room and relax," Edie said as she began rinsing dishes and handing them to Peyton, who placed them in the dishwasher.

"You know they would do the dishes if any of you asked them to," Brittany said.

Portia smiled. "And that's exactly why we don't ask them to. We all let them pretend to be the big macho men, but we also know that underneath all that bluster are pussycats with tender hearts."

That perfectly described the Grayson men and someday Brittany wanted to find a man like her brothers, a man who could protect her against the world if she needed it and who would love her to distraction.

It was after dark when the gathering began to break up. Edie looped arms with Brittany as she walked out the front door. "You want to spend the night here?" she asked. "Maybe you'd sleep better here than you've been doing at home."

The offer definitely held more than a little bit of appeal, but Brittany shook her head. "Thanks for the offer, but I'd rather go home." It felt too much like going backward to spend the night here where she'd stayed for her months of recuperation.

"Are you sure you're doing okay?" Edie asked. Benjamin and Edie had spent the most time with her after she'd been rescued. Edie had sat up with her many a night when she was afraid to sleep for fear of the nightmares that might plague her.

"Am I back to normal? No, but I'm doing okay." She gave Edie a forced smile. "Logically I know that he's dead and I have nothing more to fear, but emotionally I haven't quite embraced the notion of safety just yet."

Edie gave her a warm hug. "You never wanted to talk much about the time you were held, but you know if you ever need to talk I'm here for you."

Brittany returned the hug. "I know. And now I'm going to head home and hope for a good night's sleep."

Minutes later as she drove home, she thought about those months she'd been held. She hadn't shared a lot with her family about that time, not wanting to burden them with the details. Although physically she hadn't been molested or beaten, the mental abuse had been horrific.

The Professional had made sure she'd had enough water and food to stay alive, but he'd taunted her with all the terrible things he was going to do to her. Each time the door to the shed had swung open, she'd feared that it was the moment of her death, a horrible and painful death.

And in that place of fear, in that horrible space of

abject terror, Brittany had found the utter darkness in her heart, the depth of her shame.

"But you're going to be fine," she said aloud as she gripped the steering wheel more firmly. The danger was over and life could only get better and better from this minute onward.

What she didn't understand was why no matter how many times she told herself this, no matter how badly she wanted to believe it, there was still a part of her that was terrified that the bad times weren't over yet.

The house was clean, Emily had gone to spend the night with Rose, and the steaks were marinating and ready to pop in the broiler. Everything was ready for dinner with Brittany, except that Alex was more nervous than he had been in a very long time.

He'd spent the day at her house working on the deck with Buck and Gary but Brittany had kept herself scarce, only coming out once in the afternoon to bring them all lemonade.

He now glanced at his watch. Almost six-thirty. She should be here anytime now and he told himself it was ridiculous to be so nervous about a simple dinner with a friend.

A friend, that's all she was going to be, he told himself. A beautiful friend with eyes he wanted to drown in, with a tragic past he wished he could fix. Jeez, he needed to get his emotions where she was concerned under control.

Still, when the doorbell rang he nearly jumped out of his skin. He opened the door and the sight of her in-

stantly calmed his nerves. She looked lovely in a pair
of brown slacks and a yellow blouse that enhanced the
darkness of her hair and eyes. She also looked nervous
and that strangely put him at ease. She clutched her
purse tightly to her chest and her smile was tentative.

"No need to look so terrified. I promise I won't
bite," he said.

Her features relaxed and her smile grew more natural. "I know it's crazy, but I am feeling a bit nervous,"
she admitted.

"It doesn't sound crazy. I was feeling the same
way just a minute ago." He gestured her toward the
living room. "Maybe a glass of wine will make us
both relax."

"That sounds nice," she agreed.

He walked her through the living room and into the
kitchen where the table was already set for two and
a salad and a loaf of warmed French bread sat in the
center.

"Where's Emily?" she asked as he gestured her into
one of the chairs at the table.

"I packed her off to Rose's for the night." He pulled
a bottle of red wine from the refrigerator and smiled.
"I love my daughter to distraction, but sometimes I get
hungry for adult conversation. Besides, she and Rose
have been working on some intricate 3-D puzzle at
Rose's house. Lately I've had trouble keeping Emily
home."

He poured them each a glass of wine and then carried hers to the table. "And now the most important
question of the night—how do you like your steak?"

She set her purse on the floor next to her chair and took the wineglass from him. "Medium."

He placed the steaks in the oven and then joined her at the table, and for a moment an awkward silence descended, broken when they both started to say something at the same time.

"Sorry," she said with a small laugh. "I was just going to say that it was my sister-in-law who sold you this house."

"Layla? She's a nice woman," he replied.

"She talks a lot," Brittany replied with a small grin.

Alex laughed and felt the ice breaking between them. "Yeah, even Emily said that Layla was a bit of a chatterbox, and if that isn't the pot calling the kettle black I don't know what is."

Brittany laughed and then took a sip of the wine and eyed him soberly over the rim of the glass. "It must be hard, to be a man raising a little girl."

"It has its moments," he agreed. "It took me months to learn to paint her fingernails to her approval and I still can't get the hang of a French braid. Actually, I'm lucky that she's a great kid and is very patient with me."

"I could help you out with the French-braid thing," she replied.

"Emily would be ecstatic."

She nodded and took another sip of the wine. "The deck seems to be coming along faster than I'd expected."

"There's still a lot to do. Getting the floor down is

the easy part. The railings and finish work take a bit longer."

"Have you used Buck and Gary before as helpers?"

"Buck, yes, Gary, no. Buck helped me on a previous job and I told him I wouldn't mind hiring another kid to help with the grunt work and he suggested Gary."

"I don't know if you know this or not, but Buck has quite a reputation."

He smiled. "One thing I've learned since moving here is that the people of Black Rock like to gossip and nobody is shy about having opinions. I try not to listen to rumors and I like to judge people on their own merits."

"I'm sure you've heard more than a little gossip about me."

"A little," he agreed.

She gazed down into her wineglass and when she looked back at him her eyes were filled with a steely strength. "I was kidnapped by a crazy serial killer and held captive in an old shed for four months. During that time he kidnapped four more women and planned to torture and kill us each, one at a time. He called it a party. Thankfully we were all rescued before he could have his little party. I survived and it's just something that happened to me. It's in my past now."

A wealth of respect for her washed over him. "Must have been terrible."

"It was. But so are cancer and plane crashes and a thousand other things that happen in the world."

"What happened to the other women who were kidnapped?"

She took a sip of her wine and then answered, "They've all left town, except Layla. Suzy Bakersfield moved away with her boyfriend. Casey Teasdale married her fiancé and they also left town, and Jennifer Hightower went to live with an aunt in New York. Layla was the last one to be kidnapped and I like to think that if my brothers hadn't rescued us when they did she would have talked Larry Norwood to death before he managed to kill her."

Alex smiled and then jumped up from the table to check on the steaks. He flipped them over and then returned to his seat. "You know, I've been thinking about what you said to me the other night."

She frowned. "What was that?"

"That you don't go into town because people stare at you and whisper behind your back. I was thinking maybe if you went into town more often people would get used to seeing you around again and the stares and whispers would stop."

She cocked her head as if giving it some thought. "Maybe you're right," she finally agreed. "I think it wouldn't have been so bad if the other women were still around, but I was the one who was held the longest and so people seem to be the most curious about what I went through."

"And you'd just rather put it behind you and not talk about it," he said.

She flashed him a beatific smile. "That's right."

"I just want you to know one thing—if you need it, I can be a sympathetic ear or a comforting shoulder."

Her eyes flared with a sliver of evocative heat that

he felt deep inside. "Thanks," she replied. "I'll keep that in mind."

He wanted to kiss her. At that moment with her eyes shining so bright and her lips moist from the wine, he wanted to take her into his arms and lose himself in a kiss. Instead he jumped up from the table and went back to the oven where he pulled the steaks out.

"Is there anything I can do to help?" she asked.

"No, thanks, I'm all set." He plated the steaks and then carried them to the table.

Thankfully the dinner conversation flowed easily. He regaled her with stories about his days as an attorney in Chicago, enjoying each time he managed to make her laugh.

In turn, she told him about growing up with four older brothers who teased and spoiled her unmercifully. "When I told Tom I wanted to become a deputy he fought me tooth and nail," she said. "There was no way he wanted his baby sister on the streets with a gun."

"So, how did you convince him to hire you?" Alex asked, half-mesmerized by the sheen of her dark hair beneath the artificial light overhead. He knew it would feel like silk between his fingers, imagined the long strands whispering against his bare chest as she straddled him.

"I told him if he didn't hire me then I was sure Topeka or Wichita would be willing to take me on. He hated the idea of me being on those streets even more, so he gave me the job here."

"And you liked being a deputy?" he asked, trying to stay focused on the conversation instead of on her physical attributes.

She didn't answer for a long moment. "I did, but I think I'm ready for a change now. I'm not sure that being a deputy was a true calling for me." She looked away from him and he got the feeling that she didn't completely believe her own words.

"That's the way I felt about being a lawyer. I went into the profession because I knew it would provide a good living for my family, but my true love has always been building things with my hands."

"I'm not sure where my heart lies at the moment," she said as she reached for a piece of the bread. "I enjoy working on the computer and have gotten pretty good at making web pages." Her cheeks flushed a charming pink. "In the months after the crime when I was staying out at my brother's ranch, I was most comfortable social networking with cyber friends and teaching myself the ins and outs of web design."

"If you decide you want to do that, I'll gladly be your first client. I need to get a web page up to advertise my remodeling work. I'd love to hire you."

She smiled at him. "I think we can work something out."

With dinner finished she insisted she help with the cleanup, even though he told her she should sit and enjoy being a guest.

They worked well together, as if they'd cleaned up after dinner together a hundred times before. Afterward he poured them each another glass of wine and they went into the living room.

"You have a lovely home," she said as she sank down on one end of the sofa and he sat on the other end.

"Thanks, it's finally starting to feel like home."

Once again she studied him over the rim of her glass, her eyes dark and unreadable. "How did your wife die?"

"Breast cancer."

"That's rotten," she replied.

He took a deep swallow of the wine and then set his glass on the coffee table. "What was really rotten was that she knew she had a lump in her breast for months but she didn't tell me about it and she didn't go to the doctor." He heard the edge of anger that had crept into his voice.

"Why?"

He leaned back against the sofa cushion. "We had a whirlwind romance. I met her at a fundraiser and within six months we were married. Don't get me wrong, I loved her, but it wasn't long into the marriage that I realized she was more child than woman, and by the time she got pregnant with Emily any passion I'd felt for her was gone. She was fragile, afraid of her own shadow, and it only got worse when Emily was born. By the time she finally told me about the lump the cancer had spread everywhere. She was gone within six months."

To his surprise Brittany leaned over and touched his hand, a gentle touch that lasted only a moment before she pulled away. "I'm sorry. That must have been horrible."

"It was tragic," he replied. "She didn't have to die, but she was so afraid of living that was the choice she made. If I ever decide to marry again, and I'm not sure I will, I'd want a strong woman who isn't afraid of life."

He frowned, realizing he'd said far more than he'd intended to say about Linda…about his previous life. "Sorry, I must be boring you to death."

"Not at all," she replied quickly enough that he believed her. "It's just a reminder that life can be so unpredictable, that you have to grasp your happiness whenever you can."

For the next two hours they talked about favorite movies and food, sharing little tidbits of information to get to know each other better. And everything Alex heard from her made him like her more and more. She was funny and bright and beautiful, and as the evening drew to a close he wasn't ready for it to end.

"I'll walk you home," he said as he opened the front door and realized darkness had fallen while they'd talked.

"That isn't necessary," she protested but her eyes darkened a little as she stared outside into the night.

"It might not be necessary, but I wouldn't be a true gentleman if I let you walk home alone in the dark, and I definitely want you to think of me as a gentleman."

Brittany slung her purse strap over her shoulder and smiled. "Okay, then."

As they stepped out onto his porch he locked the door and pulled it shut behind them. "This has been really nice," she said as they started down his walk.

"Yes, it has," he agreed. The scent of flowers rose up to him, but didn't diminish the scent of her that had teased him all night long.

He'd told her he was just interested in having a friend, some companionship to fill the lonely hours of the day, but after spending the evening with her he recognized he wanted more from her.

She was so different from the wife he'd lost, so filled with life and with that core of inner strength that radiated from her eyes. She drew him, stirring a simmering passion that he hadn't expected.

"I was serious about that web page," he said when they reached her porch. "I'd like to hire you to get one up and running for me." They stopped at her door.

In the faint spill of light from a nearby streetlamp, her eyes glowed as she gazed up at him. "Are you sure you aren't just trying to be nice?"

He grinned at her. "I'm a lawyer. When it comes to business I'm not nice—I'm a shark."

She laughed, that low throaty sound that swirled warmth inside his belly. "Okay, then, why don't I work something up tomorrow while you're working on the deck and before you knock off for the day we can talk about it?" She turned and unlocked her front door.

"Sounds like a plan," he agreed.

"Thank you, Alex, for a terrific night."

"No, thank you."

For a long moment they remained standing far too

close together, their gazes locked. He realized he intended to kiss her and saw the dawning realization take hold of her, as well.

He took a step toward her and she didn't retreat. Instead she raised her chin, her lips parted slightly as if to welcome him.

He took the subtle invitation, gathering her into his arms as his mouth met hers. He'd intended only a sweet, soft good-night kiss, but her lips held a heat that transformed his intent, his initial desire.

Pulling her closer, he deepened the kiss, tentatively touching his tongue to hers. Her arms wrapped around his neck as she returned the kiss, leaning into him in surrender.

He wasn't sure who broke the kiss, he or she, but they broke apart and she gave a shaky laugh. "I'm not used to my friends kissing me like that."

"Sorry," he replied. "I don't usually kiss my friends that way."

"Don't apologize. It was the perfect ending to a perfect night."

Before he could reply she was gone, leaving him staring at the sight of her closed front door and with a well of want inside him that stole his breath away.

As he started back down the sidewalk toward his house he realized there was no way he'd be satisfied with Brittany just being his friend.

He tried to tamp down the pleasure that coursed through him. He'd misjudged a woman before and wasn't eager to make the same kind of mistake.

Alex didn't believe in happily-ever-after anymore and it was going to take more than a scorching kiss with a hot woman to change his mind.

Chapter 4

The kiss had shaken her to her very core. Alex was the wrong man for her for a million reasons. She wasn't ready for a relationship. He had a daughter and she wasn't mother material. And yet for all the reasons he was wrong for her, the kiss had felt so right.

She stood at the window and watched the men working on the deck, her gaze lingering on the man who had rocked her world with a single kiss the night before.

Each time she thought about it her mouth tingled with pleasure and her entire body enjoyed a wash of warmth that made her want to repeat the experience.

It had just been a kiss, but it had made her want more and that worried her just a little bit. Wrong man, she kept trying to remind herself.

She'd learned as much about him with the things he hadn't said as what he had shared with her. His marriage had obviously not been great, but she was certain that if his wife hadn't died he would have remained in the marriage, taking care of a fragile wife and his daughter. She instinctively knew he was the kind of man who would sacrifice his own happiness for that of his family.

He deserved better than her. She was a spoiled brat who, before her kidnapping, hadn't thought about anyone but herself and if that weren't enough she still had some baggage left from her ordeal.

She turned away from the window with a sigh and sat at the table where her laptop was open. As she waited for it to power up, she thought about her work as a deputy. She'd fibbed to Alex. She'd absolutely loved being a deputy, but just like the crime had changed her, it had also changed what she thought she could be in the future.

Once the computer was up and running she got to work. When Alex had arrived that morning he'd brought with him a sheet of paper with all the pertinent details necessary to build him a web page.

She consciously shoved away the memory of his kiss and instead focused on the task at hand. As always it didn't take her long to lose herself in cyberspace.

She stopped at noon to fix herself a quick sandwich. A glance out the back window let her know that apparently Alex and the others had also knocked off for lunch.

By the time she'd finished her lunch the three men were back to work in the yard and once again she found herself wandering to the window. She told herself it was to watch the progress being made on her deck, but she couldn't stop her gaze from lingering on Alex.

What was it about him that drew her? Physically it was an easy question to answer, but it wasn't just physical attraction she felt for him. Certainly she liked the way his smile flashed his straight white teeth against his tanned skin, and the width of his shoulders made her want to get lost in his embrace.

But it was the man she sensed beneath the handsome package that drew her, a man who loved his daughter enough to quit his job and move across the country so she could have a loving grandmother in her life, a man who from what little he'd said about his own parents hadn't had a solid support system while growing up.

From what he'd told her his parents had been in their mid-thirties when they'd had him. He'd been an oops baby and by the time he was six he realized his parents weren't cut out to be real parents. He'd become a self-reliant child who had matured into a self-reliant man.

With a muttered curse of frustration she returned to her work on the computer. By the time three o'clock came and Alex knocked on the back door to let her know they were stopping work for the day, she had a tentative site to show him.

He leaned over the back of her to view the monitor

and the scent of him coupled with his body heat made her heart flutter.

"That looks great," he exclaimed. "It's exactly what I had in mind. You're obviously very talented at this."

Pleasure washed over her. "I'm still learning, but I do enjoy it. All we need to do is set you up with a domain name and a hosting service and we can get it published to the internet."

"Can you take care of all that?" he asked as she got up to walk him to the front door. "Add it into your fee?"

"Sure, I can do that," she agreed.

They reached her front door and he turned back to face her. "I was thinking maybe after dinner to-night you could give me that lesson in French braid-ing? Emily would be thrilled if she could have her hair done for school tomorrow."

"Sure, that would be fine," she agreed.

"How about around six-thirty?"

"Sounds good."

It was only after he left that she wondered if maybe things were moving too fast. She'd already figured out all the reasons why she was wrong for him. Still, she didn't want to disappoint Emily by reneging on the offer now.

And if she were perfectly honest with herself she would admit that she wouldn't mind the company. The evening hours were the worst for her, when the dark shadows of night began to spill over everything, over her.

It was precisely six-thirty when Alex and Emily

returned to her house. Brittany opened the door and Emily danced in and immediately threw her arms around her waist.

"Thank you, thank you!" she exclaimed. "I've been telling daddy for a long time that I'm too old for pigtails and I need a French braid, but he's having such trouble and needs your help."

Brittany was stunned by how much the hug warmed her. Emily smelled of bubble bath and innocence, and Brittany returned the hug with one of her own. "By the time you leave here tonight your daddy will be able to French braid in his sleep," she promised.

She straightened and smiled at Alex. "Come on, we have work to do." She led them into the living room where she had laid out a brush and comb on the coffee table in preparation for playing beauty shop.

"I washed my hair and everything," Emily said. "And when you're all finished with me, Daddy is going to take me to grandma's to show her how beautiful I look."

"Honey, you're beautiful without a French braid," Brittany replied. She sat on the sofa and patted the space next to her. "Let's put Daddy here and you sit on the floor here in front of me."

Brittany was far too aware of Alex as he sank down next to her. His body heat wrapped around her, as well as the scent of his spicy cologne. As she picked up the hairbrush, she felt ridiculously clumsy, as if she'd suddenly grown ten thumbs.

She began to brush through Emily's hair, enjoying the feel of the pale, silky strands. "My mommy used to brush my hair like this," Emily said as she relaxed against Brittany's legs.

Brittany's heart squeezed for Emily's loss. "I'll bet you miss that," she said as she exchanged a quick glance with Alex.

"Sometimes, but Daddy tries his best and he's getting better and better," Emily replied. "He only pulls sometimes if he gets in too much of a hurry, but he's always sorry when he does."

"That's good. And now, for the fine art of French braiding." As she began to braid Emily's hair she went slowly, showing Alex exactly how it was done. He watched intently, as if it was the most important thing he might learn for the rest of his life, and that made Brittany only like him more.

"Okay," she said when she was finished. "Now we're going to take it all out and let you try."

Alex looked at her dubiously. Emily turned around and flashed him a bright smile. "Don't worry, Daddy. I know you can do it," she said as she scooted over in front of him.

Brittany could never have guessed that a lesson in braiding hair could become a study in sexual tension, but as she leaned against Alex and guided his fingers through Emily's hair, tension coiled in her stomach as she wondered what those fingers of his would feel like sliding through her own hair, over her bare skin.

She could tell he felt it, too. When his gaze met hers his eyes were darker in hue, simmering with a hunger that was unmistakable.

By the time she'd had him work the hair three times

in a row, she felt as if he knew what he was doing and she rose from the sofa, needing to distance herself from him. "Emily, want to see in the mirror?" she asked the little girl.

"Oh, yes," Emily exclaimed with eagerness as she got up from the floor.

Brittany led her into her bedroom where she had a full-length mirror on the back of the door. Emily gazed at her reflection and emitted a little squeal. "It's perfect."

It wasn't perfect, but it was a terrific effort by a terrific dad. Emily turned and looked at Brittany. "Would you like me to brush your hair? Sometimes I brushed my mommy's hair for her and since you did mine I could do yours."

The offer touched Brittany deeply. "That's very nice, Emily, but I think my hair is just fine for tonight."

"Okay, then I'll owe you one," Emily replied. She turned back to the mirror and gazed at her reflection. "Do I look older?"

Brittany hid her smile and studied the little girl thoughtfully. "You know, I think you do. With your hair like that you look at least eight."

Emily preened. "Now we have to go show my grandma," she said as they left Brittany's bedroom.

Alex stood in the middle of the living room, his gaze unfathomable as it lingered on Brittany. "Thanks," he said simply.

She smiled and nodded. "Not a problem."

"Brittany, you want to come with us to visit my

grandma? She's going to be so surprised. She couldn't braid my hair because she has bad fingers that hurt."

"Arthritis," Alex said.

"Thank you for the invitation, Emily, but maybe another time," Brittany replied.

"That sounds like a plan," Emily replied.

Alex checked his watch. "And we'd better get over there if we're going so we can get you back home and in bed on time for school tomorrow."

When they reached the door Emily gave her another hug and Alex thanked her once again, the heat still lingering in his gaze.

She felt that heat long after they'd left and she was once again alone. She picked up her hairbrush and comb and carried them back into her bathroom, her head filled with thoughts of both Emily and her daddy.

The fact that Emily had even offered to brush Brittany's hair let her know that Emily was kind and thoughtful, and Brittany knew that was a testimony to Alex's great parenting.

But it wasn't his parenting skills that coiled heat in the pit of her stomach and made her think about rumpled sheets and his scent lingering on her pillowcase.

She somehow felt as if she were on a runaway train where he was concerned, powerless to halt the careening forward motion. *But do you really want to stop it?* a small voice whispered inside her head as she turned on the television and settled in on the sofa.

Would it be so terrible to follow through on the desire she felt for Alex? To have a wild and passionate relationship with him? It didn't have to mean anything. It didn't have to lead to some attempt to build something lasting.

She wouldn't actively pursue a physical relationship with Alex, she decided, but if it happened spontaneously she wasn't sure she would try to stop it.

As far as Emily went, there was no reason she couldn't be friendly with the little girl. It wasn't as if she was auditioning to become a stepmother. They were neighbors and there was no reason they couldn't share an occasional trip to Izzy's or maybe even have lunch together.

A feeling of peace swept through Brittany, a peace that had been missing for a long time. For the first time in months she felt as if she were finally returning to the land of the living and it felt wonderful.

When Alex looked at her she didn't feel like a freak—she felt like a desirable, normal woman. He didn't treat her as if she was a fragile victim of a horrendous crime. He appeared to only have an interest in the woman she was now, and that was definitely more than a little bit heady.

She watched TV for an hour, then bored with what was on the tube, she went back into the kitchen where her laptop was still on the kitchen table.

The computer work would always be a hobby she enjoyed, but her true calling had been working the streets of Black Rock with a badge on her chest. It was one more thing The Professional had taken away from her. She no longer felt competent to wear the badge.

In the darkness of the shed, with the chilling voice of The Professional taunting and teasing her with promises of such heinous things, she'd contemplated what no deputy should ever contemplate.

Shoving these thoughts aside, she logged in to her social-networking page and for the next hour read innocuous messages from people she had never met. She rarely posted on the page, instead just reading messages and posts from friends and friends of friends.

Reading the mundane tidbits of those lives helped fill the hours before bedtime and made her feel a little connected to the outside world.

She surfed the internet until just after nine, then powered down her computer and got up to carry her soda glass to the sink. As she gazed up at the window her heart slammed against her ribs and the glass crashed to the bottom of the sink.

It was him!

The Professional.

He stared at her through the window glass, his face covered with the familiar black ski mask. His eyes glittered the way she remembered, with evil intent. This was the way she saw him in her nightmares.

For what felt like an eternity she was frozen, locked in a hellish gaze with the man who had nearly taken her life, the man who had stolen her innocence and sense of self.

The moment lasted only a moment, broken by the scream that crawled up her throat as she reeled backward and crashed into the table.

She went down hard on her butt on the floor, skittering backward like a crab on hot sand to escape. He was back! The face. That masked face. She had to get away.

She managed to get to her feet and half ran, half stumbled into the living room. Terror gripped her by the neck, trapping the scream as her throat constricted painfully.

Grabbing the phone from the end table, she sobbed as it took her two times to punch in her brother Tom's phone number. She found her voice when he answered and sobbed his name. "He's here. The Professional is here. Please hurry…hurry!"

Someplace in the back of her mind she knew it would take him too long to come. She needed help now, before The Professional somehow got inside the house, before he had the party he'd promised and hadn't had a chance to deliver.

There was only one other phone number in her head, the one that had been on the contact information Alex had given her earlier in the day to aid her in building his web page. She punched it in, and gasped in relief as he answered on the second ring.

"Alex, can you come to my house right now? There's somebody outside. I'm scared."

"I'll be right there," he replied.

She remained clutching the phone after he'd hung up, listening for the sound of a shattering window, a broken door that would indicate that The Professional had gained entry into her home.

It wasn't done. It wasn't over. She'd known in her heart, in her very soul that it wasn't finished yet. Now all she could do was hope and pray that somebody would get here before The Professional had his final party with her.

Thankfully Emily had decided to spend the night with Rose, and Alex was still dressed when he got Brittany's call. He grabbed his house keys and tore down the sidewalk, keeping an eye on his surroundings as he looked for a possible intruder in the area.

She'd been terrified. He'd heard it in her voice. Whoever she'd seen had positively scared her to death and the fear in her voice had sliced through him like a knife.

He saw nobody and when he reached Brittany's house he knocked on the front door. There was no reply. He knocked again, harder, and called out her name. "Brittany, it's me, Alex."

The door flew open and she launched herself into his arms, her slender body trembling uncontrollably as she began to weep. "Hey, it's okay," he said. "You're okay now." He moved her into the house and closed and locked the door behind him, but she refused to leave his arms.

"He was here," she said between sobs, her voice slightly muffled as she buried her head in the front of his shirt. "He came back for me. It's not over. I thought it was over, but it's not."

"Who? Honey, tell me what happened."

She shook her head and burrowed closer against him, her sobs ripping from deep in her throat in despair. He didn't try to talk to her again. He just held her until her sobs became softer and finally stopped altogether.

He'd just led her to the sofa to sit when the doorbell rang. "That should be my brother Tom," she said as she swiped the last of the tears from her cheeks.

Alex answered the door to a tall, dark-haired man who had the same coloring as and, although bolder and more masculine, similar features to Brittany. "Alex Crawford," he said in introduction. "I'm Brittany's neighbor."

"Tom Grayson," he replied. "Sheriff Tom Grayson." He walked in to where Brittany remained on the sofa, her arms around herself as if seeking some sort of warmth. "What happened?" He eased down next to his sister as Alex stood nearby.

"He was here." The words were a bare whisper as they left her lips. She looked up at her brother, her brown eyes wide and still filled with terror. "The Professional."

Tom exchanged a dark glance with Alex. "Brittany, you know that isn't possible. Larry Norwood is dead. Larry was The Professional and he's no longer on this earth. He died in that shed. He can't hurt you anymore."

She shook her head. "He's back. I saw him. He was staring at me through my kitchen window just a few minutes ago." Her voice was filled with vehemence.

"What did he look like?" Tom asked.

"He was wearing a black ski mask, just like Larry used to wear. His eyes…his eyes glittered with that sick excitement, with that horrible evil." A shiver worked through her and she tightened her arms around her shoulders.

Tom got up from the sofa and for the first time Alex noticed the man had his gun strapped to his waist even though he wasn't in uniform, clad in a pair of worn jeans and a short-sleeved navy shirt. "I'll go out and take a look around."

Without waiting for a reply he left the house by the front door. Brittany began to tremble once again and Alex moved back to the sofa to take her into his arms.

"You're okay now," he murmured against her sweet-smelling hair. "Nobody is going to hurt you."

"I just looked up and he was there, staring at me through the window. It was like a vision from a nightmare, a horrible nightmare."

He tightened his arms around her. He had no idea what had happened, but he knew true terror when he saw it, when he felt it trembling in his arms, and whatever Brittany had seen had definitely terrified her.

Within minutes Tom was back, his gaze inscrutable. "I didn't see anyone and there are no signs that anyone was back there." He stuffed his hands into his pockets and stared at his sister, who sat up and moved away from Alex's embrace.

"Are you sure maybe you didn't see your own reflection in the window and freak out?" he asked.

Brittany's back went rigid. "My own reflection usually doesn't scare me." She shook her head. "I know what I saw and it was a man in a ski mask."

"But it wasn't The Professional," Tom countered.

Brittany hesitated a moment. "Of course, you're

right. Larry Norwood is dead, but somebody was outside my window, somebody wearing a ski mask just like Larry used to do when he came into the shed."

She got up from the sofa and walked over to her brother. "Somebody is after me, Tom. I feel it. I know it in the very depth of my being. It's not over yet for me and I'm afraid."

Tom hesitated a moment and then released a deep sigh. "Maybe you should talk to somebody about post-traumatic stress."

"I'm not crazy. I saw what I saw," she exclaimed with rising anger in her voice.

"Well, there's nobody out there now and if it will make you feel better I'll have Caleb do extra drive-bys through the night," he replied. "Or if you'd feel better you can come home with me."

"No, thanks," she said stiffly. "I'll stay here, but I would appreciate the extra patrols."

Alex could tell Brittany was angry and she remained so as she ushered her brother out the front door. She whirled back around to face Alex. "I suppose you think I'm crazy, too?"

Alex wasn't sure what he believed, but he was a smart man and knew what she needed just now was somebody on her side. "Of course not," he replied.

She stared at him for a few seconds, then her shoulders sagged forward and she returned to the sofa and sank down. "I know what I saw," she said more to herself than to him. "I'm certain of what I saw." Her hands clenched into fists in her lap.

"I believe you saw somebody," he said as he sat next

to her. "And I believe he was wearing a ski mask, but we both know it wasn't The Professional."

She drew a deep breath and nodded. "In that first moment of fear when I saw him, that's all I could think about, that somehow he'd returned from the grave to finish what he'd started. But I know that's crazy." Her hands had relaxed in her lap and he took one of them in his.

"Maybe somebody is playing a very sick joke on you," he suggested.

"Maybe," she admitted as a tiny frown appeared in the center of her forehead. "There was the balloon the other day."

It was Alex's turn to frown. "The balloon?"

"Remember, the day you came to see about the deck there was a red balloon tied to my mailbox."

"I remember," he replied. "But I'm not sure I understand what a red balloon has to do with all of this."

She leaned her head back against the sofa cushion, her gaze suddenly distant. "On that last day, in the final moments before he was going to kill us all, he released a handful of red balloons to celebrate the start of his 'party.' They were like blood droplets floating upward." She shivered, as if the memory chilled her to the bone.

Alex squeezed her hand in an attempt to bring her back from the bad place she'd gone to in her memory. "But you survived and Larry Norwood is dead and now we need to figure out who might be doing these things to you." He squeezed her hand once again and then released it. "Is there anyone you can think of who might want to torment you? Or maybe somebody who might think something like this is funny?"

"No," she replied immediately. "I can't imagine anyone who would want to do something so cruel or would have such a sick sense of humor."

"Who might know about the details of what happened with you and The Professional?" he asked.

She got up from the sofa and released a small, humorless laugh. "Only everyone in town. There are no secrets in Black Rock. I guarantee five minutes after we were all taken out of that shed every detail of what had happened in there was known to everyone in town."

"But there's somebody in town who apparently is using those facts to taunt you," he replied as he also rose from the sofa.

Her features suddenly reflected a new horror. "Where's Emily?"

"Don't worry. She spent the night with Rose tonight."

"Thank God," she gasped in relief. "For a minute I thought maybe you'd left her at home all alone."

He smiled. "She's fine. And now I want to make sure you're fine. Would you like me to stay here tonight? Spend the night on your sofa? Or maybe you'd rather come to my place for the rest of the night? I've got a spare bedroom where you'd be comfortable."

She hesitated only a moment and then shook her head. "Thanks, but I'll be fine here. I have good locks on the door and Tom said there's nobody around here now. Caleb is going to do drive-bys so the excitement for the night is probably over."

"Are you sure you're okay here alone?" he asked. He still didn't know if there was any real danger to her, but the last thing he wanted was for her to spend the night in fear.

"Yes, really, I'm fine now." She looked better. The color was back in her cheeks and she'd stopped trembling. She offered him a tight smile. "It was nice of you to come running when I called."

"Anytime, Brittany. Anytime day or night if you need me I'll be here. The last thing I want is for you to be alone and afraid."

Her gaze was soft as it lingered on him. She walked to where he stood and stretched up and kissed him on his cheek. "Thank you, Alex. Thank you for believing me and thank you for being here for me."

She stepped back from him, precluding any idea he might have had of taking her in his arms for a deeper, more intimate embrace. "I'll see you in the morning."

"If you need anything more tonight, just give me a call," he said as they walked to the front door.

"Thanks, but I'm sure I'll be fine now."

A moment later as Alex headed back toward his house, he wondered about the truth of what had happened tonight. It had been obvious that Brittany's brother Tom hadn't believed there had been somebody at the window, that he thought his sister was suffering some sort of post-traumatic stress disorder.

Certainly the balloon he'd seen tied to her mailbox had been real, but there could be a dozen logical explanations for that and none of them included a killer rising up from the dead.

Was it possible that Brittany was much more fragile than he'd initially believed? It had been her strength that had first drawn him to her, but was that strength merely a facade hiding a flaw that was the legacy of what she'd been through? Was she not the strong survivor he'd thought her to be?

With the feel of her kiss warming his cheek, he now felt as if his most important decision to make was if he should invite her into his life, into Emily's life in a meaningful way or if perhaps the best thing he could do for himself and his daughter would be to cut his losses and run.

Chapter 5

"I'm not crazy. I'm not!" Brittany said aloud to herself as she locked the door after Alex left. She didn't care what her brother thought. She didn't care what anyone thought. It hadn't been her own reflection she'd seen in the window and it hadn't been a figment of her imagination.

There had been somebody there, and his eyes had sparked with malevolence. There had been somebody there, hadn't there? She sank down on the sofa and buried her face in her hands, a wild despair sweeping through her. *Maybe you are crazy,* a little voice whispered in the back of her brain.

Tears burned at her eyes at the torture of that small voice. What if she truly had imagined the face at the window? What if the trauma that she'd suffered at the hands of The Professional had left her teetering on the brink of insanity?

Her brothers certainly thought that's what had happened, that she was jumping at shadows and imagining danger behind every bush. They all thought she could use some therapy, and maybe she could, but that didn't make her believe she'd only imagined that face at the window.

She'd hated the fact that what she'd seen in Tom's eyes had been a touch of pity, more than a little compassion for somebody who might be sick. She hadn't missed the look he'd exchanged with Alex.

She'd never felt as alone as she did now. Had Alex believed her or had he just been being kind? She wasn't sure. When she'd asked him he'd replied that he believed she thought she saw something. That didn't mean that he believed somebody had really been there.

One thing was certain. Although in those first moments of sheer panic she'd believed somehow, someway Larry Norwood had come back for her, now that some of the panic had worn off she knew it wasn't possible that it had been Larry.

Larry was dead and she knew he could never hurt her again, but somebody was playing with her and she didn't know the rules of the game. What's more, nobody else apparently knew or believed that a game was being played with her.

And if it was a game, then what was the object? She shook her head and swiped her tears from her cheeks. Maybe she was making too much of everything. The balloon could have been from a birthday party on the street and the man staring into her kitchen window might have been nothing more than a Peeping Tom.

Every town had a Peeping Tom. Bored teenagers sneaking around in the night, a pervert trying to catch a glimpse of a woman in a state of undress. Generally speaking, Peeping Toms were harmless.

She certainly could live with the fact that she'd overreacted, but the idea that she was somehow losing her mind was terrifying.

Knowing that sleep would be impossible for some time to come, she got up from the sofa, went to the front window and peered out just in time to see a patrol car slowly passing her house. A brilliant light shone on the bushes by her porch, then across the front of the house itself. Caleb was taking his job seriously.

Tom had been as good as his word and a new feeling of safety swept through her. Besides, it wasn't as if the masked man had tried to break the window. He'd simply been looking at her—like some perverted peeper.

With each moment that passed, the terror she'd felt began to ebb away, leaving her with only a weary exhaustion. It was after eleven and even though an hour ago she hadn't thought she'd ever be able to sleep again, she now stifled a yawn.

Maybe a nice hot cup of tea would finish relaxing her enough that she could sleep without nightmares of what had been, without worries about what might be. She didn't want to go to sleep believing that she was slowly but surely losing her mind or that some faceless, nameless evil was after her once again.

She filled up a teakettle, preferring the traditional way to make tea to the microwave. With the water on the stove, she sank back down at the table, her gaze going to the window above the sink.

Had there been somebody there? She'd been so certain, but now doubts were slowly creeping in. There was no question that she'd been on edge lately.

She loved being back in her own space, back in the home that she'd dreamed of while being held captive. She'd bought the house two years before and each stick of furniture, every dish towel and knickknack had been chosen with care to create her own comfortable nest.

She hated the fact that the face at the window had momentarily shaken the safety, the security she'd always felt here.

The whistle of the teakettle pulled her from her thoughts. She moved it off the burner and then grabbed a teacup from the cabinet.

With her raspberry tea made she sat at the table and thought about the events of the night. It had definitely been a roller-coaster ride. She'd been surprised to find that she'd enjoyed her time with Emily. The little girl was easy to be around, delightful in a natural way.

But was it right for Brittany to get any closer to her when she might be losing her mind? She took a sip of her tea, muttering a curse beneath her breath as she burned her bottom lip on the hot, fragrant brew.

Certainly Alex and Emily had been through enough heartache in their lives. The last thing they needed around them was a woman afraid that a serial killer was somehow stalking her from his grave.

Perhaps the light from the moon had made some weird reflection in the window. Maybe she'd been stressing more than she'd realized and the stress had made her momentarily snap and see a phantom.

She finished her tea and with a sigh got up from the table. A good night's sleep would put everything into perspective. Still, as she carried her cup to the sink her heart tap-danced a slightly faster rhythm than normal.

But as she approached the back window, there was nothing there except a faint cast of moonlight illuminating the partially finished deck. No masked man, no killer from the dead—just a backyard shrouded with the shadows of night.

As she rinsed her cup and placed it in the dishwasher her heart continued the accelerated beat. What if she had hallucinated the face in the window? What if her mind was slipping?

In the four months that she had been a prisoner in a small cell in a shed, that had been one of her fears, that she would slowly go out of her mind.

It would definitely be ironic if she had survived everything that The Professional had put her through only to lose herself to madness now. That's not happening, she told herself firmly as she turned away from the dishwasher.

That's when she saw it. A folded piece of paper stuck beneath her back door. Thinking that it was probably something Alex had dropped while working on the deck, she walked over and picked it up.

She opened it and as she saw the writing in bold red letters she gasped and dropped it on the floor as if it were a poisonous snake.

IT'S PARTY TIME.

Even from where she stood she could see the letters that formed the words. Her heart beat like a pounding drum in her ears, but this time it wasn't terror that shot adrenaline through her. It was a strange form of excitement.

Proof. The note was horrible, but it was definitely proof that the man at the window had been there. He'd been real! It was proof that she wasn't losing her mind after all. He'd been real and the note that he'd delivered was also real.

With trembling fingers she bent down and picked up the note once again. It was impossible to figure out if it was a warning, a promise or somebody's idea of a terrible joke. But it definitely was meant to unnerve her.

Her initial instinct was to call Tom again, but a glance at the clock let her know it was almost midnight. He'd already been here once on what he'd considered a wild-goose chase. She wasn't going to call him away from home for a second time tonight.

She'd contact him first thing in the morning and give him the note. That way he'd know she wasn't going crazy but rather that somebody was messing with her head.

She looked at the note carefully, but there was nothing on it to identify who might be the author. The letters were written in bold by a red marker that could have been bought anywhere and the paper was the ordinary plain white kind sold practically everywhere in town.

She sensed that whatever danger had been here had passed. Apparently the masked man had wanted to deliver his sick promise and with that accomplished he was done…for now.

All she had to do was somehow anticipate what might come next and pray that all of this was just somebody's idea of a sick joke.

Placing the note on the kitchen countertop where she would see it first thing in the morning, she left the kitchen and went into her bedroom.

There was no way she thought sleep would be possible but when she next opened her eyes it was to the sound of hammering in the backyard.

She shot straight up and looked at her clock. After nine. Jeez, she'd slept like the dead. Moments later as she stood beneath a hot shower, she thought of the note and her intention to call Tom.

Funny how a threatening note could make her feel so good, but it was proof positive that she hadn't imagined the man at the window. It was also possible the night that she thought she'd seen a shadow dance across the window it had been the same person peering in at her. Bottom line, it would appear she had some kind of a stalker.

It could be nothing more than a teenager trying to get a peek at her in her underwear. Not all stalkers were dangerous lunatics. It remained to be seen what kind of animal had her in his sights.

Whoever he was, he was a living, breathing human being, and between herself and her brothers they would figure out who he was and why he was doing these things to her. And there would be consequences for his actions.

A smile curved her lips as she walked into the kitchen and saw the men working outside. Although she was still concerned about the note and the vague feeling of threat that had accompanied everything that had happened, she also felt optimistic that the perp would be caught and she could truly get on with her life.

She waved at Alex through the window, her heart beating just a little faster at the sight of him. She'd make coffee and then call Tom.

She glanced at the countertop where she'd put the note the night before—and froze.

It was gone.

Alex wasn't sure when he realized something was wrong with Brittany. She'd waved and smiled at him through the window and then the next time he glanced inside the house she was pulling drawers from the cabinets and dumping them on the floor.

Something was definitely wrong. "Hey, Buck, Gary, go ahead and knock off for the day," he said to his two helpers. "We'll start again first thing in the morning. And don't worry, I'll pay you for the day anyway."

"Cool," Gary said.

As the two young men disappeared around the side of the house, Alex knocked on Brittany's back door. Her brown eyes were wide, glazed with panic as she hurried to the door and unlocked it. She didn't wait to greet him but instead went to another drawer in the cabinet, pulled it out and dumped it on the floor.

"Brittany, what's going on?" he asked.

She fell to her knees and began to sift through the items that now littered the beige tiles. "It's got to be here. I know it's here someplace. I didn't make it up. I swear I didn't dream it." She spoke more to herself than to him as she dug through silverware and hand towels, a sick, frantic energy wafting from her.

"Brittany, what are you looking for?" Alex felt scared, not of her but for her. Her eyes were far too wild and her movements painfully jerky. He got down on the floor next to her.

"It's got to be here. It's got to be here." She didn't look at him as she repeated the words again and again. "It was here last night. It's got to be here now."

He grabbed her hands and her gaze flew up to meet his. Her fingers were cold and trembled as he held them tight. "Talk to me, Brittany. For God's sake what are you doing? What's going on?"

Tears appeared and clung to her long dark lashes while her lips trembled with emotion. "It was a note. A note from him…the man at the window…the man from last night." The words came from her with a jerky rhythm that spoke of her intense stress.

"What are you talking about? Where did you find the note?" Alex asked.

"It was under the back door. I found it after you and Tom left. I thought it was something you'd dropped, but it wasn't. It was a note from him."

"Why didn't you call Tom immediately?"

A flash of annoyance swept over her features. "He'd just been here and he thinks I'm crazy. It was after midnight and I didn't want to call him out again. I put the note on top of the counter and figured I'd call him first thing this morning." A hollow despair filled her eyes. "And now it's gone. It's gone, Alex!"

Once again Alex wasn't sure what he believed, but there was no question that she believed there had been a note and it should be someplace in the kitchen. He looked at the mess she'd made on the floor. There was no note anywhere among the items.

"It isn't here. Let's get everything put back." He began picking up silverware and setting it back in the drawer from where it had come.

For several minutes they worked side by side, neither of them speaking. He could feel the taut tension that rolled off her, but had no way to ease it.

When the drawers were put back in place he led her to the table where she sank down with a weary sigh. Her eyes still held the hollow emptiness of a woman on the edge.

"Don't you see? It was proof. It was proof that I'm not losing my mind, that I'm not suffering some sort of post-traumatic stress that makes me see phantom figures at my window."

"What did the note say?" he asked.

"'It's party time.'" The words trembled from her lips. "I put it right there on the counter before I went to bed." She pointed across the kitchen. "And when I looked for it a little while ago it was gone."

"Is it possible you put the note someplace else and only thought you left it on the counter?" He still didn't know what to believe, but he could tell that she definitely believed what she was telling him.

She leaned back in the chair. "That's why I was checking the drawers. I thought maybe without thinking I'd shoved it in one of them before I went to bed. But it's gone. I know I didn't carry it out of the kitchen. I put it on the counter and now it's gone."

"If that's the case then what do you think might have happened to it?" He kept his voice even and calm in an effort to calm her down.

She leaned forward and her eyes suddenly blazed with life. "I think somebody came in here in the middle of the night and took it." A small burst of laughter escaped her. "God, I really do sound insane, don't I?"

"Maybe a little," he admitted.

She ran a hand across her forehead, as if easing the bang of a headache. "No matter what you think, no matter what Tom and my other brothers believe, I'm not crazy. Somebody is playing games with me." She balled her hands into fists on the top of the table. "This isn't making me crazy, it's starting to really make me mad."

"Did you check the doors and windows to see if

anyone broke in?" he asked. He had no idea if he was playing into some sort of delusion of hers or not, but he desperately wanted to give her the benefit of the doubt.

"I know the back door was still locked this morning. I had to unlock it to let you in."

"What about the front door? The windows?"

"I haven't checked them."

He scooted back his chair. "Then let's do that now."

They went from room to room, checking to see that the house was still locked up tight. The front door was locked and there was no sign of tampering, but in the bathroom in the hallway they found the window unlocked.

"I just can't be sure if it was locked before last night or not," she admitted. "But the screen is still in place."

"The screen could have easily been taken out and put back in again," he replied. "I'm going to go outside and check around the window." As he started out of the bathroom she grabbed his arm.

"You do believe me, don't you, Alex?" Her voice radiated with need.

He hesitated. "I'll be honest with you. I don't know what to believe at this point."

She nodded slowly and released her hold on him. "That's fair," she agreed.

As he went out the front door Alex's head was filled with a thousand thoughts, a hundred emotions. He wanted to believe her. He wanted to believe her because as crazy as it sounded he was already emotionally involved with her.

Emily adored her and Alex was drawn to her like
he hadn't been drawn to a woman in a very long time.
But he couldn't, he wouldn't bring an unstable woman
into his life, into Emily's life.

He'd already been there, done that and had sworn
he would never go there again. But he also didn't want
to act hastily. He didn't want to distance himself from
Brittany if there were any possibility that she might
be telling the truth. He'd never thought of himself as a
knight in shining armor, but he also didn't want to be
a total jerk and just walk away because things weren't
going smoothly for her.

He saw nothing around the window to indicate that
it might have been tampered with. The grass wasn't
trampled down and the dirt didn't hold any footprints.
Of course, that didn't mean nobody had been there;
it simply meant if somebody had been there they had
been extremely careful.

When he returned into the house Brittany was still
seated at the table where she'd been when he'd left. His
heart squeezed at the sight of her. She had her face in
her hands, her shoulders slumped forward in defeat.

She didn't feel as if she could go to her brothers.
She'd told him she'd lost her friends after the crime.
She was virtually alone with her fears.

She sat up straighter and removed her hands from
her face as she heard him come back into the kitchen.
"Let me guess, you didn't find anything suspicious."

He sat down next to her. "But that doesn't mean that
somebody didn't get inside. Who might have a key to
your house?"

She frowned. "All of my brothers have keys."

"But we know none of them would be behind all this. Is there anyone else? An old friend? Somebody you used to date?"

Her eyes narrowed slightly. "Luke Mathis. I was sort of seeing him before I was kidnapped."

"And afterward?" Alex asked, surprised at a small nudge of jealousy that made itself known.

"Luke is a part-time bartender down at Harley's, a bar on the edge of town. He's a good-time kind of guy and after the ordeal I definitely wasn't a good-time kind of woman. We talked a few times on the phone after I was rescued, but that was it."

"Did he have a key?"

"He did, but I can't imagine Luke having anything to do with this," she protested, and then added, "although he does have a wicked sense of humor."

"Can you think of anyone in your life who would do something like this?" he countered. "Maybe somebody you had a run-in with when you were working as a deputy?"

She frowned thoughtfully and once again rubbed her hand across her forehead. "Nobody specific comes to mind. I'll have to think about it."

Once again her shoulders slumped slightly forward. "I can't make sense of any of this." She closed her eyes for a long moment and when she opened them again that steely strength radiated there once again. "All I can tell you is that I know what happened last night. I'm not suffering from delusions. I'm not making things up. I held that note in my hand. I saw the red lettering on the white paper and I saw that man at my window."

There was such a ring of truth in her voice, a certainty shining from her eyes that Alex found it difficult to believe she was a woman suffering some sort of delusional state. "Are you sure you don't want to call your brother and tell him about the note?"

"No, but what I plan to do is go to Harley's and confront Luke. He's always had that kind of a sick sense of humor. Maybe he thinks this is a really funny joke."

"Then the man is an idiot," Alex replied darkly.

For the first time since he'd walked into the house Brittany smiled. "He is kind of an idiot, but he was fun to hang out with for a while." She got up from the table and leaned against the counter. "This isn't your deal, Alex. If I were you I'd run as fast as I could a million miles away from me."

It had only been a little while ago that he'd wondered if that wouldn't be the best thing for him to do. But with the scent of her in his head and her appearing like a tiny speck of an island in a storm-tossed sea, he realized there was no way he intended to walk away from her, at least not right now.

He got up from the table and without saying a word walked over to her and wrapped his arms around her. She leaned into him, as if needing him to anchor her.

Despite the trauma of the morning, despite the questions that plagued his mind, he felt himself responding to her nearness.

She was like an elixir for his blood, a bane to all

the loneliness and heartache that had been a part of his life for so long.

As she raised her face to gaze up at him he knew he was going to kiss her. He had no idea if it was right or wrong. He had no idea if she was right or wrong for him and his daughter. He only knew that at this moment he wanted to kiss her more than anything else he wanted in his life.

Chapter 6

From the moment Brittany had discovered the note
gone she'd felt as if she'd flailed around in a sea of
madness, a sea that had parted and brought sanity only
when Alex's arms had wrapped around her.

She wasn't the kind of woman to depend on a man
for anything. She'd always been strong and independent. Even in the face of death she'd remained strong
except for one agonizing moment of blackness that
she tried never to think about.

But there was no question that at this moment in
time she not only wanted, she felt as if she needed
Alex to anchor her, to heat the cold places that felt as
if they would be icy forever.

When his lips met hers his warmth eddied through
her, a welcome sensation she wanted to last forever,

and as the kiss deepened she knew it wouldn't be enough. A kiss could never be enough.

She wound her arms around his neck and pressed herself intimately close to him, wanting to lose herself in his heat, in the solid, sweet embrace that promised something more.

And she wanted more. She felt as if she'd been alone for an eternity and right now the idea of being alone for another minute was excruciating.

She wanted, no, needed intimacy. She needed to feel connected with something other than her own doubts, her own fears. She wanted connection with him.

The kiss that she knew he meant to comfort her quickly became hot and greedy as she opened her mouth to his. He'd said he just wanted a friend, but she felt the way he responded to her and in any case at the moment she felt selfish.

For over eight long months she had been utterly alone except for the taunting threats of a madman, followed by the pitying looks from her brothers.

Yes, she wanted to be selfish and take what she needed and damn the consequences. And what she needed right now was Alex, naked with his body tight against hers in her bed.

As the kiss continued she ran her hands up under his shirt, caressing his strong bare back in what she hoped would be an unmistakable gesture of her want. His flesh was smooth and hot.

She felt him tense slightly, but he didn't pull back nor did the kiss end. Instead his hands slid down her back, setting fire to every place they touched until they stopped at the top of her hips.

She wanted him, not as a friend, not as a support system, but as a lover and it was obvious by his arousal pressed against her that he wasn't adverse to the idea.

When the kiss finally ended he stepped back and stared at her, his eyes like flames of electric fire. "I should probably go," he said, his voice slightly husky.

"Alex, I don't want you to go. I want you to make love to me." She took a step closer to him and placed a hand on his chest where his heart beat strong and just a little too fast. "I know you want to, Alex. We can still be friends. It doesn't have to mean anything more than that, but I need you to hold me. I want to feel you naked next to me."

She wouldn't have thought it possible for his eyes to flare any hotter, but they did, but still he took another step back from her as if afraid to take what she freely offered him.

She sensed what he was about to say before he opened his mouth. "Don't tell me I'm not in my right mind," she exclaimed. "Having the deck built was the first thing in eight months I wanted to do for me. Having you is the second."

Her words seemed to snap whatever hesitation in him that might have lingered. In two short strides he had her back in his arms, his mouth hungrily taking hers in a kiss that sent her senses reeling.

All memory of the frantic search for the missing note, the horrid face at the window and every other troubling thought in her head flew from her mind as she gave herself completely to the moment.

It didn't take long for her to tire of kissing in the kitchen. She took him by the hand and led him down the hallway to her bedroom. Her sheets were rumpled as she hadn't made the bed after getting up that morning. It looked ready for two lovers to fall in and rumple further.

"Brittany, I don't want to be part of the craziness in your life," he said as she pulled her T-shirt over her head. "I'm not looking for a wife."

She dropped the shirt to the floor and smiled at him. "That's good, because I'm not looking for a husband. I'm not even looking for tomorrow. I just want here and now with you." She unzipped her jeans and smiled at him. "Are you going to stand there staring at me or are you going to get into my bed and ravish me?"

He grinned back. "Can't I do a little bit of both?"

Within moments they were both undressed except for their underwear. Before she got into bed she opened her dresser drawer and pulled out a condom.

They tumbled together into the sheets that smelled of her favorite perfume and he pulled her tight against him, her bare skin drinking of his.

He was strong and warm and exactly what she wanted, and when his mouth found hers again she found his kiss wonderfully exciting and a testimony to herself that she'd truly survived her ordeal with her life, her very passion still intact.

When the kiss ended he rose up slightly and looked

at her. "I haven't been with anyone since long before my wife died."

"And I've only been with one other man and that feels as if it were a lifetime ago," she replied. Luke had taken her virginity after a night of too much booze and they'd been together twice more after that, but each time had been fast and fairly emotionless and she'd been left feeling as if there should be something more, something better than what she'd experienced.

"I want to go slow," Alex whispered against her ear. "I want to savor every second with you, every inch of you."

She shivered at his words, a promise of sensual pleasure like she'd never experienced before.

His mouth slid down the length of her neck as he tangled his hands in her long hair. She was lost in the width of his back, caressing her hands up and down as the muscles played beneath her fingertips.

She'd wanted him since the minute she'd opened her front door and seen him standing on her porch. She'd wanted him the first time he'd smiled, making his amazing eyes crinkle slightly at the corners and filling her with a welcome heat.

"I've been crazy with wanting you," he said, as if in response to her own thoughts. His lips moved from her throat to her collarbone as she moved her hands up to tangle them in his dark hair.

His chest rubbed erotically against her bare breasts, shooting tingling sensations from her head to her toes. And then his mouth was on her breast, nudging the nipple with his tongue and then suckling with just enough pressure to evoke a moan of pleasure from her.

He'd said he wanted slow and he took it slow. His hands and mouth seemed to touch each and every inch of her until she was gasping with need, crying out his name in a combination of despair and delight.

It didn't take long for their underwear to be disposed of and they pressed the length of their nakedness together, a sensual delight of skin, arousal and fire.

He smelled of a morning shower and spicy cologne, a heady combination that only increased her desire for him. When she wrapped her fingers around the hard length of him he gasped aloud, as if not expecting the intimate touch.

His entire body tensed as she moved her hand up and down the pulsing swell of him. His eyes bored into hers, filled with need that fought for control. "Easy." His voice was a strained whisper and the muscles in his neck were taut. "I don't want to finish before we begin."

With a sudden movement he rolled over to his side, away from her touch, and instead his fingers found her center. Her nerves screamed as he moved his fingers in a slow, circular motion, calling forth a rising tide of sensation that had her trembling uncontrollably.

Then the tide was on her, rushing over her as she cried his name again and again. He rolled away from her and grabbed the condom from the nightstand. Seconds later he eased into her, and she closed her eyes as he filled her up, both body and soul.

He framed her face with his hands and she opened her eyes and gazed at him, and in that moment of eye contact she felt more cherished than she'd ever felt in her life.

A wealth of emotion rose up in her throat. The wonder of life, of this magic moment of complete intimacy, the knowledge that if things had gone bad in that shed with The Professional she would have never experienced this time with Alex. It all rushed over her and tears sprang to her eyes.

He frowned. "Am I hurting you?" he asked worriedly.

She gripped his buttocks and pulled him tighter against her. "No, not at all. You feel wonderful."

He smiled. "You don't know wonderful yet." Then he began to move, sliding his hips back and forth in a slow motion that stole every thought from her head.

Slow and languid soon became faster and more frantic. They clung to each other as she met him thrust for thrust, dizzied by the pleasure that was almost too intense to bear.

When she thought she could stand no more, her orgasm shook through her like an earthquake and she was vaguely conscious of him finding his own release, as well.

They remained locked together, heartbeats finally slowing as she released a sigh of drowsy contentment.

He kissed her forehead, her cheek and the tip of her nose and then slid out of the bed and disappeared into the bathroom. He returned a moment later and slid back beneath the sheet and gathered her into his arms.

She relaxed against him, for the first time in eight months feeling one-hundred-percent safe. Neither of them spoke and she was grateful for the silence that spoke more than any words could say.

She was almost asleep when he stroked a strand of hair away from her face and spoke. "This has been wonderful, but it doesn't solve anything."

With that simple sentence reality slammed back in. Somebody had been at her window. Somebody had given her a note that terrified her with its implication. Was it all just a silly prank or did it imply something more dangerous?

"I know," she finally replied.

"So, what is your next move?" He sat up and reluctantly she did the same. What she wanted to do was stay in bed forever with his arms wrapped around her. But it was time to face her life again.

She worried a hand through her hair. "The first thing I intend to do is call somebody to come over and change the locks on the house."

"Definitely," he agreed.

"I guess my next move will be to go see Luke down at Harley's. He usually works Friday nights so I'll plan on going then."

Alex frowned. "Can't you just call him?"

She shook her head. "I want to ask him if he came into my house last night, if he's the one who tied the balloon to my mailbox and left that note. If I talk to him by phone I won't be able to tell if he's lying to me. If I see him in person I'll know if he's telling me the truth or not."

"I don't want you going to talk to him alone," Alex said firmly. "I'll get Rose to watch Emily Friday night and I'll go with you to Harley's."

She started to protest, but he placed a finger against her lips. "You've already told me you aren't going to your brothers with this. You need somebody on your side, Brittany, and I want to be that man."

He lay back down and pulled her into his arms. Once again they were silent for several long moments and she wondered what he was thinking.

"You ever think about having kids?" he asked.

Of all the things she thought might be on his mind, this definitely wasn't one of them. "Not really," she answered truthfully. "I don't think I'm mother material. Why?"

"You were good with Emily."

"It's easy to be good for ice cream and hair braiding, but that doesn't a mother make."

"She wants a brother or sister. She doesn't understand that I'm not even sure I want to marry again."

"You should marry again. You should find a nice woman who will make an excellent mother for Emily and give her lots of little brothers and sisters, build a family." She ignored the small stab in her heart as she continued. "I have far too much baggage to be the kind of woman you need in your life. You don't want to repeat your past mistake."

This wasn't a conversation she wanted to have. She didn't want there to be any question in his mind about exactly what she had to offer him. "Friends, Alex. That's what we said. It just so happens we're friends who fell into bed together."

"I know. And speaking of Emily, I should probably get out of here. It won't be long till she'll be getting off the school bus."

Once again he slid out of the bed and Brittany looked at the clock on her nightstand in surprise. She was shocked to see how late it was, that they had spent most of the late morning and afternoon in bed.

"I wasn't kidding about Friday night, Brittany," he said as he tugged on his jeans. "You let me know what time you want to go talk to Luke and I'll take you."

"What if I really am just crazy?"

He pulled his shirt on over his head and shrugged with a small smile. "Then I guess eventually we'll figure that out, too." Once again he walked over and kissed her on the forehead. "Why don't you just rest for a little while? I'll lock up as I leave and I'll see you in the morning to work on the deck."

She made no move to get up. The lovemaking had left her boneless and sated, and with the sleepless nights she'd already suffered the idea of a nice long nap seemed infinitely appealing.

At least she'd made it clear to him that she had no interest in being a mommy, that whatever it was they were doing together had no real meaningful future.

He'd surprised her with his talk of children and what was even more surprising was the small whisper of yearning the conversation had stirred inside her.

Maybe someday she'd have a child of her own, when she stopped jumping at shadows and no longer carried with her a terrible sense of dread. She'd think about love and family when she didn't have the ball of anxiety weighing heavy in her heart, when she knew the man who had stood at her kitchen window wasn't a physical threat.

Odd, that nothing had happened before Alex had

appeared in her life. She'd been in the house alone for almost a month and had been feeling better and stronger every day. But the day he'd stepped into her life had been the day the balloon had been tied to her mailbox, the day she thought that everything had begun to go bad.

Who was Alex Crawford? Had there really been a wife who had died of cancer? Had he really been a lawyer in Chicago? Chad had all but admitted that although the two had gone to college together they'd lost touch with each other until Alex had shown up here in town.

It felt almost traitorous to be lying in the bed where they had just made love, wrapped in the sheets that smelled of him, and entertaining these disturbing questions about him.

She rolled over and grabbed her phone from the nightstand and punched in a familiar number. "Hey, Benjamin," she said when her brother answered.

"Hi, dollface. What's going on?"

Of all her brothers, Benjamin was the easiest to talk to. He was soft-spoken, prone to compassion and had a relaxed nature that drew people to him.

"I have a favor to ask you," she said. "But it would have to be a secret just between you and me."

"What do you need?"

"I'd like you to run a thorough background check on somebody." She felt bad even asking, but she had to be sure. She didn't know who to trust right now and as badly as she wanted to trust Alex, she definitely had to be sure about him.

* * *

"How about some lemonade for the hardworking team?" Brittany asked the next day after noon as she carried a tray of drinks out to Alex, Buck and Gary.

"The only thing better than lemonade would be an ice-cold beer," Buck said as he set down his hammer and walked over to the table.

"Sorry, I prefer not to liquor up the men building my deck," she replied.

"Lemonade sounds great," Alex said with a smile as he and Gary joined them.

She poured the drinks from the large pitcher she'd brought and the three men settled into chairs to take a quick break. "It's coming along nicely," she said as she looked at their work.

"Should be finished by the weekend," Alex replied, a sense of pride in his voice as he looked over his work.

"I've always wanted to know what it was like," Buck said, his gaze intently focused on her. "What was it like to be a prisoner of that nut job Larry Norwood?"

Gary elbowed his friend in the ribs. "Jeez, Buck," he muttered beneath his breath.

"What? You know everyone has been wondering. You know you want to know, too. Did he torture you? Use cattle prods and stun guns?" Buck pressed.

"Buck!" Alex said sharply.

"It's all right," Brittany replied. She looked at Buck. "There are much worse things than cattle prods and stun guns. There are much worse things than physical torture."

"He was smart, though, wasn't he?" Buck continued, ignoring Alex's frown of displeasure. "I mean, he managed to kidnap and kill all those women in Kansas City and then he almost did the same thing here."

"He wasn't too smart. He's dead and I'm here," she replied drily.

"That's enough," Alex said. "Back to work."

As Buck and Gary moved away from the table Alex stepped closer to her. "That was inexcusable," he said.

She shrugged. "Buck's never been known for his great social skills. He's just curious like I'm sure a lot of people are."

"If he makes you feel uncomfortable I'll take him off the job," Alex offered.

"That's not necessary. Besides, the job is almost done now."

"He's an idiot," Alex said gruffly.

Brittany smiled as she recognized the protectiveness he apparently felt toward her. "It's fine, really."

"How about dinner tonight?"

She blinked at the abrupt change in topic. She wanted to have dinner with him. She wanted to go to bed with him again. She wanted all the things she shouldn't have, but she hadn't heard back from Benjamin yet and she didn't want things between them to get any more complicated than they already were.

"I'll have to take a rain check," she replied. "I'm having dinner with my brother Benjamin and his wife," she improvised.

"Okay, then maybe Friday before we head to Harley's we can get a bite to eat together."

"We'll see," she replied, refusing to commit to anything at the moment.

As he returned to work with the other two, she carried the pitcher and glasses back into the kitchen. Once she'd rinsed them and stowed them in the dishwasher she returned to the window. Only this time it wasn't Alex who captured her attention. It was Buck.

There had been a glee in his eyes as he'd asked her the questions, a faint glint of admiration in his voice as he'd spoken of The Professional.

How could anyone admire a killer? She didn't understand how, but she knew it happened. Some of the most notorious serial killers received thousands of love letters a year from women and notes of admiration from men.

Buck had little in his life to admire. His parents had been alcoholics who had virtually been unavailable to him from the time of his birth. He'd been kicked around by most people in town and had few friends. Was it any wonder he'd find an inappropriate man to look up to?

Was it possible he'd tied the balloon to her mailbox? Wore the ski mask and stood at her window? Was he a threat or playing some immature silly game?

She turned away from the window and picked up her phone and punched in her sister-in-law Edie's phone number. "I was wondering if I could invite myself to dinner tonight," she said after the initial greetings.

"Absolutely," Edie replied. "In fact you're in luck, Poppy and Margaret are coming over and doing the cooking so you know whatever it is will be good."

They arranged for the time and then hung up. Poppy was actually Edie's grandfather, Walt Tolliver. During the time that Brittany had been held captive by The Professional, Walt had become something of a small-town hero when he'd helped break a case of grave robbing and illegal dumping.

During the same time he'd fallen in love with Margaret, the older woman who had been housekeeper for the Grayson family for years. The two hadn't married, but liked to tell everyone they were living in sin and loving it.

They were a fun couple, each proclaiming to be the best cook and bickering good-naturedly about cooking styles. At least it would be an entertaining night and Brittany wouldn't feel as if she had lied to Alex about her dinner plans.

Still, later that afternoon as she got ready to head to Benjamin and Edie's, her thoughts weren't on Alex, but back on Buck and the excitement that had lit his eyes as he'd questioned her about her time with The Professional.

Chapter 7

Antonio's Italian Restaurant was the closest thing to fine dining in the small town of Black Rock and it was where Alex took Brittany on Friday night for dinner.

As the hostess led them to a small round table in the back of the dimly lit establishment, Alex couldn't keep his eyes off Brittany.

She wore a little black dress that hugged every curve and skimmed the tops of her thighs. Strappy black high heels accented the shapeliness of her long legs. Her hair was pulled up in a ponytail, exposing the long, slender column of her neck and allowing gold-and-black earrings to dangle freely.

He still wasn't sure what he believed about her and her phantom stalker. There had been no more drama for the past couple of days. The deck was officially finished except for a few finishing touches and tonight after dinner they'd confront Luke Mathis to see just how sick his sense of humor was.

But right now Alex didn't want to think about what came before or what would come after this moment. Brittany was stunning and at least for the length of the meal she belonged to him alone.

He knew he shouldn't think of her that way, but since the afternoon of their lovemaking he'd had trouble thinking of her any other way. There was a part of him that recognized that heartache might be ahead, but he wasn't sure he was completely capable of guarding his heart where she was concerned.

As they made their way to the table he was aware of the other diners watching Brittany and he could tell she was aware of them by the rigid straightness of her back.

She only relaxed when she slid into her seat, which faced away from the rest of the diners. "Feel like you just walked the plank?" he asked teasingly.

"Actually, it wasn't as bad as I expected," she replied, although she reached for her glass of water as if her throat had gone too dry.

"I keep telling you the more people see you out and around the less interesting you'll be."

She grinned. "That kind of makes it sound like the more of me you get, the more bored you are."

He laughed. "You know I didn't mean it that way," he protested.

"I know." She picked up the oversize menu. "I'm starving."

"Good, I like a woman with an appetite."

"I'm definitely not one of those women who peck on rabbit food and call it dinner. In fact, I happen to know that the lasagna here is fabulous."

"That's good to know since this is my first time here," he replied.

"You really should bring Emily here some night. They make car-shaped pasta for the boys and little purse-shaped pasta for the girls."

"That sounds fun. Maybe the three of us could come back some evening."

She lowered the menu and looked at him seriously. "What are we doing, Alex?"

He shrugged. "We're having dinner before we go to Harley's so you can talk to Luke," he replied, deliberately being obtuse.

She set the menu aside and frowned at him. "You know that's not what I mean."

He frowned for a long moment. "I don't know what we're doing. I only know that I don't want it to stop," he said truthfully.

Her cheeks flushed with a hint of color. "You know this isn't going anywhere, that we aren't going anywhere."

"Friends," he said, and then he couldn't help but add with a smile, "with occasional benefits."

"You shouldn't be wasting your time with me."

"I'll let you know when I think you're a waste of my time," he replied easily.

At that moment the waitress arrived with her order pad and a basket of warm bread and butter. They placed their orders and then she departed, leaving them alone with the slightly uncomfortable conversation they'd been having before she'd arrived.

"I just don't want anyone to get hurt," Brittany said. "Be honest with me, Alex. You aren't sure what to believe about my phantoms and my notes and whatever. Do you really want somebody around Emily who isn't cut out to be a mother? A woman who might be losing her mind?"

"You're right, I'm not sure what to believe about the things you believe have happened, but I know that you're kind and funny and caring, and why wouldn't I want Emily to be around a woman like you? I told you before, Brittany, I'm not sure I'm in the market for marriage again, but life is too short not to connect in meaningful ways with people you care about, and I care about you."

It was a long speech and when he was finished he sat back in his chair and waited for her reply. "I just don't want anyone to get hurt," she finally repeated.

"Right now the only thing I'm anticipating might hurt me is that I'll burn the roof of my mouth on the lasagna. Now, drink your wine and tell me about this Harley place we're going after dinner."

Dinner conversation remained light and pleasant and just as she'd predicted the food was delicious. They lingered over dessert and coffee, knowing that the best time to hit the tavern was later in the evening.

"I have a confession to make," she said and something in her tone of voice caused his stomach muscles to cramp.

"What kind of a confession?" he asked.

"I had my brother Benjamin do a background check on you."

Alex sat back in his seat in surprise. "You did?"

"I had to be sure that you were who you said you were," she replied, her voice holding an unspoken apology.

"And what did he find out?"

A small smile curved her lips. "That you really are who you say you are." The smile faltered. "I'm sorry, Alex, but I had to be sure."

"No need to apologize. I don't have any deep, dark secrets and I understand your need to be sure." And he did. She'd needed to assure herself that he was worthy of her trust, and after all she'd been through there was no way he could blame her for that. The stories he'd told her about his life could have been nothing but fabrications with the intent to get closer to her, especially if he had nefarious intent toward her.

"Did you go to Harley's often?" he asked, changing the subject.

"Too often," she admitted. "Especially after I started seeing Luke. I worked hard during the day as a deputy, but I played even harder at night." She shook her head and picked up her wineglass for a drink. "It's amazing how being close to death can change your priorities, transform your life."

"So, not much of a party girl anymore?" he asked lightly.

"Not at all. Life is too short to waste it partying with people who don't bring meaning to your life." She stared down into her wineglass and when she finally looked back at him her eyes were impossibly dark and equally impossible to read.

"Larry Norwood had set up a shed with five tiny cells. For almost three months I was alone in one of those cells. You can do a lot of thinking in three months. For the first week I refused to eat what little he'd bring out to me. I spent my time exploring the cell, looking for some sort of escape route, but there was no way out."

He wanted to stop her, didn't want her to relive the experience here and now, but he also didn't want to interrupt her if she needed to talk about what she'd endured.

"After that first week I started to eat everything he brought to me, knowing I'd need to keep up my strength if I were going to try to somehow escape. I woke up every morning hoping that one of my brothers would burst in and save me and I went to bed every night with a sense of despair I've never known before."

He reached across the table and took one of her hands in his. "You don't have to do this, Brittany. I don't have to know any of it."

She nodded and tightened her fingers around his. "But I want you to. I want you to understand." She leaned forward, her eyes flittering in the semidarkness of the restaurant. "The silence was terrible, but the worst part was when I'd hear him whistling right before he entered the shed. I never knew if he was bringing food or coming in to kill me or coming for one of his chats."

"His chats?"

Again she nodded and her eyes took on the glaze of somebody remembering unpleasant things. "He'd come in and pull up a chair in front of my cell and then he'd talk about all the things he intended to do to me when he finally had all his cells filled with women." Her fingers chilled beneath his. "Terrible things. Things that wouldn't kill me, but would cause excruciating pain. He never touched me in any way, but there are nights I have nightmares about the things he promised to do to me."

"Why was he waiting until he got the other women?" Alex asked in an effort to understand exactly what she'd faced.

"His real thrill came in having an audience. He wanted to torture and kill us each one at a time while the others watched. Of course initially I didn't understand that, so each time he came into the shed I thought I was going to die."

The glaze in her eyes lifted. "I can't put into words what that feels like, how it eats away at your very soul. It changes you. It changes who you are at your very core." She pulled her hand from his and leaned back. "My brothers don't get it. They don't realize how much I've changed and that's why I have trouble talking to them. They think a new pair of shoes or a fancy purse is going to make me feel better because that's what I used to love."

"I didn't know you before, Brittany. So I can only

tell you that I like the woman you are now, that to me you represent a strength of character that I admire."

Her eyes darkened once again. "I'm not as strong as you think I am. I'm not as strong as anyone believes I am."

She averted her gaze from his and for a moment he thought he saw a whisper of secrets and realized there was probably more that she wasn't ready to tell.

She released a small, embarrassed laugh. "Sorry, I didn't mean to get into all that now."

"It's okay. I told you anytime, anyplace if you need to talk, I'm here for you."

She smiled. "But you probably didn't intend for a conversation like this to take place in the middle of dinner at Antonio's Restaurant."

He returned her smile. "This is as good a place as any." He sobered. "Brittany, let's just take things slowly. Because that's all we really have—one day at a time."

She released a sigh that sounded like relief. "I just don't want to lead you on in any way."

"I'm a big boy. Don't you worry about me. Don't you worry about anything but finishing that dessert and then getting your key back and maybe some answers from Luke."

The conversation returned to more normal topics, the beautiful weather, the flowers she intended to plant around her new deck and the party she planned to throw when everything was perfect in her backyard.

"Of course you and Emily will be invited," she said and then finished the last of her wine. "And my family and I'm thinking about inviting some of my old girl-friends."

He raised an eyebrow. "The ones who made you uncomfortable after your rescue?"

She frowned and toyed with one of her dangling earrings, making him want to take it off and nibble on her earlobe. "I've been thinking about that. I think maybe in those first weeks after my rescue I pretty much pushed everyone away, including some well-meaning friends. I felt safe at Benjamin and Edie's and I was afraid that anyone else might pull me out of that feeling of safety, so I protected myself by with-drawing. I miss having girlfriends to do lunch or just chat on the phone."

She offered him a beautiful smile and dropped her hand to her lap. "I think I'm finally really healing and it's in large part thanks to you."

"To me?" He looked at her in surprise.

"You and Emily got me out of my house for ice cream. You have me here now. You've made me re-alize I can continue my life here in Black Rock, a normal life after everything that happened to me."

She might not recognize her own strength, but she obviously had no idea the core of character that ex-isted in her. And there was no question that he was as drawn to the woman she was inside as he was drawn to her physical attractiveness.

One day at a time, he reminded himself as they left the restaurant. She'd made it clear that she wasn't mother material and he couldn't seriously contemplate a relationship with a woman who wasn't.

There was no way this thing with her could have a happy, romantic ending, but he'd meant what he'd said to her. He didn't know what they were doing, but he wasn't ready to stop.

Two things surprised Brittany. The first was that she'd had a sudden desire to talk to Alex about her time with The Professional. Although she hadn't told him everything, she'd been surprised by the cathartic relief she'd felt in telling him what she had.

The second thing that surprised her was the bad case of nerves tightening her stomach as they pulled up in front of Harley's. This was the most public place she'd been since her kidnapping and rescue.

The parking lot was clogged with cars and trucks, attesting to the fact that it was a busy Friday night. Inside would be people she hadn't seen since her kidnapping.

She glanced over to Alex as he steered into a parking place. He was his usual hot self tonight in a pair of black slacks and a short-sleeved white dress shirt. She'd found the familiar scent of his cologne oddly comforting all night long and she'd found his attentiveness to her throughout the meal more than a little bit sexy.

Still, as she looked at the tavern doubts once again roared through her. What if it hadn't been Luke who had come into her house? What if there hadn't been anyone at the window? What if that note had only been a figment of her imagination?

She was feeling healthier, more ready to face the

rest of her life with each day that passed, but no matter how much rational thought she had in her head she couldn't rid herself of a nebulous feeling of dread that somehow the bad things weren't behind her but rather were racing toward her with the speed and power of a locomotive.

Maybe it would all be dispelled now, if she found out that Luke was behind everything, believing he was being funny or trying to get her attention in an inappropriate way.

As they got out of Alex's car she tried to still the nervous flutter in her tummy. Even from the parking lot the sound of the band could be heard, the bass of the drum vibrating in the air, like her heart thundering in her chest.

"Sounds like a happening place," Alex said as he took her arm in his.

"That's because it's the only place in town where you can drink and dance and get a little crazy. And I'll warn you, people do get a little crazy in there."

"Consider me duly warned. And maybe before the night is over I can steal a dance from you."

"You like to dance?" she asked curiously.

"I used to, although Linda didn't like to. She was always afraid she'd slip and fall and hit her head or break a bone."

She tightened her grip on his arm, wondering just how much he'd sacrificed by loving his wife. "Before this night is over, we'll definitely dance," she promised.

Inside Harley's it was dark, smoky and loud. The

band on the stage was a local one, not great but adequate for public consumption. But it wasn't the dimness or the smoke or the noise that overwhelmed her—it was the amount of people who immediately flocked to her.

Friends and acquaintances crowded around her as if she were a visiting rock star. She hugged closer to Alex's side as he maneuvered her toward the bar in the back of the place.

She began to relax as she realized everyone wanted to give her a hug, pat her on the back and tell her how great it was to see her out and around again. There were no awkward questions, only support coming at her in waves.

She smiled as she heard a familiar squeal and a tall blonde came rushing at her. Brittany released her hold on Alex's arm as she was smothered in a tight hug and a fog of familiar perfume.

"OMG," Melissa Winters exclaimed as she stepped back from Brittany. "It's about time you joined the land of the living."

Brittany grinned and at that moment realized how much she'd missed Melissa, who had been one of her very best friends before she had been kidnapped.

Melissa slid her gaze to Alex and then looked back at Brittany. "And when you join the land of the living you definitely do it right!" She held out a hand to Alex. "Melissa Winters, dispatcher at the sheriff's office and former partner in crime with Brittany."

"Alex Crawford, neighbor and friend," Alex replied.

"God, I hope you're more than a friend. She deserves only the best," Melissa exclaimed, making Brittany's cheeks flame with color.

"Why don't you let me buy you both a drink?" Melissa offered.

"Thanks, but I'm just here to speak briefly to Luke. Why don't we try to plan to meet for lunch this week?"

"You mean it? I'd love it, Brittany." Melissa gave her another hug and then went back to the dance floor where her date awaited her.

Brittany looked forward to lunch with Melissa. There had been a time when she and the tall blonde had been nearly inseparable. Melissa had been one of the people who had tried to be there for her after her rescue, but Brittany had pushed her away and instead wrapped herself in a cocoon of isolation.

"You okay?" Alex breathed in her ear.

She smiled and nodded. "Better than okay." It was just as Alex had told her—after the initial flurry of greetings everyone drifted away, leaving her and Alex to continue to make their way to the bar.

The moment she saw Luke she wondered what had ever drawn her to him in the first place. Although he was tall and slender he might have been good-looking without the mop of shaggy brown hair and the growth of whiskers that managed to make him appear unkempt rather than cool. His ears were pierced and a large tattoo of a skull covered one side of his neck.

He'd been her bad-boy rebellion, a choice to make her brothers crazy in an effort to declare herself grown and independent. He was nothing like what she'd choose for herself for anything meaningful or lasting. Luke had simply been a good time for a little while and nothing more.

Still, his features lit up at the sight of her and at the same time she was aware of Alex stepping backward, giving her the opportunity to greet Luke alone.

Luke stepped out around the bar and grabbed her hands in his. "Jeez, you look great, Brittany. I'm so glad to see you."

"Thanks, I'm feeling good about things."

"Man, I've missed you like crazy." He reached one of his hands up as if to caress her face, but she took a step back so his hand fell to his side. His green eyes narrowed as if with a touch of displeasure.

He shoved his hands into his jeans pockets and continued to gaze at her. "So, what's up? I thought I'd hear from you before now. I haven't stopped thinking about you. When I saw you I thought maybe you came in to see me, you know, to kind of pick up where we left off before everything happened."

"Actually, I came in to see you, but I need to ask for my house key back. Luke, we had some fun, but things have changed over the past four months for me. I'm sorry." Even though she'd already changed all the locks on her house, she wanted to see his reaction when she asked for her key back.

"Nothing changed for me, Brit. I've just been waiting for you to come around again, you know, giving you the space I figured you needed after what you'd been through."

As if she really believed he'd just been sitting around waiting for her for the past four months. "I'm sorry, Luke. Like I said, things have changed. I've changed."

"I just thought maybe by now you'd be ready for a few laughs…some good times," he said.

"You were always good for that," she agreed, wondering if his idea of a few good laughs was to scare the hell out of her. "By the way, did you come by my place the other night? Maybe use your key to come inside?"

It was impossible to read his features, but he shook his head negatively. "Now, why would I do something like that?" he countered.

"I don't know, maybe to play a joke of some kind." She desperately wanted it to be him. She needed him to be the explanation for what had happened. A sick joke. A warped sense of humor. A balloon, a break-in and a stupid note—she could accept and forgive that. She just wanted some answers that made sense.

"I don't know what you're talking about. But I see you have a new boyfriend." He gestured toward Alex. "Who is that joker?"

"He's a friend," she replied.

"Yeah, well, I've got to get back to work." He pulled his key ring from his pocket, yanked off the key she'd requested and slid it across the bar. "Have a nice life, Brittany." He didn't wait for her to reply but turned and went back behind the bar.

"You think he did it?" Alex asked as he walked up beside her.

"Hard to tell." She frowned and looked back at Luke, who was flirting with a young blonde at the bar.

"He told me no, but he also said he was kind of waiting around for me to start up our relationship again. He didn't seem too happy when I told him that wasn't going to happen."

"You want to get out of here?" he asked, obviously concerned that she might be upset.

She smiled, refusing to allow Luke's petulance or the fact that she hadn't really gotten an answer from him to ruin her evening. "Not before we have that dance we talked about."

At that moment the band began to play a ballad. "With pleasure," Alex said and led her to the dance floor where he took her into his arms.

Despite the fact that she'd reminded him only an hour before that they would be, could be nothing more than friends, his arms around her felt like home.

That scared her. The Professional had taken her innocence and dignity from her. But she had a feeling if she wasn't careful Alex would take her heart.

Chapter 8

A knock on the door sounded just after ten on Saturday. Brittany had just gotten out of bed, after having lingered for a long time thinking about the night before and dancing with Alex.

She opened the door and was surprised to see Emily clutching a stuffed pink bear in her arms. "Can I come in?" the little girl asked and without waiting for an invitation swept past Brittany and into the living room where she plopped down on the sofa with a frown.

Brittany closed the door and followed, wondering what was going on. "I don't want to be a bother. I just need a minute away from Mr. Poophead Daddy," Emily exclaimed.

Brittany bit back a smile. Ah, trouble in parenting paradise. "I was just about to fix me an English muffin with some jelly. Would you like to join me?"

"That would be lovely," replied the child who had just called her father a poophead.

She followed Brittany into the kitchen, set her bear in one chair and sat in the chair next to the stuffed animal while Brittany pulled out the package of muffins. "Does your daddy know where you are?"

"I told him I was running away and never, ever coming back again." Emily lifted her chin as if in a show of defiance.

"I see you brought a friend with you."

Emily nodded. "This is Lady Bear. She's my bestest friend in the whole wide world."

"She's a lovely bear. Maybe we should call your daddy and let him know where you and Lady Bear are so he won't worry too much," Brittany suggested as she put the muffins in the toaster.

At that moment the phone rang. Brittany was unsurprised to hear Alex's voice when she answered. "I know this sounds crazy, but is Emily there?"

"She is. We're just about to sit down to eat a muffin and jelly," Brittany replied.

"Tell Mr. Poophead I don't want to talk to him," Emily said.

"She doesn't want to talk to you right now," Brittany said into the phone.

"She called me a poophead, didn't she?" Alex heaved a deep sigh. "I'm sorry she's bothering you with this. I'll come down and get her."

"No, it's okay. She needs some time. I'll walk her home after we've had a little girl talk."

He hesitated. "Are you sure? This definitely isn't your problem."

"I'm positive and our muffins just popped up from the toaster, so I'll see you later." Brittany hung up the phone and then slathered the muffins with butter and grape jelly. "Milk or juice?" she asked.

"Milk, please."

Once the drinks and muffins were on the table Brittany sat next to Emily. "Want to talk about it?"

Emily took a bite of her muffin, leaving a smear of grape jelly on her cheek. Brittany picked up her napkin, leaned forward and swiped it off. Emily smiled gratefully and then her smile fell.

"Megan has a birthday party this afternoon and Daddy said I could go. I already got her a present and wrapped it in really pretty pink-and-purple paper and now he says he has a meeting and can't take me. Megan is one of my bestest friends in school and I have to go to her party or else her feelings will be hurt." Her lower lip puffed out a bit. "Daddy is such a poophead."

"Can't your grandma take you to the party?" Brittany asked.

Emily took a swallow of her milk, leaving a milk mustache on her upper lip, and then shook her head. "She has a woman meeting about something. Mr. Poophead said I have to go with him to his meeting and be a good girl 'cause it is about a big job for him. So, I runned away. Can I have another muffin?"

Brittany got up to fix the muffin and her mind whirled. *Don't get involved,* a little voice whispered in her head. *It's just a ride to a party,* another voice replied. *What else do you have to do with your afternoon?*

"What's Megan's last name?" she asked as she placed the second muffin in front of Emily.

"Megan Jefferson, and I bought her a really cool pink purse with sequins and she's one of my very best friends and she'll be so sad if I can't come to her party." Emily was on a tangent, repeating herself in her frustration. "You go to a friend's party, that's what you're supposed to do. It's like a rule for little girls."

Brittany knew the Jefferson family. She'd been friendly with Megan's mother, who worked at the bank. "Maybe I could take you to your party." The words were out of Brittany's mouth before she'd realized they'd formed in her brain.

"Really? You could do that?" Emily jumped out of her chair and threw her arms around Brittany's neck. "That would be so wonderful." Her kiss on Brittany's cheek was sweet and slightly sticky from the jelly.

Brittany laughed. "Why don't you finish up your muffin and then we'll talk to Mr. Poophead to make sure it's okay with him?"

Minutes later they walked down the sidewalk to Alex's house. As Emily chattered about the party, Brittany thought about the night before. She and Alex had shared not one dance, but three before leaving Harley's. She hadn't gotten the answers she'd sought from Luke, but the night out had been yet one more step in her re-emergence into life.

When they'd reached her house once again she'd

known that Alex wouldn't have minded if she'd invite him in for another bout of lovemaking, but she'd kissed him on the cheek and thanked him for the night.

She desperately wanted to make love to him again and that's why she wasn't going to let it happen. Her heart was getting too involved and she had to make decisions now that were best for both of them.

Taking Emily to a birthday party as a favor was one thing; feeling the warmth of Alex's arms around her, the strength of his naked body against hers was quite another.

She would never again be the deputy she'd once thought herself to be and she would never be the woman Alex and Emily needed in their lives.

Alex greeted them at the door, his brow furrowed with concern as he looked first at his daughter then at Brittany. "I'm so sorry," he began.

Brittany held up a hand to halt his apology. "Emily tells me she has a birthday party to attend this afternoon and you and Rose aren't available to take her."

"I'm meeting a guy this afternoon who wants his basement remodeled. Today was the only time he had to meet with me," Alex explained. "It's a big job and I tried to explain to Emily that sometimes business has to come first."

"I have an alternative plan," Brittany said.

"She said if it's okay with you she'll take me to Megan's party," Emily exclaimed. "Tell her it's okay, Daddy. Please, please!"

"Daddy? What happened to Mr. Poophead?" Alex asked with a raised dark eyebrow and a wry grin.

Emily sidled up next to him and gave him a sweet smile. "I was just upset, Daddy. I didn't really think you were Mr. Poophead."

Alex rolled his eyes and Brittany stifled a giggle. "I really don't mind taking her to the party," Brittany said. "I have nothing going on this afternoon."

"I'd hate to impose," Alex said.

"As if I haven't imposed on you before," Brittany replied drily.

"If you're sure…" he responded.

"Oh, she's sure," Emily said. "And it was all her idea, not mine." She clapped her hands together with excitement.

"That's true," Brittany agreed. "Now, all I need to know is what time."

"The party is from two to four. My appointment is at two-thirty and I'm not sure how long it will take me," Alex replied.

"Why don't I take her to the party and then bring her back to my place and you can get her there when you're finished?" Brittany asked.

"That sounds like a plan." Emily beamed at both of them.

"Then I'll be here at around a quarter till two and we'll go from there." Brittany smiled at Emily. "I know how important birthday parties are."

"I knew you'd understand." Emily gave her a smile that bordered on hero worship. "Girls understand these things."

"Why don't you take Lady Bear upstairs and make sure your present is all ready to take?" Alex suggested.

"Okay. See you later, Brittany." On light little feet she raced up the stairs and disappeared.

When she was gone Alex turned back to face Brittany. "I think perhaps my daughter is a little bit of a manipulator."

"Goes with the female genes," Brittany said with a smile. "Really, it's okay. I know the Jefferson family and it's not a big deal."

"It's a big deal to Emily, so I thank you."

When he smiled at her like that she wanted to fall into his arms. Instead she murmured a goodbye and stepped out the door. She'd been vastly relieved when Benjamin had called to let her know that Alex Crawford was exactly what he'd told her he was—a former attorney who had lost his wife. There had been no red flags in his background. The man didn't even have a speeding ticket on his record.

He was the kind of man she might have wanted in her life forever, if she were a different kind of woman. At least nothing had happened in the past couple of days to scare her. But unfortunately, nothing had happened in the same few days to clear up the mystery of the man at her window and the disappearing note.

She felt as if she were in a curious state of limbo, not quite willing to trust her own mind yet refusing to admit that she was losing it.

As she entered her house she shoved all these thoughts to the back of her mind. All she needed to

think about for the afternoon was getting a little girl
to a birthday party.

At one forty-five when Brittany pulled up in Alex's
driveway Emily danced out the door. She had Lady
Bear in one arm and a pretty pink-and-purple wrapped
package in the other. Alex followed after her and as
Emily got into the backseat he walked around to the
driver window.

"Thanks again," he said. "I should be home by the
time the party is over."

"I'll just take her back to my house and you can call
when you're home," Brittany replied.

Within minutes they were on their way to the Jeffersons'. "I'm so excited. I love birthday parties and
this is the first one I've been to since we moved here,"
Emily said. "Do you like birthday parties?"

"It's been a long time since I've been to one," Brittany replied. She hoped there were no red balloons to
remind her of anything bad.

"There's cake and ice cream and games," Emily
continued. "When is your birthday?"

"In less than two months," Brittany replied.

"Maybe I could have a party for you. We could
have a big cake and chocolate ice cream, and you and
me and Daddy could play party games. You could be
queen for the day."

Brittany flashed a quick smile at Emily as she
pulled into the Jeffersons' driveway. "We'll see." She
had no idea how things would be in two months' time,
but she had a feeling she and Emily and Alex wouldn't
be having a birthday party together.

She parked the car and then turned to the little girl. "Maybe it would be best if we let Lady Bear stay here in the car," she suggested. Brittany remembered that little girls could be cruel and Emily showing up clutching her favorite stuffed animal might set her up for some jabs.

Emily frowned thoughtfully. "Maybe you're right," she conceded.

"Why don't we put her in the backseat? We'll buckle her in with the seat belt so she'll be safe and sound."

"That sounds like a plan," Emily replied with what Brittany had discerned was her favorite phrase.

They buckled the bear in and then walked to the front door.

Mary Jefferson greeted Brittany with a smile of delight. "It's so good to see you," she exclaimed as she opened the front door. "I've missed seeing you at the bank."

"Thanks, it's good to see you, too. I just came by to drop off Emily Crawford for Megan's party."

"Oh, please join us, unless you have someplace else to go." Mary smiled conspiratorially. "To be honest, I wouldn't be adverse to adult company to kind of even the odds. You know, the two of us against thirteen squealing, giggling six-year-old girls."

Emily smiled and grabbed Brittany's hand. "It's okay. You can stay. It's gonna be fun."

"Sure, I'd be glad to help out," Brittany agreed.

By the time they'd walked through the neat living room, the sound of the party drifted in from the backyard. When Mary opened the back door Emily dropped Brittany's hand and ran toward her friends, who were gathered in a tight-knit circle and seemed to be doing a group squeal.

Mary motioned Brittany into a chair at an umbrella table nearby. "I figure I'll give them about thirty minutes to work off some energy and then do some organized games and the cake and ice-cream thing. How about a glass of iced tea or something?"

"No, thanks. I'm fine."

"You look great. I've thought about you often over the past couple of months," Mary said.

"It's taken me a couple of months to get back on my feet and feel good about getting out and around," Brittany replied. She tensed, waiting for the uncomfortable questions to come.

"Well, it's good to see it finally happening." She then began chatting about the joys of parenting a six-year-old, the challenges of birthday parties and how happy she was to have an adult to talk to while the party took place.

Brittany found herself relaxing and realized she'd done her town a disservice in not embracing the support so many of the people had offered her after her ordeal.

She gave herself to the joy of participating in the party atmosphere, and there was such joy. As she laughed with the girls at silly antics and watched Megan's delight as she opened her presents, she found a happiness she didn't know was possible.

As she ate ice cream and cake next to Emily, she

enjoyed the girlish chatter about school activities and Justin Bieber's hair and pink shoes with sparkly heels.

There was an innocence here that soothed her, a shining promise for the future among these children who had the possibility of all things good gleaming from their eyes.

Was this why people had children? Because they filled the world with laughter and believed in Easter bunnies and Santa Claus? Was it because it was impossible to be in a bad mood when a little girl giggled or gave you an impulsive hug?

"Do you miss your mommy?" Emily asked when the party was over and they were back in the car driving to Brittany's house.

"Yes, sometimes I do." Brittany slid her gaze sideways to the little girl. "Do you miss yours?"

Emily frowned thoughtfully. "I mostly don't remember mine. Daddy tells me stuff about her sometimes, but I don't really remember her by myself much at all. But I had such fun at the party. Did you have fun?"

"I did," Brittany agreed as she pulled into her driveway.

"You looked funny when you played Pin the Tail on the Donkey." Emily giggled. "You pinned the tail on his nose!"

Brittany laughed. "I guess I need a little more practice." She parked the car and saw Alex sitting on her stoop. "Oh, look, your daddy is here."

Emily jumped out of the car carrying a big purple balloon and a handful of party favors and ran toward her dad, who stood as Brittany opened her car door. Brittany tried to still the leap of her heart at the sight of him.

Drat that man with his white T-shirt, worn jeans and the tool belt that hung low around his sexy lean hips. Why did he have to make her heart beat so fast? Why did the mere sight of him have to make her want to leap into his arms?

"Daddy, we had so much fun and I got a balloon and some candy and a paper purse that I can color any color I want. I'm going to make it pink with yellow stripes. Don't you think that will be pretty?"

"I think that will be beautiful," he agreed and his gaze shifted from Emily to Brittany.

"Did you get the job?" she asked.

"I did." A sense of pride deepened his voice. "It's a full basement remodel and should keep me busy through most of the summer."

"That's good."

"I guess I'll get the kid home and try to unwind her from all the sugar I'm sure she had at the party."

Brittany smiled. "Good luck with that. I think I have a little sugar crash in my future, too."

"Emily, tell Brittany thanks for taking you," he instructed.

Emily wrapped her arms around Brittany's waist and hugged her tight. "Thank you, thank you!"

Brittany leaned down to return the hug. Just before Emily released her she took her hand and lightly caressed Brittany's cheek. Her green eyes sparkled with determination. "I know I'll never, ever forget you in my whole life."

And then she and Alex were walking away and Brittany stared after them, tears burning in her eyes. She'd been so afraid that Alex might steal her heart but already his daughter had torn off a huge chunk that she had a feeling she'd never get back.

It was almost ten and Alex sat on the sofa, Emily sprawled next to him sleeping. She'd begged him to let her stay up late since it was Saturday night so they'd decided to watch a movie. It wasn't long after the intro credits had rolled that she'd fallen asleep.

He should have moved her to her own bed an hour ago, but instead he'd remained next to her, just enjoying the sweet bubble-bath scent of her.

Getting the remodeling job had only confirmed to him that he was where he belonged, doing what he was supposed to do. With the real-estate market in the tank, many homeowners were opting for remodeling rather than selling their homes and he had a feeling that once word got out that he was good and dependable he'd have more work than he knew what to do with.

He'd consciously willed himself not to think about Brittany all day, but it had been difficult. Thoughts of her struck him at the craziest times.

As he'd slipped into his shoes that morning he'd remembered how badly he'd wanted to take hers off after they'd gotten back to her place from Harley's.

Those sexy strappy black heels had made him half-insane.

He'd not only wanted to take off her shoes, but also slide that sexy black dress from her body and carry her to her room where they would make love until dawn. But that hadn't happened. She'd shut him down with a quick good-night kiss on her doorstep.

He would be finishing up her deck Monday and maybe then it would be easier to gain some distance from her. And he needed distance. He was definitely getting too close, wanting more of her than she'd indicated she wanted to give back to him.

Friends with benefits was fine as long as nobody's heart got involved, but his heart was already pretty far gone.

He rubbed Emily's back, deciding it was time to get her into bed. When she didn't stir he rose and then scooped her up in his arms.

Her legs wrapped monkey-style around his waist and her head rested on his shoulder and his love for her roared like a lion inside him.

She needed a mom who could take her shopping and talk about girl stuff. She needed a mom who could hold her when she cried and tell her everything was going to be okay.

Alex worked at being the best father he could be, but in his heart he knew it could never be enough, that little girls needed mommies to be completely well-adjusted.

And Brittany didn't want to be a mom, didn't believe she had what it took to be a mom. How selfish was it of him to stay involved with a woman who had already told him she would never be anything meaningful in his life…in Emily's life?

Emily's room was an explosion of pink. Pink bedspread and curtains, throw pillows and lamp, it was a room for a princess. His little princess. Still holding her in his arms, he pulled down the spread and placed her on the bed.

Sleepily she opened her eyes and smiled at him, a sweet smile that shot through Alex's heart, his very soul. The moment was fleeting and then a tiny frown danced across her forehead. "Where's Lady Bear?"

Uh-oh. A sinking feeling overwhelmed Alex as he realized he hadn't seen the beloved pink bear all evening. "You stay right here. I'll go downstairs and see if I can find her."

He left her bedside, hoping he could easily find the stuffed animal, or if he didn't, that she would have fallen back asleep by the time he returned to her room and they could do a full search in the morning.

He did a cursory search downstairs without the bear showing up and then climbed the stairs once again, hoping this wasn't going to be a big deal.

Emily hadn't fallen back asleep; rather she was sitting up in the bed, a look of wild panic in her eyes. "Did you find her, Daddy?"

"I didn't, but I'm sure we'll find her in the morning," he replied.

"No! I need her now. You know I sleep with Lady Bear every night." Tears welled up in her eyes, breaking Alex's heart. He knew how important that bear was to her.

"When was the last time you had Lady Bear?" he asked, knowing that there was no way Emily would go back to sleep without that bear in her arms.

Emily's frown deepened as tears trekked down her cheeks. "I took her to the party."

Alex groaned inwardly. It was already after ten; he wasn't eager to call the Jefferson home to find out if a pink bear might have been left there.

"But I didn't take Lady Bear into the party," Emily said. She swiped at her tears. "She's in Brittany's car. We buckled her into the backseat before we went into the party. That's where she is!"

"I'll tell you what, I'll call Grandma and see if she can come up and sit with you for a few minutes so that I can go to Brittany's and get Lady Bear."

Emily threw her arms around him. "Oh, thank you, Daddy. You're the best in the whole wide world."

"You stay here in bed. I'll be right back." Alex left Emily's room and went into his own. Thankfully he knew that Rose wasn't an early-to-bed kind of woman. He was sure she wouldn't mind coming down for a few minutes while he retrieved the beloved bear.

Within fifteen minutes he was opening his front door to allow Rose inside. She'd driven down since it was after dark and she greeted him with a smile of humor. "There's nothing so dire as a missing Lady Bear at bedtime."

"You've got that right," he agreed. "At least we know where Lady Bear is and it should only take me five minutes to get it, but I didn't want to leave her here alone while I ran down to Brittany's and I also didn't want to get her out of bed and all revved up again."

"Go, get the bear and in the meantime I'll go sit with Emily and tell her a story. Maybe I can get her back to sleep before you come back home. My bedtime stories are usually boring enough to put anyone to sleep."

"Without her bear, good luck with that," he said drily.

He stepped out into the warm night air and wondered if perhaps he should have called Brittany to let her know he was coming. But he had a feeling she wasn't an early-to-bed kind of person, either, and it was only a few minutes after ten.

It was a perfect night, the moon almost full overhead and the scent of dewy grass and flowers hanging in the air. Alex walked leisurely, enjoying the sound of crickets chirping and the relative hush of a small town at night.

In Chicago at this time of night there would have been the rush of traffic, sirens blowing and bus brakes squeaking. The city had been a cacophony of noise he definitely didn't miss.

As he approached Brittany's house he saw a light shining dimly from some room in the back of the house. Good, she was still awake. Her car was parked in the driveway and by the light of the moon he could see Lady Bear in the backseat, appearing to give him a gleeful smile.

He was about to head to the front door when something caught his attention…a shadow…a faint noise… he wasn't sure what, but something drew him around the side of the house.

Noise. It was definitely a faint noise that didn't belong in the stillness of the night. Maybe somebody was trying to steal some of the lumber that was still back there. He rounded the corner to the back of the house and froze.

A figure stood at one of the back windows. The man obviously didn't see Alex as he worked to remove the screen from the window. He was clad in black jeans, a black T-shirt and wore a ski mask over his face.

Brittany's phantom. The words thundered in Alex's head. He wasn't a figment of her imagination. He was as real as the sudden rapid heartbeat in Alex's chest.

He must have made a noise…something that alerted the man of his presence. For a split second Alex saw the glittering eyes beneath the mask and then the man whirled and ran in the opposite direction.

Alex took off after him. There was no way he wanted the man to get away. The man jumped the chain-link fence that surrounded Brittany's next-door neighbor's backyard and Alex followed, easily clearing the fence without trouble.

His only thought was to catch the man, to find out who he was behind his mask, who was tormenting Brittany. What had been his intention in trying to take off the screen? To get inside? To harm her in some way?

Alex was in good physical shape but apparently so was the man he chased, who sprinted over the other side of the fence and continued to run.

By the time Alex had chased him for three blocks his heart felt as if it might explode in his chest and the only sound he could hear was his own gasping breaths. Still he pushed on, keeping the man in his sights as he tried to gain ground.

Desperation drove him, burning in his chest as they continued to race. As the masked man turned a corner, Alex pushed harder, faster but by the time he turned the same corner the man was gone.

Alex halted, eyeing the darkness before him as he tried to catch his breath. He had no idea in what direction the man had run, no way to know how to catch him. He'd disappeared, as if the very night had swallowed him whole.

For several minutes Alex remained stock-still, watching the darkness all around, trying to get a sense of where he might have gone, but it was no use.

With a sense of failure, he turned and headed back to Brittany's house. His chest ached from his exertion, as did his leg muscles, but he was eager to get to her, to tell her that she wasn't going crazy.

Then it suddenly struck him and he didn't know what was worse—the fact that she wasn't losing her mind or the knowledge that somebody was really after her.

The Real Professional, that was how he liked to think of himself. He leaned against the side of a house to catch his breath. Adrenaline flushed through him, pumping blood through his veins with a power that made him feel more alive than he'd ever felt in his life.

It had almost happened. He'd almost gotten to her. He'd almost gotten caught. He wasn't sure which made his heart pound faster.

When he knew that his pursuer was gone, he left the side of the house and hurried to his truck parked along the curb in the distance.

He'd almost made it happen...the beginning of a new reign of terror for Black Rock. He'd read and re-searched everything he'd been able to find about Larry Norwood and his crimes, crimes that had been left in-complete in Black Rock.

He intended to re-create those crimes and make sure they were done right. He was going to kidnap five women and then kill them slowly, one at a time.

He'd worked for the past month in a shed on the back of an abandoned property and now everything was ready for the party he'd throw, a party that would have the entire town talking about The Real Profes-sional instead of The Professional, who hadn't man-aged to finish what he'd started.

People would tremble in their beds at night. They would respect his cunning, his cleverness and his evil.

Sliding into his truck, he tamped down both the ex-citement and the tinge of disappointment that threat-ened to consume him. It was all supposed to have started tonight, but unfortunately his plans had been ruined.

No problem, he told himself as he started the

engine. There was always tomorrow. He placed the syringe and Taser in the glove box. It was amazing what you could buy on the internet. The Taser would have incapacitated her long enough for him to inject her with the drug that would have knocked her unconscious and lasted until he could take her to the special place he'd built.

Of course, he couldn't completely replicate The Professional's crime. Most of the original victims who had escaped had now left town and were no longer available to meet the fate they should have before.

But one thing was certain. It all had to begin with Brittany.

She had been the first taken in the original crime and she would be the first in his crimes. It was just a matter of time, but she was marked to attend the "party" that had never happened. He was The Real Professional, better and smarter than the original, and the town of Black Rock would talk about him long after he'd moved on.

Chapter 9

The rapid knock on her front door tore Brittany from her sofa with a startled gasp. She was clad only in a pair of soft black cotton shorty pajamas with tiny pink hearts all over them. She cursed the fact that her robe was in the bedroom and wondered who was at her door at this time of the night.

The knock came again. "Brittany, it's me."

She hurried to the door at the sound of Alex's voice. When she unlocked it and opened it, he flew in, his eyes wild and his breathing rapid.

"What's wrong?" she asked, immediately feeling the urgency wafting from him.

He flashed her a tight smile. "I need your phone and I found your sanity."

She pointed to the phone on her end table. "What do you mean you found my sanity?"

He walked over to the phone, picked up the receiver and quickly dialed. "Rose, this is going to take longer than I expected. She's asleep? Good. I'll be home as soon as I can."

"Where did you find my sanity?" Brittany asked again when he'd hung up. She felt as if she were going to scream if he didn't explain himself immediately.

"At your back window where I saw a man in a ski mask trying to remove your screen. Call your brother."

"You saw him?" Brittany remained frozen in place, her heart beginning a rumbling rhythm.

"I not only saw him, I chased him for almost five blocks before I lost him in the darkness. Now, call Tom. He was real and he was trying to get into your house."

She wasn't going crazy! There had been a man in a ski mask at her window, a note left behind. Somehow, someway The Professional was back and she wasn't losing her mind.

She dialed Tom's number. "You need to come here right away," she said when he answered. "Somebody tried to break into my house and I'm not going crazy. Alex caught him midact and tried to catch him but he got away."

She hung up and looked at Alex. "He's on his way." She had no idea if he reached for her or she reached for him, but suddenly she was in his arms, his heart beating as fast as her own.

"I'm not crazy," she said into the front of his T-shirt.

"No, you aren't," he replied softly.

"Somebody is really after me."

He tightened his arms around her and hesitated a moment. "Yes, apparently somebody is after you."

She raised her head and looked up at him. "Why?"

"I don't know, but we're going to find out."

She remained in Alex's arms until Tom arrived. He wasn't alone. Brittany's brothers Benjamin and Caleb were with him.

"What were you doing here?" Tom asked Alex, who had sat on the sofa next to Brittany as her brother began to ask him questions. Caleb and Benjamin had gone outside to look at the window.

Brittany looked at Alex. She hadn't thought to ask him what had brought him to her house. "Lady Bear," he said to her and then looked at Tom. "My daughter's favorite stuffed animal is in Brittany's car. We didn't realize it until I tried to put Emily to bed so I came down here to retrieve it and that's when I heard a noise and followed it around to the back of the house and saw the man at Brittany's back window."

"What did he look like?" Tom had out a small notepad and pen and was poised to take notes.

"Black T-shirt, black jeans and a ski mask." Alex fought the impulse to reach over and take one of Brittany's hands in his.

"He left me a note," Brittany said.

Tom frowned. "A note?"

"The last time I called you about seeing him. After

you left I found it. It said, 'It's party time.'" She explained about deciding to wait until morning to call Tom and then that the note had disappeared.

"Why didn't you call me back that night?" Tom asked with exasperation.

Brittany lifted her chin and glared at her brother. "Because that night you thought the man was a figment of my imagination. You thought I'd be fine with a little therapy."

Tom looked chagrined. "Okay, let's concentrate on the here and now." He looked at Alex once again. "Anything else you can tell me about the man you saw?"

"Shorter than me, slender and fast as hell," Alex replied. "I chased him for four or five blocks and then lost sight of him at the corner of Elm and Apple Lane."

"The red balloon tied to my mailbox, the ski mask and the note, it's just like before," Brittany said, fighting against the shiver that tried to creep up her spine. "I know Larry Norwood is dead. But I think this is some sort of a copycat."

"Maybe it's just a kid trying to freak you out," Tom replied.

"It's more than that," Benjamin said as he and Caleb came into the living room. "He was definitely trying to get inside. The screen was cut and half-off and the window is cracked just above the lock. I'd guess another couple of minutes and he would have been inside."

"And why would he want to get inside?" Brittany asked, but nobody replied.

"Benjamin and I are going to head out," Caleb said. "We'll check out the neighborhood, see if we find anything or see anyone."

Tom nodded and looked at Brittany. "And you're coming home with me tonight. I don't want you here alone until we can get a full security system installed."

She started to protest, not wanting to leave her home, but she also didn't want to be stupid. There was nothing to say that the man wouldn't return later that night. "All right," she agreed. "I'll go pack a suitcase and first thing tomorrow morning I'll make arrangements for a security system to be installed."

She looked at Alex. Her instinct was to run into his arms once again, to feel his warmth, the security of his strong embrace. "My car keys are on the kitchen counter if you want to get Lady Bear." The best thing she could do for Alex and Emily was distance herself from them.

Somebody was after her and she had no idea how dangerous he might be. There was no way she wanted Alex or Emily tangled up in this mess.

As Alex left to go into the kitchen to get her keys and retrieve the bear, Brittany turned back to her brother. "I want my gun back," she said.

He frowned. "That gun was yours because you were my deputy. Are you ready to come back to duty?"

She wanted to. She desperately wanted that part of her life back, but she couldn't forget that dark moment in the shed with The Professional. She truly believed she wasn't fit for duty and it broke her heart.

"No," she finally said, her voice a mere whisper.

Tom studied her for a long moment. "Go pack your bag. We'll sort things out later."

She was in her bedroom throwing things into a small suitcase when Alex came into the room. He placed his hands on her shoulders and gazed at her somberly. "Are you okay?"

"I hate leaving my house, I hate what is happening, but yeah, I guess I'm okay," she replied.

He stroked a light caress down her cheek with the tips of his fingers. "At least I'll know you're okay with your brother."

She forced a smile. "I'll be fine. Go home, Alex. Take Lady Bear and I'll talk to you later."

Within minutes Alex was gone and Brittany was putting her suitcase in the back of Tom's patrol car. Caleb and Benjamin were still canvassing the area but Brittany had little hope that they would find anything useful.

"Just what we need, a copycat," Tom said in disgust as he pointed the car toward the house where he, his wife, Peyton, and little Lilly lived.

"Are there any other missing women in town?" Brittany asked.

"None that have been reported." His jawline was tense, as was his grip on the steering wheel. "As if Larry Norwood weren't enough now we have to have some wannabe running around town."

"Running around me," Brittany replied darkly.

Tom shot her a quick glance. "I'm sorry I didn't believe you the first time. The balloon…the man at the window—I dismissed your concerns and for that I'm really sorry."

She reached out and placed a hand on his arm. "Apology accepted." She dropped her hand and leaned back in her seat. "To be honest I was beginning to think I was losing my mind."

"You should have told me about the note."

She shrugged. "When it disappeared I didn't figure there was any point in telling you. I thought you'd just write it off as some delusion I was suffering."

"But that means somebody was in your house."

She nodded. "I know. I changed my locks the next day and Friday night Alex and I went to Harley's to talk to Luke to ask him if maybe he'd been inside my house playing one of his stupid jokes. Of course he denied it."

"Maybe it's time I have a talk with Luke," Tom replied as he pulled into his driveway.

Brittany released a sigh. "I can't imagine Luke having anything to do with this. It's not a joke, Tom. If this truly is a copycat, then he'd be trying to replicate the original crime." A wave of horror swept over her as the full realization struck her.

"I was the first one taken in the original crime. If he's repeating everything, then I'll be the first woman kidnapped again this time around."

The sense of dread that had been with her for so long now roared inside her because she knew if she had to go through it all again, this time she wouldn't survive.

* * *

"I won't be chased out of my house," Brittany told Tom the next morning. She'd slept surprisingly well in Tom and Peyton's spare bedroom considering the events of the night before.

She'd gone to bed afraid and had awakened angry. She'd lost almost eight months of living her life and enjoying her home to The Professional. Four of those months she'd been locked in a cell in a shed. She wasn't going to lose another day of her life because of him. "Besides, we can't know for sure that this is a copycat at work. It still could be just some kid having fun at my expense."

"Brittany, you have to be reasonable," Tom began.

"I am being reasonable," she exclaimed. "I've already called Bob Lockheart. He's going to meet me at the house in an hour to install a state-of-the-art security system and you're going to give me back my service revolver until this is all over."

"Of course he is," Peyton said firmly as she grabbed her husband's arm. "And if he doesn't then I have my own handgun that I'll be more than happy to loan to you."

Tom looked at his wife and then back at Brittany. "What, is this some sort of a female conspiracy? Brittany, this isn't a game."

"You're right," she replied sharply. "It's my life and I'm tired of hiding from it." She drew a deep breath and released it slowly. "Tom, I'm not being stupid or irresponsible. With a security system and a weapon, nobody is going to be able to get me. I want to be in my house. I need to be in my house, living my life. If I can't do that then I might as well have died at the hands of Larry Norwood," she ended in frustration.

Tom ran a hand down his face, the gesture doing nothing to erase the lines of worry. "We almost lost you once, Brittany. I just don't want to make any mistakes here." His voice was filled with an emotion she rarely heard. She stepped toward him and he embraced her in a tight hug.

"You're a good sheriff, Tom," she said when he released her. "And Benjamin, Caleb and Jacob are good deputies. You'll figure this out and in the meantime I'll make sure I stay as safe as possible."

Half an hour later she was headed back to her house with her gun stuffed in her waistband and, if she were to admit it to herself, a little bit of fear riding in her heart.

The easy way out would have been to stay with Tom and Peyton or any of her other brothers and their wives, but that would have simply made her a prisoner all over again.

She had absolutely no idea who she couldn't trust, but she knew with certainty who she could—her brothers and Alex. Those were the only men she'd allow close to her until this whole ordeal was over.

There was no way to know if it was somebody trying to replicate the original crimes. There simply wasn't enough evidence to support the theory, but she had to function with the possibility that it might be.

As she pulled into her driveway she was surprised

to see Jacob sitting on her front porch. He was another victim of The Professional, but in a different way.

As an FBI agent working in Kansas City, Jacob had hunted Larry Norwood when he'd kidnapped five women in that city. Larry had even had phone contact with him, taunting calls that had made Jacob an intimate participant of the crime. Unfortunately, Larry had managed to complete his "party" in Kansas City and Jacob had been left to pick up the pieces, to see the victims in death.

The result had been that he'd quit the FBI and moved into a cabin on the Graysons' family property where he lived like a hermit until Norwood began his games in Black Rock.

"Don't you have anything better to do than hang around here?" she asked as she carried her suitcase up the walk to the porch.

"Figured I'd hang out until Lockheart arrives to install that security system." He took the suitcase from her. "I see you're armed." He nodded toward the gun at her waist.

"And dangerous," she added as she unlocked her front door. He followed her in and set the suitcase in the foyer. "How about some coffee? I can have a pot made in a jiffy."

"Sounds good," he agreed. He locked the door behind him and then followed her through the living room and into the kitchen.

"Sure you want to be here, Brittany?"

"No place else I'd rather be." She pulled the coffee can from the cabinet and set about getting it brewing as he sank down into a chair at the table and watched her.

"Got any ideas?" he asked once the scent of the fresh brew began to fill the air.

"Not really." She sank into the chair opposite him. "I told Tom he might want to check out Luke Mathis down at Harley's. Luke and I were hanging out before I got kidnapped and he had a key to the house before I changed the locks, but I really don't think he's behind all this." She frowned thoughtfully. "I don't know, you might want to talk to Buck Harmon."

"Why Buck?"

"He's been helping Alex on the deck and he's just said some things that make me think he's pretty fascinated with The Professional."

"Half the people in town are fairly fascinated with The Professional," Jacob replied as she got up to get their coffee. "Face it, aberrant behavior is intriguing to most people."

"But most people don't set out to emulate somebody like Norwood," she replied.

Jacob took a cup from her and smiled. "It would be nice if everyone in the world knew how to play nice with others, but if that were the case the Grayson family wouldn't have jobs. And speaking of jobs, when are you coming back to yours?"

Brittany stared down into her coffee cup. As always when she thought of her job she was taken back to that desperate moment in time when she'd realized she'd never be a deputy again.

"Talk to me, Brittany," Jacob said softly. "There

has to be a reason why you've avoided coming back to work. We've both experienced the darkness of The Professional. There's nothing you can say to me that will surprise or horrify me."

Brittany knew that if she were going to talk about it with anyone, it would be Jacob, who had seen the faces of the dead women Larry had left in his wake.

Suddenly she wanted to talk, she wanted to tell him about that moment when she'd lost all sense of herself. "You know what he was capable of, Jacob," she said, her gaze once again on the coffee in her cup. "Every day he'd sit and tell me how many ways he was going to hurt me, how long it would take him before he'd finally kill me."

She felt a swell of emotion fill her chest. "I tried not to listen, tried not to think, not to imagine what he was saying to me, but day after day his words started to seep into my head, into my very soul."

Jacob said nothing, as if knowing that no words he offered could make this any easier for her. He simply sat completely still, his gaze intent on her.

"For the first week I spent every waking moment trying to find a way out, looking for any weakness I could exploit to escape, but there was none. By the time a month had passed he'd gotten into my head, Jacob." The words clogged in her throat as she tried to continue despite the clump of guilt and shame that rose up in the back of her mouth.

She raised her coffee cup and took a sip, trying to swallow around the lump. Jacob remained patient, not blinking an eyelid as he waited for her. Carefully she set the cup back on the table. "There was one night when he left me alone that my fear spiraled completely out of control."

She stared at her brother, remembering that moment of despair that she'd never, ever felt before in her life and hoped to never feel again. "I wanted to die, Jacob." The words were a mere whisper. "I wanted to die on my own terms, not on his. I wanted to commit suicide."

Her words hung in the air, stark and ugly, and yet with them came the release of a pressure she hadn't realized she possessed.

Jacob took a sip of his coffee and leaned back in the chair. "The only difference between you and me is that you looked for a way to end your pain immediately and I holed up in the cabin and tried to end my pain by drinking myself to death and cutting myself off from any human contact. That doesn't make us bad lawmen, Brittany. It makes us human."

She stared at him. She wasn't sure what she had expected, but acceptance and understanding hadn't been it. A bit more of the pressure in her chest released.

"Brittany, a lawman who doesn't know fear is a dangerous one, one who I would never want to work with. Fear is the way your body tells you that you're in danger. And that moment when you wanted to take your own life and not let him take it, don't fool yourself—if that's what you'd really wanted, you would have found a way. You're a survivor, Brittany, and instead of feeling guilty or ashamed about that time, you should celebrate the fact that you got through it."

Brittany thought it was the longest speech she'd ever heard Jacob say and she knew deep in her heart that he was right. Had she had a moment of weakness? Of wishing she would die before Larry Norwood could torture her to death? Absolutely. But it had only lasted very briefly and then she'd gotten on with the act of survival.

Just then Bob Lockheart arrived to install the security system. Jacob hung around for another hour and then left after Brittany insisted she'd be okay by herself. By two that afternoon she was alone in a house that had the security of a castle.

Her talk with Jacob had given her a peace she hadn't had since her rescue. She'd felt such shame about giving up all hope, such despair that she'd known such weakness. But she also knew the situation she'd found herself in had been one that few people would ever experience. And Jacob was right. She had survived. With the weight of self-loathing out of her heart, her thoughts turned to Alex.

She'd scarcely had time to talk to him last night before Tom had whisked her away. She eyed the phone. What she wanted more than anything was to hear the sound of his voice, to be in his arms, and that was exactly why she wasn't going to call him.

There was somebody after her, a man who might be trying to copy the original crimes of The Professional. At the moment her world was an unsafe place and the last thing she wanted was to bring Alex or his daughter into that world.

She knew it all had to come to an end, that their relationship was going nowhere. As much as she adored Emily she wasn't in a place to take on the role of motherhood.

Friends with benefits, that's all it was supposed to be, and now it was time to end even that. He'd be over first thing in the morning to finish up the last of the details on her deck and ultimately that's all she'd wanted from him, that's all she could accept from him.

Chapter 10

Alex had thought about Brittany all night on Saturday and most of the day Sunday. He'd hoped to hear from her during that time but when he didn't he figured she was probably busy with her brothers.

He hadn't meant to fall in love with anyone. He especially hadn't meant to fall in love with her, but Monday morning as he left his house it was love for her that accompanied him.

He'd fallen in love with her and he wanted to build a life with her. She'd said she wasn't the motherly type, but every interaction she'd had with Emily had shown him otherwise.

She was not only beautiful and bright, she was also kind and loving, and that's all she needed to be his wife and a stepmother for Emily.

It was crazy that he'd only known her a little over a week and yet knew so clearly what was in his heart for her. Besides, how long was love supposed to take? Was there a time requirement for the heart to become involved with somebody? No, love had nothing to do with time and everything to do with emotion. And his emotions screamed that he was in love with Brittany Grayson.

When he arrived at her house Gary and Buck were already there. As Alex finished up the last of the woodwork, they were going to do a general cleanup of the yard, picking up scraps of lumber and whatever needed to be done.

"Hey, boss," Buck greeted him. Gary smiled and raised a hand. "We were just wondering if you planned on using us on your next job."

Alex glanced toward the back window, hoping to get a glimpse of Brittany but the window was empty and there was no sign of her.

"Sure, I could use your help. It's going to be a big remodel job that's probably going to run us into the end of summer."

"Cool," Gary said. "My folks will be happy to still see me working."

"You've both been good help," Alex replied. "And now, let's all get to work." Once again he looked at the back window, but there continued to be no sign of Brittany.

Maybe she'd stayed on at her brother's house, he thought as he got busy. It was about noon when he realized she was home. He spied her inside and waved.

What he wanted to do was ask her if she was okay, if any of her brothers had managed to figure out who had tried to break into her house. He wanted to hold her in his arms and assure himself that she was really all right.

The fact that she didn't come outside to say hello concerned him a bit, but he stayed focused on finishing up the last of the work.

By two o'clock he'd sent Gary and Buck home. The work was done, the yard was clean and there was nothing left to do. He knocked on the back door and she appeared. It took her a minute before she got the door open.

He couldn't help the smile that stretched his lips at the sight of her, the very scent of her that wafted in the air. She was dressed in a pair of jeans and a bright yellow T-shirt that enhanced the darkness of her hair, the beauty of her eyes.

When had she become his heart? When had she broken down every barrier he'd ever tried to erect against marrying again?

"We're finished," he said as she gestured him into the house. Once he was inside she keyed in several numbers on a pad next to the back door.

"New security," she said. "Anyone tries to open a door or a window an alarm rings not only through the air, but also directly into the sheriff's office."

"Good idea. How are you doing?" He sensed a distance in her, a distance that created a hard knot of tension in the pit of his stomach. He noticed the gun sitting on the kitchen table. "Looks like you're ready for anything that might come your way."

"Whoever this creep is, we think maybe he wants to re-create the original crime, and that means if he sticks to the script I'll be the first one he attempts to kidnap."

"That's what you think the man was trying to do two nights ago?"

"I can't imagine why else he would have been trying to get into the house."

"Is this the way it happened last time? He took you from here?" The mere thought of what she'd already been through moved him forward a step toward her.

"No, he took me from my car. He was hiding on the floor in the backseat and before I knew he was there he'd slapped a hand across my mouth and stuck a needle in my arm that almost instantly made me unconscious. Whoever this new guy is, it's obvious he's trying to emulate The Professional, and that means I'm probably top on his hit list."

He so wanted to pull her into his arms, to somehow make this right. He wished he had the capacity to find the bad man and put him behind bars where he could never hurt or frighten Brittany again.

But as he took yet another step toward her she stepped back and grabbed her purse. "I'll just write you the check for the balance of what I owe you." She fumbled in her purse and pulled out her checkbook.

She was definitely distant and he was surprised to realize that it scared him, that the hard knot in his chest had grown in size. "How about we have dinner together tonight to celebrate me finishing up the deck?" he suggested.

"I don't think so." She finished with the check and ripped it from the pad, then held it out to him, her dark eyes shuttered so that it was impossible for him to guess what she might be thinking.

He took the check, folded it and stuffed it in his pocket. "Then what about tomorrow night?" He was aware he was pushing it, but he needed to know where he stood, where they stood. "Or the night after that... or the night after that?"

She worked a hand through her hair, as if to unknot an invisible tangle. It was a gesture he'd come to recognize as nerves.

"Alex, my life is complicated right now. I think it's best if we are just neighbors and nothing more."

"But I'm falling in love with you." He hadn't meant to say the words. They'd just spilled from his lips as if unable to stay contained another moment.

For the first time since he'd walked into her kitchen her facade cracked and he saw genuine pain flash in her eyes. "That wasn't part of our deal. I'm not in a place to love or be loved. I told you I certainly wasn't ready to be a mother. We need to stop this, Alex, before either one of us gets in any deeper."

"But I don't want to stop and I'm already in deep. I want you in my life, Brittany. You're everything I ever wanted in a woman."

"I'm not right in your life right now," she exclaimed, the pain still sharp in her gaze. "I'm not even right in my own life right now."

She sat at the table, her gaze not meeting his. "I'm not so different from your wife, Alex. You see me as being strong and in control, but you don't know that I wake up in the middle of the night afraid to draw a breath, afraid to get out of bed and see what might be hiding in the shadows."

"When that happens I can wrap my arms around you and let you know you're safe. You are strong, Brittany. You're nothing like Linda was before her death. And what you and I were building together was something wonderful. Don't throw it all away now."

He could tell his words hadn't broken through to her. Her eyes were once again dark and emotionless. "Does this have something to do with the man who's after you? Are you trying to protect me and Emily?"

She sighed in obvious frustration. "I'm trying to protect you and Emily from me," she exclaimed. "I'm not right for you or for her, and you and I pretending to do the friends-with-benefits thing while doing otherwise is foolish. You're a nice man, Alex. Find a nice woman and build a life for yourself and your daughter."

There was a finality in her words that brooked no further discussion, no reason for him to continue the conversation except for the aching numbness in his heart.

"You'll let me know if there's anything you find with the deck that needs further attention?" he asked stiffly.

"I will."

"And you'll let me know if there's anything, anything on this earth that I can do for you?" His voice held the hollow ring of a man with a breaking heart.

"Goodbye, Alex. And thanks for everything."

He stood for a long moment, memorizing every strand of her shining hair, every facial feature that had brought him such joy. She looked toward the back door, as if wishing him through it. And at that moment he made her wish come true and left.

Brittany buried her face in her hands, fighting against the tears that threatened to fall. It had been harder than she'd expected. She hadn't realized just how deeply Alex and Emily had dug themselves into her heart until now, with the gaping wound of their absence burning in her chest.

She was in love with Alex, and she adored Emily. But she was selfish and flighty. She wasn't the woman Alex believed her to be. She wasn't cut out to be a mother to a needy little girl.

And if that weren't enough, she was now a virtual prisoner in her home, waiting for a madman to make his next move, praying that a new "party" wasn't in her future.

It was her love for Alex that had forced her to push him away, and even if Tom or one of her other brothers managed to get the man after her in jail to-morrow, nothing would change where things stood between them.

It was over. It was finished. She'd had hours of lovemaking with him, a week of the warmth of his arms and the beauty of his smiles. It had to be enough, because she'd never be enough for him and his daughter.

She pulled herself out of the kitchen chair, needing to do something, anything to take her mind off the ache of loss, the despair of what might have been that resonated through her.

She wandered through the house like a lost soul. She should be ecstatic that the deck she'd dreamed about was finished. But she couldn't have a family barbecue anytime soon, not knowing who she might be placing in danger by inviting them to her home.

Pausing in the doorway to her bedroom, the ache in her heart intensified as she remembered that afternoon with Alex in her bed. He'd been a wonderful lover, on every physical and emotional level.

And she'd never know that wonder again. She'd never see him gaze deep into her eyes again with a look that made her feel as if she were the most important person on the face of the earth.

No man had ever made her feel the way Alex had. They'd both been fools, playing with emotions they couldn't control. She moved away from the bedroom and decided to work on her laptop. She should work on Alex's website, but she had no idea where they now stood on that particular project. Maybe a couple of hours of cybersurfing would make her forget that she'd just shoved the man she loved out of her life.

She spent most of the afternoon and early evening on the computer, lost in the minutia of other people's lives. As she read posts her mind worked to try to come up with a suspect.

Larry Norwood, despite being the town vet and a married man with two children, had been a secretive man. He didn't have friends, didn't hang out with male buddies who might have made it onto a suspect list now. There was no indication whatsoever that he had worked with a partner.

She still wasn't sure what to think about Luke. The few phone conversations she'd had with him immediately following her rescue had been awkward, but he hadn't said anything that would make her believe he identified with Larry Norwood in any way.

So, who? Who would want to emulate a serial killer? Somebody powerless, somebody who felt disenfranchised by the town? Certainly Buck fit that description.

She eyed the gun on the table. She'd carried it from room to room with her throughout the afternoon, not letting it out of her sight. Security was all well and good, but there was nothing like a bullet to stop a bad man.

Her phone rang several times during the course of the evening. Each of her brothers called to check in on her. When she spoke to Tom, she told him that when this was all over she would be ready to return to her job as a deputy. He was pleased with her decision and when she hung up the phone after speaking with him she realized if nothing else good came out of this experience, at least she'd regained the dignity, the confidence that Larry Norwood had almost stolen from her.

She'd been a darned good deputy and she'd still be

a good one. She'd almost allowed Larry to take that from her, but Jacob was right, she was only human and that didn't make her less of a good deputy.

It was just after eight when the phone rang again. She steeled herself as she recognized Alex's number on the caller ID. She thought about not answering, but avoidance really wasn't her style.

"Brittany, I'm sorry to bother you but I have a huge favor to ask you." His voice was filled with urgency. "I just got a call from Rose. She thinks she's having a heart attack. I told her to call an ambulance, but I'd like to get to the hospital as quickly as possible and I'd rather Emily not be there with me."

"Of course you can bring her here," Brittany answered without hesitation. She knew Alex wasn't the type to play games. This was real and it was life-and-death and she could definitely understand him not wanting his daughter there.

"I'll be right there." He hung up before she could reply. She hurried to the front door and quickly disarmed the security system, then, remembering the gun on her kitchen table, she ran back into the kitchen to put the weapon in a safer place.

As she picked up the gun, she glanced around the kitchen, trying to figure out where a curious six-year-old wouldn't find it. She finally tucked it into the upper cabinet next to the sink.

"Emily?" she called as she thought she heard somebody at the door. She hurried back through the living room to see headlights in her driveway and Emily getting out of Alex's passenger door.

She clutched Lady Bear in one arm as she raced toward the house. Alex leaned his head out the driver window. "I don't know how long I'll be," he yelled.

"Whenever," Brittany replied as Emily came through the door. They both waved to Alex as he tore out of the driveway, then Brittany reset the security and led the little girl into the living room.

"My grandma is sick," Emily said as she sat on the sofa and hugged her bear close to her chest.

Brittany sat next to her. "I know, but hopefully the doctors can fix her right up and she'll be back home before you know it."

"I hope so." Emily's lower lip trembled.

Brittany pulled her close against her, knowing what Emily needed more than anything at the moment was a hug from a real person, not the hug from a stuffed bear.

For several long moments Emily clung to her as Brittany smoothed her silky blond hair and murmured meaningless nothings that oddly enough seemed to help ease some of Emily's fears.

She finally sat up and swiped at her cheeks. "I hope you don't think I need to go to bed or something like that."

"Actually, what I was thinking was maybe I'd paint your fingernails and then you could paint mine."

"Now, that sounds like a plan," Emily said in obvious delight.

"You sit tight and I'll go get the polish," Brittany said. She got up from the sofa and went into the adjoining bathroom off her bedroom. Beneath the sink cabinet she had dozens of different colors of polish. The desire to polish her fingernails to match her outfits had fled at the same time her desire for high heels and purses had gone, resigned to a place of unimportance in the new life she was building.

Still, she was glad she had all the polish when she carried it into the living room and Emily squealed with excitement. Emily chose a pretty pink to be painted on her nails and while Brittany worked the little girl kept up a running chatter of everything in her world.

School, boys and ruminations on life in general— Emily shared her opinions about it all with an openness that Brittany found charming.

When they were finished with Emily's nails, it was her turn to paint Brittany's and she decided she wanted to do each nail a different color.

Brittany sat patiently as Emily carefully chose each color and painted each nail. By the time she was finished Brittany had a kaleidoscope of colors and more than a little bit of polish outside her nails.

"My daddy was sad this afternoon," she said suddenly as Brittany waved her hands in the air to dry the polish.

"Did he tell you why he was sad?" Brittany asked cautiously. Surely Alex wouldn't share with his daughter any details of the scene earlier in her kitchen.

"He just said it was a blue kind of a day. That's what we call it when we're sad. I guess it was a blue kind of a day when my mommy died and it's gonna be a blue day if my grandma doesn't get better."

"It's definitely not a blue kind of day for me," a familiar deep voice said. Gary Cox walked into the living room with that goofy, friendly smile on his face and a Taser in his hand.

"Gary?" For a long moment Brittany couldn't process his presence here in her house. She stared at him blankly, trying to make sense of it.

Someplace in the back of her mind she recognized she'd made a mistake…a terrible, crucial mistake. She'd turned off the security and then had left the front door unattended while she took care to put her gun away. It had only been for a minute, but apparently that's all it had taken for Gary to slip inside.

"Gary, what are you doing here?" she asked, trying to buy some time, trying to figure out what to do. Her first thought was for Emily, who was pressed tightly against her side as if sensing danger.

But Brittany knew why he was here and she also knew that her gun was too far away to use for protection. "Gary, let Emily go," she said urgently. "She doesn't know what's happening. Just let her walk out the front door."

"Not a chance," he replied as he advanced closer. "You know what time it is, Brittany."

Emily clung tighter to her side, making it impossible for her to attempt to defend them. "Gary, stop now and nothing will happen to you," Brittany said in an attempt to reason with the young man. "Just leave now and everything will be fine."

He grinned, that open, friendly smile that obviously hid the darkness in his soul. "Nothing is going to happen to me, Brittany."

He was close…too close. She knew the Taser could be effective up to fifteen feet away from its target and he was much closer to her and Emily than that.

"What time is it, Brittany?" Gary asked as he raised the gun and pointed it at her.

"No," she whispered.

"It's party time."

He fired the Taser and instant pain crashed through Brittany. It not only roared through every nerve in her body, but fried in her brain as she felt herself crash to the floor in front of the sofa.

As she felt herself convulsing the only sound she heard was the sound of Emily screaming and then Gary was next to her, a syringe in his hand. She could do nothing as he injected her with something. Emily screamed again and then there was nothing but silence.

Chapter 11

"I feel so foolish," Rose said as she and Alex left the hospital. It was almost eleven and the moon played peekaboo amid a bank of clouds.

"Don't be silly. Angina isn't anything to take lightly," he replied as he led her to his car in the parking lot of the small hospital.

"I sure thought it was a heart attack. I've never felt anything quite so painful."

Alex took her by the arm, grateful that it had been nothing more serious. "I'm just glad you're okay now."

"I hate that you've been sitting in the waiting room so long. It felt like they ran every test imaginable while you just had to sit in that dreadful waiting room. You know I don't like to be a bother."

Alex opened the passenger door of his car for her. "You know you could never be a bother."

He closed the door after she was safely tucked inside and then walked around to the driver door. He assumed by this time Emily was probably asleep.

He felt bad about taking advantage of Brittany, especially given the fact that she'd basically told him to kiss off, but when he'd received the frantic phone call from Rose he hadn't known where else to turn.

"Hopefully Emily hasn't run Brittany completely ragged," Rose said as he started up the car.

"I'm sure Brittany handled things just fine."

As he pulled out of the parking lot he felt Rose's gaze lingering on him. "You like her," she said.

"I'm in love with her," he replied, and then flashed Rose a rueful smile. "It's a bit awkward confessing that to you."

"Shouldn't be," she said in her usual no-nonsense voice. "I know you loved my Linda, but she's gone and you have a life to live and plenty of love to give. How does she feel about you?"

He sighed, a hollow wind blowing through him. "I thought things were moving along nicely. I thought she might even be falling for me, but she told me from the very beginning she wasn't interested in marriage or a ready-made family, and today she made it more than clear that there was no future there."

"I'm sorry, Alex. I want you to have the kind of love and happiness that you deserve, the kind that Linda wasn't capable of giving to you."

He shot her a look of surprise and she smiled. "Alex, I loved my daughter with all my heart and soul, but that doesn't mean I didn't see her weaknesses, her flaws. She was beautiful and achingly fragile. She was like that as a little girl and she never really grew up to be a woman. I want you to find a woman, Alex, a passionate woman who can embrace all of life as you and Emily do."

He'd thought he'd found that woman in Brittany and even now he wasn't sure how he was going to live his life to the fullest without her in it.

When he reached Rose's house he insisted he walk her inside and get her comfortable. As she went into her bedroom to change into her nightclothes and a robe he stood at the front door and stared out into the night.

It had been a tough day. He'd tried to keep a happy face on for Emily after he'd gotten home from Brittany's, but even the little girl had sensed his unhappiness.

How could something that had felt so right turn out to be so wrong? Why was she so certain she couldn't be a mother? She was terrific with Emily and he knew his daughter was already more than half in love with her.

Had she thrown them aside because of the danger that surrounded her? Maybe that's what this afternoon had been, her attempt to protect them.

The thought put a little bit of hope in his heart. Or maybe he was fooling himself and she just plain didn't love him. The tiny blossom of hope withered and died away.

He couldn't do anything about it now. He'd pretty much laid his heart on the line and she'd kicked it to the curb and at this point whatever her reason, the end result was the same.

Rose came out of her bedroom clad in her long, flowered robe. "Thank you, Alex. I don't know what I would have done without you tonight."

He kissed her on the forehead. "I don't know what Emily and I would do without you."

"Now go on, get out of here. I'll be fine here. Get that child of yours and get some sleep and I'll talk to you in the morning."

Within minutes he was back in his car and headed to Brittany's place. He gripped the steering wheel tightly, preparing himself for seeing her again.

He'd lived through the death of a wife. He'd survived dealing with a grieving daughter. He'd dealt with girly tears and learning to French braid and yet the thought of seeing Brittany again suddenly terrified him.

He pulled up in her driveway and saw the lights shining from the front window. Emily was probably still awake, treating the night like a special slumber party.

He got out of the car and walked to the front door and then knocked, surprised when he didn't hear any sound of movement from inside.

"Brittany, Emily, it's me," he said as he rapped harder on the door. The resulting silence set off the first alarm in his head. Brittany wouldn't have gone anywhere with Emily at this time of night. They should be in there and he couldn't imagine that they would both be sleeping so soundly they wouldn't hear him at the front door.

He rang the doorbell several times and then pounded on the door with his fist, the alarm growing louder in his head.

When there was still no answer he grabbed the front doorknob and to his surprise it twisted and opened. No sound to indicate a breach of the security.

Heart pounding, he stepped inside. "Brittany! Emily?" he cried out even though he knew they weren't there. The house held the silence of a person holding their breath…a silence that absolutely terrified him.

He raced through the house, just to make sure that he was right, that they weren't there. Brittany's car was in the garage and her purse was slung over the back of a kitchen chair. It was when he saw the purse that he went to the phone and called the sheriff's office.

Thankfully it was Tom who answered the phone. "Tom, you've got to get to Brittany's house right away. Something is wrong. I just got here and the door was unlocked, the security wasn't on and she's not here. Her car is here, her purse is here, but she's not." His voice cracked as emotion swelled up inside him. "She was babysitting my daughter. They're gone, Tom. They're both gone."

The minutes were agonizing as he waited for Tom to arrive. He stood in the center of the living room where he imagined he could smell the scent of Brittany's perfume, the sweet strawberry scent of his daughter's hair.

It was easy to see how the two had spent part of their time together during the evening. Bottles of fingernail polish littered the top of the coffee table. What he couldn't make sense of were the small multi-colored tabs that littered the floor, looking like pink, yellow and white confetti from an abandoned party.

He touched nothing, except his heart, slamming his hand against it in an effort to control the frantic beat. His knees felt weak and he had to consciously tighten his knees to keep him upright.

What had happened here? Who could have gotten in with the security? Where was his daughter? Where was Brittany?

Tom didn't arrive alone. He had all three brothers with him and they entered the house as if entering a war zone. With grim faces and dark eyes, they strode into the living room looking as if they wanted to find somebody to kill.

It took precious moments for Alex to explain the events of the night: Rose's heart attack scare, him bringing Emily here and then his race to the hospital.

"Taser markers," Benjamin said as he bent down and picked up one of the yellow pieces of confetti.

Alex's heart seemed to stop in his chest. "What are you talking about?"

"When a Taser is fired it deploys little identification markers," Caleb said.

"So, you can tell by those who the Taser belongs to?" Alex asked hopefully.

"If it was bought legally, which I seriously doubt," Benjamin replied.

"We have to do something," Alex exclaimed. He felt as if he were about to jump out of his skin. They needed to find Brittany. And God…dear God, he needed them to find his daughter.

"We start by processing the scene," Tom said. "Did you touch anything?"

"Nothing—except for the phone to call you," Alex replied.

"Then stand out of the way and let us do our jobs."

Alex stood in the foyer as they all began to collect evidence, talking in hushed tones that did nothing to ease Alex's fear.

He felt as if he were dying a slow death, as if everything and everyone were moving in slow motion. He wanted to scream at them to hurry up, to do whatever it took to find his daughter and Brittany.

Caleb left and Alex knew he was probably going to canvass the neighborhood, to see if anyone had seen anything, had heard anything that might let them know who to look for.

But where would they even begin to look? He knew there wasn't even a suspect on their radar. They had no idea who might be responsible for whatever had happened here tonight.

A darkness swept through Alex as he realized they might already be too late. He might have already lost not just the woman he loved, but the daughter who was his heart, his very soul.

* * *

The Real Professional looked at the two unconscious bodies in his shed. He'd done it! It had been pure, sweet fate that had allowed him to sneak into Brittany's house, to see her reset the alarm after the little girl had come inside and to hide in her coat closet until the time he'd stepped out and confronted them.

The Taser had done the initial work and then the drug he'd used had done the rest, rendering them both unconscious while he got them loaded into his vehicle.

The setup in the shed wasn't ideal. He didn't have the finances that Larry Norwood had possessed. He hadn't been able to build separate cells. Instead the two were shackled to the wall with iron ankle rings. He'd provided a portable toilet that could be reached by the length of their chain. He'd give them food and water.

He could keep them here as long or as short of a time as he desired. Emily had been a surprise…a gift that would certainly ensure that his name would be written in the annals of famous criminals.

The Professional hadn't taken a child. But The Real Professional had and that made him badder and better. Excitement roared through his veins. If he stuck to the plan, then he'd need to take several more women before he had his own "party." But he wasn't sure he could wait that long. He wasn't sure he wanted to wait that long.

Chapter 12

Consciousness came slowly. Brittany's first thought was that she'd been hit by a car or had been in some sort of terrible accident. Every muscle in her body ached and her head banged with a nauseating intensity.

She couldn't open her eyes…not yet. She was afraid that a shaft of sunlight, an overhead lamp might make her skull split in two.

She must have fallen back asleep, for when she became conscious once again her head felt a little better. The banging was down to a manageable ache. Then the memories slammed into her brain, retrieving her headache with a vengeance.

Gary. The Taser.

Emily!

Her eyes flew open and in an instant she took in her

surroundings. An old shed. No cages, but her ankle was shackled to the wall with a thick chain.

Emily was curled up on the floor next to her, unusually pale and not moving. *Don't be dead,* Brittany thought anxiously. *Oh, please, don't be dead.* She touched Emily's arm, encouraged by the warmth of her skin.

"Emily?" she whispered.

The little girl stirred but didn't wake up. Brittany decided to let her stay sleeping. There was no question that they'd been drugged. Brittany could still feel the aftereffects—a touch of nausea and the feeling of cotton wrapped around her brain.

But she needed to peel back the cotton and take stock of their surroundings. She needed to find a way out, to get Emily to safety.

But before she could think, before she could plan, a wave of despair rushed over her. How could this be happening again? What were the odds of being held captive by a madman twice in a lifetime?

Tears burned at her eyes but she willed them away. She didn't have time to cry. She had to figure out a way to get Emily out of here. If Brittany had to die in this shed, then so be it, but Emily was just a child and somehow, someway she had to be saved.

Sucking up the tears that still threatened to fall, Brittany took a look around. The wooden shed where they were being held was old and relatively small and had probably once been used for storage.

She saw the portable toilet nearby and a new chill danced over her skin. That indicated a lengthy stay. She also saw that there were three more shackles bolted into the walls, all empty and awaiting new victims.

So, Gary had intended to emulate his hero as closely as possible by kidnapping five women, but he obviously hadn't had the financial means to make this place as spiffy as Larry had made his holding area.

She tested the shackle around her ankle, unsurprised that it was fastened tight and impossible to slip. She was also not surprised to see that it was securely bolted to the wall, bolted tightly enough that it would take more than her bare hands and strength to get it loose.

With a sigh she leaned back against the wall. Gary. Her mind still couldn't wrap around the fact that it had been red-haired, freckled Gary behind all this.

What worried her more than anything was that Gary would probably be the last person her brothers would look at as a potential suspect. Although he had been hanging around her house to work, he was so young and appeared to be friendly and eager to please. But that was obviously a facade that hid a malevolent darkness well.

She didn't have her watch on and so had no idea what time it might be. A small bare lightbulb dangled from the ceiling burned in one corner of the shed, illuminating the interior, but it had to be after midnight.

She had no idea where they were, where this shed was located. She didn't know how long she'd been unconscious, didn't know if they were still anywhere near Black Rock. She didn't know enough about Gary's background. She didn't even know where he lived.

It was possible nobody even knew they were missing yet. Alex might still be at the hospital with Rose, not knowing that his daughter was in danger.

She glanced back at Emily, who still seemed to be sleeping soundly. Fine, let her sleep through the night. Let her sleep as long as possible before she had to wake up and face this nightmare that had caught them unaware.

She tensed as she heard the sound of footsteps approaching. Gary stepped through the door, that goofy, friendly smile on his face and a plastic grocery sack looped over one arm. "Ah, I see you're awake."

"What are you doing, Gary? Let us go and I'll see that you get some help."

His smile widened. "The way I see it I'm not the one who needs help, but you look like you could use a little. Unfortunately, if I were you I wouldn't hold my breath waiting for it to come."

"Let Emily go. If you think you're re-creating Larry's crimes, he never hurt a child. He never took a child."

Gary's blue eyes lit with an electric fire. "I know. Killing her just makes me better than him. People in this town will talk about me long after I'm gone."

"What good will it do you? You'll be dead, just like Larry."

The smile fell from his lips. "Oh, no, nobody is going to catch me. I'm smarter than Larry, better than him. I'll be like the Zodiac killer," he said, referencing a serial killer who had become famous in the late 1960s and early 1970s and who had never been identified or caught. "Honestly, Brittany, who is going to suspect me?" He flashed her that bright smile once again.

He tossed the grocery bag in her direction and it landed just to the left of her. She was almost afraid to look inside. "That should hold you until I get back here," he said. "You know, I'm not completely like him. I don't have to have an audience to enjoy my work. I could kill you right now and start my own legend."

It took every ounce of Brittany's control not to explode, not to scream and rant at him, but she didn't want to awaken Emily, who continued to sleep next to her.

Gary grinned. "Guess I'll let you live for the night. We'll just have to wait to see what tomorrow brings." With those frightening words he stepped away from the door and disappeared into the darkness of the night.

For several long minutes Brittany sat staring at the darkness just outside the doorway, every muscle in her body taut, an ache in the back of her head threatening to make her sick.

They were obviously far enough out of town that he wasn't worried about them screaming for help, otherwise they would be gagged. The small town of Black Rock was surrounded by farmland with hundreds of sheds abandoned and left to rot.

She and Emily could be in any one of those places, far enough away that their screams couldn't be heard, yet close enough to safety to run to it if they could just get free of the chains that held them.

Remembering the bag that Gary had thrown at her,

she picked it up and looked inside. A couple of bottles of water, two snack-size bags of chips and what appeared to be two cheese sandwiches in bags.

At that moment Emily moaned and her eyelids fluttered and then opened. A little frown danced across her forehead as she looked around and then a sharp cry of alarm escaped her.

"Emily, it's okay, honey. I'm here." Brittany wrapped the little girl in her arms and held her tight. "I'm right here with you."

Emily clung to her and Brittany didn't know if it was the little girl's heartbeat that pounded so frantically or her own. "I don't have Lady Bear," Emily said, her voice quivering with the portent of tears.

"No, you don't. But you have me." Brittany tightened her embrace around Emily.

Emily leaned into her and released a tremulous sigh. "We're in big trouble, aren't we?"

Brittany hesitated. She didn't want to frighten Emily any more than she already was, but she also didn't want to blatantly lie to her. "Yes, we're in trouble, but I'm hoping your daddy or one of my brothers will find us very soon and get us out of trouble."

Emily sat up and looked at her. "Do you think they can find us?"

"I think it's possible." Brittany tried to inject as much hope as she could in her voice.

Emily's gaze went out the door. "It's nighttime."

"Yes, honey, it is."

"Maybe daddy will be here first thing in the morning."

"That's right. So it would be best if we both tried to get some sleep," Brittany replied, although sleep was the very last thing on her mind.

"Okay." Once again Emily leaned against Brittany and closed her eyes. She was quiet and still only a moment and then sat back up with a sigh. "I can't sleep. I'm scared." She looked at Brittany with her beautiful green eyes. "Maybe if we talk for a little longer I can get sleepy."

"Okay, what do you want to talk about?"

For the next half an hour they talked about favorite colors and what Emily wanted to be when she grew up. She wasn't sure if she wanted to be a ballerina or one of the people who arrested people who were mean to dogs and cats.

"I want a dog," she said, her voice getting drowsy. "Maybe you could help me talk Daddy into getting one. Lady Bear would like a dog."

Brittany smoothed a strand of her hair away from Emily's face. "We'll have to talk to your daddy about that."

She should be trying to figure out a way to get them out of here. She should be frantically yanking on the bolts that held the chains to the wall, screaming her fool head off in case somebody might hear and come to their rescue. But at the moment she felt as if the most important thing she could do in the world was keep Emily's terror at bay.

"Daddy is going to be so mad at Gary." Emily leaned heavier against Brittany's side.

"Yes, he is." Brittany moved her hand from stroking Emily's hair to caressing her back. Emily sighed.

"How come you aren't a mommy?"

"I'm not sure I'd know how to be a mommy," Brittany replied.

"Oh, I'm sure you'd make a wonderful mommy," Emily replied, her voice slightly slurry with the edges of sleep creeping in. "And what you don't know about it, I could teach you."

Brittany couldn't speak, not with her heart so big, so tight in her chest, and within another minute she knew that Emily was once again asleep.

Tears once again burned at her eyes as she thought of Alex, who'd already lost his wife. She didn't want him to lose his child, too.

Somehow she had to figure out a way to get Emily out of here alive. No matter what it took, she had to save Emily.

The night was endless. When the sun began its rise Alex stood at Brittany's living-room window and watched it with eyes that burned from lack of sleep, from the beginning edges of a grief the likes of which he'd never known.

Tom was in the kitchen, coordinating the search for Brittany and Emily from there. Caleb and Benjamin were out walking the streets, trying to glean any information that might help them find out who was responsible for the kidnappings. Tom had assigned another deputy to sit at Alex's house just in case the kidnapper might try to make contact there.

Alex wanted to be home. He wanted to sit in Emily's room and smell the scent of her that lingered in the air, needed to be in his familiar surroundings while his entire world fell apart.

Here the scent of Brittany that lingered in the air ripped at his heart, but Tom wanted him here, along with Jacob. Larry Norwood had taken great pleasure in calling Jacob Grayson and taunting him about the crimes he was going to commit. They were all hoping that if this was a copycat kind of situation, then the perp would try to make contact with Jacob once again.

Jacob sat on the sofa, his cell phone in his lap and dark anger in his eyes. Alex could definitely relate to the anger. If he shoved aside his fear, he knew there was a rage building inside him, a rage that scared him just a little bit with its ferocity.

He turned away from the window to face Jacob. "I love her, you know."

Jacob nodded his head slightly. "She sounds like a cute kid."

Alex frowned. "Of course I love my daughter, but I'm talking about your sister."

"She's a cute kid, too."

"She's not a kid." Some of the frustration Alex felt crept into his voice. "She's a loving, caring woman and it's high time all of you treat her like one."

Jacob raised a dark eyebrow. "Hey, I'm on your side, remember?"

Alex felt his face warm. "Sorry," he said. "I just feel like I'm about to jump out of my skin." He turned back to the window. "Where could they be? Who in the hell is responsible for this?"

"We'll figure it out," Jacob replied, but there was no real conviction in his deep voice.

It was almost ten when Caleb came in. Alex followed him into the kitchen where Tom sat at the table, a stack of notes in front of him, notes Alex knew were from the original crimes.

"Luke Mathis has a solid alibi for last night. Even though he was off work at Harley's he spent the entire night there drinking so heavily that when the bar closed Harley let him sleep on a cot in the break room," Caleb said. "He was still there, still half-drunk when I talked to him a little while ago."

A wave of hopelessness blew through Alex. He'd hoped…he'd really hoped that Luke was behind all this and that Emily had just been in the wrong place at the wrong time when an ex-lover had decided to confront Brittany.

Tom released a heavy sigh. "So, that takes care of our one and only suspect."

"What about Buck?" Alex asked suddenly.

"What about him?" Tom asked.

"He was working here with me. He asked some inappropriate questions to Brittany about her time with Larry Norwood, seemed way too excited to talk about what she'd been through."

A deep frown cut across Tom's forehead. "Buck might be a lot of things, but I can't quite see him being responsible for this. Still…" He picked up his cell phone. "Let's get him in here and have a discussion with him."

"Wait," Alex said. "Let me call him. I'll tell him

I need an hour or so of work from him. He won't be suspicious if I call and he's always up for a little extra pay."

Buck answered on the second ring. "Hey, boss, what's up?"

"I've got a little more cleanup here at Brittany's and wondered if you could come and help. I don't need anyone but you and it will only take a few minutes." Alex was pleased that his voice didn't betray any of the turmoil inside him.

"When do you need me?"

"As soon as you can get here," Alex replied.

"I'll be there in about fifteen minutes."

The call ended and Alex looked at Tom. "He's on his way. But what if he doesn't have them? What if he isn't a part of this?"

"Then we keep looking and we hope we get lucky," Tom replied.

"If he's playing the game like the original, then he won't hurt them until he has more women," Caleb said. "At least that works in our favor."

"But he's already deviated from the original. Larry Norwood never took a child," Alex said, the words falling like painful glass shards from his mouth.

"And maybe he'll let Emily go," Tom said in an obvious effort to soothe Alex. But there was no soothing. There was nothing that could ease Alex's terror, his grief until both his daughter and Brittany were out of harm's way.

By the time Buck arrived Alex was ready to tear off

somebody's head. The rage was taking hold, so much easier to embrace than the killing grief and fear.

Buck knocked on the back door and Alex opened the door, grabbed him by the arm and pulled him into the kitchen. "Where's my daughter?"

"What?" Buck look around the room, his gaze lingering on Tom, then Caleb and finally back to Alex. "Wha—what's going on here?"

"Somebody broke in here last night and kidnapped Brittany and Emily," Tom said. He gestured to a chair at the table. "Sit down, Buck. We need to have a little chat."

"You think I had something to do with this?" Buck cursed soundly. "Why is it that anytime anything goes wrong in this stupid town you come to me? I don't know anything about it. Why would I want to do something like that?"

"Maybe because Larry Norwood was your hero. Maybe you want to be just like him." Alex's need to punch somebody was overwhelming, but instead he fisted his hands at his sides.

"What, are you crazy?" Buck looked at him in astonishment. "Norwood was a sick twist. Why would I want to be anything like him?"

"You seemed very interested in Brittany's experience with him," Alex countered.

"Sure, I've never known anyone who's been held by a serial killer. I was curious." Buck frowned. "But I'm not the only one. Gary talks about The Professional all the time."

"Gary?" Tom looked at Alex.

"Gary Cox. He's the other kid I used to help build Brittany's deck," Alex replied.

"But Gary wouldn't do something like this," Buck said with a half laugh. "He's just a goofy kid."

Gary was just a goofy kid and from what Alex had heard Larry Norwood was a nice man who cared for animals. You never knew what kind of facade hid the heart of a killer.

"Where does Gary live?" Tom asked.

"In the same apartment complex where I live. But he's almost never home." Buck's eyes narrowed. "He spends a lot of time working on an old abandoned shed he says he's turning into some kind of an awesome man cave."

Alex's heart jumped as Caleb and Tom exchanged glances. "Where is this shed?" Tom asked as he got out of his chair.

"I've never been there, but I know it's someplace on the Burwell property," Buck replied.

"The Burwell property?" Alex looked at Tom.

"Raymond Burwell died a little over a year ago without a will, leaving his farm tied up in probate court with relatives all fighting over it. It's a big spread, overgrown and with several outbuildings," Tom said.

"Then let's go," Alex exclaimed with a sick urgency pressing tight against his chest. He felt sick to his stomach, so afraid that this all might be a wild-goose chase, so afraid that they were already too late.

Chapter 13

Emily had slept through the rest of the night but Brittany had found sleep impossible. As she'd held Emily close her thoughts had gone in every direction possible.

She'd relived those days...weeks when she'd been held captive by Larry Norwood and reminded herself that she'd survived once before and she could do it again.

If the very worst happened and she didn't get out of this shed alive at least she'd had those moments in Alex's arms, those moments when she'd felt more alive, more loved, than she ever had in her life.

She could have loved Alex if she'd allowed herself to. She could have easily envisioned a future with him. He was everything she'd ever wanted in a man.

She smiled as she thought about Emily telling her she could teach her whatever she needed to learn about being a mother. Her smile fell. Emily was obviously so hungry for a stepmother, she had no standards whatsoever.

Funny, the last time she'd been held against her will she'd thought about building a deck and spending time with friends and family. This time she thought about love and being in Alex's arms.

Brittany guessed that it was about nine in the morning when Emily woke up. She sat up and rubbed her eyes. "I thought it was all a bad dream, but it's real, isn't it? Do you think Daddy will come soon?"

"I hope so. Are you hungry?" Brittany opened the bag and pulled out a bottle of water and a bag of the chips. She was afraid of the sandwiches, which weren't prepackaged.

"I'm not really hungry. I just want my daddy and my Lady Bear," Emily said in a tiny whisper.

"I know, honey." Brittany pulled her back into her arms and for several long minutes neither of them spoke.

"You know what?" Emily finally asked.

"What?"

"I think if I point my toes like a ballerina I can slip my foot out of this thing around my ankle."

Brittany's heart began a rapid tattoo. "Really? You want to try it and see?"

Emily bent down and unlaced the tennis shoe she wore. The sight of her pink polka-dot socks nearly made Brittany lose it. No little girl in pink polka-dot socks should be in this place, at the mercy of a young man who was obviously unbalanced.

Once the shoe was off Emily pointed her toe just like a ballerina and she could easily pull it out of the shackle that was intended for an adult's foot.

Brittany's heart nearly exploded. Emily was free! She could run and get help. But wait… Brittany's head whirled with suppositions. What if Gary was right outside the building? What if he lived close enough that he would see if Emily ran outside? The last thing Brittany wanted was for Emily to run into more harm.

A plan began to formulate in her head, a dangerous plan that might get them both killed or could possibly be their salvation. As she heard footsteps approaching the shed she quickly whispered her plan, not once, but twice, to Emily. She prayed the little girl understood and obeyed. It might be their only hope.

With Emily's stockinged foot covered by the plastic bag that had held their food and her tennis shoe behind Brittany's back, Brittany prepared to meet the devil in his lair.

Gary appeared in the doorway, his bright smile like nails on a chalkboard screeching up Brittany's spine. "Well, looks like you both made it through the night."

"You're a bad man," Emily said, surprising Brittany with her show of bravado. "You're a bad man and you're going to get punished."

Gary laughed. "You got a little smart mouth on you, girl. What are you going to do? Put me in time-out?"

"And you've got delusions of grandeur, Gary," Brittany said, wanting to take his attention off Emily.

"You're just a freckle-faced punk pretending to be a bad guy."

Gary's nostrils pinched together, letting her know her remark had gotten under his skin. "You know what's interesting about serial killers? Nobody ever remembers the names of the victims, but they always remember the name of the killer."

"Oh, yeah, and have you picked your killer name yet?" She kept a taunting tone in her voice. She had to make him mad. She had to make him mad enough to get closer to her. "Maybe Howdy Doody or Tom Sawyer?"

"You've got a smart mouth on you, too," Gary said, no longer smiling. "I'm The Real Professional." He said the words as if he were proclaiming himself the King of Siam.

Brittany forced herself to laugh, as if finding him immensely amusing. "Gary, Gary, nobody is going to remember your name. A year from now nobody here or anywhere else on the planet will give you a minute's thought, except maybe your parents, who will wonder for the rest of their lives where they went wrong."

"My parents don't give a crap about me," he scoffed.

"Ah, poor baby, so you're planning on using the 'I've been neglected and abused by my parents and that turned me into a monster' defense. Larry Norwood was The Professional—you're not even a pale imitation."

Her heart jumped as he took a step toward her. She felt Emily tense next to her and prayed the child remembered every single detail of their plan, prayed that Emily would do exactly what Brittany had told her to do.

"Shut up," he said as he narrowed his eyes and took another step closer to her.

Just one more step or two and he'd be close enough. Her heart screamed in her chest. She forced a laugh again. "At least Larry had a real place to keep us, with cells and cots to sleep on. He was a genius. He pulled off his plot in Kansas City and almost got away with it here. You'll never be like him, Gary. You'll always be just a pathetic pretender. Hey, there's a name for you, The Pathetic Pretender."

He lunged at her, rage twisting his features into something unrecognizable. Brittany was ready for him. She wrapped her arms tight around him, gripping him at the knees with all the strength she possessed.

"Run!" she screamed at Emily at the same time Gary's fist crashed down on Brittany's head.

Emily scrambled to her feet and ran. As she disappeared out the door Brittany tightened her arms around Gary's knees, keeping him from chasing after the child.

Run, baby, run, she thought as Gary delivered a blow that struck her upside the face. The pain crashed through her. She tasted blood and almost immediately felt her lip swell, but she didn't loosen her grip on him. She knew the longer she could hang on the more of a chance Emily had to get away.

Run fast, she thought. *Get as far away from here*

as possible. Despite her pain her heart swelled with the hope that Emily had truly escaped.

Gary railed like a madman, screaming and cursing as he hit her again and again. He smashed his fists into her ribs, slammed her in the gut over and over again.

She sobbed with the pain, afraid that he would beat her to death if she didn't let go of him, but knowing if she let go he'd run after Emily.

Finally he delivered a blow to her head that made stars dance in front of her eyes and a sickening nausea well up inside her. In horror she felt her arms slipping from him and her last conscious thought was that she hoped she'd given Emily enough time to get away.

As the men prepared to leave Brittany's house, Alex realized they didn't intend for him to go with them. Tom had been on his phone, arranging for several other deputies to meet them at the Burwell property.

As Tom walked out the front door and headed for his car, Alex caught up to him. "I'm coming with you."

"You're a civilian. It's best if you stay here and wait," Tom replied.

"Not going to happen." Alex met the man stare for stare. "It's my daughter, Tom. And it's the woman I love. I can either ride with you or I can follow you in my car, but there's no way in hell I'm staying here."

Without waiting for Tom's reply Alex slid into the passenger seat of his car. "You're a stubborn cuss, aren't you?" Tom said as he got behind the wheel and started the car. "I suppose you'll have to be if you plan on sticking around Brittany for any length of time."

They both fell silent as Tom pulled out of the driveway and tore down the street with Brittany's brothers following in their own vehicles.

A hard knot sat where Alex's heart should be. What if they were headed in the wrong direction? What if they were too late?

He couldn't think that. He couldn't imagine his life without his Emily. She was the best part of him, the very core of the heart that beat in his chest.

And Brittany, how his heart ached with thoughts of her. It didn't matter if she couldn't see herself in his life, he just needed to know that she was someplace on earth living in the kind of happiness she deserved.

The drive to the Burwell place seemed to take forever and when they arrived at the small farmhouse all the law-enforcement officials gathered around Tom.

"If Gary is the person we're looking for then we have to assume that he's armed and dangerous," Tom said. "I want us to search in teams of two." As he assigned the areas he gestured toward Alex. "You stay with me."

Alex nodded, eager to get started, hoping and praying that they were at the right place at the right time. Any other thought was simply too painful to entertain.

"I want us to go in quietly," Tom continued. "Put your phones on vibrate and keep your eyes and ears open." With those final words the men all parted ways.

Alex wanted to run through the overgrown grass toward the half a dozen outbuilding in the distance.

He wanted to rip open doors, tear at old lumber, do whatever it took to find Gary Cox's man cave.

Was Gary simply building a place to party? A place where he could bring his friends to drink and play music and not have to worry about the complaints of neighbors?

As he and Tom grew closer to one of the buildings, Alex recognized Gary's car parked nearby. The knot in his chest twisted tighter.

Okay, so the kid was here, but that didn't mean Emily and Brittany were here, as well. Tom had his gun drawn, his eyes cold and dark as they drew closer to the building.

They paused just outside the door and that's when Alex heard it—the sound of a man cursing softly, the moan of somebody hurt and the sound of fist meeting flesh.

All cautions that Tom had given his men, any orders Alex was meant to follow, flew out of his head. With the adrenaline of an enraged bull, Alex flew inside the building.

In an instant he summed up the nightmarish scene. Gary stood over Brittany with his fist raised to deliver another blow. Her face was bloodied and she looked unconscious and there was no sign of Emily.

He didn't make a sound as he attacked. He grabbed Gary by the shoulder, whirled him around and then delivered a punch to the center of his face. As Gary stumbled back and fell to the ground Alex wasn't finished yet. He leaped on top of Gary's prone body and began to pummel, all his fear, his anger centered in his fists.

"What did you do to Brittany? And where's Emily?" he screamed as he pounded. "Where's my daughter?"

"If you kill him he won't be able to tell you," Tom exclaimed as he pulled Alex up and off Gary.

Alex immediately rushed to Brittany. Her mouth was bloody, one of her eyes blackened and swollen shut. She seemed to be hanging on to consciousness by a mere thread, but at least she was alive.

Alex whirled back to face Gary, who Tom had gotten to his feet and handcuffed. "Where's Emily?" he asked, vaguely aware of the shed filling with Brittany's brothers and some of the other deputies.

"I killed the little brat," Gary said as Tom dug through his pockets for the key to the shackle that bound Brittany to the wall. "I killed her and buried her body in the field outside."

"No, he's lying." The words left Brittany on a soft pain-laced whisper. "She got away. I held him so she could run as fast and as far away as possible. Go, Alex, she's somewhere out there and she needs her daddy."

At that moment the scream of a siren sounded from the distance and Alex realized one of the brothers had called for an ambulance. Brittany would be cared for, but he had to find his daughter. "Thank you," he said, knowing the words would never be enough to convey his gratitude for the woman he knew had saved his daughter's life.

He tore out of the shed, unsure in which direction to run. Had Gary beaten Emily, too? Was she lying in the tall grass somewhere slowly dying?

"Emily!" He screamed her name as tears began to blur his vision. The overgrown brush and weeds were so tall and she was so little. "Emily, where are you?" The words tore from his throat, from a place of such pain he nearly fell to his knees.

As the ambulance pulled up, several of the other men left the shed and began to search, as well, calling out Emily's name. It was such a big field and there was no way to know what direction she might have run, how far she might have been able to go in whatever time she'd had.

Agonizing minutes passed with Alex continuing to yell her name until he was half-hoarse. He couldn't think about Brittany's injuries. The thought of her bloodied features made him want to weep, but knowing she was being attended to, he had to stay focused on Emily.

And then she was there…rising out of the tall grass in front of him. Her green eyes wide and filled with tears. "Daddy?"

Alex fell to his knees and opened his arms and she ran to him. He wrapped his arms around her and squeezed her tight, sobbing into her hair as relief coursed through him.

"I knew you'd come, Daddy. I just knew it," she whispered fiercely against his ear, her arms wrapped in a near death grip around his neck as she began to cry.

"It's okay, baby." His heart swelled tight in his chest. "You're safe now and Daddy is never going to let anything like this happen to you again." He scooped her up in his arms and rose to his feet.

Benjamin approached them, his relief evident on his handsome features. "I recommend you take her to the hospital, get her checked out by a doctor and then Tom will want to talk to her."

Alex's first impulse was to take her home and never let her go again, but he knew Benjamin was right. She needed to be checked by a doctor and then she'd have to tell her story to Tom.

"It won't take long," Alex said to his daughter. "We'll get some things taken care of and then we'll take you home where Lady Bear is waiting for you."

"I don't want Lady Bear. I just want Brittany," she replied.

So do I, Alex thought. At that moment the ambulance pulled away, sirens screaming as it raced toward the main road. He had no idea what kind of internal injuries she might have suffered. She'd looked half-dead from the beating she'd taken.

"Let's get out of here," Alex said.

Gary was taken away by Caleb as Tom offered to take Alex and Emily to the hospital. As they made the drive Tom asked Emily questions and it didn't take long for a picture of what had gone down to appear.

It also didn't take long to realize that Brittany had sacrificed herself for Emily's escape. "She held on to him so he couldn't run after me and he hit her hard, but she screamed at me to run," Emily said as she rubbed tears from her cheeks.

If Alex had believed himself in love with Brittany before, this information only intensified the depth of his love for her. He couldn't wait to find out how she was, but it was a long process when they arrived at the hospital.

Emily got a clean bill of health and then they sat in the waiting room to hear word about Brittany. Emily sat on his lap, curled into his chest and sharing bits and pieces of the long night with him.

"I think I lost my shoe," she said and pointed at her stockinged foot.

"We'll get you a new pair of shoes," Alex replied. "We'll get you a dozen pairs of new shoes."

"I just need one pair. Daddy, I would have really been scared, but Brittany made me feel not so scared. When can I see her?"

"I'm hoping soon," he replied. He needed to see her, to thank her for what she'd done for Emily…for him.

It was another hour before Jacob finally came into the waiting room. Emily was almost asleep, but she perked right up at the sight of the lawman and the news that she could go see Brittany.

"She's going to be fine, although she's banged up pretty good," he said. He looked at Emily. "She has a black eye and her mouth is kind of puffy, so she doesn't look too good." Alex appreciated him warning Emily. "They're going to keep her overnight for observation, but you can go see her if you want. Room 112."

Emily scrambled off Alex's lap, as if not wanting to wait another minute. Alex had to hurry to keep up with her as she raced toward Brittany's room.

She turned into the room and then stopped and gasped with her hands over her mouth. Alex nearly bumped into her and his heart cried as he saw Brittany. One side of her face was black-and-blue, that eye swollen shut. Her mouth was swollen, with a cut on the corner but she offered them both a wobbly smile.

She looks like this because she saved my daughter, Alex thought. Her sacrifice weakened his knees, ached in his chest. He was positively humbled by the half-broken woman in the hospital bed.

"Oh, Brittany," Emily exclaimed as she lowered her hands and raced to the side of the bed. "You look awful."

"It doesn't hurt as bad as it looks," Brittany replied drowsily. "They gave me a shot that pretty much made the pain go away."

"I don't know how to thank you," Alex began, his voice thick with emotion.

Brittany held up a hand to stop whatever he was going to say. "Please, just let it go."

"At least your fingernails still look pretty," Emily said as she moved to the side of Brittany's bed. Alex noticed that Brittany's nails were each a different color, obviously his daughter's handiwork.

"Can I give you a hug?" Emily asked.

"Honey, I don't think that's a good idea," Alex protested.

"I think it's a wonderful idea," Brittany replied, her

voice slurring slightly. To Alex's surprise she patted the bed next to her.

Emily crawled up on the bed and curled into Brittany's side. Brittany placed an arm around her as Emily ever so gently kissed her on the cheek. "I love you, Brittany," Emily said softly.

"I love you, too," Brittany whispered softly as she closed her eyes. Within minutes both of the women who held Alex's heart were sound asleep.

When Brittany awakened she was alone in the hospital bed. The room was semidark with only the light from the sinking sun coming in through the window. Alex sat in the chair next to her bed and he smiled at her as he realized she was awake.

"Emily?" she asked.

"Is with Rose," he replied.

"Gary?"

"Is in jail."

She sat up, wincing as every ache and pain in her body made themselves known. "And all is right with the world."

"I don't know how to thank you for what you did. You saved Emily's life."

There was such emotion in his eyes, those beautiful blue eyes that she'd thought she'd never see again. "I was just doing my job. And it is going to be my job again. I've decided to go back to being a deputy."

"That's good if that's where your heart is," he replied.

"It is."

"So, you feel competent enough to keep an entire town safe but not enough to help parent a six-year-old little girl who loves you desperately."

He didn't give her a chance to reply, but continued as he got out of his chair and stepped closer to her. "I love you, Brittany, and I believe in my heart that you love me, too. I think we could have something magical between us if you'd just allow it to happen."

"There's a difference between being a deputy and being a mom," she said. There was no place on her body, on her face, that ached more than her heart.

"Yeah, you need a gun to be a deputy, but all you need to have to be a mom is love. You sacrificed yourself for Emily in that shed. You already proved yourself to have a mother's heart."

She stared at him, at the face she'd grown to love. There had been a little part of her that hadn't believed in herself, that had been afraid that she wasn't the woman she wanted to be, the woman he and Emily needed in their lives.

She'd faced not one, but two serial killers and she'd survived. She wasn't crazy and she had grown from the immature girl she used to be into a woman who wanted something meaningful, something lasting in her life. And that something was here right in front of her. All she had to do was reach out and embrace it.

"When we were in that shed, Emily told me that being a mom was easy, but that if I had problems with it she could teach me all I needed to know about it," she said.

Hope lit Alex's eyes and in that hope she saw a

reflection of the woman he saw when he looked at her—a strong woman with a loving heart, a woman ready to take on the responsibilities of a ready-made family.

"Yes," she said.

"Yes, what?" he asked, looking perplexed.

"Yes, I'd like to be a part of your life, of Emily's life. Yes, I want Emily to teach me everything I need to know about being a mom. I love you, Alex, and I'm ready to take care of the town and then come home to a loving family. This thing between us, I'm not ready for it to stop, either."

His eyes blazed with love and desire and he made a sound of frustration. "I desperately want to kiss you, but I'm afraid no matter where I kiss I'll hurt you."

Brittany held up her hand with the multicolored fingernails. He took her hand and brought it to his lips where he kissed each and every finger with a gentleness that promised the kind of happiness Brittany had never dreamed possible.

She was not the child her brothers thought of her as, nor was she simply a victim of the crimes that had been perpetrated against her. She was just a woman in love with a man and his daughter and she was eager to discover the future with them that awaited her.

Epilogue

Chaos reigned on the deck that Alex built. Conversations filled the air along with the heady smoke scent of barbecue. An explosion of colorful flowers lined the deck and tumbled into a flower garden in the yard where Emily was playing with Lilly in the grass.

Nobody complained about the late-July heat, especially not Brittany, who was seeing the final version of the vision that had sustained her when Larry Norwood had held her captive for so long. The only additions to that vision were Alex and Emily.

No matter how long Larry would have held her she never would have been able to imagine the kind of love she'd experienced in the three months since Gary Cox had been arrested.

She and Alex had taken things slow, maintaining their own residences and dating. But her love for him and Emily had blossomed with each day that had passed.

Loving Emily was easy. Loving Alex felt as necessary as taking her next breath. He'd melded in with her brothers as if he'd always belonged.

She looked around at all the people who had gathered for her barbecue, the people she had envisioned when she'd been kept in that shed, and more. There was nothing better than seeing her brothers with their loved ones.

As Tom flipped burgers his gaze went often to his wife, Peyton, and Lilly out in the yard. Caleb sat next to Portia and occasionally rubbed his hand against her bulging pregnant belly. Benjamin had turned in his badge and was now ranching full-time and Edie looked happy to have him at the ranch day in and day out. Finally there was Jacob, who was sitting in a chair next to Layla and smiling indulgently as she talked incessantly without seeming to take a breath.

Over the past year the Grayson family had faced many trials, but they'd all come out stronger, better in the end, and discovered that ultimately the only thing important in life was love.

"I've got the burgers ready," Tom yelled from the grill.

It was like calling cattle to a feed trough. The entire group headed for the table that was already set with salads and condiments, with chips and baked beans.

Brittany wouldn't have thought the cacophony

could grow any louder, but it did as everyone found a seat and the meal commenced.

Alex slid into the chair next to hers and lovingly touched her thigh beneath the table. "How's my woman?"

"Happy," she replied. "Happier than I've ever been in my life."

"That's what I like to hear," he replied, his amazing eyes filled with love.

"I have a little announcement to make," Caleb said. "Portia and I went to the doctor yesterday and it looks like there's going to be another little Grayson boy in the family."

Portia rubbed her big belly with a smile. "And right now we're still fighting over what his name is going to be."

"As far as I'm concerned, this works for now." Caleb leaned over against Portia's belly. "Hey, Boy, how you doing?"

Everyone at the table laughed and the sound wrapped around Brittany's heart. There hadn't been enough laughter in the Grayson family lately but they'd been catching up on that over the past three months.

Brittany had started back to work as a deputy a month earlier, and between that and Alex and Emily, her life was as full as she wanted.

"I also have an announcement to make," Alex said and rose from his seat. "Well, actually, it's not an announcement. It's a question."

Brittany looked at him in surprise as he fell to one

knee at the side of her chair. Her heart fluttered wildly in her chest as she gazed into Alex's eyes.

"Brittany, we've had over three months together," he said as the others fell silent. "Months that have been the best of Emily's and my lives. I want more. We both want more." He pulled a velvet box from his pocket and opened it up in front of her.

The diamond ring caught the sun and sparkled with a brilliance that couldn't compare to the shine in her heart. "Will you marry me, Brittany?"

"Say yes!" Emily said and jumped out of her chair. "Oh, please, say yes and be my mom."

There was never any question in Brittany's mind what her answer was going to be. "Yes," she said. "Yes, I'll marry you."

"Now, that sounds like a plan!" Emily exclaimed with excitement.

Alex pulled Brittany up into his arms, and as they kissed, the family who loved her cheered as if they knew what she did, that the future was bright with love and happiness.

Brittany had survived not only The Professional, but also an imitation of the monster, and that she had survived for one reason—because fate had wanted her here to step into the role of wife and mother. It was her true destiny, she knew as Alex's mouth found hers once again, and she was ready to embrace him and Emily as her very own.

* * * * *

A sneaky peek at next month...

INTRIGUE...

BREATHTAKING ROMANTIC SUSPENSE

My wish list for next month's titles...

In stores from 16th March 2012:

❏ Special Agent's Perfect Cover – Marie Ferrarella

& Copper Lake Secrets – Marilyn Pappano

❏ Rustled & Stampeded

   – B.J. Daniels

❏ High-Risk Reunion – Gail Barrett

& Millionaire's Last Stand – Elle Kennedy

❏ The Spy's Secret Family – Cindy Dees

Available at WHSmith, Tesco, Asda, Eason, Amazon and Apple

Just can't wait?

Visit us Online

You can buy our books online a month before they hit the shops! **www.millsandboon.co.uk**

0312/46

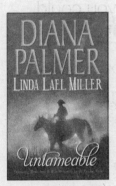